Three-times Golde— learned to pack her learned to read. Bor— lived in the United S—, Puerto Rico, Portugal and Brazil. In addition to travelling Tina loves to cuddle with her pug, Alex, spend time with her family, and hit the trails on her horse. Learn more about Tina from her website, or 'friend' her on Facebook.

With two beautiful daughters, **Lucy Ryder** has had to curb her adventurous spirit and settle down. But because she's easily bored by routine she's turned to writing as a creative outlet, and to romances because—'What else is there other than chocolate?' Characterised by friends and family as a romantic cynic, Lucy can't write serious stuff to save her life. She loves creating characters who are funny, romantic, and just a little cynical.

THE DOCTORS' BABY MIRACLE

TINA BECKETT

RESISTING HER COMMANDER HERO

LUCY RYDER

MILLS & BOON

Published in Great Britain 2018
by Mills & Boon, an imprint of HarperCollins*Publishers*
1 London Bridge Street, London, SE1 9GF

The Doctors' Baby Miracle © 2018 Tina Beckett

Resisting Her Commander Hero © 2018 Bev Riley

ISBN: 978-0-263-93339-0

THE DOCTORS' BABY MIRACLE

TINA BECKETT

MILLS & BOON

To my kids.
You make me laugh and support me no matter what.
I love you!

PROLOGUE

Two years ago

TUCKER STEVENSON WALKED out of the clinic a new man.

Only he didn't feel new. He felt old and cynical and very, very tired. But at least he'd severed himself from his past, in more ways than one. What was that old Grimm's fairy tale he'd read as a child? *Seven at One Blow?* Well, he hadn't struck down seven, but two was enough: a vasectomy and a divorce. It did seem kind of ironic that his test for "swimmers" should be scheduled for the very same day his divorce became final.

He'd never in his worst nightmares suspected he and Kady would end this way. Theirs had been the stuff dreams were made of. Or so he'd thought. Yet here he was, making sure what had happened to them would never happen again.

He glanced back at the clinic before pulling his sunglasses off his head and dropping them onto his nose, dimming the view around him as he made his way to the subway station.

It was done. There was no going back.

His doctor, while arguing against the procedure, saying Tucker was too young to make that kind of decision, had finally acquiesced and given him the old snip-snip eight weeks ago. He would not make another woman pregnant, or cause her to go through the horrors and heartache he and Kady had lived through. She'd tried to talk him out of it, saying they were through if he went through with it. But it hadn't changed his mind.

It hadn't changed hers either. Four years of marriage gone, in the blink of an eye.

He bumped shoulders with someone with a muttered apology as he stepped into the crowded station. On his way back to the hospital, a twelve-hour shift stared him in the face. But at least work kept him from thinking. And the change in venue from Atlanta to New York had meant a fresh start, even if it hadn't dulled the heartache of the past. Bracing his feet apart and wrapping his fingers around the grab bar over his head, he closed his eyes and let the steady *whooshing* of the metro keep the painful memories at bay.

If only they'd known when they'd met, things might have been different.

No, they wouldn't. Because while the pregnancy—a year into their relationship—had come as a shock, the tearful yearning in Kady's eyes as she'd shown him the pregnancy test had won Tucker over. She'd desperately wanted that child. Had wanted him to be happy about it. And in the end he had been. A hurried elopement and whirlwind honeymoon had been just like the rest of their relationship, full of explosive passion that left him breathless. It had been that way the moment they'd laid eyes on each other. The rest was history.

"No regrets," she'd said, lifting her glass of sparkling cider and clinking it against his with a laugh. And when Grace had been born… Magic. Pure magic. The perfect world they'd created had seemed complete. Their love unbreakable.

And yet look at them now.

He opened his eyes and hardened his heart. This solved nothing and only put him in a bad place. His patients needed him. And he needed them.

So that's what he would focus on, and leave all the other stuff behind.

At least until he hit his bed tonight and fell into an exhausted sleep.

The subway lurched to a stop, the doors peeled apart, and Tucker joined the throng of people vying for the exit. Seconds later he was headed up the escalator where a shaft of sunlight beckoned, promising a brighter day.

And, with a little luck, a less painful future.

CHAPTER ONE

Present day

KADY MCPHERSON STUFFED the letter from the IVF clinic into her purse as she stepped out of the taxi onto the sidewalk of the conference center. She paused and took a deep decisive breath. As much as she hated being late, nothing could blot her happiness. She was finally going to take charge of her life after all this time.

One glance at her watch had her racing up the concrete steps. She was supposed to have been here five minutes ago. But who knew that getting a cab would be so hard? At least she wasn't the first speaker. But she still had to somehow slide onto that stage without disrupting the symposium.

She showed her badge to the official manning the registration desk. He pointed her toward the second door on the left, where a large cardboard placard was set on an easel: *Managing High-Risk Pregnancies and Deliveries*.

High-risk.

Her tummy squelched just a bit. As much as she loved her job, there were moments like this, when seeing it spelled out in crisp emotionless text sent her mind spinning into the past. As did each case that didn't go the way she hoped it would. She'd spent nights staring at the ceiling in her bedroom, trying to make sense of it all. Which inevitably led to trying to draw her own baby's face into sharp focus. Instead, the image had blurred with time.

Pregnant women were her passion. And she was committed to doing everything in her power to make each one's delivery process as safe as possible. Was it because of the pain she'd gone through when she'd lost her child? Maybe. All she knew was that she was driven to help every woman she could. And every baby.

So here she was in New York, substituting for a panelist at the plea from a sister hospital. She'd come straight from the airport to the huge Westcott Hotel complex—her home for the next week. Hopefully the rest of her stay would be less chaotic than today had been.

She avoided looking at the sign again, instead tugging the heavy door and peering inside. The sound of chattering voices had her sagging with relief. People were still milling around the huge room, looking for empty seats, while someone passed out bottles of water to the panel members on the dais. Evidently she wasn't the only one running late.

Making sure that envelope wasn't sticking out, she shifted her purse higher onto her shoulder and made her way up four steps to the top of the platform.

So far so good. No one had noticed her entry.

She edged past the first three panelists as she tried to figure out where she was supposed to sit. The crisply folded nameplates were facing the audience, so she had no idea who anyone was. There were still two empty seats up here. Which one was hers?

She reached the first empty chair and leaned over it, tipping the paper name card so she could see it. Someone named Abe Williams. Okay, it wasn't this one.

The person sitting to the left turned slightly to look up—did a second take.

Shock and horror snaked up her spine just as the lights from the huge overhead chandeliers faded and came back up. A signal that they were getting ready to start.

A signal she ignored, her tummy muscles spasming in protest. She pressed a hand to it, gritting her teeth to keep the sudden slash of pain from exiting her throat.

She couldn't think, couldn't speak…couldn't *move*. *Oh, God.*

All of a sudden, Grace's face swam before her eyes in focus once again. Because she was the spitting image of this man, mirrored in those familiar features—that sharp nose, high cheekbones, those blue-gray eyes.

Saliva pooled in her mouth. A quick swallow sent it rushing to join the acidic lagoon growing inside her.

The lights winked again.

"Hello, Kady. Small world." The low, graveled tone that had once driven her wild with need was now tight. With anger? Hatred?

If so, it wasn't reflected in his eyes. They didn't flicker away, just held hers with an impassivity that made her want to cry. The same impassivity he'd shown at the end of their marriage.

It had been two years since their divorce…three years since their daughter's death.

Hurt made her draw a shaky breath, unsure what to

do or say. The lights came back up a third time, and the moderator moved behind the podium. He gave them a pointed glance that sent her hurrying down the row without a word. She felt Tucker's gaze follow her.

It could be worse. She could be sitting right next to him.

Worse?

What could be worse than attending the same convention as a man who'd had a vasectomy just to make sure he never fathered another child with you?

She'd pleaded with him. Had begged him to reconsider.

Remembered humiliation quickened her steps.

Never again. She would never rely on another man for her happiness. This time around she would be one in charge of her future. Of whether she had another child or not.

She dropped into the padded metal seat and scooted it under the table, cringing as the legs made an awful squealing sound against the polished wooden floor. The man at the podium glanced her way again, a frown on his face. She mouthed, "Sorry," then dug into her attaché for the notes she'd brought. How was she going to speak when it came her turn?

The crowded room would have been nerve-racking enough, but to have someone who'd once known the most intimate details of her life sit there and weigh her every word?

Her thumb scrubbed over the spot on her finger. Empty, but not forgotten. Neither had her muscle memory erased the habit of reaching for it whenever she was nervous.

Or missing him.

No, she didn't miss him. Not anymore.

The moderator gave a quick summary of the topic and then started down the line of presenters, reading from a sheet that evidently contained each person's professional bio. She stared at her notes, willing the words to make sense. Willing herself to drown out the well-modulated voice from seconds earlier. Her thumb searched for that missing ring yet again.

Stop it, Kady.

She should have been counting people, so she could brace herself for the mention of her ex's name, but since she didn't remember how many seats there were, all she could do was sit there in dread.

"Dr. Tucker Stevenson, pediatric surgeon specializing in fetal surgery at Wilson-Ross Memorial Hospital, New York City."

Her heart twisted. Even the best surgeon in the world couldn't have prevented what had happened three years ago. And Tucker was one of the best.

The moderator moved on to the next panelist, listing dry facts that barely scratched the surface of what made each person live and breathe…and grieve.

"Dr. Kadeline McPherson, maternal-fetal medicine, at Wilson-Ross Memorial Hospital, Atlanta, Georgia."

No mention of anyone's personal life, how many children, spouse's name. Thank God. And she was even more thankful that she'd gone back to her maiden name. Kadeline Stevenson might have caused awkward questions that she'd rather not answer. She suspected Tucker would prefer that little tidbit to remain buried as well.

She gulped.

Buried.

She hated that word. Avoided using it like the plague.

Speech. Read your speech.

Fiddling with her thin sheaf of papers that contained words she'd recited hundreds of times, she prayed for a clear head. The question-and-answer phase was the trickier part, trying to think up responses on the fly.

With Tucker sitting in the same room.

Forget about him, Kady.

The table microphone inched its way down the line as each person finished.

Tucker's turn came, and his voice cut through her all over again. So much for forgetting about him.

His words were sure and firm, with a confidence that came with being the top in his field.

Kady closed her eyes and tried to drown him out with a bawdy mental rendition of "Ninety-nine Bottles of Beer on the Wall", but it didn't work. Especially since he'd sung that very song to her during her labor to take her mind off the pain.

If only she'd known the real pain would come months after the baby's actual birth.

"Fetal surgical intervention is necessary in any number of cases. My most recent involved an obstructed urethra in an eight-month-old fetus. Surgery removed the blockage and mother and baby were both fine."

They were both fine. How many times did he say that in a day?

Light applause followed his speech, just like it had everyone else's. Kady realized she was the only one not clapping, but just as she went to join in, the sound died away, leaving her with her hands up, palms facing each other.

Tucker chose that very moment to glance her way.

One side of his mouth quirked up, a crease coming to life in his right cheek.

Her breath caught as a spark of something dark arrowed through her abdomen. For a few awful seconds she couldn't look away. He evidently didn't have the same problem, giving his attention to the next speaker, who talked about controlling blood pressure in patients with preeclampsia.

She wasn't making that mistake again.

She focused on some nameless audience member as the microphone moved again, capturing the topic of twin-to-twin transfusion syndrome. So far no one had mentioned genetic abnormalities, but no symposium of high-risk pregnancies would be complete without that element. Normally she could just sit there stoically, an expression of polite interest superglued to her face.

But with Tucker sitting just down the row? Almost impossible.

Was he thinking the same thing?

Doubtful. He'd somehow seemed to be able to push Grace out of his life and thoughts with the same ease that he'd signed those divorce papers. Out of sight. Out of mind. Was that how it worked with him?

No, she'd seen his grief firsthand. Raw and angry and ready to wreak havoc on the gods for what had happened. In the end, the only true havoc he'd wreaked had been on their relationship when he'd stated they were having no more children. Ever. She'd had no say. Her request to him to go with her to genetic counseling had fallen on deaf ears. Nothing had moved him from his stance.

And yet a second ago he'd tossed her a smile that had

napalmed her senses as if nothing had ever happened between them. As if they were old friends.

They were not friends.

The drone of voices went silent. Glancing up in a panic, she realized it was because it was her turn to speak. The microphone was already in front of her. How had she missed that?

Clearing her throat and hearing it amplified through the whole auditorium made her wince. As did the light laughter that accompanied it. "Sorry. It was a long flight."

More laughter. Louder this time. Maybe because the flight from Atlanta to New York only took a little over two hours.

The emotional distance, though, was much, much longer.

She forced an amused crinkle to her nose. "Long day at the office?"

This time the laughter was with her rather than aimed at her. It helped put her at ease and allowed her to temporarily block out all thoughts of Tucker Stevenson. Plunging into her brief five-minute speech, she allowed her passion for the subject at hand to propel her through to the end. Wasn't her specialty all about empowering women during difficult times?

And wasn't that what her IVF quest was all about?

The audience clapped, and she couldn't stop herself from sneaking a glance back down the line of presenters. Tucker was leaning forward, his elbows planted on the table, head swiveled in her direction. This time he gave her a nod that she could swear contained at least a hint of admiration.

For her?

A shiver went through her.

No, she had to be mistaken.

A thought came to mind. Had he gone through with the procedure?

The thought of her ex-husband never fathering another sweet baby girl like their Grace pierced straight through her. He'd been a wonderful daddy—once he'd got over his initial fears of inadequacy. He'd loved their daughter in a way that had made her go all gooey inside—had made her hot for him and him alone. No other man could touch what she'd once felt for Tucker.

Watching as that pristine white casket was slowly lowered into the ground had changed him, though.

It had changed both of them.

Gone had been the days of frantic lovemaking. Of being unable to wait to get each other's clothes off. In fact, Tucker had moved into another bedroom soon afterward, cutting himself off from her completely.

The difference between them was that Kady had never completely let go of hope. Even in the aftermath of Grace's death.

It took two recessive genes coming together to cause Tay-Sachs. He could have had children with someone else and not had a problem. Although since neither of them were of Ashkenazi Jewish heritage, it had never dawned on them that they could be carriers until it was too late. What were the chances?

Enough to land them with a horrific diagnosis.

Any future children they'd produced would have had a one in four chance of having the same deadly genetic imprint.

But there were other ways to have kids. Adoption. Even genetic selection of embryos, although that thought made her stomach swish sideways.

The last panelist finished and not one of them had spoken about genetic abnormalities, which she found odd. Unless there was a dedicated workshop just focusing on screening. She would have to look at the schedule and avoid any such session like the plague.

The moderator opened the floor to questions—the moment she'd been dreading the most.

The first one came from a female audience member and was directed at Tucker. "How many fetal surgeries have you done? And what are the most common things you've corrected? The last question goes along with that. Have you ever had a case that you knew was hopeless?"

The long seconds of silence that followed the query would have made any librarian proud. Only Kady knew exactly what had caused it. And why.

A thousand pins pricked the backs of her eyelids and she had to steel herself not to let them take hold. Instead, she clasped her hands tightly together and willed him the strength to get through the question.

"I've done a few hundred surgeries, although I don't have an exact number. The most common procedures I've run into have been neural tube defects. And, no, I've never had a case where I've given up without at least exploring every available option."

That answer jerked her head sideways to stare down the line at him. He most certainly had. The fact that he could sit there and let that answer fall from his lips made the pendulum swing from sympathy back toward anger.

Only this time he didn't look her way, so her mad face was useless.

Two questions later, someone asked Kady what her toughest case had been.

"That would be my divorce." She laughed as if it was all a big joke, even though that barb had been sent straight toward the hunk to her left. "Sorry. No, my toughest case was a mother who came in at six months carrying quadruplets. She'd had no prenatal care and was seizing—in full eclampsia." A whisper of gasps went through the audience. Kady waited for it to die down, knowing the worst was yet to come. That case had made her cry, and had almost, *almost* made her quit medicine completely. But they needed to know the realities of what they would face.

She forced herself to continue. "Only one of those babies survived. That was hard. I can't stress enough the need for early intervention and care, and you should stress it to your patients as well. Knowledge really is power in cases like this one. If she'd been followed from her first trimester, we probably could have given her a good outcome that ended with four live births."

Even as she said it, she knew—from experience— there were some conditions that no amount of care or intervention could fix.

An hour later, the questions had been exhausted and people filtered from the room, leaving her to stuff her papers back into her bag and plan her escape. The moderator handed her a note. She glanced at it and frowned. The head of maternal-fetal surgery at Wilson-Ross wanted her to stop by his office when she had a chance.

Why? Unless it had something to do with the conference. She made a mental note to swing by the hospital as she dropped the slip of paper into her purse. Her fingers brushed across the IVF clinic's letter, and she couldn't stop herself from glancing at it. It was a huge decision. But maybe it was the best one for her.

"I didn't realize you were going to be here." Someone settled into the vacated chair next to her.

She snatched her attention from the letter, jerking the edges of her handbag closed.

Get real, Kady. It's nothing to be embarrassed about.

"I could say the same thing about you." She hadn't meant that to come out as surly as it had.

His glance traveled from her face to her hand, making her realize her fingers were still clenched around the opening to her bag.

"The difference is," he said, "I work here."

"I was a last-minute substitution. Your administrator asked me to come."

"Ah, so you're taking Dr. Blacke's place, then. I'd wondered who they got."

"Is he traveling?"

"No. He found out he has pancreatic cancer last week."

Up came her head, her eyes finding his. "Oh. I'm so sorry, Tucker. I had no idea. Does he have a good prognosis?"

"Unfortunately no, although all of us have seen hopeless cases turn around completely."

"And sometimes they don't." She forced her fingers to release their death grip on her purse, afraid he'd read some kind of telling emotion into the act.

Ha! As if there wasn't.

"You're right. Sometimes they don't." He studied her for a few seconds before continuing, "Our divorce was the toughest thing you've ever handled?"

"It was an icebreaker. It was supposed to be funny."

Especially since they both knew the correct and not-funny-at-all answer would have been Grace's death. "None of them know we were ever married, much less divorced."

"And yet we've been both." His mouth tightened slightly. "Maiden name?"

"Easier, don't you think?" If he could do short, concise questions, so could she. Especially as her heart was beginning to set up a slow thudding in her chest that spelled danger. She needed to get out of there.

"Easier? Possibly."

Possibly? That drew her up short. How did that even make sense? Of course it was easier.

"I think it is. People won't automatically see the last names and wonder if we're brother and sister. Or something else."

One side of that mouth quirked again. "Oh, it was definitely something else."

The thudding became a triplet of beats. Then another. How was it that he could still turn her knees to jelly with the single turn of phrase?

"Tucker…" She allowed a warning note to enter her voice.

He leaned back in his chair. "So how are you?"

"Fine."

Sure she was. Right now, she was anything but fine. Why had she let herself be talked into this stupid trip?

He leaned forward. "Okay, let's cut to the chase. Are you staying for the entire conference?"

"Yes. You?" It was a stupid question, since he lived here, but her brain was currently operating in a fog.

"Hmm…"

She would take that as a yes.

"Do you have a place to stay?" he asked.

A weird squeaking sound came from her throat that she disguised as a laugh. "I take it that wasn't an invitation."

He smiled the first real smile she'd seen since she'd been there. "I take it you wouldn't accept, if it was."

"That probably wouldn't be wise." Not that they hadn't done some very unwise things over the course of their relationship. "The hospital booked me a room at the hotel across the street. It's convenient. And close to both the hospital and the conference center."

"Convenient. That's one word for it."

Was he saying that her being here was making it awkward for him? Of course it was. Just like being around him was uncomfortable for her. In more ways than one.

She took a deep breath and asked a real question. "How are you, Tucker…really?"

"I'm busy." His smile faded, the words taking on an edge that made her tilt her head. And it didn't answer her question.

"You always were in high demand."

"With some people. Not so much with others."

Was he talking about their marriage? Because she hadn't been the one to withdraw. He had. She'd loved this man. Deeply. Passionately. It was why it had devastated her when he'd shut down completely during Grace's illness—pulling away from everyone except for his patients.

She'd been his wife! Grace's slow downward spiral had been just as painful for her. The worst thing was, she'd felt frighteningly alone during those first few months after her death, while Tucker had slept in the guest bedroom and spent longer and longer hours working at the hospital. Desperate to reconnect with him on whatever level she could, she'd casually said maybe they should try to have another baby. If she'd thought that would lure him back into their bedroom, she couldn't have been more wrong. He'd looked at her as if she'd taken leave of her senses, his next words chilling her to the bone.

I'll never have another child.

When she'd started to say something more, he'd cut her off with a shake of his head and walked out of the room. Any time she'd brought up the subject after that, begging him to talk to her, she'd been met with the same stony response. Rather…no response. And his hours at the office had increased so that he'd barely been home at all.

Then had come the final blow. On the first anniversary of Grace's death, he'd announced he'd decided to get a vasectomy, as if it was something people did every day. He'd probably hoped that would end all talk of having more children. It had.

His unilateral decision had floored her. And infuriated her.

The powerlessness she'd felt had been crushing. All-encompassing.

That had been the beginning of the end. Actually, it had been more like a rapid slide to home base, only to find out that the ball had arrived long before you had.

Three strikes and they were out. Bags packed. Papers filed. Divorce decree signed.

Being bitter solved nothing, though. So she stuffed all that back inside.

She went back to his cryptic comment about being in demand. "I'm sure your patients appreciate all you do."

A softness came back into his eyes. "I wasn't trying to be the big bad wolf back then, Kady."

"I can see that…now."

Back then, though, things hadn't been so clear, and he'd seemed like the villain in their particular tale.

To her, anyway. Even now the memory of those days pinched at her heart like a pair of surgical clamps, causing a strange numbness to come over her.

But not so numb that it staunched the weird waterworks sensation that was inching its way back onto her radar. God, she wished things could have been different between them. They hadn't been, though. So she needed to stop looking at him with glasses that magnified those old hurts. "That's all in the past, where I think it should probably stay."

He stood. "You're right. It is. I just wanted to stop by and say hello."

"I'm glad you did. It was really good to see you again."

Good and sad and filled with all kinds of regrets.

He walked away, leaving her on her own once again. Only this time she was ready. All decisions about whether or not to have children would be made by her. And as soon as she got home, she was going to act on them. Seeing him again had just brought home all her reasons for wanting a child, and that longing she'd had as she'd carried Grace over those nine months.

All she needed to do was select a sperm donor and she'd be ready to start a family of her own.

For a few brief seconds she'd wanted to throw that letter from the clinic in his face, the way he'd thrown his decision about not having children in hers, but what would it solve?

Nothing.

She didn't want to hurt Tucker. She just wanted a baby. Not to replace Grace. That would never happen. She would always love her little girl and be grateful for the time they'd had together. At times, Grace's loss still caused her lungs to seize in the middle of the night as she lay there alone in bed. Any tiny sound in the dark would make her sit up, sure she'd heard a familiar cry. Wishing with all her might that she *had* heard that cry. And when she realized no one was there, Kady would be the one who cried.

Surely her daughter wouldn't have wanted her to be stuck in limbo like this, never moving forward. She'd like to think Grace would have wanted her to go on living, to love and be loved. And she was finally ready to share that love. With another baby.

She tried to focus on that and block out the negative thoughts that were steadily creeping into her head.

And the best way to hold those at bay was to stay as far away from Dr. Tucker Stevenson as possible.

CHAPTER TWO

TUCKER HAD NO idea why Phil Harold, the department head, wanted to see him. He was already running behind on his appointments and had a surgery scheduled at two o'clock this afternoon. At this rate, he'd be late to the convention workshop today. The convention. Great. Where he'd probably see Kady again.

How in the hell had any of this happened? He'd come to New York to get away from her. No, not from her. From the pain and memories of what had happened in Atlanta. Except some things—unlike his old golf clubs—weren't as easy to leave behind. Some of them had followed him. And seeing Kady again had been like a punch to the gut, reawaking the guilt of not being able to give her what she'd wanted.

It was just for a week, though. Surely he could maintain some kind of poker face for that long. Then she'd fly back home. Life would return to normal.

Or some semblance of normal.

He rapped on the door, irritated that his thoughts seemed to keep circling his ex.

"Come."

The curt command didn't faze him. Phil was that way

with everyone. And, as far as he knew, he hadn't done anything to tick the man off. Not this week, anyway.

He pushed through the door and paused. Someone else was already in there. "Sorry, I can—"

"No, come in. This concerns both of you."

Both?

Taking another look at the chair's occupant, his stomach curdled in protest. Talk about circling. Think about her, and she appeared.

What the hell was Kady doing here?

He'd figured she'd be out lounging by the pool this morning, wearing one of those skimpy bikinis she tended to favor. Memories of creamy skin and long, lithe limbs flashed through his skull, only to be ejected in a hurry.

Not even going there.

That was what had gotten him into trouble in the first place.

He chose to remain standing by the door, even as Phil took his seat again. "You have a group of medical students scheduled to shadow you this week between conference sessions. Are you ready for them?"

Oh, hell, he'd completely forgotten about that. Since most of his workshop responsibilities were in the late afternoons, Phil had asked if a small contingent of students who were interested in obstetrics and pediatrics could follow him on his rounds.

That still didn't explain why Kady was here.

"I am. Thanks for the reminder, though." Even he could hear the tightness in his voice.

Kady was just as tense. He saw it in the stiff set of her spine, in the way her neck was set squarely between her shoulders. And her hands were clutched together, pressed against her belly. A protective posture. Remembered from her pregnancy all those years ago? His own stomach muscles squeezed against each other.

She'd known Phil was going to call him in here.

"Dr. Blacke was going to help originally, but since he can't be here, I thought Dr. McPherson might agree to take his place, since your specialties tie together in some areas. I've been trying to coax her into it. She thinks you might object for some reason. You don't. Correct?"

He waited for Kady to offer up some other kind of excuse, but she just sat there like a stone. It was up to him to derail this train.

"No objections, but I'm sure Dr. McPherson didn't come here expecting to practice medicine."

Phil's glance went from him to Kady. "Can we count on you to help a sister hospital train up a new generation of doctors?"

Leave it to the department head to make it almost impossible to refuse. It was a weapon the man used well.

"Well… Of course. If you think it would help."

The hesitation was obvious. But he knew Phil well enough to know that he would purposely ignore it. And there was no way he could signal her without his boss seeing it.

And Phil wasn't asking anything out of the ordinary. He and Dr. Blacke normally did a kind of back and forth dialogue with medical students.

"Yes, it would help Dr. Stevenson out immensely."

Of course it would.

Tucker was barely able to suppress the eye-roll he felt coming on. He covered it by asking, "Any idea who will take Gordy's place during his treatment?"

"Not yet. We're still looking for his replacement." He

glanced at Kady, a speculative smile curving his lips. "You wouldn't consider transferring to our neck of the woods, would you?"

Kady's hands uncurled and her thumb went to the back of her ring finger and scrubbed at it. Trying to remove any reminders of what was once there? She'd mailed the rings back to him. He still had them somewhere. Why, he had no idea.

"No, I'm sorry. I'm getting ready to—" Her voice came to an abrupt stop, along with her thumb, before starting up again. "I have a lot going on in Atlanta right now. And my family is there."

Kady's grandparents. They were good people who'd raised her after her parents had been killed in a car accident. He respected them. And Kady loved them like crazy. He'd left for New York almost immediately after they'd separated.

He hadn't talked to them about the split. He probably should have faced her grandfather and tried to explain. But what explanation was there, really? He and Kady disagreed on a fundamental part of their life together. She wanted more children. He didn't. Had taken steps to make sure that option was never on the table with Kady, or any another woman.

His and Kady's wants and needs had landed them in opposite corners of the ring, and neither of them was willing to come to the middle.

Middle? There was no middle. One of them would have had to give in completely. He couldn't ask that of Kady. Whispers of guilt surrounded his heart and mind, his teeth clamping tightly to ward them off. She deserved to have kids if that's what she wanted. He just…couldn't. A divorce had seemed better than forcing her to live a life she didn't want. Maybe she already had another child. The thought of that made his jaw lock tight. She wasn't married again, judging from the lack of a ring on that finger she'd been worrying a moment earlier.

Phil nodded. "We'll just have to take whatever you're willing to give while you're here, then. Since Dr. Stevenson is fine with you pairing up, then we're good?"

One side of Tucker's mouth twitched to the side at the way Phil had worded that. He and Kady used to do a whole lot of pairing up—in a completely different sense. There was no way he or Kady were going to admit to that, though, so it looked like they were both stuck. Unless they told Phil they were divorced—from each other—they were going to have a hard time explaining why they couldn't work together.

"I'm happy to help, of course."

Those words were soft. Unsure. Not like the Kady he knew who took the bull by the horns and wrestled it to the ground. Then again, she'd lived through a lot of heartache since their youthful days when they'd been carefree and crazy in love.

"Good. I'll leave you two to work on coordinating your schedules. I appreciate you giving us some of your time, Dr. McPherson. If you go down to HR, they can reimburse you for your hours. Not as much as you'd get for practicing medicine, but we do have a small budget for consultants."

"It's okay. I'm taking Dr. Blacke's place at the conference anyway. If it will help patients in the future, then it's for a good cause."

"We at Wilson-Ross thank you."

It wasn't like Phil to stand on formalities. Or to suggest that a visiting doctor transfer to his department on a permanent basis. He took a closer look at the man as a tinge of something dark and ugly rose up inside him. He didn't see any overt interest, but Phil was divorced too, and Kady was a beautiful woman.

Even if the man was interested, there was nothing he could do about it. Nothing he *would* do about it. His ring was no longer on her finger. She could do as she pleased.

And if Phil pleased her?

Give it a rest, idiot!

Maybe interpreting Phil's words as a dismissal, his ex climbed to her feet and reached to shake Phil's hand. Her blouse rode up, exposing a sliver of her back in the process.

His fingers curled into his palms.

Damn.

How he'd loved to explore each ridge and hollow of her spine, his index finger slowly working its way from her neck all the way down the vertebral column, whispering the names and numbers of each in her ear. By the time he'd reached the bottom, she'd been shaking with need.

So had he.

Sex between them had always been volcanic. Greedy and generous. Two words not normally associated with each other, but that described their lovemaking perfectly.

"Thanks for the opportunity," she murmured.

The opportunity to spend more of her time with her ex? Of course not. That was just his feverish brain lusting after what it couldn't have. What it *shouldn't* have.

Which was why he'd had to let her go two years

ago. His body had never listened to his head where she was concerned. If he'd stayed, he would have ended up making them both miserable. He'd seen it in her face. Heard it in her voice.

He waited for her to leave the room, then threw a nod to Phil and followed her out. He fell into step beside her. "You don't have to do this, you know. If you said no, Phil would have to understand."

"And what would we tell him exactly?"

"We'd think of something."

She sighed. "I think it's already been decided. Besides, I want to do it."

"Why?" He was genuinely curious. The last thing they should do was spend any more time than necessary together. Hadn't he already proven that a minute ago? Or maybe she wasn't still as affected by him as he was by her.

"I don't know exactly. It's an exciting chance to see how things are done at the main campus of Wilson-Ross."

"Trust me. It's the same as Wilson-Ross in Atlanta."

"Maybe, but we follow protocols set by New York. You see the first new wave of treatments."

He nodded. "You could get that by meeting with the folks in Maternal-Fetal. I could set up a face to face with them, if you want."

"I would love that. But I'd still like to help with the medical students." She turned her face to look at him. "Unless it would make you too uncomfortable."

That was exactly what he had been thinking just moments earlier. But it wasn't something he wanted to admit. Not even to himself.

"And you wouldn't be?"

The colorful lines on the white linoleum floor helped guide patients and staff alike to different sections of the hospital. He followed the blue stripe, although he knew the route by heart. His office was on the other side of the hospital.

"We've lived through things that were a lot worse than a few hours of awkwardness."

"Yes. We have." He hesitated. It was none of his business, but he had to ask. "Did you ever have more kids?"

Her face paled for a few telling seconds before turning a bright pink. She opened her mouth. Closed it. Then opened it again. "No. I haven't."

"I'm sorry, I shouldn't have asked that."

She stopped in her tracks, her chin popping up. "No. You shouldn't have." Then her face softened. "Thank you for sending the flowers, though."

He didn't have to ask what she was talking about. The monthly daisies for Grace's grave. "The florist sends them. I just put in the order."

"I thought they were from you, but there is never any card attached."

"Grace can't read a card." His jaw tightened again. "Or anything else."

The florist had told him that daisies symbolized innocence and purity. Exactly what he thought of when he remembered his daughter. It had made the suffering she'd gone through all the more terrible somehow.

"Then why send them?" The question didn't have the challenging tone he would have expected. Instead, she seemed to be searching for something.

He had no idea what, and even if he did, Tucker didn't have an answer for her. He had no idea why he sent them. It was true. Grace would never see or touch or bury her face in those white petals. A tightness gripped his throat that wouldn't let go.

That first trip to the florist's shop had been hard. He'd sat in the parking lot for almost an hour before he'd been able to make himself go inside. The woman at the desk had taken his order, the compassion on her face almost his undoing. But once it was done, it had become almost a ritual—a sacred remembrance of what she'd meant to him.

He shrugged. "I know she would have liked them. It's the only explanation I have."

As she turned to start walking, something made him snag her wrist and pull her to a stop. When she turned to face him again, he took a moment to study her before letting go of her hand. She'd lost weight in the last two years. She wasn't emaciated, by any means, but there were hollows to her cheeks that hadn't been there when they'd been together. Maybe it was because her hair was longer than it had been, those vibrant red waves throwing shadows across her face. But whatever it was, her green eyes were the same, glowing...alive. Only now they were a little more secretive than they used to be. He didn't like not being able to read her the way he once could.

"Are you...?"

Her brows puckered. "Am I what?"

"Are you okay with me sending them? The flowers, I mean." He'd set out to ask her if she was really and truly okay. But since he wasn't sure he really wanted to know, he'd changed it at the last second.

"Yes." Kady reached out and touched his hand. "I think it's sweet. And Nanna and Granda' like seeing them when they go to visit her grave."

"How are they?" Kady's Irish grandparents had taken some getting used to. As had her extended family, which was huge. And loud. And fun. He and his parents had been close, but their family gatherings had been small, reserved affairs. And as an only child, Tucker had learned to imitate that…to remain quiet and stoic no matter what was happening around him.

Not the McPhersons. They all wore their hearts on their sleeves, holding nothing in.

Only Kady did. At least, the Kady standing in front of him did.

She dropped her hand to her side. The urge to reach down and enfold it in his came and went. "They miss Grace, obviously, just like I do. But they're doing okay. Nanna has been a bit forgetful recently, which has Granda' worried."

"Anything serious?"

"I don't think so. I don't see the signs of Alzheimer's there. But time will tell. If it gets worse, I'll talk her into getting some tests."

"A very smart idea."

Tell them I said hi. Send them my love. Tell them I'll see them soon.

None of those responses were appropriate anymore. And it set up an ache inside him that wouldn't quit.

"They're thinking of selling the house and getting something smaller."

The McPhersons' home was huge by any standards. They'd held large family gatherings there. Thanksgiving. Christmas. Any holiday had been an occasion to be celebrated. He couldn't picture them living anywhere else. The family's wealth had been another thing that had come between him and Kady at the end. She had insisted her grandparents were willing to hire a fertility expert to make sure the odds of having another baby with Tay-Sachs were as low as possible. He'd been dead set against it. Not because of the money it would take. Her grandparents could afford all of that and more. His argument had been more along the lines of not being able to guarantee with a hundred percent certainty that they would not have another child like Grace.

"That would take some getting used to for them, wouldn't it?"

"I think they're ready for a change."

Just like Tucker had been. Looking back, though, he wondered if it wasn't so much that he had been ready for change as it was that he'd been running from his grief. The hopeful look on Kady's face whenever she'd spoken of another baby had been enough to send an icepick through his heart. Eventually the organ had become a sieve, any emotional involvement leaking away until there had been nothing left.

"I hope it all works out for them."

"Thank you."

And on that note it was time for him to get back to his own retooled life. "Well, I have a surgery today at two. I'm assuming the medical students will be coming tomorrow, since Phil didn't mention them being at the hospital today." He paused. "Do you need anything while you're here?"

He wasn't sure what he would do if she came up with something personal.

"No. I think I'm good. I guess I'll see you later this afternoon, if you're in any of the sessions."

"I'm scheduled for the anesthesia and pregnancy track."

She nodded. "I'm not in that one. I have 'Monitoring

the High-Risk Pregnancy from Beginning to Delivery.' So I guess I'll see you tomorrow, then. Any idea at all on when we're supposed to meet the students?"

He hadn't thought to ask, although Phil had probably told him at some point. "I'm not sure. I'll get hold of him and give you a call at the hotel, if that's okay."

"Yes. I'm in room 708. You can leave a message if I'm not there."

No offer of her cellphone number. But then again, he'd told her he'd call her at the hotel, so maybe she thought he didn't want it.

He didn't.

Did he?

Hell, no. It would just give his fingers an excuse to push and erase those numbers again and again. Or, worse, call her with some trumped-up excuse just so he could hear her voice.

That was all he needed—one more thing to brood over. Not that he'd tried to call her since the divorce. Her cellphone number could be the same, for all he knew.

She said goodbye, and this time when she turned to leave he didn't try to stop her.

Even though there was a small part of him that wanted to do just that.

And he had no idea why.

Kady had the morning to herself. It was still early and the pool was deserted. Dropping her towel onto a nearby lounger, she went over to the water's edge and dipped in a toe. A shiver rippled over her at the difference in temperature. All the windows were fogged up, but the heat and humidity of the room were a welcome change from the icy interior of the hotel. She kind of liked the misty atmosphere. It gave her a sense of privacy. As if this was her personal luxury spa.

She hadn't seen Tucker at the convention the previous night, but then again they'd been in separate sessions. As soon as her part had ended, she'd gone straight to her room. She'd had a headache, and a dull listlessness had stolen over her, something she hadn't felt in a while. The result of seeing Tucker again?

Probably.

It was a shock, that's all. Anyone in their right mind would feel a big old jolt of disbelief at seeing their ex after all this time.

All this time? It wasn't like it had been ten years since she'd seen him. From her horrified reaction, it might as well have been, though.

And he hadn't called to say what time they were supposed to meet the medical students, so she assumed that wasn't happening until later. Or maybe he'd told Mr. Harold that he preferred she didn't come. That made her frown. She would have expected him to let her know, either way. Unless he'd tried and couldn't reach her.

She probably should have given him her cellphone number, but it hadn't even crossed her mind until she'd been almost out of the hospital. To run back and breathlessly give it to him smacked of teenaged infatuation. And Kady had long since passed those days of young love.

Young love. Ha!

"Cynical, Kady. Cynical."

Okay, it might be cynical, but better that than be hurt by another man. Tucker had talked about never having any more children? Well, she was pretty sure she wasn't getting married again. She hadn't even wanted to date since they'd broken up.

She could just take the plunge and put up a profile on one of those date matcher-upper things. Instead, she took a different kind of plunge and jumped into the pool. The chill shocked her system, almost causing her lungs to contract and blow out all her air reserves. She controlled the urge and then kicked her way to the very bottom. She tooled around, following the downward curve until she reached the deep end. Nice. This was the only kind of plunge she wanted to take. Her eyes burned slightly from the chlorine, but she was used to that. She drifted to where the light was, putting her palm over it before she went even deeper, glancing up at the surface above. She couldn't remember if the pool had an eight- or twelve-foot depth.

What did it matter? She could just stay down here forever.

Except she couldn't.

As they always did, her lungs sent the first twinges of protest to her brain. Just another few seconds.

She closed her eyes and let herself "be." Something she could only seem to do in the water. But her lungs' distress calls had now been taken up by other parts of her body. Time to go. She pushed off the concrete floor and shot toward the light above, breaking the surface and sucking down one huge gulp of air after another, before reaching toward the edge. Instead of a cold tiled surface, she encountered something firm but warm. Curling around her hand.

Blinking the water out of her eyes in a hurry, she glanced up.

"Tucker?" The name rasped across her vocal cords

right before shock took control of them and rendered her silent. She wasn't even sure why she'd asked, other than letting her brain in on what her heart already knew: it was him. It had to be, even if the light behind him cast his face in shadow. That, along with his dark jeans and black shirt, gave him a slightly sinister look. He could be a dark god. Or a fallen angel. She couldn't quite decide which fit him better.

Neither.

Breathe, Kady, breathe.

She did just that, trying to figure out if she was just imagining it or if Tucker was really crouched by the side of the pool, gripping her hand. His skin was warm. She could just curl into his palm and…

And nothing.

"I was just about to go in after you."

"You were?"

"You looked pretty lifeless down there. One minute you were swimming like a fish and the next you went into some kind of suspended animation." His thumb made a slight movement across the back of her hand. Small enough to make her wonder if she'd imagined it. Imaginary or not, it sent raw sensation skittering down her nerve endings, making them scramble to interpret it.

There was nothing to interpret.

She struggled to get her tongue to wrap around the words. "You've seen me like that before." He had. Many times.

He paused, fingers tightening slightly on hers. "Yes. I have."

Were they talking about the same thing? "Okay, so you know that I'm fine."

"I do now. You're a land creature, Kady. You belong up here."

Next to him? When he looked like that? When just the touch of his hand on hers was making her picture all kinds of crazy scenarios? Like pulling him into the pool and seeing what it started?

There was no way in hell she was going to do that. "What are you doing here, anyway?"

"I lost the slip of paper with your room number on it." The pad of his thumb shifted again. This time there was no way it was her imagination. Why was he still holding onto her anyway? And why the heck wasn't she pulling away?

"How did you expect to find me when you came over, then?"

"I hadn't thought that far ahead." He smiled. "Want me to help you out?"

She took stock of the situation. Her towel was way over there. And she was dressed in a pretty skimpy bikini. He'd seen her stretch marks and the changes in her abdomen from carrying Grace before. But they'd been married back then. When things between them had been easy and comfortable.

She was no longer comfortable in his presence. She was self-conscious and nervous. And she didn't like it.

Better to just face it. "Sure. Thanks."

She gave a quick kick of her legs to help him, and Tucker hauled her up and out of the pool. His eyes skated across her torso, then he dropped her hand as if he'd grabbed the wrong end of a scalpel. Then he swore, his gaze moving up and out—landing on anything except her.

What the...?

When she glanced down, she shrieked. The side strings on her bikini top had come undone, something she would have noticed had she not been so busy trying to figure out if he was stroking her hand. And getting worked up over it.

Well, she wasn't worked up anymore!

Turning away quickly, thankful now for the fogged-up glass, she yanked the strings behind her back and attempted to tie them. Except she normally turned the top around and tied it in the front before twisting it to the back once more and then knotting the top.

Why couldn't she have worn a one-piece?

Well, she hadn't expected Tucker to walk in on her, for one thing.

Why do you care? The man has seen you naked, for heaven's sake. He's seen you giving birth. He cut the cord afterward.

But that noise he'd just made hadn't been an "Oh, big deal" sound.

It had been more like, "Did I just see what I think I saw?" In the old days, she would have thrown him a sexy quip and invited him closer. Much closer. They then would have spent the next couple of hours tangled in a heap, finding the first available surface. The bed. The sofa. The dining-room table.

On the fourth try with the strings she let out an exasperated breath.

"Do you need help?"

"No." She wasn't going to admit it, even if she did.

"Here, let me."

Warm hands brushed her icy ones aside, fingers gliding across her skin. Prickles broke out, rippling

across her body and ending at her nipples, which tightened unbearably.

Because this time the slow, soft touches weren't in
her imagination.

Lordy!

She hadn't invited him to come closer, but he had
anyway.

It wasn't for the same reasons, but her body thought
it was. It was busy rolling out the red carpet for the man
while he worked on unaware.

As embarrassing and awkward as her reaction to the
workings of his fingers was, it was even worse when he
suddenly stopped. "I think that's got it. Do you need it
double knotted?"

There was a low roughness to his voice that made
her stomach contract. She should tell him, no, that she
was fine, that she was done anyway.

"Please."

Was that her head talking? Or her overly eager li-
bido?

She had no idea, only knew that her eyes slid closed
as soon as he touched her again. What he didn't know
wouldn't hurt him. And, God, she had missed this part
of their relationship.

His movements weren't quite as sure as they'd been
a few minutes ago. His palm brushed her back, all five
fingers trailing down her spine in a way that was burned
into her memory. Then his touch was gone.

Was that an accident? Or was that blast from the past
done on purpose?

Accident. It had to be.

Snapping herself back to reality, she made sure
her boobs were fully contained before turning to face

him—praying her errant nipples weren't as prominent as they felt. "So why didn't you just call the hotel and ask them to connect you with my room?"

His gaze was glued to her face as if a single shift might spell disaster. It very well could. For both of them.

"I was right across the street and thought I'd just leave a message at the desk. Then they told me they'd seen you come in here, and I thought I'd tell you in person. I didn't know you'd be…" He gestured toward the pool.

"What else would I be doing in here?" As soon as the words left her mouth, she knew they were a mistake. They'd had a very sexy encounter one time at a private pool at a cabin they'd rented in the mountains.

She gulped. "What was the message?"

"That the medical students will arrive at around ten this morning."

"Ten? *This* morning?" Panic fluttered in her chest. "You just found this out?"

"I did. Phil called, but I wasn't in a position where I could answer, so he left me a voice mail. I assumed he left you one as well." His voice tightened. "I just wanted to make sure."

Tucker hadn't been able to answer his phone when his boss called? Why not?

It was none of her business what he did or didn't do. Except when he barged into where she was swimming and almost gave her a heart attack.

And then made her want him all over again.

At least he didn't know. Or did he?

"I haven't checked with the front desk yet, so maybe he did leave a message."

He glanced at his watch, not quite meeting her eyes.

"It doesn't matter. Since it's eight thirty, we have time for you to change and get some breakfast, if you haven't already eaten."

She hadn't, but she wasn't sure she wanted to spend any more time with him than necessary outside the hospital or the conference center. He'd been in close proximity to her for, what? Ten minutes? And those nimble fingers tripping down her spine had set off all kinds of cravings.

A week. It's only a week. Surely you can contain your impulses for seven measly days.

"Good thing you got the message to me, or I might have had to show up to work in my bikini."

Yikes. She'd meant it as a joke, but it didn't sound quite as blasé as she'd hoped it might.

So much for containing her impulses.

"I don't think Phil would approve of drool-lined hallways. Someone might slip and hurt themselves."

That made her smile. "I take it you aren't talking about you?"

He chuckled. "I would be too busy beating them off with a stick to worry about slipping."

"Would you beat them off?"

He was just kidding. He had to be.

"I wouldn't have to. Because you *are* going to change out of that. Otherwise things are liable to get…complicated."

A shiver went down her spine at the memory of his fingers skipping across her skin.

Complicated?

Hell, they already were. If he touched her again, she'd be the one slipping. As in slipping under his spell all over again. That would be disastrous for everyone.

She did her best to pass it off with a laugh. "Well, I'm all about things staying uncomplicated. So I'll go up and change. And I'll take you up on your breakfast offer, if it still stands."

"It does."

"Then if I can have fifteen minutes, I'll be back down in something more suitable for work."

And more suitable to hold herself in line. Although she wasn't sure she had anything in her suitcase with the power to do that.

But she was going to have to somehow dredge up a hefty dose of willpower. Before someone slipped and went down, like Tucker said they might.

And that someone was most likely to be her.

CHAPTER THREE

THEY ENDED UP taking breakfast back to Tucker's office, while he tried to figure out why he'd gone into that pool room. But the windows had been fogged up enough that he hadn't been able to make out anything inside. He was still shaken by the image of Kady floating in that pool. He'd truly thought something had happened. His heart had galloped in his chest, and he'd just reached for the bottom of his shirt to pull it off when she'd darted full force toward the surface.

That had to be why he'd reacted to her bikini the way he had. Or rather her wardrobe malfunction. Thank God it hadn't been the upper strings that had come loose. It had been bad enough to get that tantalizing glimpse of the lower curve of her breast. His body had released a sudden rush of endorphins and brought with it a craving for this woman he'd never truly figured out how to suppress and he had no idea why. But he'd better damn well find the page in the instruction manual if he was going to survive this week.

At least now she was dressed in tan slacks and a black scoop-necked top. Very professional. If he'd expected that to be his get-out-of-jail-free card, though, he was sorely mistaken. Because his memory was just fine, thank you very much. And it wasn't likely to forget that tiny drop of water that had clung to that exposed strip of flesh. He'd wanted to lick it off. To lay her down on that concrete floor and make love to her. The urge had erupted out of nowhere, shocking him with its intensity. Only it wasn't love.

It was lust. Pure and simple. Their sex life had never lacked for anything.

Until Grace had died. After that he hadn't been able to…

"How's your omelet?" Kady's voice broke through his thoughts.

He forced a brow up as if he hadn't a care in the world. "It's hospital food. How do you think it is?"

"My mixed fruit is pretty good."

"Because it only requires chopping. The fruit does all the work as far as taste goes."

"Which is why I chose it."

Although his office was fairly large and comfortable, it felt the size of a cramped work cubicle at the moment. Kady was perched on his leather sofa…the same one he normally stretched out on when he put in long hours, snatching bits of sleep when he could.

He'd put plenty of space between them. At least he'd thought he had. But even though she was on the sofa and he was on a nearby chair, he could still see a tiny vein that pulsed at the base of her throat, could enjoy the way her brows puckered and moved as she talked. The way she moistened her lips when she paused to collect her thoughts.

He recognized it all. Recognized the slight lilt from her Irish roots. Not an accent per se, just a slightly different rise and fall to her voice than most Americans had. A carryover from living with her grandparents.

Forcing a smile, he decided to change the subject. Put it firmly back in the business court. "So, Phil said there are thirteen medical students who'll be joining us. We'll head to Maternity and look over the cases down there first, and then head up to the surgical unit."

"Okay, tell me what I need to do."

"Well, one of my cases yesterday came about after an ultrasound uncovered a problem with a fetus's digestive tract, and the patient's OB/GYN called me. A section of the abdominal wall hadn't closed properly, allowing the baby's intestines to slide outside of the body."

She leaned forward, her interest obvious. "Were you able to close it? How old was the fetus?"

"The mother was thirty-three weeks along and, yes, I was able to close it." He paused. "That's where we can help these students see how certain specialties work together. If you'd come across a similar ultrasound, would you have referred the patient to a surgeon?"

"I'd have to look at all the data but, yes, if it was as straightforward as you say, I would have called you in as soon as we spotted it."

"Good. That's what Phil was looking for, I think. To show them how cases can flow back and forth between doctors."

"I see. Is there anything in the maternity department right now that might land in your court?"

He allowed himself to relax slightly. "Nothing at the moment. But we're going to concentrate on high-risk pregnancies and talk about when surgical intervention is considered and why."

"That sounds pretty straightforward."

"It's actually hard for me to think like a medical student these days. Is it the same for you?"

Kady's lips twisted to one side for a moment as if she was thinking. "I think so, although I probably haven't had as much contact with students as you do here in New York."

"We were so young back then, weren't we?"

Back when passion had been without thought, and he hadn't had to worry about whether or not he would ever make love to a woman again. That fear had turned into a self-fulfilling prophecy, which in turn had sparked a vicious cycle. Even the thought of trying caused acid to churn in his stomach and made his heart pound in his chest. He lived in dread of intimate glances or, worse, a candlelit dinner. Those days had been one endless nightmare.

In the end, his problem had been all in his head. The vasectomy had both cured him and doomed him.

"As if you're ancient now."

"Sometimes I feel like it." And if that wasn't the truth, he didn't know what was.

She took a bite of one of the strawberries on her plate and took her time chewing and swallowing before speaking again. "So do I. But I think that's the long hours talking. This conference is actually like a mini-vacation to me."

"So I saw."

Perfect. He was back to the bikini scene. Leave it to his mind to somehow find its way to the very place he didn't want it to go. And there had been no hint of his body hesitating at what it had seen. It had wanted it. Wanted her. What he wouldn't have given for that back when they'd been together. But that hadn't happened.

His mind had wanted her, but his body had been too paralyzed by fear to respond to his mental commands. The humiliation had been crushing. Damning.

From all appearances, those days were over.

"Hey, it's a hotel. I don't always have access to a pool. I looked up the amenities and came prepared."

"You always were good at that."

She smiled. "Not always. That's how we wound up with Grace."

His entire body chilled in an instant. Yes. It was how they'd wound up with Grace. He'd often wondered whether, if he could have seen the future, he would have chosen for her not to be born.

His innards wound tight, clenching and releasing. Would he? He couldn't imagine never seeing that sweet baby's smile. Never feeling her tiny fingers clamp onto his. And there was his answer. He wouldn't change it. Even though the agony of those days was still almost impossible to look back on without deep sadness.

Kady must have sensed the change in him because she set her plate down next to her hip and leaned across to touch his wrist. "It wasn't your fault, Tucker. It wasn't either of our fault. We were in a hurry. We were young and in love. We'd been talking about marriage from the time of our second date. The pregnancy just fast-forwarded all of those plans."

Did she think he was upset that they'd gotten married because of the baby? He never regretted marrying her. What he did wish was that they'd known about the possibility of Tay-Sachs right from the beginning. And he wished he'd talked to her after Grace had died about what was going on in his head.

It would have solved nothing, though.

"There's no way we can change any of it, so it doesn't really matter."

"Would you, if you could?"

At the look of hurt on her face, he frowned, realizing how brusque he'd sounded. But when she moved to pull back, his fingers lightly encircled her wrist, holding her in place. "I don't know, Kady. It's not something I would choose to go through a second time." He'd made sure he wouldn't. And he didn't regret it. Not for a second.

"I don't think any of us would."

And yet she'd wanted another baby, despite the possibility that it could happen a second time. Was it probable? No. But the slim chance that it could tied his stomach in knots, making it impossible to make love to her. What if she'd accidentally gotten pregnant a second time? Part of the reason he'd pulled back emotionally had been because of that. And part of it had been that he'd just been unable to perform, knowing that any type of birth control could fail. Any except for one.

"It's over and done with." And so were they. Yet seeing her in that pool had coaxed a reaction from his body that he hadn't been able to manage for the last year of their marriage.

Why now? Why not back then?

Was she dating anyone? It was none of his business, but it would be a lot easier to resist the tug and pull of need if she was. His gaze dropped to her stomach. What would it be like to see her swollen with someone else's child?

A faceless form appeared in his head, only to have Tucker kick it away as hard as he could.

Thank God that wasn't something he would ever have to witness.

She tugged her wrist free from his grip. "You're right. It is."

"Kady." This time it was he who leaned forward. "I never wanted it to end the way it did."

"The fact that you filed for divorce says you did."

His gaze raked her face. "You gave me no option."

"'There are always options to be explored.' Isn't that what you said at the workshop that first night?"

He shook his head. "You wanted another child. I didn't."

"You made that rather obvious."

Hot air stuck in his lungs. Was she talking about how he'd avoided the bedroom?

She went on, "When you moved into the guest room, I figured a divorce was inevitable."

He had moved out of their bedroom. But he hadn't had much of a choice. It had been either that or have her discover his secret. And add one more thing to her plate? Kady had always been good at blaming herself.

So was he.

"We were both dealing with so much at the time." They had been. Decisions that had been impossible to make under the weight of grief. "I wanted to give us both some space."

"You succeeded. We had a whole lot of space. And not just in terms of the bedroom."

"I know. Maybe we can get off to a fresh start."

"Fresh start?" She met his eyes. "What do you mean?"

"We were once friends. Maybe we could start there."

Friends. Was he kidding?

"What makes you think that's even possible?"

Tucker propped a foot on his left knee. "Because

we're mature adults. We've both moved on with our lives. We should be able to let the past go, right?"

They should. Except that her sitting across from him was sending messages to all the wrong parts of his body. Parts that were definitely showing signs of functioning around her again.

"We've never made very good friends, Tucker."

She was right. The sex had always been too intense. So crazy hot that they hadn't been able to stop and nurture some of the deeper stuff.

"No. We didn't, did we?"

And there it was. That glitter of green eyes that said she knew exactly what he was talking about.

"Nope. But I don't remember either of us complaining about it." Their gazes locked, her tongue peeking out to moisten her lips. And suddenly there was a familiar pressure behind his zipper and a big old hole where common sense should have been.

His body was functioning, but right now he needed it to take a few deep breaths and hit pause before they wound up somewhere they would both regret. "No, we didn't. But maybe we should have."

She reeled back slightly in her seat. "I'm sorry?"

"I didn't mean that the way it sounded. I just want us to tread carefully. You're here for a week. I don't want to do something that I can't undo."

The image of that undone bikini top wandered through his head before he pushed it aside.

"I don't either. So what are you proposing?"

"That we use self-discipline. Self-control. The very things that carried us through medical school. Surely we can do that."

Not that Kady hadn't shown both of those things.

But since he was the one who seemed to be struggling, maybe he needed to voice the words to give her fair warning.

"That sounds reasonable. But maybe you should stay away from the pool from now on."

He smiled. "For once, we're in agreement."

"Shake on it?" She held out her hand.

As he rose to his feet and moved over to do as she asked, he hoped he could remember what he'd said. And start practicing a little of that self-discipline he seemed to be lacking.

"Well, now that that's settled—" he let go of her hand "—shall we go down to the maternity ward and see what cases they have?"

She'd thought he was going to kiss her a moment or two ago. And she wouldn't have stopped him. Her lungs had greedily held onto every scrap of air, just in case.

And then he'd shut the whole thing down with a single line.

A little voice whispered that it was for the best. Of course it was. But that didn't mean her body agreed with that voice. Or even listened to it. Ever. At least not where Tucker was concerned. She should be glad he'd come to his senses. Because she sure hadn't come to hers.

Smoothing her blouse down and waiting for him to gather what he needed off his desk, she tried to get her errant heart and her crazed thoughts back under control. There was nothing to worry about. Tucker was just taking precautions.

But she was worried. Maybe not about him but about herself. How easy it would have been to slide back into his arms. To forget all the pain and heartache that had happened between them.

But he was right. Once it happened, there would be no undoing it.

"Ready?" He glanced back, his hand on the door lever.

"Yes."

Please, let's go out and rejoin the real world, where exes don't fantasize about each other. At least, they shouldn't.

People streamed up and down the corridor, lanyards designating some as staff, while others were either patients or visitors. The hospital was busier than the one in Atlanta, but at least it gave her a chance to catch her breath. Not easy with Tucker's tight haunches and broad shoulders striding ahead of her. His phone pinged twice, but the messages couldn't have been important because he glanced down and then kept walking, not bothering to respond.

Or maybe he didn't want her to know who they were from.

Ridiculous.

It didn't matter one way or the other. He didn't have a ring on, though, so he hadn't remarried. And she knew him well enough to know there was no way he would have hinted about things happening between them if he was involved with someone.

A minute later they joined several people in front of the elevator. "What floor is the maternity ward on?"

"Third. The surgical department is here on the fifth floor, which is where I spend the bulk of my time."

She cocked her head and said in a low voice, "Is it hard to do the surgeries?"

"What do you mean?"

A quick shrug as she tried to blow away the impulsive question. Then the doors to the elevator opened. They waited for those who were getting off to do so, before moving into the cabin. It was a quick trip, since they only had to go down two floors. Then they were in the lobby of the maternity unit where a huge sign over the main door gave the department's mission statement:

> *To give every pregnant woman who crosses the Wilson-Ross threshold the safest, most respectful birthing experience possible.*

She paused. It was worded differently than the one at her hospital, which was interesting. She had assumed both hospitals would be cookie-cutter versions of each other, but that wasn't the case. She was already seeing subtle differences. The way the hospitals were laid out. The decor was individual as well, probably to reflect the flavor of the host city.

Tucker paused by one of the doors. "Yes. Sometimes it's hard to do the surgeries. Especially when it's a case where genetics are involved." He glanced at her. "But then there are those days when everything just falls into place and I feel like I'm doing what I wasn't able to do for Grace—give a baby a chance for a normal life."

"Oh, Tucker..." She paused, trying to gather her thoughts. "I feel the same way. There are times I think I see her, when I'll pass a child's room and see what I think are Grace's blond hair and blue eyes."

"I know."

He really did know.

She touched his arm and went to say something

else when a bustle of movement caught her eye as they turned a corner. The pace on the floor was frenetic, which might have been normal, except for the… Her vision sharpened as nurses rushed from room to room, and several alarms beeped at the unattended nurses' desk. Her grip tightened on his arm as a sliver of fear went through her. "Is it always this way?"

"No." He stopped the nearest nurse. "What's going on?"

"There was a fire at the Heritage Birthing Center a few streets over. Ten patients in various stages of labor are either here or on their way over."

Kady let go of Tucker's arm, her chest tightening. She knew all too well the pain, fear and confusion some of those women were experiencing. She'd felt the same panicked helplessness firsthand, which was why she'd specialized in this area of medicine. And yet it was an area in which there was at least hope for a good outcome. Unlike with Grace.

She took a step forward. "I'm a maternal-fetal doctor from Wilson-Ross in Atlanta. Tell me how I can help."

Tucker nodded as well. "We'll both help. Put us where you need us."

CHAPTER FOUR

THE BABY'S HEAD finally crowned. Three hours of pushing had exhausted the young mother, whose chart said she was just seventeen years old. Tucker had thought for sure that Kady was going to order a C-section, but instead she had manually maneuvered the baby several times, the patient groaning in agony with each attempt. She'd arrived at the hospital in the pushing stage, too close to delivery to attempt an epidural unless they were going to take the baby.

"You're almost there, Samantha. Deep breaths and rest until the next contraction."

Kady's face was beaded with perspiration, and fatigue rimmed her eyes. This was the fourth delivery they had assisted with, having had to leave this patient to attend others who had given birth quicker than their current patient.

Picking up a cup from a nearby table, he offered Kady a sip from the straw so she wouldn't need to swap out her gloves after touching the glass. She leaned forward and pulled a couple of long drinks of cold water, nodding her thanks up at him.

She had always been good with her patients, empathy mixing with skill. It was the perfect combination in any physician, but it was even more valuable in an obstetrician.

Did these deliveries seem mundane to her, since she was used to dealing with the sickest of the sick? If so, there was no evidence of it in her face.

The patient moaned. "It's starting again."

She had no one with her, whether it was because of the fire or just because she was alone in this thing, he had no idea. There hadn't been any next of kin listed on her chart, and Kady probably didn't want to put any unnecessary stress on her by asking about a significant other.

He imagined Kady all alone, raising a child, and a rock formed in his stomach. She had been such a great mother to Grace, but it was something they'd shared in together. To do it all by herself... There were women like Samantha, though, who did it all the time—from birth to high-school graduation and beyond. Kady would at least have her grandparents. But if her grandmother really was beginning to lose her memory, how long would she be able to count on her?

If Kady decided to have a child, she'd do it with someone. Wouldn't she?

"Okay, Samantha, take a deep breath and bear down."

That was Tucker's cue to count. Banishing everything else from his mind, he laid a hand on the patient's shoulder and did just that, counting down the seconds and letting his ex do her job without interference from him.

Not that he would. This was her area of expertise. His was in infants far smaller than this one. "Ten. Deep breath and go again."

Samantha's face turned red as she continued to push, pulling up on her legs, limbs trembling with effort.

"Head's out. Stop pushing."

"I—I can't. I have to…"

Tucker stepped into her line of vision. "Blow through it, Samantha. You can do it." He huffed along with her, knowing that Kady was working to make sure the shoulders could be eased out. Tears streamed down the girl's face, tugging at something in his chest. Samantha had red hair, much like Kady's, and it brought back memories from years earlier of Grace's birth. He shoved those thoughts from his mind in a rush.

"Okay, we're ready. Not much longer, Samantha."

He guided her through counting once more, praying Kady was right.

Two more pushes and then a thin cry drifted his way. Samantha's head fell back to the pillow, eyes closed as she struggled to catch her breath.

A nurse brought the baby up to the young mother, easing her gown aside to allow the skin-to-skin contact that the birthing center would have wanted. Wilson-Ross did this as well if mothers requested it, but sometimes traditional methods were slower to change. Kind of like the difference between turning a barge and turning a speedboat. The smaller operations were able to make those shifts in methodology a lot quicker than a bigger hospital could. But sometimes there were trade-offs to be made.

Kady was still working on delivering the afterbirth evidently, but when he looked over at her, he noted the tight white lines on either side of her mouth immediately. Something was wrong.

He glanced back at the mother, who, although she

had one arm around the baby's back, was very quiet. Too quiet.

Then he saw a splash of blood on the floor just as Kady raised the alarm. "I have a PPH here! I need two large-bore IV lines started."

Postpartum hemorrhage.

The two nurses both went into action, one removing the baby from the mother's arms and carrying her over to a nearby table. The staff was already bare bones because of the added caseload from the birthing center, so Tucker jumped to help, checking the chart for blood type and calling down to get the wheels turning. He then called the surgical department, in case they needed to take the patient in for emergency surgery.

The urge to take over bubbled up inside him, but he held back, knowing that Kady was well qualified to call the shots. He couldn't stop his head from going through the steps he would take, though, were this his case.

The patient's eyes were now closed, face much paler than it should have been. Dammit. How much blood was she losing?

"Tucker, I need fluids and Pitocin pushed. I want to try to close off these vessels."

"On it. Can you see what's causing it?"

"Not yet. Looking now."

He let her work, another nurse coming in to get the baby and take it to the nursery. Lines were started with the Pitocin drip. If they could get the uterus to contract down on the leaking vessels they might be able to avert a catastrophe. "Do you want me to apply pressure manually?"

Sometimes massaging the abdomen would also help encourage the body to get back on track.

"Yes."

He applied deep rhythmic massage to the area over the uterus, glad that the woman was unconscious. After five minutes his forearms began to burn. Kady was still working feverishly, trying to figure out what was causing the bleeding.

"It's slowing."

Relief filtered through his system. "Do we need a couple of units of blood? They're standing by with some."

"Give me another minute. If I can get it stopped, we may be good with just the fluids."

"Do you want me to keep going?"

"Yes. I'll take whatever help I can get."

There had been a time when he had prayed that very prayer to a God who'd remained silent. In the end, Grace's condition had remained unchanged, and she'd died.

Was life really that arbitrary?

He wasn't sure, but he was glad that in this case things seemed to be turning around.

"Okay, I think we're close to normal levels. Let's stop and see what we've got."

Tucker halted his manipulations and waited, as did the nurse who was working to keep track of times and vitals. Silence enveloped the room as they waited for Kady to either set them back in motion or call off the alarm.

"Still holding. Let's ease up on the Pitocin and see if things continue. Is she conscious?"

"No." He and the nurse said the word together.

"Let's get a blood count so we can see how much volume she has left."

During pregnancy, a woman's blood volume increased by about fifty percent, so some bleeding was normal. It was just when it went beyond a certain level that it turned into a crisis. At its worst, they would have had to perform a hysterectomy in order to save the mother's life. Thankfully it hadn't come to that.

It was as if the lab had been waiting right outside. Or maybe the pediatric nurse had alerted them, because they were there in less than thirty seconds.

Samantha's eyelids fluttered as they were doing the blood draw.

A few minutes later they had their answer. The red-cell count was low, but not dangerously so. With the help of the two nurses, he and Kady worked to clean her up and make her as comfortable as possible.

"Can I see my baby?" The patient's voice was a mere whisper. "Is she all right?"

Kady came around and held her hand. "She's fine. You're the one who gave us a little scare. I can let you see her, but just for a few minutes. I want to send you to ICU for observation to make sure the bleeding doesn't start back up again."

"What caused it?"

"When the placenta detaches it can cause some bleeding, which is normal. You just lost more than we expected. You were also pushing for a long time. The important thing is that your body was able to do what it needed to do to stop it."

"What about the baby? Can she go with me?"

"To ICU? No, I'm sorry. But I'm hoping you'll be able to have her with you before the night is out. I'll check on you periodically to see how you're doing."

That made Tucker frown. She'd already been working for six hours straight. And she wasn't even a resident at this hospital. She could very easily turn the case over to another doctor.

But that wasn't the Kady he knew. She cared deeply about her patients, even ones she hadn't followed through the prenatal phase.

When he went to say something, though, she gave a quick shake of her head. She'd evidently known exactly where he was headed. It was fine. The hospital was undoubtedly glad to have her on hand during this crisis. And because she worked at a sister hospital, it made the process a little more fluid than it might have been otherwise.

"I'll get the nurse to bring your baby in to you for a few minutes."

"Can I nurse her?"

Kady paused as if thinking. "Yes, I think that might be a good idea, actually, if you're feeling strong enough."

Nursing was another way to trigger the body to clamp down on the uterus, signaling that childbirth was over and it was time to close up shop.

The baby latched on without difficulty, and Kady smiled and squeezed Samantha's shoulder. "We'll be right over here, if you need us."

She wasn't going to step out of the room, not while her patient needed her.

"I can stay with her," Tucker said. "Why don't you take a break?"

"I'm fine. I'd rather be on hand."

He smiled. "You always were stubborn."

"No more stubborn than you."

The urge to put his arm around her and give her a

quick hug came and went. Not smart, Tucker. You're colleagues now, remember? Nothing more. What he felt right now, though, went far beyond professional admiration. Kady's calm determination had been one of the things he'd loved about her. She never gave up.

Not even when it came to wanting another baby.

"Good job, by the way. I thought for sure she was going to need more aggressive measures."

"I did too. I just wanted to give her body another minute or two to figure things out."

The process for a PPH was similar to resuscitating a cardiac patient. It was a tense situation that could quickly deteriorate into a life-threatening emergency. Tucker had seen a woman die from blood loss. Not common in this day and age of emergency surgery, but when a patient arrived who had already lost over half her blood volume, there sometimes wasn't enough time to reverse things. Thankfully it had only happened once in his memory, but since he didn't deal with this end of things very often, it could occur more than he'd thought.

"You made the right call."

"This time. You're never quite sure when things are happening so quickly."

He knew what she meant. Sometimes you had to go with your gut instincts, because there wasn't time to think through every remote possibility. Had his gut instinct been wrong about getting a vasectomy?

It was too late to do anything about it now. He could see now that his head hadn't been screwed on straight during Grace's last days or afterward. He'd been operating on a ball of pure emotion and grief, while doing his best to hide both of those things from his wife. Not exactly the best conditions under which to make decisions.

It hadn't been a rash one, though. He'd wanted to save his marriage—had hoped that by having the procedure they could have normal relations again. Instead, he'd ended up sending a wrecking ball straight into it.

Divorce had seemed inevitable by then. They had wanted different things out of life.

No, not out of life. Out of one area of that life. She wanted more kids, and he didn't. And the fear of her getting pregnant again messed with a certain region of his brain, which in turn shut down an important region of his body.

"I think the baby's done."

Their patient's quiet voice called him back from his thoughts. Kady had been silent as well. Had she been thinking about the past? Probably not. She'd been able to move on quite easily after the divorce. And she certainly hadn't seemed brokenhearted during the workshop. Or afterward. Shocked to see him maybe. But distraught. Not hardly.

Even the bikini mishap hadn't seemed to faze her, unlike Tucker, who'd almost turned her around to see if that part of his body could follow through to completion.

Another line of thought he needed to stay away from.

Samantha gave her baby one last kiss on the forehead, her eyes filling with tears, before allowing her to be wheeled away in her bassinet. "It's so hard to let her go."

A pang went through him. At least Samantha was only handing her daughter over on a temporary basis. Not letting her go forever.

"It's not for long. We want her to leave with a strong and healthy mom." Kady's words rang with a sincerity that made a believer out of him. There was no hint of remembered grief in her voice. "Let me check you one more time before we have you transferred."

The gloves snapped off a few seconds later. "The flow looks normal."

"Does that mean I can just go to a regular room?"

"Let's play it safe, okay? It'll just be for a few hours. You don't have anyone you want to call?"

Okay, so Kady was going to ask. He'd wondered.

Samantha shrugged. "My roommate, maybe, but she's at work until midnight."

"Do you know her number?"

Once Kady had written it down, she tucked it into her pocket. "We'll see if we can reach her."

We? A figure of speech, surely. She wasn't looking to spend more time with him than she already had. They'd worked these cases together for almost seven straight hours. She had to be dead on her feet.

He was tired too, but that didn't necessarily mean he wanted to go home. Sometimes the rush of adrenaline needed to carry you through a difficult case also made it hard to sleep when the time came. He just wanted to go and get something to eat and get away from the noise of the hospital for a while.

They got their patient prepped and an orderly came up to wheel her to ICU. "I'll check on you a little later tonight."

Surely she wasn't planning on staying at the hospital all night? Then again, knowing Kady…

With their patient gone, Tucker surveyed the room, still cluttered with the evidence of their battle. "I certainly didn't expect the night to end this way."

"It's not over yet. I need to see if they need help with any other cases."

When she went to leave the room, he stopped her with a touch. "What you need to do is take a breather."

"I'm okay. Seriously. I'm just happy to be useful."

"I thought you were taking a mini-vacation."

"Sometimes things are taken out of your hands." She paused. "I needed this, Tucker."

He could agree with that. Sometimes things were taken out of your hands, even when those hands tried to hold on as tightly as they could.

"If you're going to insist on staying, I'll go with you. I probably couldn't sleep anyway."

Strangely, after some of his most devastating cases, he had come home and held Kady all through the night. She'd never asked for details about what had happened, just hugged him back, maybe sensing that's what he'd needed more than anything. Those days were gone. It was one of the things he missed the most about their life together. He doubted he'd find that kind of intimacy with another person.

But he wouldn't find it with her either. Not now. A wisp of regret curled through his skull, searching for a place to land. He hardened his heart. He didn't need intimacy. Not when it involved losing a piece of your soul.

The earlier chaos in the hallway had died down considerably. They had changed shifts somewhere in the middle of it. He went over to the nurses' station where one of the regular RNs, Gloria Luther, was tapping away at a computer keyboard. "Any other cases from the birthing center?"

"I think yours was the last one. Thanks for your help, Dr. Stevenson, and…" She slid her glasses a little further down her nose and sent a glance to Kady. "Things have been so busy I didn't even get a chance to learn your name. I take it you are a real doctor."

Kady laughed. "About as real as they come."

"This is Dr. McPherson from Wilson-Ross in Atlanta. She's here for the conference and is helping orient some of our medical students so you'll be seeing her from time to time this week."

"Nice to meet you." The woman reached across the top of the desk to shake her hand. "And great timing, by the way."

With graying hair scraped back in a severe knot and a gruff appearance, this was one case where appearances were deceptive. Gloria was one of their patients' favorite nurses. She didn't put up with any nonsense but would stand toe to toe with any doctor who wasn't moving quickly enough to help those in her care.

"Thank you." Kady smiled at her.

The nurse looked at her a little longer than necessary and then back at Tucker, before saying, "Oh, I see."

"I'm sorry?" he said, frowning.

"Nothing. You've been at the Atlanta hospital for a while?" she asked Kady.

"I've been there ever since graduating from medical school."

"I think Dr. Stevenson came from that same hospital, didn't you?" She sent him a sly glance. "Did you know each other there?"

You could say that. But he wasn't about to admit they were ex-spouses, although if she went looking on the internet, he was pretty sure there would be pictures of the two of them together at some of the Atlanta hospital's functions. Back when they had probably still been smiling.

Kady saved him from answering. "Yes, we knew each other. We were married for a while, actually."

His gut sucked tight. Why had she admitted that? Gloria wasn't known for being part of the rumor mill, but word could still get around and make things awkward for both of them.

"I thought maybe that was the case. Well, at least you can get along well enough to still work together. My ex and I aren't nearly as lucky."

It was lucky, wasn't it? They weren't ranting and raving at each other, and he was pretty sure Kady didn't actively hate him, although she'd probably felt pretty strongly about him when he'd filed for divorce. But all of that had to be looked at based on where they'd been in their lives at the time.

And that had been in separate bedrooms.

Grief combined with fear of discovery was a potent combination, he'd found out. In all the wrong ways.

"I'm not sure I would call it lucky." Kady threw a smile at the other woman. "But being angry doesn't do either of us any good."

He well remembered that anger…and the pleading. But neither had changed his mind.

Nothing had. And he still didn't regret his decision. It had given back a part of him that he'd feared dead. Not that he'd slept with many women in the years since the divorce, but at least he knew he could, if he wanted to.

And with Kady at the pool? Oh, yeah, he'd wanted to.

"Well, I'm happy for you. You put in a long shift together, from what I heard. And you both came through it alive." She sent them a quick smile.

Yes, it really had been a long day. And those words brought back the bone-weary tiredness he'd been struggling with for the last half-hour. Maybe he'd be able to sleep after all. "Yes, it was. You're sure that was the last case from the birthing center?"

"Yes. It looks like it's going to be a quiet night from here on out. Our beds are full from the new arrivals, but we should be able to cope."

"Any losses?"

"No, thank God."

Samantha Peters had probably been the closest call they'd had. And Kady had handled it all like the pro she was.

"We're going to take off, then." He paused, realizing something. "We missed the evening's conference sessions."

Kady shrugged. "It's fine." Then she glanced at the board to the right, where a long string of names and room numbers were listed. "I want to be kept updated on Samantha Peters, if you don't mind. I'll be in to check on her around midnight."

Gloria wrote something down. "Will you be close by?"

When his ex looked flustered for a moment, Tucker stepped in. "She will. I'll set her up in my office."

"Okay." She glanced at the board in front of her. "Room 301's call button just went off, so that's my signal to skedaddle. If you'll leave your number on the desk, I'll let you know if anything changes."

How would the nurse even know if there were changes since Samantha had been transferred out of the unit?

"She's not in Maternity anymore—she's in ICU."

Gloria's brows went up. "You're not the only one who likes to check on their patients' progress. I'll call up to ICU from time to time and see how she's doing."

"Thank you."

With that Gloria hurried toward a room to the left and Tucker was left wondering what the hell he'd been thinking, offering to let Kady sleep in his office.

It was just for a few hours.

Then it would be one more day down.

And not many to go.

Tucker had no idea how he felt about that. Neither was he going to try to figure it out.

He was just going to put his head down and keep moving. Until Kady finally caught her flight back to Atlanta.

CHAPTER FIVE

KADY DOG-PADDLED AROUND CONSCIOUSNESS, going past it a few times before circling back to find it.

Where was she?

Even when she opened her eyes, the darkness remained. She'd been sleeping, but this wasn't her hotel room, since her cheek was against something that was like leather, only cushier.

If not the hotel, then where?

She allowed her senses to drift, snuggling a little further under the thin blanket or whatever was on top of her.

Wait. She'd been at the hospital. Was supposed to check on someone.

A patient!

This time she sat up, struggling to see.

"It's okay. It's not midnight yet."

Low earthy tones drifted across the space as her eyes tried to adjust—as objects began materializing through the gloom. A desk. A chair. The shape of a person.

Tucker.

How long had she been asleep? From her groggy, cotton-stuffed head, she was going to say it was only a couple of hours.

Had he been sitting in that chair the whole time, watching her?

The thought unnerved her. "What time is it?"

"Eleven thirty. I was going to wake you up in fifteen more minutes."

"I'm awake. Did you get any sleep?"

"Not yet."

Well, now she felt horrible. He had to be as exhausted as she was. They could have taken turns. Kady was used to getting in power naps when things were busy at the hospital in Atlanta. And the cots in the doctors' rest area weren't nearly as comfortable as this couch was. Which was probably why she'd slept so long.

Or maybe it was the way his scent clung to everything in the room, including the throw pillow.

Damn. Not a good thing to be thinking about when the room's occupant was just a few yards away.

He clicked on the light, and what she saw made her breath catch in her chest. Not because he looked atrocious. Tucker could never look anything other than gorgeous. But right now that attractive face was shadowed by a haggardness that made her heart ache. He looked like he'd gone to war and come out on the losing end. Well, he had been through a battle. They both had. And there was nothing she could do to make it better. That was what hurt the most. Her husband had ducked out of her life back then, and no amount of begging or pleading had brought him back.

"Sorry. You should have woken me up. Why don't I take the chair for a while? Or, better yet, you could go home, if you wanted to."

"I have to scrub for surgery in a few hours."

"And you've had no sleep?" Anger zipped up her

spine, more at herself than him. "You needed the rest more than I did."

"I said I didn't sleep. But I did rest. I've done this before. And it's not a complicated surgery."

Was there really any uncomplicated fetal surgery? From her perspective, no. But maybe there were degrees of difficulty in his field the same way her high-risk pregnancy field had different levels. Preeclampsia was different from full-blown eclampsia.

"What type of surgery?"

"The fetus has a diaphragmatic hernia."

Uncomplicated?

She didn't think so. A diaphragmatic hernia meant that a hole in the diaphragm was allowing abdominal organs to move into the chest cavity. Mortality rates could be high. "How bad is it?"

"It's one of the better cases I've seen. The heart and lungs are displaced, but the hole isn't large enough to allow widespread movement between the chest and the abdomen. If I can stretch an abdominal muscle over the spot as a kind of patch, it should help everything to stay put."

"What about the heart and lungs?"

"They should move back into place on their own. The patient is at twenty-nine weeks, so if we can keep her from going into labor right away, things should have a chance to right themselves before Tony is born."

"Tony?"

One side of his mouth quirked as if he'd been caught doing something he shouldn't. "It's the name they've chosen for the baby."

He'd cared enough to learn the baby's name?

Oh, God. A truckload of memories careened her

way: Tucker speaking to her abdomen when she'd been carrying Grace. Tucker saying the baby's name over and over, believing she would hear it and have a sense of identity from the moment she was born.

He'd been right. She had seemed to know her name, eyes flickering with what could have been recognition soon after birth. Did he even remember?

"You used to talk to Grace before she was born, remember?"

He leaned back in his chair. "I do."

Not the most elaborate response, but at least he hadn't shut her down. She wished they could have sat and shared what they'd each loved most about their daughter, but they'd been too busy fighting each other to sit down and remember the good times.

"Do you talk to your patients while you operate?"

She could very easily imagine him doing that, telling them to hang in there, that he was going to try to fix whatever was wrong with their tiny bodies.

"The sedation we use for the mothers carries over to the babies, so they can't hear me." He paused for several long seconds. "But, yes. I talk to them."

She'd watched him operate before, cradling those tiny forms in his hands, moving with such care.

And he talked to them. The way he'd talked to Grace.

A rush of strong emotion welled up inside her, blinding her for an instant. She took a deep breath and let it out in a long silent stream, trying not to examine her feelings too closely, afraid of what she might find lurking there.

She stood, dropping the blanket onto the sofa, and went around to the other side of the desk. "I'm so glad."

"Glad about what?"

A strange hoarseness had invaded his voice.

"That you talk to them."

Before she realized what was happening, he'd wrapped an arm around her waist and dragged her onto his lap. Then his mouth was on hers. And her world exploded. He hadn't wanted to touch her in a very long time, so to have him kissing her as if he couldn't get enough was heady. And terrifying.

Right now, she didn't care about patient charts or medical conferences or anything else.

A kaleidoscope of memories sent her reeling back through time, bits and pieces of the torn fabric of their old life sliding together to form something old but something totally different from what had been before.

The man who hadn't wanted to touch her, who'd shunned her embrace was suddenly not that man anymore. Instead, he was the person she'd known while they'd been dating, the husband who'd talked to his daughter through her stomach. The lover who'd shown her peaks she'd never known existed.

His lips turned hard and demanding in an instant, his tongue delving deep into her mouth as if he hadn't tasted her a thousand times over during their years together.

It was all new—all old.

One hand went to the back of her head, his fingers diving into her hair, his palm cradling her skull as he deepened the kiss even more. A sound erupted from the back of her throat. She tensed, afraid it would drive him away from her. It didn't. If anything, it pushed him closer.

He lifted her off his lap with a suddenness that left her reeling.

"What's wrong?"

"Nothing. Absolutely nothing."

He stood, scooping her up until she was cradled against his chest, and then he was moving toward the other side of the room.

Her mouth watered when she realized where he was going. All kinds of mental images flashed through her mind and she already knew that all of them would fall far short of what Tucker could make her feel. Was already making her feel.

He lowered himself to the cushion of the couch, still holding her tight. Her mouth found his again, and the kiss deepened, his tongue seeking entrance.

Yes!

She welcomed him in, the fiery sensation so familiar that an ache settled in her chest. But only for a minute.

Tucker's hands went to her waist, urging her to face him, mouths coming unlocked for a second or two as she scrambled to find a way to do what he wanted. Then she had a knee on either side of his thighs. And the second she lowered herself onto his lap, she knew it was over. This night was not going to end the way she'd expected it to when she came through the door to that office.

What did it matter? Because in this moment in time there was absolutely no place she would rather be than in his arms.

CHAPTER SIX

IT HAD BEEN so long. Too long. And the engine that couldn't all of a sudden could. And how.

It had roared to life with a suddenness that had sent his whole world spinning through space.

Why had it seemed so impossible before? He had no idea.

His hands went to her hips and shifted them down and forward, using the pressure to ease the ache that was forming in his groin. Only it didn't ease it. It made it jerk with a need that had him groaning for release.

"Damn." His hands went under her blouse, fingers scraping up the length of her spine before tangling in her hair. Those glorious, lustrous strands that had driven him crazy with need time after time. Oh, the things he'd done with them. With her.

Too many wants and needs to satisfy all at once. So he would start with this one.

The buttons on her blouse were calling him, so he undid one pearly bauble after another, revealing white lace beneath it all.

God.

Soft swells of pale flesh rose and fell with her breathing. And if she lowered herself onto him and pumped, that flesh would jiggle in a way that would drive him over the edge.

She was gorgeous. She always had been. But motherhood had added something that fit her to a T.

A squiggle of unease went through him.

No. Don't think about that. Not right now. A gentle tug on her hair had her neck arching back and soon his mouth was on her throat, sliding up to her ear, nipping the lobe. "Do you want this as much as I do?"

"Can't you tell?" The words rumbled against his skin, her breath warming his cheek.

"Not yet. Let's find out for sure. Stand up for a minute."

She blinked down at him, her confusion apparent, but she did as he asked, getting her legs under her, forcing him to let go of her hair. The lack of pressure against his zipper caused a pointed protest to go through him.

That was okay, because he had more important things to do right now. He undid the top of her slacks and slid the zipper down. Then he slid them down her hips and kept going until he reached her calves. Kady took it from there, kicking the garment off the rest of the way. But when she went to reach for her underwear, he stopped her, pulling her forward until she was standing on either side of his legs, her shins pressed against the front of the couch.

And he couldn't resist. Filling his hands with her ass, he held her still and pressed his face against the lower curve of her belly, feathering his lips across the silky underwear, making circles that gradually traveled lower and lower until...

A moan from somewhere overhead and hands that were suddenly in his hair, holding tight, said he'd hit just the right spot. Her parted legs provided the perfect opportunity for his tongue to dip out and find a damp warmth.

"Mmm, yes, I think you do want this."

He should have let her take those panties off, but it was too late now. Besides, he was afraid he'd be tempted to finish things off too quickly. And the last thing he wanted right now was fast.

So he gently allowed his tongue to push forward and back, the increase in her breathing and tightening of fingers in his hair saying it was having the desired effect.

He loved driving her crazy. Always had.

It wasn't long before he was no longer satisfied with having the thin fabric between them. So he slid a finger beneath the elastic of her leg and eased it over. This time he was skin to skin and the first touch set up a pulsing in his groin that wasn't going to be denied.

"Tucker. Oh, God."

The sound of his name on her lips undid him. He didn't want slow any longer. One hand left her butt and moved to his fly, maneuvering until he'd freed himself. All he wanted to do was yank her down and feel that soft flesh slide over him, but he had to do something first.

He parted her. And kissed her. Right where he knew it counted. Right where experience had told him she liked it.

His lips closed around that tiny nub of flesh and sucked. Licked. Pulsed against it with rhythmic intent. Suddenly she was frantically pumping, ragged breaths telling him she was almost. Almost. *Almost*.

There!

He felt it the second she went off, and he wrapped

an arm around the backs of her thighs, forcing her onto
the couch. She was in as much of a hurry as he was,
evidently, because she fought against his pull, scooting
forward until she was above him, hands on his shoulders, eyes closed. She hesitated for the slightest second.

"Do it. *Hell*. Do it, Kady."

Then she was pushing down, encasing his aching
flesh in a tight velvety space. Dammit. She was still
pulsing, the sensations ripping right through any rem-
nants of control he might have had. In an instant he was
thrusting up into her, a massive surge of energy propelling him at a frantic rate. He erupted hard, the muscles
in his legs turning to rock as his hands forced her down
as far as she would go, his mind blanking out everything
except the fierce waves of pleasure. Waves he never
wanted to end. Hoped would go one and on and on.

Little by little, they subsided, his muscles starting to
uncoil. His strokes slowed until her bottom was resting on his thighs. He tipped her against his chest as he
leaned back against the sofa cushions behind him. His
eyes had long since closed, and he had no desire to open
them again. Except things were still happening. The
rational side of his brain, which had been idling along
in the background, began to move forward, a million
questions starting to swirl and form actual thoughts.

What had just happened?

When could it happen again?

And how was he going to talk her into it?

Um, he was not going to talk anyone into anything.

He wasn't the only one who was starting to come to
the conclusion that something enormous had just taken
place. Kady shifted against him. He realized that he
hadn't even gotten undressed. And Kady was barely

undressed, her underwear pulled to the side, her bra still fastened in front.

And he'd forgotten to watch them jiggle.

That thought made him smile. He hadn't been in any condition to watch anything. He'd been on a fast track to disaster.

No. It wasn't a disaster.

Was it?

Oh, hell. Maybe it was.

Before he could ease her away from him, she sat up, her hands propelling her up and off his lap with a suddenness that made him grunt.

"Sorry," she said.

She didn't look sorry. And he wasn't sure if he should be apologizing or what. His head was still fuzzy and his mouth felt like it had been sucked dry by a vacuum. And he didn't know what the hell he was supposed to say. Or feel.

Her fingers hurried to her shirt and yanked it closed around her, buttons going back into their holes. Something was wrong.

Well, yeah, that was pretty obvious.

No. Not that.

Something was going on that was different than simply having sex.

Did she still have feelings for him?

His chest stuttered with something he could have sworn was fear.

What the hell had he been thinking?

By the time she'd yanked her slacks on, he'd decided he was definitely going to issue an apology. A big one. One that would cover any number of wrongs.

Before he got a chance, though, she scrubbed her

hand up and down her other arm and took a deep breath. "I have something important I need to ask you."

No. She wasn't going to talk about feelings, was she? He was in no shape to try to stop and dissect what they'd just done. Not with his legs still shaking, and his head still trying to figure out where it was. Or how he'd let any of this happen.

It was just sex.

Right?

He forced the words out of his throat. "What is it?"

Dropping on to the couch next to him, she clasped her hands in her lap. "I'm not quite sure how to phrase this."

The feeling of impending doom that had been slowly circling overhead for the past three or four minutes darkened to storm cloud proportions. Irritation swept through his system, blotting out much of the pleasure he'd just experienced. "Just ask your question, Kady."

"Is there any chance I could get...? Um, did you...? Is there any way I can get pregnant from what we just did?"

He frowned, trying to form her words into something that made sense. "Pregnant."

His brain seized, sending bile washing up his throat when he realized what she was asking. She was wondering if he'd done what he'd been so determined not to do after Grace's death.

What in the name of everything holy was she implying?

Or maybe it wasn't what she was implying. Maybe the whole encounter had been planned, hoping to get around his refusals and get what she wanted.

No. Kady wouldn't do that. It was one thing he could

state with all certainty. She didn't operate by subterfuge. If she wanted something, she asked.

At least the Kady he'd known before had. And this new, independent Kady? Was that how she operated as well? Did she think that if she somehow got pregnant, she could force them back together?

She'd given no indication that she was interested in him that way anymore. Until that kiss.

But…pregnant?

He was going to shoot down any tiny fragment of hope before it could form. In either of them.

"I had a vasectomy. I told you I was going to." He zipped himself back in. "So no. There's no chance. I've had follow-up exams just to make sure."

Her brows puckered. "Did you really hate being a father that much?"

"No, I hated losing a daughter that much."

And I hated not being able to make love to her mother afterward.

The fear of another pregnancy had paralyzed him. Obviously the surgery had fixed whatever had been broken.

No. It hadn't. It had simply fixed the symptom of that broken part of him. Yes, he could function again—and hell if it hadn't felt great—but the second she'd said the word *pregnant*, his heart had frozen into a block of ice that nothing could reach.

"I lost a daughter too, Tucker."

He got to his feet. "I realize that. Did you come to New York with an agenda?"

"What? No, of course not." The area between her brows puckered in anger. "How can you even say that? I never expected tonight to happen."

"Sorry." He dragged a hand through his hair. "This whole idea of pregnancy came on awfully quick. It never even crossed my mind."

She gave a dry laugh. "Maybe because *you* knew it was impossible. But I certainly didn't. And I needed make sure that if I *did* get pregnant anytime soon, I would know with certainty you aren't the father."

If she…

"How the hell would you get pregnant?"

Up went a brow.

"Let me rephrase that. Who would you be getting pregnant with?" If she said she had a boyfriend, he was going to punch a hole through the nearest flat object.

She crossed her arms under her breasts. "That's none of your business."

Anger threaded through his innards. "Lady, you just asked me if there was any possibility I was going to father a child with you. I think I have a right to know why."

Kady moved behind his desk, maybe needing to put some space between them. Well, she needn't have bothered, because right now there was an emotional gulf the size of a couple of universes between them.

"Fine, you want to know? I'm looking for a sperm donor."

A couple more layers of ice coated his chest wall. "And you thought I might be willing to oblige? Only you forgot one tiny detail. To ask permission."

Up went her chin. "I never needed your permission, because you were the last person I would have asked. I didn't mean for any of this to happen." Her hand swept toward the couch.

He couldn't stop the obvious question. "So who *were* you planning to ask?"

"No one. I've gone to a sperm bank. I'm in the process of selecting the best match."

The thought of Kady carrying someone else's baby made him feel physically ill. But he was the one who'd told her no over and over again. Not that he would have been able to get her pregnant back then.

"You're going to do artificial insemination?"

She shrugged. "I'm going to start there, and if that doesn't take, I'll try in vitro."

"You really do want another child, don't you?" His anger disappeared in an instant and regret took its place. Regret that he hadn't been able to give her what she needed. Regret that she'd needed it so badly that she hadn't been able to see past it.

"I told you I did." Her eyes turned sad. "Many times."

"I know. And I'm sorry it couldn't be me."

"It's over and done with. We're moving on." Her gaze went past him.

Was she talking about what had just happened between them? Yes, that was over and done with. But as far as moving on went? He was pretty sure the aftershocks of that encounter were going to be wreaking havoc with his system for a long time to come.

"So where do we go from here?"

Her head tilted, the confusion on her face plain. "What do you mean? *We* don't go anywhere from here. We decided that two years ago when we got a divorce. You go back to your life, and I'll go back to mine as soon as this conference is over."

"Of course." He wasn't even sure why he'd asked that question. It was better to bury any weird sentimental notions before they could take root and fester below the surface. "I phrased that badly. I meant how do we put what just happened behind us so we can finish out the rest of the seminar without it becoming awkward?"

This time she laughed, but there was no humor in the sound. "I think it became awkward the moment I landed in New York and realized you were at the conference. Wouldn't you agree?"

"No doubt about that." And yet they'd had sex.

"Are you going to be able to get past this?"

Said as if the only one she had doubts about was him. He was going to blow that idea out of the water. "I already am."

A skitter of some strong emotion passed through her eyes and then was gone replaced with a wary nod. "Me too. So we have nothing to worry about, then."

"No, nothing."

But deep in Tucker's heart he knew he just told the biggest lie of the century. Because the word *worried* didn't begin to cover the thoughts that were currently ricocheting through his head and threatening to explode into something far worse. It wasn't worry. Or concern. Or uneasiness.

This was more like the heavy dread that came with knowing something big was just on the horizon. Something that would rock his world and change it forever. And no matter how hard he tried, he knew there was probably nothing he could do to stop it.

Tony's surgery was underway.

Kady had asked to observe, something about the case pulling at her.

Obviously...since it was what had sent her into his

arms in the first place. Hearing him call that baby by name had touched a part of her she'd thought was dead. It wasn't.

And now that she was here, she was having trouble thinking about anything other than what had happened in Tucker's office. They hadn't even locked the door.

Anyone could have walked in.

The janitor. A patient. Even the department head.

Her stomach twisted.

At midnight? Not very likely. Even if anyone had known Tucker was in his office, they would have thought he was getting some much-needed sleep before the surgery.

And he had. At least she thought he had. After they kind of hashed out a tentative agreement for how to proceed professionally, he had stretched out on the couch again. But this time Kady hadn't stuck around. She'd told him she was going up to check on her patient and would be back before his surgery. She had peeked in on Samantha, but the young woman, of course, had been sound asleep. So Kady had gone down to the waiting room and curled up in one of the most uncomfortable chairs known to man and waited for the hour hand on the clock to creep around to five o'clock.

Then she'd met Tucker back at his office. When she'd arrived, he had already showered and dressed. He offered her the use of the tiny cubicle in his bathroom, which she gladly accepted. But even his shower carried his clean masculine scent, a stark reminder of what they had done hours earlier. Once his surgery was over, she was going straight to her own hotel room and rid herself of any trace of it.

At least she hoped she could.

She glanced down at the operating-room floor again, and every thought suddenly vanished when Tucker lifted something, his lips moving as he said something to someone…

Yes, I talk to them.

She swallowed hard. He was talking to the baby he held in his hands.

Tony.

Her ex bent low over the tiny form, his big body now blocking her view. But she'd seen it. It was unbelievable that surgery could be done on a fetus that size. But she'd watched Tucker operate more than once during their marriage, so why was it so surprising to see him do it now?

Maybe because she couldn't reconcile the Tucker who under no circumstances wanted another child—who had gone so far as to guarantee it would never happen—with the Tucker who could take a baby from its temporary home and treat it with such tender care. To repair the little one so that it had the best possible chance of living and thriving once it entered the real world.

Which man was the real Tucker Stevenson?

Maybe he was both. Or neither. Maybe the true man was somewhere in between.

He was still young. The fact that he'd made such a permanent decision about his fertility should tell her how strongly he'd felt about the whole thing. When they had been together she'd thought his reluctance was a result of his grief and that with time he would work through it and come round. That hadn't been the case.

Just then he glanced up at the observation window, causing her thoughts to freeze. It only lasted a second or two, but even that brief look made a shiver go through her. How was she going to get through the rest of the day, much less the rest of the week?

They were set to meet the medical students for rounds almost immediately after this surgery and then they had the conference later this afternoon.

He took a step to the side, glancing up at her again. Why was he…?

He was trying to make sure she could see. That gesture made her heart squeeze. No matter how often she'd tried to cast him in the role of bad guy, he proved her wrong time and time again: sending flowers to Grace's grave; the funny tone he'd had when asking her who she was getting pregnant with; the way he'd just taken a few steps to the left.

The way he'd made love to her?

No, that had been sex.

Just sex.

Are you sure?

Oh, Lord, she'd better hope so. For her heart's sake.

Because even if it meant something more to her, there was no future in it.

And Kady was not willing to have a meaningless fling. Even with her ex-husband.

Tucker's low voice came over the speaker, detailing each step of the procedure just as he'd done the entire time. He was steady. Steady hands. Steady voice. Steady presence.

At least he had been.

"Kady, do you have any questions up there, before I close up shop?"

Questions? Oh, she had plenty. But none of them were about Tony. Or the procedure.

But now every head in the surgical suite had swiveled toward her, probably wondering how Tucker knew her or, worse, if they were dating.

Ha! They hadn't dated in a very long time. And when they had…

Think up something intelligent! Professional.

She leaned close to the tiny microphone hanging in front of her, glad her earlier thoughts hadn't been captured by it. "Will the surgery have to be redone in the future? Or will this procedure be the only repair needed?"

Tucker's eyes found hers and held them. "We can hope this will be it. But there are never any guarantees."

Just like she'd hoped that their divorce would bring an end to all the heartache she'd endured. But it never quite went away. She'd had opportunities to date over the last couple of years, but she just hadn't had the energy or desire to start over.

Maybe that's what looking for a sperm donor was all about. A new start. A chance to finally make that break with the past.

Except, even in death, Grace would always be a point of connection. Like the fresh flowers she found whenever she went to visit her daughter's grave.

"Well, I hope for his sake that he can go on from here without ever needing to think about what happened today."

And if that didn't sound like wishful thinking, she didn't know what did. Because she would never be able to get away from thinking about what had happened in his office last night.

"That's the hope. Okay, let's get this little guy back where he belongs. Good job, everyone."

With one last glance up at where she was sitting, Tucker bent over his patient once again and began closing up the gaping wounds his scalpel had created.

If only they could each find someone who could do the same for them.

Whoever had said time healed all wounds had either been crazy or a damned liar.

Because looking at Tucker still hurt.

And she had no idea when that ache would finally go away.

CHAPTER SEVEN

HE'D HOPED THE conference would be a refuge.

No such luck. He and Kady had been thrust once again into the same workshop after a disastrous day following an even more disastrous night. The medical students who'd followed them around had had questions. Lots of them. Some of them having to do with colleague relationships. Platonic ones, but it still made Kady's face light up like a neon sign.

Afterward, they'd had to rush over to the conference center together. This was the seminar he'd been dreading the most: Genetics and Pregnancy—identifying common abnormalities. And, of course, Kady was the replacement for Dr. Blacke so she was there with him. Seated next to him this time. Colleague relationships indeed.

If he'd known, he might have feigned a patient emergency and risked the wrath of Phil Harold if someone checked up on his excuse.

But since they'd come together, Kady would have known immediately why he was skipping out on the session.

He glanced over at her. Nothing was in front of her. No notes. No computer tablet. Well, that made two of them. He had no intention of saying a word other than his short canned speech, unless one of the audience members asked him something point blank.

Like about interdepartmental relationships?

Why would anyone ask something like that? He was imagining things that weren't there.

Or were they?

Dammit, Tucker, knock it off!

The microphone passed to the third panel member, who, according to his bio, was a researcher in the area of bioengineering. "Okay, so true story—I went to college to get a degree in music. I wanted to be a concert pianist. I had it all going for me—hard work and a drive to succeed. And then... I met a girl." He paused when knowing laughter erupted across the audience.

"Well, things got serious, and she got pregnant. We got married, and we both continued going to school. She went into labor five weeks early. We were scared but unbelievably happy. And then our life together changed forever. Our boy—Alexander—was born a harlequin baby. He never came home from the hospital."

He swallowed hard.

Harlequin ichthyosis was a terrible condition where thick scalelike armor encased a newborn's body. It created treatment challenges that were difficult if not impossible to overcome.

It was equally impossible not to notice the parallel threads that ran between the bioengineer's story and Tucker and Kady's saga.

Unexpected pregnancy. *Check.* Quick marriage. *Check.* Baby born with devastating fatal condition. *Check.*

Tucker couldn't even bring himself to glance at Kady to see if she was thinking the same thing he was.

"In a matter of months, I changed my major from

music to medicine, studying how genetics affect the human story. It was the only way I could think of to make sense of my son's death."

Was there a way to make sense of a thing like that?

Maybe each person dealt with tragedy differently. Tucker peered sideways at the woman next to him. Kady's head was down, and she was staring at a closed manila folder to the right of her.

Yes. She was thinking of Grace too. Or at least he thought she was.

He couldn't stop his hand from covering hers.

When she glanced up at him, her eyes glistened, but that was the only sign that this topic was affecting her. Him? It was damn well ripping his heart from his chest.

She squeezed his fingers and then let him go, maybe afraid someone would see them and wonder what was going on.

He used to be weirdly fascinated with genetic abnormalities. Had been called in to consult on a number of them. Now he tried to avoid them whenever possible. So whatever had driven the researcher to abandon his goals and dive into the deep end of the very condition that had killed his child had passed Tucker over.

He'd never operated on a Tay-Sachs baby. It didn't normally show up until six months after birth. Or when routine testing revealed the lack of an enzyme needed to break down fatty material.

Tay-Sachs was a death sentence. Grace had slowly lost her ability to do things, her motor skills decreasing at an alarming rate until she had been paralyzed.

And unlike the man who'd just laid his heart on the table for everyone to see, Tucker had no intention of mentioning Grace. Or anything else personal. That was his cross to bear.

When it was his turn to speak, he just rattled off a few obvious areas where genetics and fetal surgery overlapped. He then nodded to Kady, giving her the floor.

"Thank you, Dr. Stevenson. Almost every inherited condition that we are able to identify prenatally automatically changes that patient's status to high risk. Obviously we wish we could identify every anomaly before birth, but we just can't. The best option, if you know you carry a certain gene, is to get genetic counseling. *Before* getting pregnant, if possible." She paused and drew a deep breath. "But even if you find out about the condition *after* having a baby, I strongly urge you to get counseling. Not to is irresponsible."

By the time she finished, his abdominal muscles were rock-hard. Maybe she wasn't talking about him. But what else could she be referring to?

There'd been no need to get counseling, since they weren't going to have more children together. Ever.

Or maybe she had been talking about herself, since she was thinking of getting pregnant through a sperm donor. His gut tightened even further.

How the hell was she going to make sure her donor wasn't a carrier, unless the sperm bank tested everyone? Or maybe they did nowadays. He had no idea, because the thought of donating sperm made him sick.

By the time the Q & A portion of the seminar came around, Tucker had a raging headache that started at the back of his neck and stretched like a band over the top. Maybe because he'd gotten less than five hours' sleep last night and had done surgery, led around a pack of medical students for most of the afternoon and now was here at the conference. A sixteen-hour day. And less than twenty-four hours since he and Kady had made love.

"Dr. McPherson, can you give us an idea of what types of cases you would refer for genetic counseling?"

There was a long pause while Kady waited for the microphone, which had moved further down the table. Her fingers were pressed tight against the laminated surface, but other than that telltale sign of nerves, there was no indication that the question bothered her.

The microphone landed in front of her.

She cleared her throat. "There are any number of inherited disorders that I've seen or worked with over the years. Sickle cell, thalassemia, hemophilia, some types of breast cancers, and Tay-Sachs are a few of them."

The words *Tay-Sachs* hit him like a hammer blow.

"Thank you. Can I ask one more question related to that?"

"Certainly." Her fingertips seemed to push harder against the table, turning white.

"Do you ever have patients who refuse genetic counseling? If so, would you refuse treat them if they were to become pregnant again?"

"I would never refuse to treat anyone." If anything, she sounded surprised by the question. "As for patients refusing testing, there are more of them than you might think."

Like Tucker?

She went on. "As for why, I think most of it boils down to fear. But what people should realize is that knowledge is a powerful tool."

And sometimes it wasn't. He'd pretty much read the

whole encyclopedia when it came to his daughter's illness. He had a whole lot of head knowledge. But it changed nothing. Not then. And not now.

That person sat and another stood.

Hell, how long was this going to go on?

"This question is directed to the panel as a whole. If someone knew they had a recessive gene and it was unlikely that their significant other had the same gene, should they tell their partner?"

The harlequin baby's father motioned for the microphone. When it arrived, he looked the person straight in the eye. "Yes. Always. What Dr. McPherson said is true. If you know and don't tell, and your partner unknowingly carries that same gene, you could endanger any child you might have. Are you willing to take that risk?"

His vasectomy had kind of taken care of that. And now Kady knew about it.

Damn.

He'd let things go way too far last night.

His head told him he was a fool. His body told him he was a fool too. A lucky one. One who wanted more of what it had just gotten.

Not happening. Ever again.

As in never.

Three more days and the convention would be over. Caput. In the history books. And his ex would be out of his life all over again.

It was only when people started getting up and bunching at the exit that he realized the workshop was over.

Kady turned to him. "I hope you didn't think I was directing any of that at you."

"Any of what?"

She frowned, making him revise his answer. "It doesn't matter who it was aimed at. It was good advice."

"Thanks. I had a patient a few months ago who was a carrier for sickle cell. She and the father were dating on and off, and she got pregnant. When the baby was born he had the condition. Unfortunately the couple was on the outs with each other and she refused to allow us to notify him."

"Wow. So he might not have even known he was a carrier."

"No." She sighed. "Think about what could happen if he fathers another child with a different woman and she finds out he already has a child with sickle cell."

"It wouldn't be his fault."

"No. But the child would pay the price."

"The first child paid the price anyway." Most people weren't tested unless they had a familial history.

"Maybe, but why let it be for nothing?"

A thought came to him. "Did you go through counseling? After Grace's death, I mean."

She swiveled her chair to look at him. "I did. I found out there are options."

"Such as?"

"Like having any potential sperm donor tested for the mutation. Or fertilizing a couple of my eggs and having them tested for Tay-Sachs before they're implanted."

It all sounded logical when you looked at it with the objective lens of science. It was obvious she'd given this a lot of thought. Had done her research. But didn't she know that it wasn't just Tay-Sachs that was a danger? Anything could happen to that future fetus. A rogue mutation. A glitch during implantation. During the first trimester.

And she was willing to risk losing another child? The thought of a second gravestone next to Grace's was eerie. Lightning couldn't strike twice, right?

It could with them.

"Does having a baby mean that much to you that you're willing to risk it?"

"It does." Her eyes sought his. "I'm sorry that's something you never understood."

"I understood." He just hadn't agreed with her. As much as he'd wished he could have given her what she wanted, neither his head nor his body would cooperate. It was why he'd been so willing to let her go. To let her find what she needed elsewhere. He was only surprised that it had taken her this long to go through with it.

Someone clearing their throat made him glance up sharply. He was surprised to find a young woman standing in front of them, the snug waistline of her dress showing off what was obviously a pregnancy. Third trimester, if he wasn't mistaken.

He had no idea how much of their conversation she'd heard. Kady must have been wondering the same thing because her face was stiff and wooden-looking. "Can I help you?" he asked.

The woman nodded, her dark hair sliding forward to cover part of her face. "Did you mean what you said?"

The question was directed at Kady.

"About what?"

"About informing partners of your genetic history." The softness of her voice gave her away.

"Absolutely." Kady's head tilted. "Why do you ask?"

"My mom recently found out that she has breast cancer. She's turning fifty this year. She has the BRCA 1 mutation." Her hands twisted under her belly. "I was tested a couple of months ago. I have it too. What if my baby…? It's a girl."

Kady stood to her feet. "Just because you have the mutation it doesn't mean you'll get cancer. Or that your baby will develop it."

"What if I pass the gene on to my daughter? Can she be tested?"

That was a tricky question. And it was in a gray area as far as ethics went. "My gut reaction is no. There are no preventative guidelines in place for children."

"So she just has to wait?"

"Most health professionals I know would say yes. Is there a partner in the picture? If so, what does he or she say?"

"Her father—my husband—doesn't know yet."

Kady went to the edge of the dais and sat on it, putting her a little closer to the young woman. "Tell him. He has a right to know."

"That I might pass a terrible disease on to our baby? How does that help anyone?"

"You two are in this together. That means trusting each other with sensitive information." She glanced over at Tucker.

"I know you're right. But what if he leaves me?" The words were barely above a whisper.

Hell. That was always a possibility. Tucker had left, hadn't he? But only so she could have the freedom she needed to go after what she wanted in life.

"Wilson-Ross has a genetic counselor on staff. Why don't you go and talk to them? They can help you come up with a plan."

The woman drew a deep breath, whether in relief or resignation he wasn't sure. "Do you think they can?"

"That's what they're there for. Do it, if only for your own peace of mind." She smiled. "And give that husband of yours a chance to do the right thing. He might surprise you."

Kady had given Tucker the same chance by asking him to go to counseling with her and he'd refused.

Would counseling have changed his mind? He didn't think so. But she'd asked him to go. Had looked into his eyes and forced him to make a choice. He had. It just hadn't been the one she'd been hoping for.

Had he done the right thing? He'd thought so at the time but he was beginning to wonder.

"Thank you." Her soft words were directed at both of them, even though he hadn't said a thing. Hadn't been able to think of one helpful comment.

And yet Kady had known just the right thing to say.

"Tucker, can you hand me a pen and a piece of paper, please?"

Frowning, he tore off the back cover of the booklet for the workshop and handed it to her, along with one of the monogrammed pens that Wilson-Ross had given them.

Kady scribbled something and handed it to the woman. "This is the hospital's main number. Call them. Tell them you need to speak with a genetic counselor. Let them help you, like they did me."

"You act like you have the gene or something."

"Let's just say it's the 'or something.' My daughter was born with an incurable, inherited gene. She died when she was two years old."

"I'm so sorry."

"It was the hardest thing I've ever gone through. Do I wish she'd never been born? No. Not for a second. So I think I might understand a little more than most people what it's like to receive a piece of devastating news."

"How did the father take it?"

Without skipping a beat, she said, "We're no longer together. But it doesn't have to be that way for you. Talk to a counselor, and then talk to your husband."

It was like taking a stomach punch to the gut. Was she saying she could have done something that would have given their marriage a different outcome? He didn't see how.

"Okay, I will. And I'm sorry your husband didn't think your relationship was worth fighting for."

Not worth fighting for? Hell, he'd fought for her with all he'd been worth. None of it had been enough to change her mind. And she hadn't been able to change his. Their marriage had been as doomed as his daughter.

As the young woman walked away, Kady turned to him. "I don't think that, you know."

He shrugged. This wasn't something he wanted to talk about over a cup of coffee or anything else. In fact, he'd rather they not discuss it at all. Especially not after the day he'd had.

"It's okay. She obviously didn't overhear as much of our conversation as I thought she did." He picked up his packet of notes. Notes he hadn't needed after all. "Do you want me to give you a ride back to the hotel?"

"No, it's only a block away. I think I'll walk. I need the exercise."

Or did she just not want to be stuck in a car with him?

"You sure?"

"Yes. I could use some fresh air. See you in the morning."

And he could use some time alone to get his head

back together. Somehow being with this woman made him crazy. And brought back feelings both good and bad, that he hadn't felt since he'd left Atlanta.

A sense of foreboding stole over him. He'd thought his life would go back to normal in three more days. Once she got on that plane and headed out.

The door to the conference center closed, leaving him standing in an empty room. Would life really go back to normal? Or would he just realize how alone he really was? In more ways than one.

CHAPTER EIGHT

KADY'S PHONE WAS RINGING. She could hear it through the door to the shower, but with suds in her hair and an ache in her heart she decided to just let her voice mail pick it up. She wasn't in Atlanta, so it wasn't her hospital calling with an emergency regarding one of her patients.

Tilting her head back to let the sharp spray power-wash the shampoo from her wet locks, she tried to clear her head. Something that no amount of fresh air had been able to do last night.

She still had an hour before she was supposed to be back at the hospital for another round of medical students. God, how was she supposed to face Tucker again after yesterday? She didn't have any choice, unless she went home early. A tantalizing thought, but not something she was going to do. People had to face exes all the time in the real world. She just needed to suck it up and deal with it.

Most people didn't wind up sleeping with those exes, though.

Well, that had been a one-time thing. It wasn't like they were going to hook up every night while she was here. A tingle stole across her belly and slid lower, following the trail of water from the shower.

"Not happening," she told it. "Forget it."

As if forgetting it was an option. If Tucker was anything, he was a great lover. Except for those last horrible months of their marriage when he hadn't been able to stand the sight of her naked. When every touch from her had been met with a cold shoulder and an even colder heart.

And yet the night before, he'd kissed her as if he couldn't get enough. As if having sex with her was the only thing he could think of. Just like in the early days of their relationship.

That was what had done her in. What was still doing her in. What had changed in the two years since they'd seen each other? He'd gone from cold to very, *very* hot.

Whatever it was, she wanted nothing to do with it. Maybe she should say that out loud, just in case.

"You want nothing to do with it. Nothing to do with him."

Ha. Well, that did a whole lot of nothing, because that tingle spread to an uncomfortable level. Finishing her shower in a hurry, she dried off then wrapped the oversize towel around her hair and padded into the bedroom to check her phone. The missed call was an Atlanta number she didn't recognize. Maybe it was about a patient after all.

Sitting on the mattress, she pushed the button to return the call, adjusting the towel so she could get the phone to her ear.

"Atlanta Fertility Services, may I help you?"

Her heart skipped a beat. This was the firm she'd contacted about finding a sperm donor for her. She still had the envelope from them in her purse, as far as she knew. She just hadn't planned on contacting them again until she got back to town.

"This is Dr. Kadeline McPherson. I had a missed call from this number."

"Oh, yes, Dr. McPherson. Dr. Torres would like to speak to you personally. Can you hold for a moment?"

"Yes."

The soft sounds of a vaguely familiar melody drifted across the line. Why was the fertility clinic calling her? Of course they didn't realize she was in New York. It had never dawned on her to tell them. Maybe they'd found something in her application that needed to be redone.

Her heart stuttered. Or maybe they'd found something else in her lab work. Another genetic anomaly that would knock her out of the running for ever having a child.

No. She'd run a gamut of tests when she'd gone through genetic counseling. She had the Tay-Sachs gene but nothing else had turned up. At least, nothing known.

The music cut off. "Dr. McPherson?"

"Yes."

"I wanted to check in. We've identified several donors who would be excellent prospects. Tay-Sachs testing is negative, along with any other known genetic factors. Do you want to come in and look at the files?"

Her stomach squirmed and she had no idea why. She'd been excited to move on to this next phase in her life a few short weeks ago.

Before she'd come to New York?

No, that had nothing to do with it. She was just nervous. This was a huge step. "I'm actually out of town at the moment. Would you be able email the files to me, so I can take a look?"

"That's not a problem. Our front desk should have your email address, correct?"

"It was on my paperwork."

There was a pause. "Is everything okay?"

No, but she wasn't sure why. "Yes, it's just hectic here. I'm at a medical conference."

He chuckled. "I understand. I've been to a few of those myself."

"You know what I'm talking about, then." Her words sounded stilted even to her. "But I should be home in a few more days. I can look them over and let you know my thoughts. Is that okay?"

"Perfect. I'll let Jessica up front know. You should get the files sometime today."

"Thank you."

"You're welcome. If you have any other questions, just give us a call."

She ended the call, a chill washing over her. Was it her imagination or did Dr. Torres sound a little more eager than he had when she'd originally met with him? She groaned and dropped her phone onto the bed. It was her imagination. He didn't sound any different now than he had a month ago. Maybe it was her who had changed.

Seeing Tucker again had turned her world on its head. Everything seemed upside down and inside out—a place where the words *simple* and *uncomplicated* no longer existed. But they would. Once she got home.

The phone rang again. "Surely not."

She picked it up and pressed the green button. "Hello?"

"Kady? Where are you?"

This time, it was Tucker's voice that came over the line. Her heart thudded and it took a couple of swallows before she could speak. "I'm sorry?"

"Didn't you get my message?"

"What message?"

"I called you about ten minutes ago. Your patient is asking for you." She'd given him her cellphone number after she'd left his office that fateful night. At the time she told herself it was to make reaching her a little easier in case of a schedule change.

Pulling the phone away from her ear, she looked at the time. It was just eight o'clock. She wasn't supposed to be at the hospital for another hour. "My patient?"

Wow, she sounded like an idiot responding to everything with a question. But Tucker put her head in a spin every time she heard his voice…felt his touch. Like the moment he'd unsnapped the button on her pants and…

No more touching. No more kissing. No more anything except work. Hadn't she just had this talk with herself a few minutes ago?

"Your patient from the birthing center."

The name and face came to her in an instant. "Samantha? The PPH patient?"

"Yes, she's leaving today and wants to see you."

The chill from a few moments ago disappeared. "Did someone get a hold of her roommate?"

"I think she's on her way to pick her up."

"Tell her I'll be there in fifteen minutes." The medical students would have to forgive her wet hair and lack of makeup. Some things were just more important.

Like having a baby of her own?

Maybe.

* * *

True to her word, she arrived in fifteen minutes. And she'd obviously just showered not long ago. Her hair was twisted up in one of those clawed contraptions that she used to wear at home all the time.

If he undid it and let those silky strands tumble down her back, he knew just what scent would cling to them. Vanilla, coconut…and Kady. He forced the air in his nostrils to exit, hoping to avoid searching for any hint of it. He'd been knocked on his ass last night during her conversation with that young woman. It seemed everywhere he'd turned recently, something had done just that. Making him rethink decisions he'd once thought were irrevocable. Like having children?

Kind of hard to do that with a vasectomy.

"Is she still here?"

"She's waiting for you in her room. Four forty-one."

"No more problems?"

He shook his head, forcing his gaze from her wet hair to her face. It looked fresh scrubbed as well, her pale lashes bereft of mascara, the smattering of freckles across her nose on full display. More memories crowded into his skull, each less welcome than the one before. And there wasn't a damn thing he could do about it.

"They wouldn't release her if they thought there was."

"Thank you for calling me."

"I tried to let you off the hook, but she insisted."

"I was planning on checking on her this morning. I didn't realize they were going to discharge her already. I'm used to making those kinds of decisions, but I guess she wasn't really mine."

"Yes, she was. You pulled her through that crisis."

"I'm glad I was here."

She put a hand to her hair, as if checking to make sure it was still secured, then went back to worrying at that empty ring finger. He hated that it was bare, hated that she kept drawing his attention to it.

She stopped fiddling and looked at him. "I'm glad you were there too."

"Are you?" A clod of something stuck in his throat, making his voice come out rougher-sounding than it should have.

"You did a lot to help keep her calm."

The wind went out of his sails in a hurry. Of course she hadn't meant she was glad in a more personal sense. He decided to change the subject.

"You didn't have to rush right over. I'm sure she would have waited for you."

"That bad, huh?"

He frowned. "I'm not sure what you mean."

"The way I look. I didn't put on any makeup."

Ah, that's what…

"I think I remember telling you I liked you without it. Many times."

"Patients always looked at me like I was a kid without it."

No one would mistake her for a kid anymore. Not because she looked older. Yes, there were tiny lines beside her eyes and a crease on the right side of her face where her smile reached slightly higher. The biggest change was in those green eyes. Eyes that had seen things no one should ever have to see. Had held her daughter in her arms as she'd taken her final breath.

She wasn't older. There were just moments he caught a fleeting sadness in her eyes. Or was that resignation?

He had no doubt the experience had aged him too.

Only he hadn't handled it nearly as well as she had. Grace's death had nearly crippled him emotionally. He'd never been as open as Kady and her family were about showing their feelings. Their grief had been almost palpable—expressed the way healthy people were supposed to. Tucker, on the other hand, had built a dam, shoving his emotions behind it.

After everything had gone south, he'd retreated into himself with the lame excuse that he needed to be strong for his wife. In the end, she had been the one who'd been strong for him. She'd been able to function emotionally…sexually, even in the midst of her grief. And he hadn't been able to deal with that. So he'd shut her out. Along with her family and most of the world. When Kady's grandfather had tried to talk to him, he'd slammed that mental door as well.

For Tucker, shame and grief had gone hand in hand and created an unholy alliance. A wall had gone up that had never come down. It still hadn't.

"I can go home afterward and dry my hair at least."

Damn, she'd taken his lengthy silence for disapproval.

"Leave it. I like it."

As if that should matter one iota. He always managed to say the wrong thing around her.

"Okay, I will."

And with that simple answer and the smallest glimmer of a smile she started walking toward the room. She glanced back and tossed her head in a *come on* gesture. "You were in that treatment room as well."

"I don't think she even remembers me. It was you she wanted to see."

"Somehow I doubt that very many people forget you, Tucker. You kind of blow through like a hurricane."

He blinked. "Is that a compliment?"

"It's just the reality."

And leaving him to wonder what the hell she meant by that, she headed toward the room, leaving him to follow behind.

Once they got there they found someone already there, holding the baby. "Dr. McPherson, thanks so much for coming. This is my roommate, Phoebe."

"I'm glad I got to see you before you left." Kady's thumb went to town on her ring finger, like she should be doing something but wasn't sure what.

Ah, she wasn't used to being with a patient without checking vitals or doing something doctorly. He understood that all too well. It wasn't always easy to have relationships that weren't based on either professional courtesy or trying to help patients. It was why doctors sometimes had a hard time switching off once the last patient had been seen. There were days there just wasn't anything left for anyone else. Not fair to families sometimes. Tucker had always thought he and Kady had had the perfect arrangement, because they'd understood that and had given each other space when it was needed.

But when the same two doctors couldn't fix what was wrong with their daughter, that house of cards came tumbling down. Nothing known to man had been able to reconstruct it. Maybe he'd never have another real relationship ever again. And maybe it was even easier that way.

Was work enough?

It had been. At least until now. And once Kady went home? Would it be enough again?

He had no idea. But he sure as hell hoped so. When his eyes ventured to that black hair clip, though, all bets were off. Because the cycle of remembering and rejecting began all over again.

"Do you want to hold her?" Samantha's voice brought him back from the brink, and he realized she was talking to him. At some point the baby had passed from Samantha's roommate to Kady.

She was standing with the newborn tucked into her arms, gently rocking the infant back and forth. Nothing had ever looked more right than seeing her with a baby. His breath stalled in his throat, even as he noted her eyes on him, a worried crease between her brows. Had Samantha already asked him once?

"Oh, no. I'm good."

"Aw, come on," the young woman coaxed. "I know you know how to hold a baby. You operate on ones smaller than this one all the time, right? At least, that's what Dr. McPherson told me. How about holding one that's healthy?"

Healthy.

Had Kady told her about Grace?

No. They were talking in generalities. And if he refused to hold the newborn, someone was going to wonder why.

The breath he'd been holding in stagnated in his lungs and his throat tightened. Somehow, though, he managed to hold his arms out when Kady came over, allowing her to gently deposit the tiny bundle into his care.

No one should ever trust him with a baby.

And yet patients did it every day.

This was different, though. This baby had weight. And substance. And…health.

What he was feeling now was probably the same thing Kady had felt a few moments ago.

Grace had felt just like this once upon a time. Just a day old, but with a solidness that had felt very right in his arms. Smoky blue had eyes met his and blinked. Blond tufts of hair had stood straight up. Small fists had waved in the air as if…

He couldn't do it. "Take her, please." He held the baby out for Kady to take back, while chunks of his heart seemed to peel away and fall to the floor.

How could she bear the thought of having another child? Holding it close? Loving it?

He could treat preterm babies because he knew they weren't his. And it was his way of doing what he hadn't been able to do for Grace: give them a cure. But there was no attachment. No sentimental feelings attached to any of them. He made sure of that.

Then why did their names run through his head as he operated on them? Why did he murmur to them, even as his scalpel cut deep?

He was just trying to remember that what he did was important to someone.

Samantha took the baby from Kady with a smile. "Thanks again for everything."

She acted like there was nothing weird about the way he'd rushed the infant back into Kady's arms. Maybe he hadn't been as transparent as he'd thought. Or maybe he was better at hiding his emotions than he gave himself credit for.

They walked the trio out to the curb, waiting while

the baby was strapped into a car seat in the roommate's car. Then they waved goodbye.

This was the last time they would ever see Samantha and her new baby. He tried to drum up the last time he'd seen his own baby, but failed miserably.

"Tucker, are you okay?"

Kady's soft voice called him back from the depths. "I'm fine. Just didn't expect to have to hold her, that's all."

"I could tell." She linked her arm through his for a moment as they stood there on the curb, the noise of traffic and voices outside very different from the canned silence inside the hospital. "You were a good father to her. Don't ever forget that."

A sudden wash of emotion spurted from behind the wall, stabbing at the backs of his eyes and clogging his throat. Oh, hell. Not now.

He pulled his arm from hers, afraid if they stood there any longer, she would see.

"We did everything we could for her. So did her doctors." His cool businesslike tone had to be a slap in the face after what she'd just said. But it was all he could manage without the past pouring out in a very real way.

She gripped his arm again. "Hey, don't do that. Don't you *dare* do that."

"Do what?"

"Act like she was nothing more to you than one of your patients. She was our *daughter*, dammit."

"You think I don't know that? That I don't have to deal with what happened every single hour of every single day?" The dam broke and he turned, yanking her against him. "I remember the second she was born, the second she smiled. The second she…"

Then his lips were on hers, hand going to the back of her head and clutching her to him. Grief and want and need all melded together into a huge tangled ball that was impossible to unravel.

Kady seemed to understand exactly what he was feeling, arms wrapping around his neck, giving back every bit as good as she got.

And it *was* good—too good—the heat and pressure of her mouth changing the tone in an instant. He deepened the kiss, and a familiar stirring took place, reminding him that he could indeed do things. *Wanted* to do them.

With Kady and no one else.

"Woohoo! Go, Dr. Stevenson!" The cheer, along with several catcalls, had him yanking away from her so fast that she tripped backward, might have fallen if he hadn't reached out to grab her arm.

Thirteen figures stood on the sidewalk, staring at them. Some of them grinning, some of them shocked as hell. Well, no one was more shocked than Tucker himself.

What did he do about it? This was his fault. He'd initiated that kiss. It was bad enough that the medical students had seen it. Who else had spotted them?

Great. How was he supposed to explain this to anyone?

Worse, how was he supposed to explain this to himself?

This was why he didn't let his emotional responses come out to play more often. They ran amok, doing whatever the hell they wanted to.

He took a breath.

"We just had a… This was…"

Kady took a step forward. "Remember when we talked about interpersonal relationships? This was a lesson in what not to do with a colleague. I hope you all got the point."

Whether they believed the hogwash she was dishing up or not, they didn't dare contradict her. While he willed his body to turn off the fireworks she'd unwittingly ignited, Kady was busy running over the latest case study with the group. A case he couldn't even remember going over with her.

Because he hadn't given her the chance. He'd whisked her back to that hospital room to see their patient and things had slalomed downhill from there.

Until that kiss, when things had started going up in ways they shouldn't have. But Tucker had proved one thing to himself.

He hadn't forgotten the smell of her hair.

Or her touch. Or anything else about her.

It was still there. In the back of his memory bank.

And there wasn't any power on earth that was going to erase it. Not three days from now, when she went home. Not three months from now. And probably not three hundred years from now.

CHAPTER NINE

KADY SAT BY the pool and tried to make out the words on the documents. Not easy on her phone. Making the text bigger helped, but then she had to scroll repeatedly back and forth to follow the sentences from beginning to end.

She should probably just wait until she got home to go over the sperm donors' information, but she'd wanted to give it a chance to percolate for a while.

Anything to take away the memory of that scene in front of the hospital. She'd been shocked by the outpouring of emotion from a man who hadn't let her see the real him in a very long time. She'd glimpsed it when he'd been so desperate to hand the baby back to her. But during that kiss? Lightning had cracked through the air, singeing them both. And something had woken inside her. Some vital part that had tunneled into the earth had sprung back to life, leaves unfurling and seeking the sun.

But if she'd hoped Tucker would declare that he'd never stopped loving her, that he'd changed his mind, she'd been sorely disappointed.

But, then, she'd been disappointed before.

She focused on the information on the screen.

It was all there. Height, weight, body type, ethnic background. The first two she rejected outright, although she wasn't quite sure why. They seemed perfect on paper. What wasn't to like? They were both evidently tall, dark and handsome. So what was wrong?

She had no idea.

Tipping her sunglasses to the top of her head, thinking maybe the artificial darkness was injecting some kind of pessimism into the process, she tried again. The glare from the white paper hurt her eyes. There was no foggy residue on the windows today to mute the sunlight. She squinted and forced her eyes to keep moving, trying to pinpoint the problem.

She found nothing.

Why was she having such a hard time differentiating between one application and the next? Maybe it was having the sanitized, clinical reality laid out in front of her. This was not a love match. Or computer dating. Then again, it wasn't meant to be. It was scientific data, nothing more, nothing less.

But taking the human element away made it seem like all three applicants were painted with the same brush. No mention of a dimple. No stray acne scar on any of their right temples. No crooked little toe from a break when he'd been three years old.

He?

She swallowed. *God.* Those things belonged to Tucker.

Was that why none of these physical bios measured up?

She should have been long over him by now. And she'd thought she was. Had thought that having a baby on her own meant she was finally moving forward with her life.

But when he'd stood there on that curb and suddenly grabbed her, she'd come face to face with the flesh and blood man she'd fallen in love with. Passionate and loving, but reserving those feelings for her alone. She hadn't seen that side of him in so long that she'd almost forgotten it existed. And then it had been there. Right in front of her. Making her want to lose herself in his touch.

She hesitated. She'd been disappointed that he hadn't expressed any deeper emotion afterward.

Was it because she was still in love with him?

No. She couldn't be. Not possible when they wanted such different things out of life.

But that was back when the mechanical Tucker had systematically shut her out of his life in the most devastating way imaginable. He'd withheld his touch. His affection. His words of love. They'd inhabited the same physical space but not the same world.

These last three days had been different. It had been like Tucker had woken from a deep slumber.

Could he be changing before her eyes? Or, like her sunglasses, was it all just an illusion?

She didn't know, but she couldn't bank on something that might be confined to her fantasies. Or to a five-day working vacation. She needed permanence. Shared ideals.

Her eyes went back to the last donor's file, turning her phone to the side to see better.

"Must be some interesting reading there."

"Ah!" She let out a scream, the cellphone tumbling out of her hand and landing on the towel she'd tossed down a few minutes earlier. Thank God the pool room was empty this morning.

"Sorry." He bent down to scoop up the phone.

"No, don't—"

Too late. His gaze was on the screen, head cocked to the side. Then twin shutters slammed across his eyes. When they lifted to meet hers there was a blankness she remembered all too well.

The Tucker from the end of their marriage.

"Donor bios? Is this what you were talking about in my office?"

She reached up and grabbed her phone from him. "If you must know, yes."

There was a silence that seemed to stretch on forever.

"Why would you go this route?"

"It's less complicated."

The shutters lifted a little. "Less complicated than what?"

Was he serious? "Than the whole relationship thing. That didn't seem to work out for me all that well."

A muscle pulsed in his jaw. "I'm sorry, Kady. For everything."

No, no, no.

She did not want her future to go hacking around with her past. She needed them to stay in separate realms where she could manage them. When they mixed, things got…complicated. It made those bios look unappealing all over again.

"It doesn't matter. I'm just doing what I think is best for me."

He lowered himself into the chair beside hers. "And going it alone is best?"

"At the moment? Yes."

He nodded at the phone. "Mind if I look?"

"Yes, I mind." She was very aware that she was sitting there clad in nothing but her red bikini. Again. "Did you want something?"

She allowed the crabbiness in her voice to come through. Today had not been the stuff of which dreams were made.

Well, except for that kiss. And even that had turned into a disaster when their medical students had shown up in the middle of it. Just when Tucker had been getting to the good part. And then they'd had to pretend to simply be colleagues for the next two hours while they'd tried to overlap cases without overlapping anything else.

And hell if Kady hadn't wanted to be overlapped. By him. The whole damn time.

She still did, despite her every attempt to banish it from her head.

That was part of the reason she'd decided to come back to the hotel and focus on her future baby. The baby she was going to have.

Not fun. Not fun at all.

She'd been fine with that. Until Tucker had come along with his stupid kisses and super-sexy sofa-loving and ruined it all.

"I actually came by to apologize for coming unglued this morning."

And that was the icing on the cake she'd had in the oven all day. His "coming unglued" was the thing that had given her the most pause about going through with the IVF.

"Nothing to apologize for. It was a kiss. We've certainly done that before."

"Yes, we have." He leaned back and put his hands behind his head, his khaki slacks seeming completely out of place in the steamy humidity of the pool room. "What I'm trying to figure out is why it's happening *now*."

"We're both under a lot of stress right now."

"So you're saying I'm a stress reliever?"

"You're twisting my words out of context." Like him, she had no idea why this was all suddenly happening now, when it hadn't happened three years ago.

He turned his head and nodded toward the phone. "So how many prospects have you got in there?"

Her brain had to hop around a bit to follow his train of thought. This was still none of his business, but maybe by talking about it she could regain her earlier excitement.

"Three." It was insane to be sitting here, discussing this with him.

"I take it all of them are genetically engineered perfection."

"Funny. You're a real funny guy." Okay, now she was mad. Mad because he'd hit on the very nerve she'd been worrying all morning long. How could she even tell what kind of men these were? They might seem like perfect physical specimens, but what were they like? *Who* were they?

She was over-thinking this. People chose sperm donors all the time. And no one ever seemed to regret doing it. At least, not from all the glowing testimonials emblazoned on the walls of the fertility clinic.

"Can I see them?" No sardonic humor in his voice now. He seemed deadly serious.

"Why?"

His dark gaze landed on her. "I'm curious to see

who is going to father Grace's half-brother or -sister, that's all."

A shaft of pain went through her. He was right. Any baby she had would be Grace's half-sibling. She would tell them all about her. But she wanted to get one thing straight. "He won't be his or her father. Just a sperm donor."

In reality, the baby wouldn't have a father, just some nameless figure who had masturbated into a plastic cup.

Dammit, why was she making something that should be beautiful into a sleazy backroom thing?

Like her encounter with Tucker in his office?

No, that hadn't been sleazy either. It had been exciting and powerful.

And she was thinking about it far too much to be healthy.

She should be grateful that there were men who were willing to help people like her. They were good, caring men. Men she should be glad had chosen to go this route.

Tucker held his hand out for the phone. Against her better judgment, she handed it to him. "It's kind of hard to read on that format."

"What's your password?"

Her chin tipped up, the numbers rolling off her lips. "Zero-eight-sixteen."

He started to punch the numbers in then stopped. His Adam's apple jerked up before settling back into place. "August sixteenth. Grace's birthday."

"It seemed appropriate somehow."

"And yet what you're using it for isn't."

A thread of anger uncoiled inside her. "I would have

to disagree. She's part of who I am. You admitted yourself that any new child would be Grace's little sister or brother. It's my way of making her a part of the process."

He typed the numbers in and looked at the screen, his thumb and forefinger moving in a way that made her earlier efforts at resizing the wording seem ridiculous.

"Nope. Not this one."

She craned her neck to look at the screen. "Why?" It was one of those Kady had rejected. Maybe Tucker's reasons would be a little more objective.

"He looks like he could be your brother."

Her insides took a dive. Now that he mentioned it, he did look a little bit like the male members of her family.

He scrolled to the next candidate. "A body builder, huh? Is that the type you're drawn to?"

No. It wasn't. But there was no way she was going to tell him who she *was* drawn to. Because it was the man hunched over the small screen, khaki-clad legs on either side of the lounge chair as he kept reading.

He looked gorgeous.

His profile showed a strong nose, a slight bump in the bridge that he said had come from a skateboard accident when he was a teenager.

She couldn't imagine the Tucker of today on a skateboard.

Instead, he frowned. A lot. His serious demeanor had put a dent between his thick brows, wiping away the carefree young man she'd once known. By Grace's death? By their divorce? Or just by life in general?

Could she blame him? She didn't laugh nearly as

much as she used to either. Losing a child was an experience that no one should ever have to face.

And Tucker never would again, thanks to his vasectomy.

"What about this third guy?" His voice jerked her attention away, glad he hadn't found her staring at him.

She'd already ruled the fake brother and the body builder guy out. She didn't need to look at this one to know she wasn't going with him either.

How was she going to tell Dr. Torres that she couldn't decide on anyone? Maybe it was like a menu. If there were too many choices, nothing looked good.

Three was hardly too many.

But none of them seemed right.

She was trying to think up an answer when the dent in Tucker's brows became more pronounced. He'd found something he didn't like.

"What is it?"

"Nothing."

That did not look like a nothing kind of expression. "Give me my phone, please. This is ridiculous. You are not going to help me choose a donor."

Surprisingly, he handed it to her. "Thank you."

"So do you accept my apology?"

"Apology for what? Making fun of something that's very serious to me? No."

He swung his legs over the side of the lounge chair and regarded her, elbows on his knees, hands loose between his strong thighs. "I'm not making fun of you, Kady, I know how much this means to you."

A knot formed in her chest. It did. Until now, and she wasn't sure why. "Thank you."

Maybe the mechanical man hadn't returned after all.

Actually, he seemed a little different this afternoon, a little softer than when she'd first arrived. Or was that wishful thinking? She'd just been sitting there dreaming about that kiss in front of the hospital and whether or not he'd changed.

Could he have?

His gray eyes moved from her phone to rest on her mouth, as if reading her thoughts. When his attention slid higher, heated shadows now moving through his gaze, she shivered.

He wanted to kiss her. Just like he had in front of the hospital.

"What's happening to us, Tucker? Is it just nostalgia?"

"I didn't behave very well after Grace's death. I think maybe I'm seeing that for the very first time. Some of my choices might not have been very well thought out."

She blinked. Was he talking about having children? "We were both hurting. We just handled it in different ways."

Maybe they'd both been a little impulsive. She'd jumped right to wanting another baby. And he'd leapt in the opposite direction. She might have pushed a little too hard to get her way, but three years after Grace's death her desire to have another child hadn't faded.

"Is that what we're doing now? Handling it? By handling each other?"

She smiled. The first real smile since yesterday. Maybe that's exactly what they'd been doing. And handling hadn't been all that bad. "Maybe it's what we both needed. The question is, now what do we do about it."

Especially since a little voice inside her was whispering to her that they could just keep going on like they were. And after that?

"Hell if I know." His tone was playful, like old times.

Her smile grew. "There are only a few more days left of the conference. Surely we can keep our 'handlings' to ourselves."

"I'm pretty sure about me, but you…?" One side of his mouth went up in the devastating smile he wore so well.

Ha! She wasn't confident about herself either. "Are you saying I might not be able to control myself?"

"I'm saying I know you can't."

She swallowed. He was right. She couldn't. The second he touched her she was toast. Just like she always was.

Not good for a woman contemplating having a child with a complete and utter stranger.

Well, Tucker sure hadn't stepped up and offered his services.

Oh, yes, he had. He might not be able to get her pregnant, but he got the job done. The job of needing and wanting and…

Loving.

Oh, no. No. *No!*

The word games between them had just become deadly serious.

She drew a steadying breath, even as her world tipped from side to side like a rowboat faced with frenzied seas. The reality she'd been toying with earlier washed over the side of her little craft, dumping her into the ocean in a second. She sputtered to the surface and headed back to the overturned vessel as the truth sank in.

She loved him.

That's why none of those applicants seemed right. Why she was looking for some sign of him in each prospect. There wasn't any, because Tucker wasn't in those files.

But it did her no good. She might love him but he didn't love her. Or want children with her.

His very presence was messing with her future happiness.

She needed to tell him in no uncertain terms to stay away from her for the rest of the conference. Otherwise they were in danger of becoming colleagues by day, lovers by night.

"I'm pretty sure I can control myself quite well, thank you very much."

"Really? Let me see that phone again."

"What?"

What had seemed humorous a few minutes ago now left a bad taste in her mouth. He really was okay with letting her go through with using a sperm donor? Not that he had any say in the matter, but after what she'd just realized, it would have been nice to see at least a glimmer of misgivings.

Fine. If he was okay with it, then she would be too.

She handed him the phone. Instead of opening the screen, he set it down on the lounger and then stood to his feet. "What are you doing?"

"Making a point about the boundaries of self-control. It's pretty damned hard to talk about sperm when you're lounging around, wearing practically nothing." He waved his hand over her midsection.

"Nothing? It's called a bikini. This is a pool after all."

"I know. And a bikini and water go together like…" He smiled. A very knowing, cunning smile.

"Don't you dare." She suddenly knew where this was headed.

He scooped her into his arms. "Oh, I dare all right."

"Tucker! Put me down! This is definitely against pool rules."

"It's definitely against our own rules too, but you don't see that stopping me." He started walking toward the edge of the concrete surround.

"Don't."

He paused. "You didn't come out here to swim?"

"Yes, but I changed my mind."

"That's good, because I've changed mine too." He swished her from side to side as he started counting down. "One…"

"No, Tucker, I hate—"

"Two…"

"I am going to kill—"

"Three!"

At the last second she locked her arms around his neck, so that when his hands went to toss her she held tight. If she was going in then so was he, dammit.

They both crashed into the water in a tangle of arms and legs and shockingly cold water. At least in her boat analogy from earlier, the water had been warm.

She pushed to the surface, checking her bikini top this time before she actually stuck her head out of the water. All secure. Tucker was already at the side of the pool, lifting something out of the water.

His phone! Oh, God. She swam over to him.

"I'm sorry! I had no idea you were carrying that."

He gave her a lopsided grin that carried none of the

anger she was expecting. "At least I did you the courtesy of setting yours aside." He shook water droplets from the device, making her cringe.

"Maybe you can put it in a bag of rice or something."

"I don't think rice is going to do any good in this case."

Kady lived on her phone. It had her notes, her contacts, her appointment reminders. Everything. "Did you back it up somewhere?"

As if she did. She never backed up her devices. She would after this, though.

"It's okay. I deserved it. And, yes, it's backed up. And insured."

Was throwing an ex-wife into the pool covered under that particular warranty?

There were lots of things that didn't come with guarantees. Like relationships. And life.

She wished they did, because then, just like the products that lined the shelves, you could avoid those that carried a "buy at your own risk" label. But if she and Tucker had never gotten involved, she wouldn't have those sweet memories of her daughter. The heartache afterward had been almost as horrible as Grace's death, but she would gladly go through it all again if it meant she could hold her baby girl one more time.

But, of course, she couldn't. And there were no do-overs in life. Moaning and groaning about the past did nothing but make you a bitter, angry person.

Like Tucker had been?

If she were honest, she had been pretty bitter and angry herself. About Tucker's attitude, about the fate that had given them both a recessive gene that would destroy not only their daughter's life but also their relationship to each other.

She said the only thing she could think of. "I'll pay to have it repaired."

He tossed the item over to her towel, hitting it on the first try. "I think you already have."

"Ha! Since you were the one who was going to toss me in while you stayed up on the surface high and dry. It seems like you got what was coming to you."

The water had gone from cool to languorously warm as her legs paddled back and forth, her arms supporting her upper body on the side of the pool. Maybe the warmth wasn't so much the water as it was being next to the man she'd been unbelievably intimate with.

With his black polo shirt clinging to his body in all the right places, he was a figure to behold. His khakis were plastered to his legs as well and... "Oh, no. Your shoes!"

"At the bottom of the pool. And they're not insured."

She peered through the water to the bottom and saw two black shapes, one beside the other as if he'd neatly placed them there on purpose. She started laughing, the sound coming up from the depths and carrying across the room. She suddenly felt giddy and carefree—couldn't remember the last time she'd felt this way.

"I'm glad someone finds my monetary outlay funny."

"It just..." She tried to suck down a quick breath before going on, the words broken apart by giggles. "It looks like you planned where each one would land. That's a surgeon for you." Her laughter picked up again, and she had no idea why. It wasn't all that funny. Well, probably not to anyone but her. But Tucker was such a precise man in every way—he liked to be in control of his actions, that tendency carrying over into his surgeries. It's what made him one of the best fetal surgeons in the country.

"It's a good thing I don't invite you in to my surgical suite very often. I don't think my patients would appreciate you chortling your way through their procedures."

"Chortling." She coughed, trying to staunch the weird flow of sounds. "What kind of word is that?"

"It means laughing."

Her nose crinkled as she struggled to regain control over her breathing. Not easy when every time those damn shoes came into her line of vision, her lungs started tightening in preparation for another round.

Not good.

"I know what it means. I've just never heard it used in an actual conversation."

He turned his head to look at her. "There are lots of words and sounds that aren't used in actual conversations."

Her laughter dried up in a rush.

"Sounds?"

He answered with the lifting of his left brow.

"Boundaries and self-control?"

"Say the word and I'll stay firmly on my side of that line." His finger came up and trailed across her collarbone, belying his words and sending a shudder through her.

He would stop if she asked him to. But right now she was caught under a spell she didn't want to break.

Making a decision, she leaned up to whisper in his ear, "Lines can be stepped across. Can't they?"

"Yes, they can. It's as easy as this." One arm sank beneath the surface of the water and slid across the small of her back, just above her bikini line. "Too far over?"

Unable to trust her voice, she shook her head.

The arm curled around her side, his fingers brushing the indentation of her hip. "How about now?"

"No."

One finger dipped just below the elastic at her waist and stroked just above the juncture of her thighs. When the sensation made her give a low moan, there was no mistaking where this was headed.

He bit her earlobe. "How far across the line am I allowed to go, Kady?"

"A-as far as you want." The words came out thick with need.

Message received.

Tucker's head dipped, his lips seeking and finding hers. All the playful banter of moments earlier disappeared. And something deeper and far more dangerous rose up to take its place. She was ready for it. Had been ready for the last two years.

CHAPTER TEN

THEY CRASHED THROUGH the door of her hotel room, lips still locked, Tucker kicking it shut behind him. It was as if she'd released a latch on some primitive side of him and let loose a beast that was intent on devouring her. And she was more than happy to let him do just that.

The bed was a few feet away, and they fell onto it, Tucker's weight pressing her deep into the mattress. His clothes were wet and chilly against her superheated skin, but it was okay. She would take whatever she could get of him. His hands went to either side of her face and dark eyes stared into hers. "You're gorgeous. You know that, don't you?"

He made her feel that way.

When she went to draw him back to her, though, he stood, pulling his phone and sodden wallet from his pockets. He then tossed them onto the other side of the king-size bed. Impatient, she sat up, her fingers going to the button on his slacks and making short work of that and the zipper. It took a little bit of effort to see-saw the garment down his lean hips until he could step out of them. "You get your shirt while I get…" She hooked her thumbs into the waistband of his briefs and eased them over the bulge in front. As soon as she did, he sprang free.

God.

She'd almost forgotten how much pleasure this part of his body could bring her. And how much pleasure it could bring him when she touched it. When she…

The hands that had been undoing his shirt stopped the second her lips met his skin. He swore, palm reaching to grip her hair. A half-hearted tug that changed nothing made her smile, although that was hard to do when her mouth was…she opened wide…full.

It was. Full and heavy and incredibly sexy. She loved the intimacy of it. Loved sending him to the brink and watching him try to fight against the rising tide. The thing was, she always won. And he always tried to stop her.

"Kady."

Her gaze went up, brows arching slightly in challenge as her tongue swirled around him. Stroking, tasting, doing everything in her power to make him come unhinged.

Instead, he did the unexpected. He stepped back, breaking the suction. "Not this time."

She licked her lips again. "Not good enough? Then come here so I can do it even better."

"Witch." He came forward, but not to take up where she'd left off. Instead, he reached for her wrists and bore her back to the bed. Arms over her head, he transferred her hands to one of his, then held her in place. "Now it's my turn."

He leaned over her, lips trailing down her neck and collarbone in a way that missed being ticklish by a hair's breadth. Instead it crossed the line into breath-stealing, especially when he cruised the V of her bikini top until he arrived at the other side. And then he found one of her nipples.

Hard, tight, aching.

Breath whooshed from her lungs when he took a long, hard pull on it. Then another.

"I want you so much it hurts."

There was a sound of wonder in his voice that she didn't quite understand, but it didn't matter—she wanted him just as much. Between her legs, inside her, all around her. If she spent her whole life holed up in this room, she wouldn't care.

"Lift your head, honey."

She did as he asked, the fingers of his free hand fumbling with the strings to her bikini. Then he peeled the top down, exposing her breasts. This time, his lips touched bare skin. Her eyes fluttered shut as he teased and nibbled, traveling back and forth. The need inside her expanded faster than she wanted it to, her insides melting. "Tucker, let go of my hands."

His teeth bit down, and she arched up off the bed. "Not yet. Maybe not ever."

She couldn't do anything but moan and thrash as he continued the onslaught, leaving out an important part of her body. And there was nothing to push against to help staunch the growing ache. Her hips pumped into empty air, trying to squeeze her thighs together, anything that would help give her the sensation she was looking for.

He lifted his head and stared down at her. "Spread your legs."

"Not unless you're ready to put something between

them." She didn't recognize the thin, raspy voice that spoke those words.

"Trust me."

She did as he asked, and he moved between them, removing any hope of squeezing herself to orgasm in an instant.

Her groan was met with a smile. "Patience."

A fingertip went to the base of her throat and slowly traveled the midline of her body, between her breasts, down her abdomen, into her bellybutton until he reached the top of her pubic bone. He didn't dive off the edge like she'd hoped. Instead, he zigzagged slowly in place, just above where she wanted it to be.

There was a tenseness in her breasts, her nipples drawn into rigid peaks. They knew what was coming. Only Tucker wasn't giving them the satisfaction that lay just beyond reach. He slid his finger down a smidgen and tracked it back and forth again, a little harder this time.

She moaned, eyes closing. He was so close.

God! *She* was so close.

His voice sounded in her ear, the low, insistent tone adding another tremor to her system. "I'm going to make you come."

There was no doubt of that. She wasn't sure why he was announcing it. She was ready for him to touch her. To *really* touch her.

But a minute went by, then two, while her body strained toward that point of contact. Except there was nothing to push against.

"You're going to come." The voice came again, that finger tracing a circle millimeters away from her pleasure center. "Just with this. Because I need to be inside you. And can't. Until you come. Hard."

She believed him. Already a familiar tingling was gathering speed.

If she thrust her hips hard enough, she might be able to jolt him to the right spot, but she wanted to do this. For him. Wanted his mere presence to send her into the clouds.

"Kady." His tone was now a tense whisper. "I need you to come for me, baby. Please."

It took two seconds, then her body fluttered, a sharp clench of her inner muscles driving her forward. Then another. The spasms and his stroking finger rendered her powerless to retreat to safety, even if she'd wanted to. The next contraction did it.

"Ah-h-h…" She climaxed with a fury that stole her breath. She didn't have time to think about any of that, though, because he was suddenly there inside her, pumping hard and fast, that ravenous beast back to finish off his prey.

"Dammit, yes!" His triumphant oath came just as he let go of her hands and clutched her hips, raising them as he continued to thrust inside of her. "Yes."

He slowed but still pumped, drawing out both their climaxes.

"Yes."

That final word was full of masculine satisfaction. Of satiation.

Drawing a shaky breath, and feeling pretty satisfied herself, she kissed his neck. "You are a very bad man."

He chuckled, making no move to pull away and separate them. "I thought women were drawn to bad boys."

"There is bad and then there is *bad*."

"And which one am I?"

"I haven't decided yet."

He rolled over, drawing her with him. "I can be as bad as you want me to be. Or as good."

Planting her hands on his shoulders, she pushed up so she could look at him. "I can't believe you did that."

"Did what?" He feigned innocence, but his smile said he knew exactly what she was talking about.

"You know."

"It was payback for what you tried to do." His arm hooked around her back, holding her in place. "In fact, I don't think I've been paid in full yet."

He drew his nose up her temple. "Were you picturing any of those donor's faces when I was inside you?"

Was that a hint of jealousy in his voice? "Would that make it more exciting for you?"

"No." The growled word made her laugh.

"We can play who's behind curtain number one."

He kissed the corner of her mouth. "I'm behind all the curtains."

"Are you? Those were supposed to be for the donors. Unless you want to pretend to be one of them. Maybe you're vying for the top spot."

His index finger tickled the lobe of her ear. "And what would you do with me if you chose me?"

"Mmm... I would coax what I needed out of you." She frowned. "Except that's impossible now."

"Let's say things were magically reversed through the wonders of modern technology." His lips pressed against her neck. "Now, how would you coax me?"

Her brain was having a little trouble concentrating, since his mouth had skimmed to her collarbone, his voice low and seductive. "I would use anything I could. My hands. My mouth."

Teeth connected with the sensitive skin at the crook of her neck. When air hissed through her teeth, he licked over the spot, generating a languid warmth that drugged her system. "And after you got it?"

"I'd have to make sure things took, so we might have to make multiple attempts."

"Multiple attempts. Oh, yes, I think we would. And once it took? Would you throw me away?"

"Never."

His fingers found one of her nipples, wrenching a moan out of her. "So now you have me. And you've coaxed and coaxed and coaxed. What comes next?"

Her breath was coming in shorter spurts. "W-we'd have to get busy, choosing names."

"Bueller." He squeezed the tight peak of her breast, making her writhe against him.

"No."

"No, Kady? Are you sure?" The pad of his thumb brushed over her and her eyes fluttered closed.

"No to Bueller. Not to that."

"How about Gregorian?" The pressure of his thumb increased slightly.

"Isn't Gregorian…a type…of chant?" She was doing some chanting of her own and it had nothing to do with baby names. "Why are we only having boys?"

A sense of euphoria was making it increasingly hard for her to think. This was a conversation he never would have participated in three years ago. And now he was smiling. Kissing her. Thinking up outrageous names, even as he was driving her wild with need. Was this their new normal? She hoped so.

"We're only having boys because…" His hands moved to her hips, shifting her just a little to the left. Something magically began stirring down below. "Right on cue. Saved by the hoisting of the mainsail. And it didn't need any coaxing after all."

She gave an over-dramatic sigh that sounded more like a whimpered plea. "You're taking all the fun out of it."

Actually, he wasn't. He was putting all the fun back into her life. Fun that she'd almost thought obliterated forever.

"Want to bet?" He positioned her, thrusting upward in a rush.

She gasped as he filled her completely. "Didn't you just…?" Her voice squeaked to a stop when his palms glided over her backside and squeezed. "You can't mean to…"

"I can." He smiled up at her. "And I do. Maybe it's time I did a little coaxing of my own."

Coaxing. It had worked. A little too well.

Tucker needed to wake her up, even though it was the last thing he wanted to do. But they had missed their conference session, spending the afternoon making love again and again instead. He was exhausted. In a good and familiar way. A way that once upon a time he'd thought he'd never feel again.

Those days were over.

At least, he hoped they were.

Were they falling in love all over again? If so, what did he do about it? He could stop it in its tracks with well-placed flippancy once those gorgeous green eyes opened.

But he didn't want to do that. He didn't want to hurt her.

So what *did* he want to do?

What he wanted to do and what he *should* do might be two different things. He had to tread carefully. Maybe he could start by reexamining some of his choices. And sharing those with her. He'd tried to do a little of that during the game they'd played this afternoon, hopefully letting her know that he really did want to be behind the curtain.

Kady squirmed in her sleep, a soft sigh and a puckering of her lips making him wonder if she was dreaming about what they'd done together. His gaze trailed over the naked line of her back and the spot just above her ass where the edge of the sheet rested.

The same finger that he'd used last night went behind her ear, brushing back and forth over the tender skin. As much as he wanted to stay here with her all night, his stomach was beginning to protest that, at seven thirty, it was past his dinnertime.

He leaned down and replaced his finger with his lips, dropping tiny kisses behind her ear, her scent drifting up in intoxicating little eddies. She murmured something unintelligible and tilted her head closer, as if seeking out his touch. His body stirred all over again.

God, he loved this woman.

The kisses stopped.

Loved.

Loved.

He did. Had never stopped. He'd just buried those emotions beneath a load of fear when all the talk of babies had started.

But she still wanted children. Was looking to find a sperm donor to get her there.

Maybe she would rethink that. Especially after their afternoon play date.

Was that what he wanted? To make her change her life plans so they could be together?

Maybe. Would she be willing to? Or maybe he was the one who needed to be willing to change. He'd meant what he'd said about being behind all of those curtains.

He wanted her to choose him. Even if it was on her terms? Playing around with baby names hadn't been as gut-wrenching as it had been at one time. In fact, it had been—

"Tucker." She groaned his name, and his body hardened further. He loved hearing her say his name in that cute, almost-accented tone. Especially when it came in on one of those breathy little sighs that said she liked whatever he was doing.

He kissed her again. "Time to wake up. We have somewhere to be."

"Somewhere to be?" Her eyes blinked open and she rolled onto her back, her breasts gloriously exposed to his gaze.

Right now the only place he wanted to be was in this bed with her.

"We are going out to dinner."

"Mmm…" Her eyes met his. The spot between her brows puckered as she processed that thought. Then she sat up, her frown growing deeper. "What time is it?"

"Seven thirty."

"Oh, no! We missed the conference. And it's the last night. Why didn't you wake me up?"

He smiled. "I believe I was trying to do just that. I'm insulted that my kisses didn't have more of an effect."

She muttered something under her breath.

"What was that?"

"Nothing."

That adorable just-woken grumpiness. He even missed that.

His lips pressed against her temple. "Maybe my kisses were having an effect after all. Was that the problem?"

"No."

He nipped the edge of her jaw, moving just close enough to her mouth to make her wonder. "Are you sure?"

"Do we really have to eat?" She turned slightly until they were lined up lip to lip. "Because if the answer is no, you could just lie back and let me demonstrate some truly effective kissing techniques. Or there's always pole dancing with a very special pole."

The groan this time was all his. "Don't go there, Kady."

She laughed. "You are so transparent."

A slight cloud came over him. Hell, she probably could see right through him. Maybe even knew that he loved her. If so, why did she find that amusing? Because nothing about what he'd just realized was funny.

At least, not to him.

A thread of warning coiled around his heart. He should just tell her how he felt and see if she felt the same way.

Their time together was almost over. If he was going to confess, it needed to be now—tonight—or she would disappear back to Atlanta and he would miss his chance.

You already missed your chance.

The whispered words went through his head and the string tightened further.

He ignored it, glancing at the clock next to the bed. "I want to go someplace fancy. But for the place I'm thinking of, we need to be there by eight thirty. Did you bring a dress?"

The big confessions could wait until they'd eaten. Or during dinner. Maybe once he had some food in his stomach the memories of last night wouldn't clog his thoughts. He needed to be clearheaded about what was best for the both of them. Even if he hadn't yet figured that out.

Still, it couldn't hurt to drop little hints, could it? Threading his fingers through her hair, he turned her head again and kissed her, the cling of her lips filling him with wonder. Okay, they were both awake. Their sex drive had been satisfied and she was still willing to kiss him. Scratch that. Satisfied for the moment. Because he was back to wanting her every moment of the day.

This time it was Kady who whispered. "Fifty-nine minutes until the witching hour. And, yes, I brought a dress. A slinky red one, as a matter of fact."

He didn't want to know what had possessed her to pack something sexy. Had she been planning to go to a club and meet men? When a frisson of what he knew to be jealousy crawled through his gut, he pushed it away with a shake of his head. What did it matter, as long as she used that dress on him?

"Ugh." He swung out of the bed with a muttered curse. "I guess it really is time to get moving. Do you want the shower first?"

"No, you go ahead. I need to dig some clothes out of my suitcase."

"I don't like you in clothes."

She laughed again. "Wasn't it you who said the hospital might frown if I showed up for rounds in a bikini? Or, worse, naked? I think they would be equally upset if we were pulled over for a traffic stop, and they saw I was sitting there without a stitch of clothing on."

"It might get us out of a ticket." But that thin thread of jealousy was rearing its ugly head again. On second thoughts, he wanted her in clothes whenever they were outside the bedroom.

"How about if you were out of a job afterward, if the hospital caught wind of it? I know how much you like to eat."

"I *love* to eat." He said it with a wicked lift of his brows that had her out of bed in a flash.

"Later. Right now, you need to go get your shower, so we can both eat." Before he had a chance to think of a rejoinder, she added, "At that restaurant you mentioned."

He scooped his clothes off the floor. Damn, he didn't have any clean clothes here in her hotel room. It didn't matter. They'd have to swing by his apartment anyway, so he could put a suit on. Danali's was fancy enough to have a strict dress code. He went there about once a week, mostly for business meetings, but something made him want to show it off to Kady. Or maybe it was just that he wanted to show her off.

He got in the shower and lathered up quickly. Those tight cords he'd housed in his chest for the last three years were cut in two by a burst of true happiness. She hadn't acted weird or stilted or awkward or any of those

things that could have occurred once she'd woken up.
They had played and laughed and made love just like
they used to.

Could they make this work? For real this time?

He was dried and dressed in ten minutes, brushing
his teeth with the complimentary toothbrush in a plastic wrapper he found propped in a cup. Another toothbrush was nearby, this one not covered by plastic. He
dropped his in next to hers.

Looked good. Right.

As did the thought of sleeping in her bed every night.

Something pinged in the back of his head. Nope, not
going to think about it. Not right now. Whatever happened when her time in New York ended, he could at
least enjoy being with her right now.

He would worry about tomorrow…

Tomorrow.

Tucker looked gorgeous in his black suit. With his dark
hair slicked back from his broad forehead and freshly
shaven, he had taken all of ten minutes to get ready.
Even so, they had barely made the eight-thirty cutoff.
But it probably wouldn't have mattered. The waitstaff
knew him and seated them immediately.

How often did he come here anyway? And who did
he come with? Probably not a colleague slash lover. At
least, not if he was smart.

She'd learned the hard way that interhospital relationships were not a good idea. Another doctor had asked
her out on a date soon after her and Tucker's divorce.
She'd turned him down in the nicest way possible, but
the man had kept coming back for more over the next
several weeks. She'd finally had to tell him point blank

that she wasn't interested. And then it had started. The harassing phone calls. Going to her patients and making little digs about her with thinly veiled hints that she was incompetent.

It had taken a patient complaint to make him lose privileges at the hospital. But it was something she hadn't forgotten. Now she simply remained as aloof as possible with male colleagues. She was sure there was whispering about that behind her back as well, but at least it kept them away. It was difficult and went against her character. In hardening her heart, she had become almost like… Tucker.

That made her smile. Because Tucker was not acting very Tucker-like right now. He was anything but aloof, his glances holding a smoldering promise that said there might be more of this afternoon headed her way tonight. And that was fine with her.

She fluffed her napkin on her lap and accepted the menu the waiter handed her. "Thank you."

She tried to study the choices, but the words blurred until they were undecipherable.

How long could they keep this up?

She swallowed. Not very long. She was scheduled to fly out of New York tomorrow afternoon.

She didn't want to go. A complete turnaround from that first day, when she hadn't wanted to stay.

"Do you see anything that interests you?"

She glanced up. Yes, she did. And it was sitting across the table from her. But there was no way she was going to say that. "Do you have any suggestions? It seems you come here quite often."

"I do. But only for business reasons. Meetings with

hospital bigwigs or sponsors." He reached over and took her hand. "I'm glad I'm not the only one."

"I'm sorry?"

"I was worried about your reasons for packing that dress."

She glanced down. The red silk creation, with its spaghetti straps and curve-hugging fabric had been a last-minute addition to her luggage. She'd somehow thought she might have time to catch a show on Broadway. Little had she known that every spare second would end up being spent in the company of this man. But, oh, was she glad it had wound up that way.

"I'd hoped to catch one of the musicals New York is famous for."

"Alone?"

She blinked. "Of course. Who would I have gone with?"

"No one." He squeezed her hand. "I wish I'd known. I'd have taken you."

"You would?"

The thought of actually sitting beside Tucker at a Broadway musical made her heart flutter. With nerves? With anticipation? She wasn't sure what she felt right now. Forcing a cheery note into her voice, she said, "Next visit?"

He paused and studied her. "Why does this visit have to end?"

"I'm scheduled to fly out after our meeting with the students, for one thing."

She waited for him to respond, only to be disappointed when the waiter appeared to ask if they were ready to order. Kady gave Tucker a nod, hoping he would order for her. He knew what she liked.

Yes, he did. In more ways than one.

Maybe it was time for them to have a heart-to-heart talk and see what happened.

And if he loved her? Did she dare hope? He'd certainly talked last night like he wanted a future with her. That wasn't the only surprising thing. The talk about reversing his vasectomy had sent shockwaves through her system. She'd thought he was joking. Until he'd started naming any children he might father. Yes, the names had been outrageous. But at one time this topic of conversation would have been off limits. In fact, they wouldn't have made it past the mention of babies.

This was a whole new playing field, it would seem. But what did it mean?

He'd hinted that some of his decisions after Grace's death might have been impulsive. Did that include his vasectomy? Was that why he'd mentioned having it reversed?

They'd talked more about Grace this week than almost ever before, but past experience still had her tiptoeing around the subject. Maybe it was time to test the waters again.

As soon as the waiter poured their wine, she took a careful sip.

"I think we should talk about things."

He nodded. "I have a few things I'd like to talk about as well."

That surprised her. But at least he seemed willing to open up and have an actual conversation. At least she hoped they both had the same topic on their minds.

"Why don't you go first?"

There was a pause while Tucker repositioned his cutlery. Stalling. She could certainly understand that.

None of this was easy—for either of them. Finally he glanced up at her.

"I think I'd like you to reconsider going through with the in vitro procedure. And to reconsider going back to Atlanta."

"You want me to stay here? With you?"

"Yes."

She swallowed hard. It couldn't be this easy. Could it?

Oh, God, what if it was? What if it really, truly was?

Pulling up to the curb in that taxi and exiting in their evening dress had seemed like some kind of fairy tale. The twinkle lights at the front of the restaurant, the formal waitstaff, the quiet intimate atmosphere all contributed to that feeling. If Tucker had planned for this to be a new start, he couldn't have chosen a better venue.

This was the moment of truth. To bare her soul and see what happened. She paused to take another sip of her drink. A bigger one this time, needing a shot of courage. "So you were serious about all of that stuff you said last night?"

"I was never more serious in my life."

She set her glass down, the breath catching in her lungs. "You're actually willing to have the procedure reversed?"

He looked at her, head cocking to the left, his warm and sexy expression gradually fading until careful neutrality was all that remained. "Reversed?"

"Your vasectomy."

Neutral went to something a little darker. Was that fear around the edges of his pupils? Or just dismay? "I never said I was going to have it reversed."

"You did. I heard you."

"You mean when we were in bed?" He sat back in his chair. "It was a hypothetical situation. We were pretending. About a lot of things. Remember?"

Pretending? Yes, they had been. But she'd thought there had been at least a modicum of truth buried beneath all that pretense. Like him being the one she chose.

Hell, they'd made love as if nothing else had mattered. And he'd joked about falling back into bed tonight. Like they were on the cusp of a new beginning.

As if nothing had happened in their past.

Was that it?

He was willing to pretend that none of those bitter times had ever happened.

And what about Grace? Did he want to pretend she had never happened either?

That was not an option. He might like games of make-believe, but there were some things she wasn't willing to wave a magic wand at.

And what about future children? Had she misunderstood those veiled hints. Maybe he hadn't been talking about that at all.

"What else were you pretending about, Tucker?" She lifted her chin. "Or did this week not mean anything besides sex?"

"You know that's not true. I asked you to stay in New York not five minutes ago." A grain of irritation had appeared in his voice.

"You also asked me to reconsider having the IVF treatment. Why, if you're not going to have the vasectomy reversed?"

There was a longer pause this time. So long that she

could hear her heartbeat in her ears, hear the exact moment it began picking up speed.

"I was seeing where things stood."

The pounding in her chest became a low roar. "Would it be a problem if I said I still wanted to go through with it?" Maybe he was just worried about the risks involved in getting things reversed. Even as she thought it, the rational side of her rejected that possibility.

She didn't want to be rational. Not about this. She wanted the fairy tale, dammit! She wasn't quite willing to give up on it just yet. He wanted her to stay. Surely they could work something out?

Then he touched her cheek. "Can you live without it, Kady?"

All her hopes washed out in a split second, leaving behind an ugly, slippery stain.

"Are you asking me to?"

"I thought I could consider the possibility—"

"Consider?"

As in merely tolerating the idea? The last time they'd gone down this road, she'd begged and pleaded for him to change his mind. It had gotten her nowhere. And now he'd moved only as far as considering it?

After all those words to the contrary earlier today?

Like he'd said, they'd only been words. Just a whole lot of pretend. Had he thought it would make her even hotter for him?

It had. Oh, Lord, it had.

Her eyes watered, and her hands clenched the napkin in her lap. She willed the tears not to spill over.

Never again. Not with this man. She would not fight this battle a second time.

She might have acquiesced if there'd been any kind of actual give and take on the subject. But there hadn't been.

Raw anger clutched her innards, making it hard to speak. But she had to.

"I'm sorry, Tucker, that's not good enough." Her clenched hands moved to the top of the table. "I'll lay this out as plainly as I can, so there are no more misunderstandings. I am going through with the IVF treatments. With your blessing or without it."

If he was stunned, he didn't show it. He simply nodded. "I thought that might be the case. I'm happy for you, of course."

Said as if she were an acquaintance who had shared a bit of good news with him. No "we" anywhere in there.

God, how could she have been so stupid? This afternoon she'd been so sure he was reexamining their relationship the same way she was, hoping that maybe somewhere in their individual plans there was room for something more. Something lasting.

If she was going to kill the dream, she was going to kill it completely.

"So that means you're not interested in children. Not ever."

His gaze held steady. Too steady. Robot Tucker had taken up residence again.

"I think I made that pretty clear three years ago."

He had. And she was a fool to think that might have changed over the course of a week.

With the tears still lingering in the background, she tried to think of some way to avoid going down opposite sides of the highway. She looked for some kind of intersection. A fork in the road. Anything that might mean their worlds might be able to meet in some way, shape or form. All she saw were two parallel lanes that stretched as far as the eye could see.

There was no bridge. No crossroad. No body of water connecting the two, and there was a space in between that was impossible to leap across.

How was she going to survive meeting with those students in the morning when all she wanted to do was get on a plane and run home?

"You did. You made it crystal-clear."

And she was done. So very done. In more ways than one. With this trip. With this dinner. With this man.

She stood to her feet, dropping her napkin onto the table in front of her.

"I think this is where we part ways once again. I'm going back to Atlanta. Just like I planned." Drawing in a deep breath, she was aware that people were beginning to glance her way, but she didn't care. "And since you enjoy pretending so much, I'll let you in on a little secret. Once I get home, I'm going to pretend that none of this ever happened. I bet I'll even fool myself in the process. After all, I had the best teacher around."

With that, she turned and walked away, throwing the waiter a shaky smile as she passed him. When he made to say something, she held up her hand to stop him. "Unfortunately, I think Dr. Stephenson has decided to change his reservation at the last minute. He's now officially a party of one."

CHAPTER ELEVEN

SHE WAS GONE. And Tucker was sitting in his car alone.

He couldn't believe she'd left without so much as a goodbye—although after the way she stormed out of the restaurant last night, he should have had a pretty good inkling of what was coming.

He hadn't gone after her, partly because he'd been stunned that she'd thought he'd been serious yesterday about the vasectomy thing.

He hadn't been, had he?

It had started out as a hypothetical situation, but by the end even he'd had a hard time differentiating between fantasy and reality. So he couldn't blame her for being confused.

But to just walk away?

He'd thought she would at least show up for their rounds with the medical students. A little voice had warned him that probably wasn't going to happen.

Even so, he and the students had waited for her for a good fifteen minutes before a niggle in the back of his mind told him to call the hotel. When they'd patched him through to her room the number had rung and rung and rung. And he didn't have her damn cellphone number anymore, because the pool water had wiped everything in his cellphone clean. His phone wouldn't even start up. And to go to the department head meant an awkward explanation as to why he wanted to call her.

By that evening she'd checked out of the hotel and was gone. Because of him.

He sat in his car, toying with his new replacement phone. All his contact information had been saved to the cloud—who knew?—so he had her number again. Unless she'd changed it.

So why hadn't he tried to call?

Because deep in his heart he knew it wouldn't change anything. It was about her wish to have children. The second he'd realized she was serious, he'd panicked, just like he had in the past. All his vows not to act rashly had been wiped away in the course of a single sentence.

Can you live without it?

He knew Kady well enough to know that it would take a force of nature to change her course.

Maybe the correct question should have been, could he live *with* it?

After they'd made love, the answer would have been…maybe. Until she'd mentioned the reversal, then when he shot that down, she'd said she was going through with the IVF.

Kady wasn't looking to repeat their experience with Grace. He knew her well enough to know she'd be careful beyond belief either with screening the embryo before implantation, or if she went the IVF route, screening the donor with equal care. So her child wouldn't have any genetic anomalies if she could help it.

So what was the real problem? Was it children in

general? Or was it that he had never come to terms with Grace's death?

Staring at the church across the way, he drew in a deep breath, because he already knew the answer. What he decided in the next few minutes would set the course for the rest of his life.

Could he live with it?

Maybe the time had come to find out once and for all.

He'd looked up support groups, surprised to find one that met less than ten miles from the hospital.

Whether he could go in or not remained to be seen.

To stay or leave.

Kady had left.

But in his case, leaving would be the coward's way out. In her case, it had been because she'd seen no hope for the future.

He could go back to life as it had been—keep sending anonymous flowers to Grace's grave without actually dealing with the deep pain caused by her loss.

The three years since her death had been miserable.

Until Kady had walked back into his life with her eternal optimism and a smile that had turned him inside out. She'd somehow been able to come to grips with what had happened to Grace. At least he thought she had. So why couldn't he?

Someone parked beside him and a young couple got out of the car. The woman clutched a book that reminded him of…a photo album. He looked down at his own empty hands.

He didn't have one. The only thing he had was a faded mental image of what his child had once looked like. When he'd come to New York, he'd left everything behind, intending to start a new life.

He hadn't. Not really. He'd just coasted along, bouncing from patient to patient, until it had all become a big blur.

The couple walked up the steps to the church. It was then that he realized the woman was pregnant, the wind plastering her shirt to her rounded belly and giving her away. He frowned. Were they going to the same meeting as he was? He glanced at his watch. It was supposed to start in five minutes.

Stay? Or leave?

He counted down the minutes. He reached the minute and a half mark before he released the latch on the door and stepped onto the pavement. Then, with a tightness in his chest and a queasy sensation in his gut, he walked up the steps and opened the door.

There were eight people seated in a circle. Three couples and two people by themselves. At a long table a woman was arranging pamphlets. In a dark skirt and a white blouse, she had an official look to her. That must be the leader of the support group. She turned and caught sight of him and walked over with an extended hand.

"Hello. I don't think we've met. I'm Nadya Rosenberg. Are you here for the Tay-Sachs meeting?"

She said the word matter-of-factly, no hesitation, as if it was something she said every day. Maybe she did.

"Tucker Stevenson. And, yes, I'm here for the meeting."

"Feel free to pick a seat. We'll get started in just a minute."

He picked a chair as far from the couple with the

photo album as he could, not that there were a hundred places to choose from.

Nadya opened with some announcements about upcoming events and learning opportunities.

Opportunities? He'd assumed that everyone in this group had lost a child to the disease.

"So last week we talked a little bit about genetic counseling. Did any of you have a chance to do that or find out more? Or, if you've been, can you tell us your experience?"

A couple of people said they were looking into it. He glanced at the couple who were expecting a baby, wondering what their story was. Maybe they'd lost a nephew or niece and not a child.

Once that topic of conversation petered out, Nadya redirected the group to something else. Just when he'd decided that this wasn't going to benefit him at all, she turned to the couple with the album.

"Heidi, why don't you share what you told me after the session last week?"

Fingers gripping the book in her lap, her husband put an arm around her shoulders and gave her an encouraging nod.

"Well. Most of you know that we're going to have a baby, and if not…well, it's pretty obvious."

A few chuckles met her words.

She smiled. "I wanted to share that losing a child to Tay-Sachs doesn't mean you can never have another baby. I mean, I'm not trying to tell anyone how to…" Her voice faded away.

"This is your story, Heidi. Yours. There are no judgments here."

She smoothed a hand across the book. "We lost

Logan—our first child—ten years ago. We were devastated obviously. We still miss him. That will never change."

Several people nodded.

"We don't regret having him. He brought us so much happiness in the four years he was with us." She opened to the first page of the album. "I recorded everything I could, especially after the diagnosis. I'm here to say it's okay to be sad. To be angry. To put life on hold for a while."

She took a breath. "But you can't do it forever. I did, for ten long years. Until I realized that Logan would be horrified at the way I set my whole life orbiting around him, long after he was gone. We went through counseling—and it was the best and hardest thing I've ever done in my life.

"This new baby is going to be a girl. Could she have Tay-Sachs? No. Because we had the embryo tested before implantation. But she could be born with something equally devastating. Or get cancer. Or die in a car accident." Her glance touched on him and then skipped away.

"Life has to be lived. With all its happiness. And all its terrifying uncertainty."

She might have been speaking directly to Tucker, even though he sensed she wasn't trying to convince anyone of anything.

The woman's chin quivered for a second and her husband whispered something in her ear. She nodded. "If anyone wants to see pictures of Logan, feel free. Just know that you can't stop living. Educate yourself, yes. But live. For our children's sakes. Don't make them the punctuation mark that ends your story. Life goes on. Yes, stop. Take time. As much time as you need. But don't let it stop you from celebrating life. Theirs. And yours."

One of the people next to her asked to see the album and it started to make its way around the circle. Tucker watched as people smiled at whatever was in that book. He hoped he could get out of there before it reached him.

Nadya glanced his way. "I know you're new, and if you don't want to say anything it's okay. But if you do, we're here to listen and help each other. Tay-Sachs has touched all our lives in some way. Do you want to tell us how it touched yours?"

He sat there for a long moment. That moment turned into two. As he looked around at the faces in the room, he saw…understanding. Maybe all that pretending with Kady that day had been his subconscious, telling him it was okay to let the past go. To look to a new future… with a woman he loved. And that having children didn't mean he loved Grace any less.

Suddenly he wanted it all. To laugh with Kady as they chose outrageous baby names. And to be willing to deal with the nitty-gritty—and sometimes painful— business of living, in between all that laughter.

Then the book landed on his lap. A photo of a tow-headed little boy graced the cover of it. Probably a year old and still able to smile, he was dressed in a blue and white sailor suit. Tucker stared at the picture, unable to look away. A celebration of life, she'd said. Of her child's life.

Maybe he should start celebrating Grace's life. And beyond that?

His fingers closed around the album, gripping it so tightly he half expected it to break in two.

And after that, maybe he should allow himself to be open to the possibility that he might be able to experience the joy he'd once felt with Grace…with another child.

Kady should be here. He should have called her and asked her to come. They could have gone through this together.

And maybe they still could.

If he hadn't completely destroyed any possibility of that.

Taking a deep breath, he passed the photo album on to the next person and leaned forward. "I had a daughter. Her name was Grace. She had blond hair. Blue eyes. And the most beautiful smile you've ever seen."

Kady felt no different than she had a week ago in her doctor's office. Except now she had two tiny embryos inside her. And a lingering numbness that had nothing to do with the procedure and everything to do with her ex-husband. Every day, she'd wondered the same thing: Had she done the right thing in leaving like she had?

But how could she have stayed?

Tucker had made it more than clear that he hadn't changed his mind. Hadn't the actual vasectomy warned her of that?

Evidently not, because she'd allowed her hopes to creep up. Then she'd taken his words about having it reversed as fact, only to have Tucker roll down his steel doors, locking her out. Locking everyone out.

Just like before.

She wasn't willing to go through that kind of pain ever again. Not even for the man she loved. The sex had been great. The emotional cleanup afterward... not so much.

She dropped into her office chair. Her twelve-hour shift was just ending, and all she wanted to do was go home and sleep. Maybe that was the hormones talking. Or maybe it was just normal physical and emotional exhaustion. The top of her desk looked pretty damn attractive right now. She could just put her head down and take a few hours to recharge before heading home.

Except it brought back memories of a few hours spent in another office in another city. Where she'd made love to a man she'd once considered her soul mate.

Her cellphone chirped a text at her, and she groaned aloud. Please, don't let there be another emergency. So far she'd dealt with one crisis after another. And that didn't include the ones in her personal life.

She glanced at the screen. Needed at nursery. Can you come?

No name was attached to the message, just a phone number. That was weird. Maybe it was the parent of one of her neonates. She often gave parents her cellphone number in case one of them had questions. It relieved their minds to know she was within reach.

Sighing, she stood and stretched her back and then smiled. If she thought her back ached now, just wait a few more months when those babies started growing. "Please stay put, little ziggies." The embryos had grown past the zygote stage, but the pet name had stuck. She went down a floor and exited the elevator, turning left only to stop dead in her tracks.

She swallowed. Okay. Exactly how tired was she?

Pretty damn tired, unless the hormones were causing her to hallucinate.

Tucker stood in front of her, holding what looked like a pink balloon in the shape of a heart.

Neither of them moved. She tilted her head to the side, hoping he would blink into nothingness before she did something stupid. Like rush into his arms. Or start blubbering. Hormones. It had to be.

He didn't disappear. But he wasn't smiling either. Why was he here?

"Did I leave something in New York?"

If that wasn't the dumbest line ever. If she'd left something, the hotel or hospital would have just mailed it. They wouldn't have sent Tucker. And she was *not* going to ask about the balloon. Maybe he was visiting someone in the nursery.

Oh, God, had he fathered a child with someone else?

You really need to get a grip, Kady. He made it pretty clear he was never getting that procedure reversed.

"It's not what you left. It's what you *didn't* leave."

She didn't what? It took her a second to realize he was answering her question. "I don't understand."

"You forgot to leave me a little wiggle room—or a chance to do the right thing."

He hadn't taken a step toward her, and she realized there was more than one person staring at them. Just like at that restaurant. She swallowed.

"Let's go to my office."

"I'd rather do this here." He glanced to the side. "But we can go over by the windows if you'd like."

"Okay." He led the way across the room, that ridiculous balloon bouncing with every step he took. She stopped next to him, gazing out over the park for a minute, then she turned back to him. If he was here to talk her out of it, he needed to know he was too late.

"Before you say anything, I want to let you know that it's already done."

"What is?"

She clasped her hands in front of her, not because she was embarrassed but because she had to steel herself not to touch him. "I had two embryos implanted last week."

"Okay."

She tried to read something into his tone. Panic. Anger. Resignation. But there was nothing. Nothing that she could sense, anyway.

"Okay? Just okay? Is that all you have to say?"

"No. I have a whole lot to say."

She shrugged. "I don't know what you could possibly say that would make a difference at this point."

"Maybe not, but I need to at least tell you this. I didn't mean what I said at dinner. I was stupid. And tired." He took a step closer. "And terrified."

"You shut me down the second I tried to talk to you about it. Just like you did when we lost Grace. I'm sorry I misunderstood about the vasectomy thing, but can you at least see how I could have gotten that idea?"

"I do."

Okay, it was a start.

"I'm not sure they're both going to take, but I want these babies, Tucker. Not to replace Grace. They could never do that. But I can't live my life in the shadow of her memory. And you shouldn't either."

"I know that now. And I think I finally understand."

She doubted it, but if that's what he wanted to think, good for him. "You came all this way to tell me that?"

"No. I came to give you this." He placed the string of the balloon in one of her hands and closed her fingers around it.

Had he somehow heard about her pregnancy before he'd come? He only had one balloon so probably not. "What is this for?"

"You said this was something you were going to do. With my blessing or without it. I know you don't need it, but I wanted you to know that you have it." He paused again. "I went to a support group for the families of Tay-Sachs patients."

Shock rippled across her belly. "You did?"

He nodded. "I told them about Grace. About us. About all of it."

"You…you…"

She had a sudden need to sit down, so she dropped into the nearest chair, fighting the urge to put her head between her knees.

You are not going to faint.

He'd actually told someone about their daughter? That was…it was…

Unbelievable.

She gripped the string of the balloon, afraid to let go. He'd said it was his blessing. For children?

"What made you want to go?"

"It was time. It was past time." His fingers wrapped around hers. "I lost you once. I didn't want to lose you again. I hope I haven't."

He wasn't making any sense. "You don't want children."

"I didn't. The thought scared the hell out of me. So much so that when you talked about it all those years ago, I froze. I couldn't touch you because I was afraid you would get pregnant. It got to the point that I wouldn't have physically been able to make love to you, even if I'd wanted to."

"You didn't want to. That much was obvious." The pain of those days came rushing back.

"I did. But my body wasn't going to cooperate. I simply couldn't perform. The long and the short of it was that I didn't deal with Grace's death the way I should have. I pushed it away and tried to forget it ever happened. And then I pushed you away as well."

"Why the vasectomy?"

"I'd told myself that if I could take away the fear of an accidental pregnancy I could get back to normal. But you were so against my having the procedure that we both said things we shouldn't have. Things got tangled into a knot that neither of us could untie."

"I thought you no longer wanted me. It almost killed me."

"I never stopped wanting you. Ever. And I'm sorry that I didn't talk to you about it. I was embarrassed and angry. At the world. At the doctors." He raised their joined hands and kissed her fingers. "At myself. So am I too late?"

"I think so, as I'm pregnant." Those words should tell him all he needed to know. She wouldn't go back and undo it, even if she could.

He smiled. "What if I said I'm finally okay with that?"

"Are you?" Something had gotten lost in translation here. The last time she'd seen him, nothing had changed. He hadn't wanted children. Had only *pretended* to want them. Was he still pretending?

"I once asked you if you could live without it, Kady. What I should have been asking was if I could live with it. I came to the conclusion at the support group that I can. I think maybe my heart knew it, but my thick skull just couldn't process it."

"What?" Okay, maybe her head really was lying on her desk and she was deep in some kind of dream world.

"I'm still scared as hell, Kady. But I'm here to tell you I'm on board on hundred percent. I want the baby—babies—you're carrying."

"Y-you're okay with becoming a father again?"

"The support group was the first step in healing, I think. But yes." His smile grew. "You really have two of them in there? I guess I should have brought more balloons."

She felt she had to warn him. "There are no guarantees that they'll take."

"I know. I'm willing to risk it. If you are pregnant or not, I still want you in my life. And if both of these babies make it, then I want them in my life too."

A sliver of sunlight came through one of the windows and hit the floor in front of her, and she allowed herself to hope. "Are you sure?"

"Yes. I am."

She closed her eyes, and thanked whatever gods were looking down at them. When she opened them again, Tucker was still there. Strong and steady. The Tucker she'd fallen in love with.

"Where do you want me?"

His head shifted sideways to look at her. "Excuse me?"

She laughed. "I mean, where do we live? Here in Atlanta? Or do you want to go back to New York? Maybe my grandparents could be talked into relocating, since they're ready to downsize."

"So you're willing to give me a second chance?"

She let go of the balloon and watched as it drifted toward the high ceiling above. "I've been willing for a very long time."

"You're going to be sorry you did that." He nodded toward the balloon. "Because now we're going to have to go after it."

"I'm sure it'll come down eventually."

"I'm sure it will, but since your wedding rings are in there we might want to make sure we're here when it does."

"My wedding rings?"

He nodded. "Although if you don't want any reminders of the past, I'll understand. We can always buy a new set."

"I loved those rings."

"And I love you, Kady. We'll get the balloon back. Once I do this." He lowered his head and captured her lips in a kiss that was sweet, gentle and filled with a longing she understood far too well.

She would have told him she loved him too, but her mouth was busy at the moment. And she figured there would be plenty of time for that. And for decisions about where to live. And to catch that runaway balloon.

They had their whole lives ahead of them.

And if they were very, very lucky, they would have the lives of two special babies to celebrate somewhere along the way.

EPILOGUE

THE MOMENT HE held his newborn daughter, he knew it was going to be okay.

And she *was* his daughter, no matter what any paternity test might say. The rush of love he'd been so afraid he wouldn't be able to feel came hurtling toward him, stopping right at his feet. Just like his love for her mother.

"She's gorgeous." He pressed her tiny form to the skin of his chest, the contact branding him for life. They hadn't done this with Grace, and he was glad Kady had insisted on him unbuttoning his shirt before he held her. He was also glad she'd so steadfastly said she wanted a baby. With or without him.

He'd chosen with.

It was the right choice. He knew it.

In the end Kady had chosen both sperm and eggs from donors, just so there would be no chances.

He smiled. And both embryos had implanted exactly the way they should have. He held Bethany Michelle, while Kady cradled Nathaniel Eric. These were it for them. Their children. Their little family. They would raise and love them and cherish every moment they had with them. Just as they'd done with Grace.

Tucker hoped they both lived long happy lives. Someday they would talk to them about their older sister, show them pictures, and they would visit her grave together. She would always hold a special place in their hearts. She'd taught him that the important things in life might not last as long as one might like. Any of them could be taken in an instant. Life carried no guarantees.

It had taken him far too long to learn that message. He could have saved both Kady and himself a lot of heartache if he'd been able to understand this truth, that they needed to be grateful for the blessings of life and to take nothing for granted.

Carefully keeping Bethany against his chest, he leaned down and kissed Kady. "The nurse said your grandparents are here. They'll want to see the babies."

"They'll spoil them rotten." She sighed. "But I wouldn't have it any other way."

"I wouldn't either. Do you think your grandfather has finally forgiven me?" Tucker had been accepted back into the fold as if nothing had ever happened. As if he hadn't been a huge jerk for the last two years.

"He loves you. My whole family loves you. Probably more than they love me."

"Not true, but thank you. And I love *you*. Thanks for knocking some sense into me."

"You came to your senses all by yourself. I'm the one who had to be convinced in the end. No more secrets, okay?"

They'd caught the balloon back at the hospital, and Kady's original wedding rings were now back on her finger. Watching her thumb rub across those bands again and again was satisfying in a way that nothing else was.

"No more secrets." He'd been afraid that Kady's pregnancy might affect him physically, but it hadn't. They'd talked through his reservations, and she'd told him even if they never had sex again, she was okay. She loved him. Wanted to be with him.

They'd had sex, though. Lots of it.

He'd gone through genetic counseling with her, insisting even when she said it was no longer necessary. He'd done it anyway, the way he should have all those years ago. He never wanted her to feel that alone ever again.

He'd even asked if she wanted him to have his vasectomy reversed, saying for future babies they could use their own sperm and eggs and have the embryos tested before they were implanted. Kady said she was happy with the two babies they were going to have. They were enough.

Yes, they were.

And so was she.

He was back in Atlanta. Back in the house where they'd spent time with Grace. It had taken some careful planning as the New York hospital hadn't wanted to let him out of his contract, but in the end they'd capitulated when he'd worked out a compromise. He had to promise to come up for a month once a year when the new crop of medical students was doing its shadowing. Once the babies were old enough, Kady would join him.

Bethany squirmed against him and gave a thin cry. Tucker immediately tensed, only to find Kady's hand on his arm. "Hey, it's okay. She's okay."

He took a careful breath and blew it out. "You may have to talk me down from the ledge from time to time."

"We'll probably take turns standing on it. When that happens we'll just hold hands and get through it together."

"Together. That's one of my favorite words." He lowered himself into a chair beside the bed. "Why don't you try to get some sleep? I can either hold the babies or call the nurse to come and take them."

"You're actually willing to let them out of your sight?"

"What? No. I'd go down with them and wait until you're awake again."

Kady couldn't contain her laugh. "I want them to stay up here. There'll be plenty of time to sleep later." She tilted her head so it leaned against his arm. "Besides, I'm afraid I'll wake up and find this is all a dream."

"It is a dream. But it's very, very real. I'll be here when you wake up. So will Bethany and Nathaniel." He grinned. "Well, the babies and I might be in the nursery, depending on how strict they are about time schedules." The hospital did offer rooming in, but since Kady had needed a C-section they might be a little less accommodating to their request, even though Kady worked in this very unit. Doctors supposedly made the worst patients. Who knew?

"You look good holding her," Kady said. "I never believed this was possible."

"You look good holding him."

Settling a little deeper in the recliner, he did his best to soak in this moment, to imprint it on his memory— where he could retrieve it when times got tough.

One thing he knew for sure—he would never walk away from this woman ever again. Or his children.

He was right where he belonged. And this was where he would stay. For as long as they both should live.

* * * * *

RESISTING HER COMMANDER HERO

LUCY RYDER

MILLS & BOON

As always, to my family.
Especially my daughters Kate and Ash.
You are, and always will be, everything to me.

CHAPTER ONE

"LOWER THE BASKET!" yelled paramedic Francis Abigail Bryce into her headset over the whop-whop-whop of the helicopter hovering a hundred feet overhead. Wind and rain lashed at the ledge on which she was crouched, shielding the fallen climber.

If she slipped it was a long way down and probably wouldn't end well. It wasn't exactly how she'd envisioned spending her Friday evening but when word had come through from the rangers' station earlier that a climber had fallen, Frankie had been dispatched to the scene.

Further up the coast from the large seaside town of Port St. John's on the Olympic Peninsula in Washington state, heavy rains had caused a huge landslide and rescue teams were busy digging out survivors. With the storm wreaking havoc on the Juan de Fuca Strait, rescue personnel were stretched to the limit.

Frankie had returned with a few of the injured and then been the lucky candidate in the wrong place at the wrong darn time. Now, instead of providing emergency medical care at the site of the slide, she was clinging to a slick ledge only a few feet wide and a couple hundred feet from certain death because a group had thought it smart to go climbing in torrential rain.

She looked down into the guy's youthful face and shook her head. Probably a student on spring break, she thought. EMTs were always busy this time of the year, rescuing kids from their own ambitions.

"Hang in there, handsome," she yelled, aware that in the fifteen minutes she'd been there, he'd been slipping in and out of consciousness. She suspected a ruptured spleen and she'd already wrapped his leg in an inflatable compression cast.

Concerned about what was taking so long, Frankie looked up as a deep voice in her ear warned, "Heads up," and the next instant a large figure dropped onto the ledge. Dressed in a red and black jumpsuit and wearing a half-face helmet with comms mouthpiece, he looked like a huge bug from an alien world.

Frankie didn't need to see his eyes to know who it was. The hard, masculine jaw and the unsmiling line of his sensual mouth would have been a dead giveaway even if the hair on the back of her neck hadn't stood up like a freaked-out cat.

Nathan Oliver. The man who'd been back for months without at least letting her know he was home.

What the hell was he *doing here?* Wasn't he some super-secret commander of the Maritime Security Response Team or something? Unless her patient was a terrorist, or a foreign national in the country illegally—which Frankie doubted—she was pretty sure a member of the nation's deployable operations group stationed at Port St. John's wouldn't normally be part of search and rescue.

Then again, maybe the landslide and current conditions in the strait had put all coasties on call, including the MSRT. And, yeah, wasn't it just peachy that *he* had to be the one dropping from the sky?

Unhooking his line from the chopper, he gave a couple of hand signals to the pilot above before his safety line disappeared into the lashing rain.

With her heart in her throat, Frankie ruthlessly squelched the urge to reach out and grab him before rotor wash blew him off the ledge. Or maybe before she gave him a little shove over the edge herself.

Okay, fine, so maybe she was tempted for about a nanosecond, but even though Nathan Oliver was the last person she wanted to see, she didn't want him to die either.

They'd meant too much to each other—once.

Besides, balanced on the rocky ledge and sure-footed and powerful as a mountain lion, Nate was more than capable of rescuing them both. He'd been a Navy SEAL before transferring to the Pacific North West unit of the US Coast Guard as Lieutenant Commander of the MSRT. Granted, the present conditions probably weren't the worst he'd experienced, but even *he* couldn't walk up sheer cliffs in this weather.

He dropped to his haunches beside her and she felt the sweep of his penetrating gaze. The resultant shiver, she told herself, was from being soaked through and freezing. It couldn't be that he still affected her.

That ship had sailed a lifetime ago and Frankie didn't make a habit of repeating her mistakes. Especially the very public ones that had devastated not only her pride but also her heart.

She saw his mouth form words that looked like, "You okay?"

But instead of replying, she yelled, "Where's the basket? He's going into shock."

He pointed skyward and she looked up to see the rescue litter swinging wildly in the gusting wind as it descended toward them. Nate barked out an order to the chopper and the pilot edged closer to the cliff face. But instead of controlling the swing, it caused the litter to spin.

He rose to his feet in one smooth move and stretched out a long arm to snag it. Almost in slow motion, Frankie watched as it abruptly shifted in the wind. She opened her mouth to yell a warning as the medevac litter flew through the air toward him.

He saw it coming too late to get out the way and it clipped him on the side of his helmet, sending him staggering backward toward the edge.

Time slowed and stretched, narrowing into an endless tunnel of pure horror as Nate fought to regain his balance. Then his foot slipped and in that split second before he went over, his gaze caught and held hers.

In that timeless instant, all the wild conflicting emotions she'd managed to suppress for twelve long years exploded through her, blinding her to everything but him.

Everything but the need to keep him from disappearing from her life forever. And before she realized she was moving, Frankie rose and leapt for him in one desperate move.

She reacted. As she always did.

Fear gave her strength and speed and before she could even process her actions, her icy fingers closed around his harness. Her momentum sent her thudding into him and Frankie wrapped her legs around him like a vice as they shot off the ledge.

Through the frantic yelling in the comms, she heard him curse as his arms enveloped her like banded steel. Her line went slack and for one awful moment she thought they were headed for the bottom of the gorge. She sucked in a breath, tightened her grip and pressed her face into Nate's throat, thinking stupidly that maybe it wasn't such a bad way to go.

Wrapped around his big tough body and with his uniquely potent masculine scent filling her lungs, Frankie could think of a dozen worse places to be.

It was the closest she'd been to him in twelve years. The closest she'd been since the night of her eighteenth birthday, the night he'd completely humiliated her in front of half the town.

He'd been around forever and as well as she'd thought she'd known him, she couldn't have known how much he'd changed or that he'd lost friends on his last mission. He'd looked the same—although bigger, harder and fitter—and acted the same as the boy she'd known her whole life. And if she'd noticed the closed-off expression in his eyes, the tight line of his mouth and jaw that night, she'd put it down to typical male arrogance and the fact that he was a member of the nation's elite fighting force, mixing with a bunch of wild immature teenagers all because she'd begged him to come to her party.

She should have known better than to try to measure up to all the women in his life. To him she'd always just been his best friend's kid sister; wild, reckless—always wanting to tag along.

Besides, she'd never measured up, to him *or* to her brother Jack. At least not in her parents' eyes. Jack had been their golden child and Nate, popular, sporty and incredibly smart, was like their second son. They'd excelled at everything and it had been daunting, living in their shadow.

The birthday incident had been humiliating and she'd said things that filled her with guilt and shame whenever she thought about them. She'd lost him that day... and then seven years later she'd lost Jack in a mortar attack.

Her champions. Her own personal superheroes.

Frankie's heart squeezed. And now she and Nate were heading for the bottom of the gorge and she'd never get the chance to prove that she'd—

The safety line abruptly snapped taut, halting their graceful pendulum arc into empty space; halting the wild, regretful thoughts flashing through Frankie's mind. The next instant they were headed straight for the unforgiving rocky surface of the cliff face.

She tensed, because this was going to hurt.

Nate tried to turn, probably to take the brunt of the impact, but Frankie was attached to the safety line and the collision was hard enough to force the air from her lungs...and Nate's big warm muscular body between her thighs.

Stars exploded behind her eyes. Whether they were from the jolt to her skull or his hard, tough body, Frankie wasn't sure. But it was enough to rattle loose her good sense and cause some seriously inappropriate thoughts to flash through her mind, sending heat exploding through her body.

Nate Oliver was still the hottest man she'd ever known. The kind of hot that made women think inappropriate thoughts even while dangling hundreds of feet in the air by a slender nylon rope, and one wrong move away from falling to their deaths.

"Don't look down," he ordered. "And for God's sake don't let go. Not yet."

Of course Frankie didn't listen. Craning her neck, she looked down and then promptly wished she hadn't when a distressed squeak escaped without permission. All she could see beneath her was a dark cold emptiness. Vertigo abruptly clamped queasy fingers around her throat and her belly churned.

"Dammit, Frankie," Nate growled in her ear. "I said don't look down."

She wanted to tell him that he wasn't the boss of her but her breath was lodged in her throat and she could only gasp.

Oh, God. How mortifying. Inside, Fearless Frankie—Port St. John's former wild child—was freaking out.

"I'm going to let you go," Nate said calmly, and it took a couple of beats for his words to register.

When they did, she snapped, "No!" and tightened her grip on him. No way was he letting go.

"Just enough to free my hands and feet," he explained quietly. "Then I'm going to crab-walk us to the ledge. Okay?"

She wanted to say no, but she knew it would take a little strain off the safety line and keep it from shearing off on the rocky outcroppings.

She really, *really* didn't want that to happen.

She looked up at the suspended medevac litter, which was now hanging motionless a few feet to her left.

Go figure.

Gritting her teeth, she nodded jerkily, tightening her grip on Nate's harness. Her thighs clenched around him until they ached, and all she could think was, *Thank God for all those squats and lunges I've been doing lately.*

"Good girl," he murmured, and she wanted to snort because she was about as far from being a good girl as they were from the ground. He eased his grip until all that kept him from succumbing to the law of gravity were her arms and legs.

He murmured into his comms and then with his feet planted flat against the cliff face, he began to move them toward the ledge.

It couldn't have been more than a minute since Frankie's spectacular leap off the edge but her muscles had begun to shake and she didn't know how much longer she'd be able to hold on.

Beneath Nate's jumpsuit, muscles bunched and flexed, giving her a few more inappropriate thoughts. Thoughts that might have freaked her out if she hadn't been closer to death than she liked. Frankly, in the circumstances, she figured she was allowed.

Besides, it had been so long since she'd had inappropriate thoughts of any kind that she might as well enjoy them. They were the closest she'd had to actual sex in forever.

Finally, the tension on her harness lessened and Nate straightened, big feet planted shoulder width apart.

After a couple of beats he said, "You can let go now, Francis," the dry tone as much as his use of the hated name bringing her head up. The first thing she saw was his mouth, beautifully sculpted and much too tempting.

Tearing her gaze away, she looked up into eyes as dark and fathomless as the death they'd just escaped.

Sometime in the past couple of minutes—probably while she'd been having those hot thoughts—he'd lifted his visor and the warmth in his usually unreadable gaze stunned her.

"You okay?" His mouth was barely an inch away and all it would take was one tiny move from her and—

Spooked, Frankie flashed a quick look to the left and saw they were once more on the ledge. Her patient, wrapped in a silver emergency blanket, was a few feet away, waiting for her to get her act together.

"I'm fine," she croaked, her throat desert dry and tight with tension while adrenaline still pumped through her at their near disaster.

Eager to put a little distance between them, Frankie released the stranglehold she had on him and slid to the ground until all that connected them were her fingers still locked on his harness.

"Francis."

She opened her mouth in a snarled protest but it gave her the impetus she needed to let him go. She might have pushed away from him if they hadn't been perched on a narrow, slick ledge and she hadn't just taken a decade off her life with that one daring leap.

"You good?" he asked again, ducking his head to look into her eyes. He must have been reassured because he didn't wait for her to reply. "Help me secure the PEP so we can get off this ledge."

Frankie shook her head even though she knew he meant the patient extrication platform. Sucking in a shaky breath to still the churning in her gut, she shoved all her messy emotions aside and got her head in the game. She had a patient who needed her undivided attention and the litter swaying gently just over their heads was waiting to airlift him to the closest trauma center.

Everything else could wait. Including her freak-out because no way was anyone witnessing that.

Within minutes, they'd transferred the student to the backboard and strapped him into the litter. Nate then reattached the hoisting strapline and with a hand signal from him, Frankie's patient rose into the air. She watched as hands reached out to snag the litter and pull it aboard the chopper before expelling the breath she'd been holding.

Litter rescues occasionally went bad but, despite the rocky start that had almost cost Nate his life, this one had gone relatively smoothly. But she wanted to be off the ledge before something else went wrong. Before she lost the tight grip on her emotions.

She wasn't looking forward to climbing back the way she'd come either. Her arms and legs shook, which would make the ascent a little tricky even though the rangers at the top had set up a standing body belay and would take most of her weight as she "walked" up the cliff face.

She'd wait until Nate left with the chopper before attempting the ascent for fear of completely humiliating herself any further.

Out of the darkness the hoisting strapline appeared again and Frankie let out a tiny relieved breath. Any minute now she'd be free to fall apart without an audience.

She watched Nate catch the metal connector clip and murmur something that she couldn't quite catch. Now would be a good time for Fearless Frankie to regain control, she thought, because smartass and cocky was way better than cowering, trembling and freaked out.

She gave a cocky grin and quipped, "So long, soldier," adding a snappy salute for good measure.

"It's *sailor*, not soldier," he growled, as he unclipped her line and gave it a quick tug.

"What are you *doing*?" she snapped in outrage, making a grab for it, but it was already out of reach as the rangers above reeled it in. She turned on him with a snarled "Are you insane?" but he ignored her, snapping her onto his harness capture strap. Of course, she tried to stop him but he brushed her hands aside with a quick impatient flick and hooked them both to the hoisting line.

Eyes on hers, he wrapped his arms around her and said, "Trust me."

The words had her heart lurching as the truth landed like a punch to the solar plexus. God, she did. Didn't want to…but did.

"No," she lied, but he must have read the reluctant truth in her eyes because he said, "Bring us in, Boom," and the next instant they were airborne.

Frankie swallowed as they swung away from the ledge. She didn't like the feeling of being suspended in a sea of blackness while wind, rain and rotor wash lashed at them from every side any more than she liked being vulnerable.

To *any*one…let alone this man.

She'd tried it once and he'd devastated her, stomping on her tender heart with his size thirteen tactical boots. It was the last time she'd allowed her feelings to show.

"I'll get you for this, soldier," she warned through clenched teeth and squeezed her eyes closed against the overwhelming pull of the man pressed intimately against her.

Gone was the cocky, handsome boy who'd treated her with all the indulgent impatience of an older sibling. In his place was a man whose powerful cocktail of tightly coiled testosterone and simmering pheromones was even more treacherously compelling.

Even the expression in his eyes was different—sometimes intense, sometimes brooding but always distantly watchful.

This Nate might look like an older, hotter and harder version of the boy she'd once loved but somewhere along the line he'd acquired a darkness that made him more than dangerous, more than lethal, to women everywhere.

Over the sound of the chopper she heard him yell, "You falling asleep there, spider girl?"

Her eyes popped open and she looked up to see the red and white fuselage looming closer. A couple of visored men watched and controlled their ascent, reminding Frankie of a movie she'd seen about alien abduction.

"No," she muttered. "I'm pretending I'm on a beach in Hawaii."

He must have heard because his mouth kicked up at one corner and before she could fully grasp the sudden transformation, hands were reaching for them, pulling them in. The instant she felt the capture strap release, Frankie scrambled over to where a crewman was tending her patient and wondered what she thought she was doing, because she had a feeling that getting sucked into Nate Oliver's force field again…would be an unmitigated disaster.

Fortunately, she was too smart to let that happen. *Way* too smart.

Her patient's eyes were open but he appeared dazed and disorientated. "Focus on me, handsome," she yelled over the noise of the engine, and quickly freed his arm to set up an IV. "You hang in there, okay?"

Looking up briefly to gauge their ETA, she noticed several pairs of eyes on her and became aware of the grins.

Frowning, she looked around and caught sight of Nate's expression and by the firm unsmiling line of his sexy mouth, he wasn't happy. But then again—apart from that flash of wry humor—unsmiling seemed to be his default expression.

At least when it came to her.

Her belly clenched.

"What?"

"*Yowza*, lady," a crewman yelled, his wide toothy grin and smooth cheeks all she could see beneath the bug helmet. "You saved Sammy in the most awesome move I ever saw. Ever think of joining the circus?"

Sammy? she thought with a frown. *Who the heck is Sammy?*

Thinking maybe they were talking about her patient, Frankie drawled, "I'm allergic to rings," laughing when she was rewarded with confused looks. She shook her head. "Never mind."

No way was she explaining that one. She'd decided a long time ago that marriage wasn't for her and guys seemed to think all a woman wanted was a wedding ring and a white picket fence.

Determinedly pushing aside unpleasant thoughts, Frankie willed the chopper to move faster through the air. The sooner they arrived at the hospital, the sooner her patient could be rushed into surgery. And she *really* needed to escape this inexorable pull Nathan appeared to still have on her double-X chromosome.

CHAPTER TWO

HOURS LATER FRANKIE dragged her weary feet through the ambulance bay doors into ER. The adrenaline had long since faded and she was feeling every strained muscle and ache as though she'd been through a marathon workout session.

Fortunately, the mud slide hadn't been as extensive as everyone had feared and most people had managed to escape the worst of it. Those that hadn't had already been admitted or treated and released.

It had probably been the longest shift of her career. Her jumpsuit clung wetly to her skin and her boots squelched with every step. There was also something wrong with her back that she could no longer ignore. She'd check it herself but one of her superpowers wasn't the ability to make her arms bend the wrong way or her head swivel like an evil toy in a horror movie.

Fortunately, the ER was quiet after the earlier rush and she found the person she was looking for in the staff lounge, stuffing her face with one donut while searching through the bakery box for another.

Paige Carlyle looked as exhausted as Frankie felt. At the sound of the door opening, the petite doctor looked up guiltily—cheeks bulging like a chipmunk's—as though she'd been caught doing something illegal.

"Those things will kill you," Frankie announced, snagging the full to-go mug off the counter. She swallowed a large mouthful and grimaced. "And so will this."

"Hey," Paige objected around a mouthful of pastry, and snatched the cup away, cradling it protectively against her chest. "It's hot, delicious and I need the sugar."

"No, you don't. You need some veggie juice and a nice long soak in a hot tub."

Paige made a face at the mention of veggie juice. "Yuk, I'm not drinking pond scum," she declared, gleefully washing down her donut with hot chocolate and making sounds that were a little too disturbing in Frankie's opinion. Paige reluctantly closed the bakery box and slumped against the counter. "But a long hot soak sounds like heaven. My feet hurt and I haven't been home in so long Ty's probably forgotten what I look like."

"Stop whining. It's unattractive," Frankie said with an accusing frown. "And so are your constant reminders that you have a sexy hunk waiting for you with home-cooked meals and daily massages."

Paige's mouth curved in a secretive smile and she made another sound that ratcheted Frankie's irritation level a couple of notches. "You sound jealous," Paige observed mildly. "Like you want a sexy hunk at home too."

Frankie snorted. "Who doesn't?"

"Well, I do know another unattached sexy hunk you might be interested in," the doctor said craftily.

"Your brother? The air force top gun?" Frankie

gave a dramatic sigh. "He's hot and I just *love* a man in uniform."

Paige gagged. "Yuk. *No.* I was talking about someone in another sector of the armed forces. Say…the Coast Guard?"

"Not interested," Frankie said promptly. "And I can handle my own love life, thanks." Or lack thereof, she reminded herself dryly. "You just concentrate on Terrible Ty."

Tyler Reese had been Nate and Jack's best friend until the summer they'd turned eighteen. Something had happened that had landed the three friends in a lot of trouble and it had been the last time Ty had been in Port St. John's—except for Jack's funeral—until an injury had threatened to end his surgical career. He'd returned to recuperate and had run into Paige on his first night.

Or rather into Paige's flashlight, which had clearly knocked some sense into him because he'd left his life and big city career to move north.

Paige cleared her throat and stared at Frankie expectantly. "Is there something you need to tell me, Ms. Bryce?" she asked with excruciating politeness.

Frankie frowned at her friend's tone. "No," she said warily, and when the doctor just narrowed her eyes, she shrugged and couldn't stop the sharply indrawn breath at the movement.

Paige must have seen something in her expression because she demanded, "What did you do?"

Of course Frankie answered with an affronted "Nothing," hoping Paige would drop it because the doctor looked like she needed a break as much as Frankie did. She'd just go home, have a hot shower and fall into bed. She could deal with everything after about twelve hours of shut-eye.

Paige scoffed. "Tell me before I call Ty." She paused and her gaze turned crafty. "Or better yet, maybe I'll call a big bad coastie. He can hold you down while I examine you." Knowing exactly who Paige was talking about, Frankie narrowed her eyes dangerously but her expression clearly didn't intimidate the medical center's newest specialist.

"Let's go," Paige said, tossing her to-go cup in the trash before moving toward the door, turning impatiently when Frankie didn't move. "Well? What are you waiting for?"

"An ER physician?"

Paige rolled her eyes because everyone knew that though she was a qualified pediatrician, she was still paying off her state-granted tuition by working in ER. "Your smart mouth doesn't intimidate me, Ms. Bryce," she drawled. "Room Four. Stat," she ordered, before disappearing through the door.

Frankie closed her eyes, her boots rooted to the spot. It wasn't that she was being deliberately difficult. She was just too tired to move. Oh, yeah, and every breath reminded her of her flying trapeze stunt. Moving required skills she'd temporarily misplaced.

A second later the door opened again and Paige stuck her head inside, scowling when she saw that Frankie hadn't moved. She narrowed her gaze and gave her cell-phone a peremptory waggle. "Now," she snapped.

Frankie frowned. "Does Ty know how annoying you are?"

"Of course he does," she announced cheerfully. "It's one of the things he loves about me."

Frankie rolled her eyes because Paige was right. Ty did love her. His feelings for the pint-sized Attila the Hun were so obvious that it made Frankie just a little bit jealous.

She wanted someone to look at *her* like that.

Sighing, because now she was feeling sorry for herself, she followed Paige down the passage into an empty ER room.

"Okay," the doctor said with her hands on her hips. "What hurts?"

Finding levity in the situation, Frankie snorted and reached for the zipper tab on her jumpsuit. "Maybe you should ask what doesn't hurt…and go from there?" Maybe she should have gone home before she tried this because there was no way she was going to be able to dress again without bawling like a baby.

Paige pulled on a pair of surgical gloves and studied her. "Lemme guess. You acted rashly during that mountain rescue and you've hurt your back."

"What mountain rescue? How do you know it's my back?" Frankie demanded irritably. "And I'm never rash—at least, not any more—and not unless I need chocolate. Then all bets are off."

Paige arched her brow. "It's the way you're holding yourself." She leveled a mildly irritated yet softly understanding look that made Frankie squirm. "And I know you hate being a burden because you harbor what you think is a super-secret need to make amends for your past, Frankie. So you were wild and rebellious." She shrugged impatiently. "Big deal. We all do dumb stuff when we're kids."

Frankie spluttered. "That's ridiculous. I bet you—"

But Paige interrupted with, "You're an excellent paramedic—the most advanced one on the coast, actually—but maybe you should think about saving yourself."

"What does *that* mean?" Frankie demanded with a scowl.

"It means no woman is an island. It means that you should accept help once in a while. Now would be good…while we're both still standing." Paige huffed out a laugh when Frankie rolled her eyes. She reached out to peel the jumpsuit off Frankie's shoulders and had barely got it halfway down her arms before sucking in a sharp breath.

"Ooh, that's nasty."

"What?" Frankie demanded, craning her neck at the tone in Paige's voice. "What?"

"You really should have had this seen to ages ago," Paige scolded, and gently pulled Frankie's wet under-shirt away from her back. Frankie must have made a sound because Paige cursed. "Did this happen before or after your Fearless Frankie stunt?"

"I don't know what you're talking about."

"Sure you do, since everyone *else* knows about it," Paige groused. "And how come I have to hear via the grapevine that you made a superhero save, anyway? I thought best friends told each other everything?"

Not everything…because there were some things a person didn't share. With anyone. Especially things that made Frankie cringe with shame whenever she thought about them.

Paige huffed and eased Frankie's bloodied tank top over her head, leaving her in a black sports bra, jump-suit pooled at her waist. She made a sound of exasper-ation at what she'd uncovered. "I know we joke about it but, Frankie, really, taking a flying leap off a ledge? What the heck were you thinking?"

Wincing as Paige gently probed a particularly tender spot, Frankie demanded, "Who told you about that?"

"So it's true?"

She sighed irritably. "It's complicated… *Ouch*. That hurts."

"Not as much as it's going to," Paige said shortly. "But seriously? It's like you have a death wish or something." Frankie opened her mouth to object but Paige beat her to it with a snapped-out "I'm busy here." But after a couple of beats she said almost absently, "There's bruising, a couple of lacerations and some bad grazing. What really happened?"

Frankie gave a negligent shrug. "I got caught between a rock and a hard place." Paige sighed and began cleaning Frankie's injuries. "Wanna tell me about it?"

"No," Frankie said.

At the same time a deep voice drawled from the door, "Yes, Francis, let's hear all about it."

She closed her eyes wearily and thought, *Not now. Not ever.* Or at least not while she was feeling exhausted and raw and couldn't think of a snappy comeback.

She'd hoped to avoid the lecture she knew was coming but she should have known he would eventually hunt her down. He'd hunted terrorists for a living, for God's sake. What had made her think she could continue to evade him?

She'd only managed to avoid him since the night of her eighteenth birthday because he'd wanted it that way. She'd wanted it too, she reminded herself, mostly to forget that the boy she'd idolized had called her a selfish willful brat who didn't think about how her actions affected others. He'd also called her reckless and told her to grow up.

Then he'd left town. Getting as far away from her as possible.

Well, she was cool with that. *Really* cool, she thought fiercely. She just wished he'd stayed away.

Turning, she eyed him with what she hoped was cool disinterest, ignoring the fact that even after the long night, he looked bigger, badder and hotter than ever.

While she looked like a complete mess.

Go figure.

"This is a medical examination room," she said flatly. "Only medics allowed."

One dark brow rose in silent challenge. "Want to call Security, Francis?" he drawled with a hint of amusement that did nothing but raise her blood pressure. And not in a good way.

"No," she snapped, because he had awesome SEAL skills no security team could match. "I don't want any witnesses when I use a scalpel." Her unspoken, *on you,* hung in the air between them.

It had genuine amusement lighting his eyes and curling his mouth in a smile that had *her* gritting her teeth in aggravation. Arrogant BAB, she snarled inwardly, using the acronym she and Paige had thought of one night when they'd been a little tipsy. But "badass boy" fitted Nate like a pair of snug boxer briefs. Except seeing him now, it was clear he was no longer a boy.

"You thinking of taking me on, Francis?" he drawled smoothly, his gaze hot and intense one moment, dark and unreadable the next. The lightning-fast changes left her confused and more than a little irritated.

"You think I can't?" she challenged, furious with

the shiver crawling up her spine that had nothing to do with Paige using alcohol swabs on her scrapes and cuts.

Besides, taking him on while she was tired and hurting wouldn't be smart. Not to her pride and certainly not to her heart.

She glared at him. Why couldn't he take his sexy self off and leave her alone?

"You can try." He smirked with typical male arrogance that had Frankie barely restraining herself from snarling.

Casually propping his shoulder against the door frame as though he had every right to be there, Nate locked his dark brooding eyes on his hapless target—*her*—his sensual mouth an uncompromising and disapproving line. All humor had gone.

Frankie shivered. Yeesh. She'd forgotten that about him, about his ability to focus so intently on a person they felt like the most important person in the world. Like they were under a microscope.

She turned away to stare at a wall chart without seeing a thing. But her body, the traitor, was locked like a tractor beam on him. And then…and then her nipples tightened and tingles spread across her skin like a heat rash that she blamed on the fact that she was cold and wet.

"Excuse me, *Doctor*," she drawled, ignoring the hunk in the doorway. "But isn't there a rule that says only family members are allowed in an ER room?"

Paige sent Nate a quick look and muttered something that sounded like, "Don't pull me into whatever is between you two."

Frankie felt guilty for about two seconds. She didn't want to involve Paige but she wasn't above using her friend as a buffer either. Especially when it came to Commander Cool.

"There isn't anything to get between," she said smoothly, ignoring Nate and mentally celebrating the complete disinterest in her tone.

"Frankie." Paige protested her rudeness, but Frankie ignored the rebuke, watching Nate out of the corners of her eyes while pretending to ignore him too. For long moments he studied her until she was ready to start squirming.

Finally, with a casual roll of his shoulder, he pushed away from the door frame.

"It's all right, Doc. I'll go." A big hand landed palm flat against the door in preparation of pushing it open. He paused and with a hard look at Frankie said to Paige, "For you."

Meaning he'd never do it for Frankie. The notion stung, and before she could stop it, hurt sliced through her. Quickly squelching it with the full force of her will, she reminded herself that getting her feelings hurt by Nate's attitude would not only be stupid but self-defeating. Besides, she was over her silly adolescent infatuation and the last thing she needed or wanted was someone with a hero complex.

She turned and locked gazes with him just as he pushed open the door. His mouth twisted with faint irony and the next instant he was gone.

Heavy silence descended on the room but Frankie could literally feel her friend vibrating with questions and maybe a bit of exasperation. She slid a sidelong look at her and caught Paige chewing on her lip. She could practically see the wheels spinning away in the brunette's head and counted the seconds until the other woman cracked.

She reached nine.

"Seriously, Frankie?" Paige finally burst out. "You blew him off? Are you sick, dumb or just insane? And what the heck is going on between you two anyway?" she continued, without waiting for a reply.

"Nothing." Frankie sighed, tension draining abruptly and leaving her beyond exhausted. "Nothing I want to talk about anyway. But I am confused about why everyone keeps referring to Nathan as Sammy."

Paige was silent for a couple of beats as she studied Frankie. She must have decided not to probe because all she said was, "It's his coastie handle."

"Handle?"

Paige rolled her eyes. "His nickname, his moniker."

"I know what a handle is, Dr. Cutie," Frankie said, because she knew *that* moniker irritated Paige. Besides, why should she be the only frustrated person in the room? "I'm just not sure I understand this one."

Paige shrugged and swabbed a particularly tender spot that had Frankie sucking in a sharp breath.

"I'm guessing it might have something to do with him transferring from the SEALs." She sprayed her back with iodine. "Lie down, will you? I need to put in a few stitches."

Frankie's gut clenched. "Can't you just glue them or something?"

"No. I can't."

"But—"

"I know you, *Francis*," Paige briskly interrupted when Frankie opened her mouth to argue. "The first thing you're going to do when you get home is ignore

doctor's orders and shower. Next thing you know you're
back here with an infection. Besides, I'll make sure
they're small and won't leave any scars."

Her mouth snapped shut. Okay, so maybe Paige did
know her. "Fine." She lay facedown on the bed and
propped her chin on her stacked hands. At some point
she must have dozed off because the next thing she
knew, Paige was tapping her arm.

"All done, sleeping beauty," she said cheerfully, "and
before you object, I've booked you off for a few days.
Now go home and get some sleep. No picking up heavy
objects or taking flying leaps off ledges. And absolutely
no physical activity or you'll undo all my hard work."

Frankie sat up with a yawn and twisted to see Paige's
handiwork but her back was a patchwork of waterproof
dressings. She tentatively rolled her shoulders to test
her flexibility and was pleasantly surprised to discover
that, though it pulled a little, it didn't hurt.

"While you were snoring, I gave you a shot of pain
meds and antibiotics," Paige said, clearing up the mys-
tery. "You should be good till the morning."

"Which is in about an hour," Frankie said, sliding off
the bed and blinking blearily at her wristwatch. "How
long was I out?"

"About twenty minutes." Paige helped Frankie pull
her jumpsuit up her arms and over her shoulders. "I'd
let you sleep but Andrews is in charge tonight."

Frankie brushed her hands away.

"I can dress myself, Mom, thanks."

Paige backed off with a snicker and picked up a clip-
board. She scribbled something then looked up. "Are
your tet shots up to date?" Frankie grunted out a reply
that the doctor must have understood because she tore

a sheet off a pad and held it out. "I've prescribed anti-biotics and pain meds. Get them. With all that bruising, you're going to be sore in the morning."

Frankie mustered a snappy salute. "Thanks, Doc," she said, and with a quick hug headed stiffly for the door. "You're the best."

"Yes, I am." Paige chuckled. "Just be sure to put that in the patient survey on your way out."

Frankie stopped abruptly at the door when she remembered their earlier visitor. She wouldn't put it past Nate to hang around and ambush her while she was spaced out on pain meds and couldn't defend herself.

"What's wrong?" Paige asked, alarmed. "Are you hurt somewhere else?"

Shaking her head, she quickly stepped aside and nudged Paige into the doorway. "Tell me what you see. Go on," she urged when her friend looked at her like she was a crazy person on the verge of a meltdown.

When she made a get-on-with-it gesture, Paige gave a dramatic eye-roll and stuck her head out, looking around with dramatic furtiveness. "What am I looking for?" she whispered loudly, clearly enjoying the cloak-and-dagger moment.

Frankie growled and pulled her back into the room. "Any…um…*thing* that doesn't belong in the ER?"

Paige's eyes widened and sparkled with enjoyment. "You mean like a…a seal?"

"No." *Of course a SEAL.* She huffed out an exasperated laugh, both at herself and Paige.

"Well, no sign of seals or any other wildlife," Paige said with a quick head-shake.

"Okay, good. Because I'm not in the mood to fend off any marine mammals or any other wildlife."

She wasn't in the mood to deal with Nate, especially not in his disapproving big-brother role.

No wait, she amended. Not in any role. She just wanted to go home, shower for about an hour and then fall into bed and sleep for a week.

"Thanks, Paige, I owe you," she said quietly, and walked stiffly from the room.

"Yes, you do, Francis Abigail," Paige said, popping her head into the passage. "And I plan to collect…in the form of an explanation. About sea mammals."

"Sure," Frankie said agreeably. "I know a lot about whales and dolphins." She smirked when Paige sighed loudly, but no way was she sharing her humiliation at the hands of Nathan Oliver. She'd never told a living soul about what had really happened that night and had no intention of discussing it now.

Or ever. Even with her best friend.

CHAPTER THREE

LIEUTENANT COMMANDER NATHAN OLIVER leaned against the wall in the dark and drank from a disposable cup. He hadn't wanted the sweet, black coffee but it was warming his hands and keeping him awake while he waited for the one woman on the face of the planet with the ability to drive him completely nuts.

Nate hunched into his wet-weather Coast Guard jacket and blinked his gritty eyes. He was cold, wet and exhausted after a thirty-hour shift and wasn't in any kind of mood to deal with Frankie. But it needed to be done before her stupid recklessness got her killed. Besides, being cold, wet and exhausted was nothing compared to what he'd survived in the teams. Nothing compared to what *could* have happened up in the mountains.

But last night wasn't what he wanted to think about; he got icy chills just recalling the expression of horror on Frankie's face as she'd risen to her feet and launched herself at him in that split second before he'd gone over.

From experience, he knew the memory would be replaying in an endless loop for weeks, if not months, to come. His belly cramped into a tight ball and he felt a dull pain in his chest—right next to his heart. Massaging the ache, he reminded himself that he wasn't having a coronary.

It was probably just indigestion from having to drink hospital coffee.

And since it was her fault he was drinking the swill, he added it to her already lengthy list of transgressions. Transgressions that included keeping him from his warm bed, acting without thinking and…and being all grown up and too damn beautiful for her own good.

Okay, and maybe for his good too, but no way would he ever admit that out loud…or go there. Not with her. Not after he'd promised Jack that he'd look out for his wild and willful kid sister if anything happened to him. Only Frankie was no longer a kid; something he'd been forcibly reminded of when he'd walked into that ER room.

Nate sucked in a breath at the memory of her sitting there, her back a patchwork of bruises, scrapes and lacerations. Injuries she'd sustained when she'd gone all Queen of the Jungle and saved his ass.

In that moment he'd wanted to grab her and shake some sense into her but the sight of her had hit him like a bullet to the chest. Gone was the wild skinny tomboy… in her place was a tall, stunning beauty with lush curves in all the right places.

Frankie was all grown up.

But the last thing he wanted to notice was…that. Besides, she'd been like a sister to him. And then there was the blood oath he and Jack had made the day they'd left to join the armed forces.

He was going to honor that promise, preferably from afar, but right now he needed to make her see that her actions had been reckless, thoughtless and dangerous.

He'd had every intention of doing it last night but they'd been surrounded by people and she'd been playing "evade and escape" since touching down on the hospital helipad. It was a game they'd been playing since his return to Port St. John's. A game he was beginning to tire of.

Granted, after that first week when he'd surprised Frankie chatting with his mother and sister in their kitchen, he'd deliberately kept his distance, needing to deal with being back in Port St. John's and his new MSRT commission. He'd also had his hands full, helping his mother cope after a climbing accident had left his sister, Terri, a paraplegic.

He'd never admit it, but he'd also been having nightmares about the last SEAL mission that had taken the lives of several teammates. Bleeding from his own injuries, he'd tried to rescue his fallen buddies but he'd been pinned down. Waiting for air support, all Nate had been able to think about had been the wild grief in Frankie's eyes at Jack's funeral and wondering if she would grieve for him if he was killed in action.

The wild jumble of emotions had terrified him and he'd done what any man did when dealing with stuff he didn't know how to handle. He'd shoved everything deep and stayed away. Partly because she would have prodded and poked until he'd told her all his dark secrets and revealed his pain and feelings of failure. But mostly because, well…he didn't trust himself around her because she drew him in as no other woman did.

His mother swore Frankie had changed since her wild adolescence days but Nate wasn't so sure. That crazy stunt was exactly what the wild child would have done in the past. And damn the consequences.

His jaw clenched when he imagined what those con-sequences would have been if she hadn't been hooked to a lifeline. She would have plummeted to her death with him.

What kind of reckless fool did that?

But even as the thought occurred, he knew. It was the kind that put someone else's life ahead of their own. The fiercely loyal kind that had your back; no questions asked—no matter what. The kind he'd known only in his best friends Jack and Ty, and then his buddies in the teams.

Yet, without hesitation, she'd dived off a slippery ledge to save him. In spite of everything he'd done to push her away.

Scowling down at the rapidly cooling contents of his cup, Nate wondered if he was punishing Frankie for all his confusing emotions. A prickle of warning tight-ened the back of his skull and his head came up just as the very woman he'd been thinking about sauntered through the automatic doors. Francis Abigail Bryce. His best buddy's sister. The wild, exuberant girl he'd watched over for too many years while growing up—and had spent a further twelve trying to forget.

Sucking in a slow deliberate breath, Nate pushed away from the wall and willed his body to relax, his mind to calm. It was a trick he'd learned in the teams. A trick that helped him focus only on the mission ahead while ignoring everything else.

Dealing with Frankie was guaranteed to be as dan-gerous, as unpredictable and explosive as any of the classified missions he'd survived.

Without taking his eyes off her artfully messy red-gold hair, he threw the rest of his coffee into the bushes and tossed the cup in the nearest trash bin.

He was about to head after her when the door burst open and a young medic ran out, only to stop abruptly when she saw him. "Nate," Paige said breathlessly. "Th-thank God."

Despite his impatience, Nate paused and eyed his best friend's fiancée. "Problem, Doc?"

"Yes," she huffed worriedly, craning her neck and squinting into the darkness. "She shouldn't be driving. I was just about to go wrestle her into my car so she didn't have to drive home but I'm on duty."

"What I wouldn't give to see that?" he drawled, leaning forward to plant a quick kiss on her forehead. "Don't worry, Paige. I've got this."

"Are you sure, Nate? Because Frankie is—"

"I'm sure, Doc," he interrupted gently. "Don't worry, I'll get our girl home safely." And with his hands shoved into his pockets, he took off into the darkness, not about to admit that he still thought of her that way.

Our girl.

How many times had he, Jack and Ty said the same thing? *What's our girl up to now? Surely our girl wouldn't be so reckless as to dive off Devil's Point into the sea?*

He caught up with Frankie in the far corner of the car park where she'd parked her battered SUV. He'd trawled the parking earlier and deliberately found a space a couple of cars down from her vehicle so she couldn't sneak off.

He knew the instant she became aware she was being followed when her stride faltered, so imperceptibly he would have missed it if he hadn't been a trained observer. Or watching her long shapely legs.

She stiffened and, without turning, said, "Go home, soldier." As though she knew who it was before he could announce himself.

"We need to talk," he said, ignoring her continued use of the "soldier" moniker. She was determined to annoy him and Nate was just as determined not to be riled. He'd decided to pick his fights where Frankie was concerned and this one wasn't worth getting into. Not now anyway. He was too tired and had other more important issues to address.

Like was she really okay and...*what the heck had she been thinking on the mountain?*

Clenching his jaw against the impulse to yell at her, Nate growled when she stopped at her SUV and dug around in her shoulder bag for her keys. So much for calming his mind, he thought with frustration.

Without looking at him, she asked, "About what?"

"Let's start with you making a target of yourself in a dark parking lot, and ending with driving after being medicated on top of a long shift."

"Don't be ridiculous," she snorted, causing his jaw to harden. "I'm perfectly capable of driving myself. Besides, *all* my shifts are long."

"All the more reason to be careful after taking meds," he snapped, reaching out to snag her shoulder bag. She tried to snatch it back but the move had her sucking in a sharp breath. She abruptly swayed and in the light from the nearby security light he watched her face drain of color.

Cursing, he wrapped an arm around her waist and yanked her roughly against him. The feel of her body, warm and soft against his, had him sucking in his own sharp breath. Putting his hands on her hadn't been part of his plan.

But this pale and terrifyingly fragile woman tugged at something buried so deep he'd forgotten it was there. Something he didn't want to examine too closely.

"C'mon," he muttered wearily. "I'll drive you home."

"I can get myself home, Commander Big Shot," she announced, but her bold statement was ruined when it emerged all slurred and weary. It must have annoyed her because she planted her palms against his chest and shoved. "I'm fine," she grunted, when her efforts failed to move him. "Especially as I've been taking care of myself for a while now, thank you very much."

"That's *Lieutenant* Commander Big Shot," he corrected mildly, allowing her some space but snagging her arm when she tried to stomp off in the opposite direction. He tugged her toward his brand-new four-by-four. "And it's not you I'm worried about, wild thing. It's the other poor saps on the road. Your driving is enough to scare even the most seasoned speedster."

"Hey," she protested, stumbling into a parked car before he could steer her out of the way. "I'm an excellent driver. You should know. You and Jack taught me."

At the mention of Jack, they both seemed to freeze because the last time he'd tried to talk to her about her brother, she'd kind of freaked out. He'd wanted to tell her how much Jack had meant to him—of the promise he'd made to look out for her—but Frankie hadn't wanted to listen. She clearly didn't want to talk now either because her expressive face abruptly closed down.

It had been more than five years and Nate still missed Jack, especially being back in Port St. John's.

Injecting as much normality and humor into his tone as he could, he said, "That's why I know you suck. Maybe you should get a siren installed." He pulled her upright and was relieved when she allowed him to steer her to the driver's side. "That way people will know to get out of your way. Besides, I'm surprised that piece of junk you drive hasn't fallen apart."

"Hey," she objected again, this time more strongly. "Just because it doesn't fit your lofty idea of perfection it doesn't mean it's ready for the scrap heap, Mr. Everything-is-Better-Newer-and-Shinier. It's just like you to be—"

She stopped abruptly when she realized she wasn't at the passenger side. After a couple of blinks, a slow smile tugged at her full lips and she flashed an upward gaze. For the first time he realized that her smile was wonky and her eyes were a little glazed.

Great. She was as high as a kite.

"You're letting me drive?"

His snort was enough to bring back her scowl. "You're no fun," she accused sulkily, and in the abrupt silence that followed he heard her suck in a sharp breath.

It was the same accusation she'd flung at him the night of her eighteenth birthday. The night she'd pretended to drown in the surf when she'd been an excellent swimmer. The night he'd lost his temper when he'd realized she'd done it to get his attention.

It was also the night he'd realized that a grown-up Frankie—with all the curves of blossoming womanhood—was more dangerous to his mind and body than a whole mountainside of terrorists with their crosshairs on his center mass.

"Get in, Francis," he murmured dryly, disengaging the locks and opening the door. "*I* drive."

"You're still bossy and annoying," she muttered beneath her breath as she gingerly climbed into the cab. "And if I wasn't so tired, I'd tell you that you're not the boss of me."

His lips twisted wryly. "Of course you would. Get in, woman, before my patience runs out and I toss you into the harbor."

She uttered a soft snort and lurched over the gearshift, giving him an eyeful of her curvy bottom. He wanted to look away but he couldn't because, in spite of everything, a grown-up Frankie would tempt a saint.

"I'd like to see you try," she muttered grumpily, and Nate's amusement faded. *None* of this was funny, least of all the sight of her pale, exhausted face. Knowing he was partly to blame made his chest ache.

He pulled himself into the cab and shoved the key in the ignition, studying her out the corner of his eye.

"You okay?"

Her soft snort was accompanied with a dry "Peachy," drawing a long-suffering sigh from Nate. The skinny girl with wild red hair, a smattering of freckles across her nose and a wide contagious smile had turned into a stunning woman.

But the joyful sparkle in her clear green eyes had been replaced by shadows and secrets. Secrets she was keeping from him.

Nate shook his head at himself and started the engine. He shoved the gearstick into reverse and with quick economical moves backed out of the parking and headed for the exit.

At this time of the night it was a quiet drive across

town to the little bungalow she called home and he
waited until he turned into her driveway before saying,
"You ready to talk, Red?"

Out the corner of his eye he saw her go still and it
took him a couple of seconds to realize the old nickname he'd given her when she was ten had slipped out
without thinking. Maybe it had been the mention of
Jack, as though they were still all young, and alive…
and together.

Her lush mouth firmed and she turned to face him,
gaze unreadable when she'd always been an open book.
To him at least.

"About what? I thought we'd settled the issue of me
driving in a drug-induced state when I allowed you to
shanghai me?"

"It's about your reckless behavior."

"Reckless? Hardly," she snorted, gathering up her
shoulder bag and reaching for the door handle. "I was
just going to drive home, for God's sake. Not take a joy-
ride through town and along the coast. Besides, I sur-
rendered to your bossy manhandling, didn't I?"

"You know what I'm talking about, Francis," he said
wearily. "I'm talking about what you did on the mountain."

"I don't know what your problem is," she half
snarled, lurching upright in her seat as though prepar-
ing for a fight. "It's not like I was the one without a
safety line. *You* were," she pointed out shortly. "I'm
not the one who thinks she's a big, bad indestructible
SEAL too cool to die."

"What's that supposed to mean? Of course I'm not
indestructible. What gave you that idea?"

"Oh, I don't know," she tossed over her shoulder as

she reached again for the door handle and shoved the door open. "Maybe this insatiable need you have to be a damn hero."

She hopped out before he could answer and slammed the door with way more force than necessary before stomping her way up the garden path.

Muttering curses, Nate got out and followed, wondering what he thought he was doing. This was exactly why he needed to keep his distance, because five minutes in her company and he was ready to howl with frustration.

Taking the stairs three at a time, he moved beneath the light to where she was digging in her shoulder bag for her keys. Without looking up, she snarled irritably, "Go away. I'm not in the mood for any of your annoying lectures."

Controlling himself with difficulty, he said mildly, "Humor me," and folded his arms across his chest. Propped against the wall, he studied her pale face in the glow of the overhead porch light. "You owe me that at least."

"Excuse me? I owe *you*?" She gaped up at him for a couple of beats before a scoffing laugh escaped. "I think you have that backward, *Commander Big Shot*," she drawled. "The way *I* remember it, *bub*," she said, poking his abs with a hard finger, "you were on your way over that cliff when *I* saved *you*."

He grabbed her hand before she could drill a hole in his chest, tightening his grip when she tried to snatch it back. Her growl of frustration had his brow arching with amusement.

"Exactly," he said with masculine superiority, knowing it would get a reaction out of her. Besides, why should he be the only one with escalating blood pressure? "You seem to forget how well I know you, Francis," he said quietly. "That daring leap off the ledge was impulsive. You never gave a thought to that safety line and you know it."

"You don't know anything about me, *Nathan*," she snapped, and pulled free. "You just *think* you do. You left here when I was a girl to go off to prove what a big badass you were. What's more reckless than that? Besides, I'm not that adoring little kid you once knew, and even if what you say *is* true—and it's not," she snapped, jabbing the air with her keys, "you're lucky I did make that leap, or you'd be whipping poor soldier angels into shape instead of standing here now, annoying me."

It wasn't in the least bit amusing. He sighed. "Frankie—"

"I'm sorry." Her voice hitched. "I wasn't thinking." She was quiet a moment before adding, "I meant you'd be stomping around in hell with your size thirteen boots, trying to save lost souls. Isn't that what you always do, *Lieutenant* Commander? Save lost souls?" She drew in a deep breath as though that brief flash of fire had exhausted her. "I'm not a lost soul," she said flatly, shoving a shaky hand through her hair as she leaned back against the door to study him through drooping lids. "I never was. Only you could never see that."

"Have you forgotten I how many times I saved your skin over the years?" he demanded tersely, recalling how they'd all—he, Jack and Ty—tried to make up for Frankie's parents' disinterest in their daughter, only to have her run circles around them.

She closed her eyes and wearily pushed herself upright, ramming her elbow into his gut when she turned to shove the key into the lock. "I don't need saving,

Nate," she muttered. "I can save myself. And even if I did need a savior, it wouldn't be *you*."

Her words burrowed beneath his skin. "I get that," he growled furiously, because that's what she *had* wanted once. "But what you did last night was reckless."

"Don't let it go to your head, stud," she dismissed coolly, pushing the door open before pausing with one foot inside. "I would have done it for anyone. You're just mad because I beat you to it. Mad that the badass Navy SEAL got rescued by a girl."

"Don't make this about me, Frankie," Nate said irritably, ignoring her accusation because what she'd said was ridiculous. Besides, *he* was the trained professional. It was *his* job to save people.

"Why not?" she shot back heatedly. "It's not like I was alone on that ledge. It's not like I was just going to—" She stopped abruptly and sucked in a sharp breath, turning away.

"It's not like you were just going to what, Frankie?" Nate demanded. "Use your head? Think before you acted? Because that's your usual MO, isn't it? Wade into the fray and damn the consequences?"

The look she sent over her shoulder was filled with hurt and fury. "You know what? Never mind. You brought me home. Thanks." She turned away as though she couldn't bear the sight of him. "You can leave. You're good at that."

He caught her arm. "Excuse me?"

She tried to yank her arm free but he tightened his grip, not wanting her to disappear inside where she'd no doubt continue to ignore him. "If I have to tell you," she drawled smartly, "you're not half as smart as I thought you were."

"And *you*, babe?" he growled. "How smart are *you*?"

She froze, her fiery green eyes turning arctic as she glared up at him. "Tell me you did *not* just call me 'babe'." Her mouth curled in distaste. "Take it back and I might consider letting you live."

It was such a Frankie thing to say that Nate couldn't help the low laugh that escaped him. It was clearly the wrong thing to do because she sucked in a furious breath and punched him.

She tried to punch him again but Nate was expecting it and reacted with lightning-fast reflexes, wrapping his hand around her much smaller fist and yanking her against him.

Dark satisfaction filled him when a shocked squeak emerged from between her parted lips. "You only get one shot, *babe*," he warned silkily, staring into eyes gone dark with surprise.

Infuriated by his warning, by the name he'd used on her when it was what he called all his other women, his laughter—heck, all of the above—Frankie stared up into his hard, handsome face, and with her free hand punched him again. Harder.

Her fist practically bounced off his steel-hard abs and before she could growl her frustration he'd backed her against the wall, both wrists imprisoned in his inescapable grip. She ignored the slight discomfort in her back, furious with the easy way he pinned her hands beside her head.

Her startled protest was interrupted by a low, rough curse that ended on, "You just had to, didn't you?" And then he did something that shocked her even more. He swooped in and slammed his mouth down on hers.

Frankie went utterly still, shock reverberating through her. To be perfectly honest, she'd been hoping to get a reaction from him, but she'd never expected him to…to… *Oh, boy.*

The next instant she thought, *How dare he kiss me?* and tried to bite him, but he broke the kiss, his breathing furious and choppy in the predawn silence. As though he was restraining himself from throttling her. With a great deal of effort.

Yeah, well, she was restraining herself too. From melting into a puddle at his feet. But there was no way she would ever admit it. Even on threat of dismemberment.

"You little hellion," he rasped against her lips, and roughly took her mouth again. This time the kiss lasted longer than those first furious seconds and, completely against her will, Frankie found herself kissing him back. Tentatively at first and then… Wow.

The man certainly knew his way around a woman's mouth. Knew exactly how to use *his* lips to drive her crazy with hard punishing kisses one minute and soft deep caresses the next.

He was warm and solid against her, radiating heat and the kind of strength she needed to keep her knees from wobbling and dumping her at his feet. Was, in fact, keeping her upright with his big hard body.

Someone moaned—she was pretty sure it was her—the sound so breathy and needy she might have cringed if she'd had the capacity to do anything more than respond, feel and…oh, God…make another muffled sound in the back of her throat. Every thought, every protest was stripped away—along with her resistance.

The instant her mouth softened against his, he broke

away, drawing back far enough to mutter a string of curses. Even before she managed to fill her lungs, Frankie's first thought was, *What the heck just happened?*

She finally sucked in air and opened her eyes, her body absorbing the hard press and heat of his, her mind struggling with the fact that he'd...that he'd...

"Wha—" she croaked, then snapped her mouth shut before any more embarrassing sounds emerged and he realized that she was speechless. That the woman who usually had an answer for everything had been rendered speechless by a kiss.

By Nate's kiss.

With a low muttered curse, Nate pushed away from the wall and turned, impatiently thrusting a hand through his mussed hair as he headed for the porch stairs.

"Go inside, Frankie," he ordered, his voice low and intense, sounding unbearably weary.

Feeling her hackles rise at his bossy tone, the easy way he always seemed to dismiss her, the way the kiss appeared not to have affected him when it had practically floored her, all seemed to crash in on her at once.

"What the hell was that?" she demanded, mortified to discover that her voice shook almost as much as her knees.

With his back toward her, Nate shoved his hands in his pockets and sent her a hooded glance across his shoulder. His face was a study of light and shadows— just like the man himself—and the side of his mouth lit by the porch light twitched at the corner.

"If you don't know," he drawled dryly, "then you're not half as smart I thought you were."

It took a couple of moments for Frankie to realize he'd used her earlier words against her but before she could respond, he had walked away and was pulling open his truck door.

He paused to stare at her across the distance and with a low "Do everyone a favor, Francis. Stay out of trouble," he slid inside and started the engine, leaving Frankie spluttering as his taillights disappeared into the predawn light.

CHAPTER FOUR

FRANKIE HAD BEEN asleep for what felt like mere seconds when she was awakened by banging on her front door. For a moment she thought she'd overslept and jerked upright to stare wide-eyed at her bedside clock.

Twelve fourteen? That couldn't be right, could it? Had her clock stopped during the night?

Her heart pounded a furious drumbeat in her ears and she struggled to remember what day it was. But when her body strongly objected to the sudden move, memory returned in a rush and she sank back into her pillows with a groan.

She'd barely managed to get any sleep, having been awakened several times by confusing dreams that had left her shaking like a leaf one moment and burning up the next. She was tired, achy and needed her sleep or someone was going to pay. Big time.

She carefully found a comfortable spot and was just drifting off when— *Bang, bang, bang.*

"Seriously?" she snarled, throwing back the covers and easing her stiff body off the bed. Her legs felt like cooked noodles and about as useful.

With a muttered curse about the dire consequences to the idiot on her doorstep, she stomped—fine, shuffled—

down the stairs, wincing and cursing when every step practically vibrated up her spine into her head.

Sheesh. She felt like she'd rolled down the mountain, hitting every rock on the way or…or spent an entire weekend on a bender. But she was way past the bender stage and no longer did stupid things.

Correction: she *mostly* didn't do stupid things. Last night had been the exception. She'd been so out of it she'd let *him* manhandle her and…and *kiss* her.

She was hugely embarrassed to recall that she hadn't put up much of a fight, especially as there had been some anger and a lot of frustration behind his kiss.

As if he'd wanted her to shut up and kissing her was the only thing he could think of.

Yanking open the door, she squinted up…*way up*… at the huge figure leaning against the wall looking far too rested and relaxed to be the last person she wanted to see. The person responsible for disturbing her sleep. The person who'd left her at four thirty in the morning feeling confused and strangely buzzed.

"Do you know what time it is?" she rasped irritably, carefully lifting an arm and shoving her fingers through her tangled hair. She hoped he hadn't caught the fine tremor in her fingers or the careful way she moved but Nate always saw more than she wanted.

"Had a rough night?" he asked mildly, his mouth— the mouth that had sucked the sass right out of her and the one she'd been dreaming about—twitching when her reply to his asinine observation was to curl her lip in a silent snarl.

Frankie didn't care how she looked. Pausing, she gave a mental eye-roll. Correction. She didn't *want* to care but she'd fallen face first into bed with damp hair and could only imagine how she looked.

"You should be sleeping."

For a few incredulous moments she blinked up at him as though she hadn't heard him correctly. "Sleeping?" she practically yelped. "I *would* be sleeping, but some idiot is breaking down my door before the sun is even up."

Nate studied her silently from behind his aviator shades before lifting his arm and pointedly looking at a big black navy diving watch. "It's just after noon."

"What are you doing here, Commander?" she demanded huskily. "I told you I don't need a babysitter."

"No, you said you don't need a *keeper*," he corrected. "There's a difference. I happen to disagree but this is being a friend—a *brotherly* friend."

Frankie stilled at his reminder that his interest was fraternal and nothing more. And the guilt that always accompanied the pain when someone mentioned Jack had her retorting, "I have enough friends, and I certainly don't need or want another brother."

For a couple of beats Nate stilled, his jaw flexing as he studied her. And just when she expected him to turn and walk away, he expelled his breath in a half exasperated, half amused whoosh.

"Good thing I know how grumpy you are in the morning before you've had your caffeine," he drawled dryly, "or your sunny disposition might scare me away." He held out a large to-go mug.

When the aroma of fresh coffee finally hit her brain, Frankie reached out and grabbed it, tempted to forgive him for disturbing her sleep. "I'm only grumpy when

I'm trying to sleep and idiots interrupt me. Why are you here again?"

"I brought you breakfast."

"I'm not hungry but thank you for the coffee," she said politely, taking a huge sip and sighing as the hot brew hit her stomach. "Now go away."

Nate chuckled and pushed away from the wall. "She said you'd say that," he said with amused resignation. "Now, either you back up and let me inside or I get ugly because I'd rather face you than an angry Paige."

Frankie narrowed her eyes at him over the top of the to-go cup. "How ugly?"

"I'm trained in close-quarters combat," he said mildly. "How ugly do you *think* it can get?"

The last thing she wanted to be reminded about was his close-quarters combat move from that morning, so she demanded instead, "Why?"

"Why what?"

"Why now?" She took another sip of coffee and felt her head begin to clear. It paid to have her wits about her when dealing with Nate. "You've been home for nine months and not once in all that time did you even pick up the phone and say, 'Hey, how about a drink to catch up on old times?' So I repeat…why now?"

Nate was quiet so long Frankie thought he didn't intend to reply and before she could stop it, hurt lodged like a hard, hot lump in her chest. She stepped back and reached out to close the door before she did or said something she'd regret.

"Never mind," she clipped out frostily. "I can see that you're trying to come up with some lame excuse you think I'm stupid enough to swallow," and was about to close the door when a size thirteen boot stopped her.

Annoyance at his gall edged out the hurt and she put all her weight behind it, trying to force it closed, but all it did was remind her that she'd given the mountain a full-body hug last night.

She grunted. "Move your big clumsy foot before I break it in half."

"Yeah," came his darkly amused voice, "I can't see that happening."

Furious at his masculine display of superiority, Frankie shoved again and nearly whimpered as pain shot up her spine to explode in her skull. She must have made a sound because Nate muttered a few choice curse words.

"Stop before you hurt yourself," he growled. "And before you start yelling at me again, I thought Paige told you to take it easy?"

She curled her lip to snarl at him when long tanned fingers curled around the door and with little visible effort he pushed it open—moving her backward with it.

Only because she didn't want to spill her coffee.

Feeling a little light-headed, she turned and headed for the kitchen before she embarrassed herself by passing out. "Don't let the door hit you on your way out," she snapped over her shoulder, sighing when she heard the door click shut. "Yeah," she muttered. "So much for friendly concern. But thanks for the coffee," she said, then yelped when she turned her head and discovered him right behind her.

"Holy…" she gasped, stumbling into a kitchen cabinet and almost dropping her coffee before managing to set it on the counter with shaking hands. "What the heck are you doing?"

Having nothing to occupy her hands, she folded her arms beneath her breasts and glared at him.

He'd removed his sunglasses and shoved them onto the neck of his white T. "I brought you breakfast and I plan to stay while you eat it." His eyes were sharp and intent as an eagle's and she wished she was wearing more than ancient PJs—wished she'd had more time to dress and put on her mental makeup, because dealing with the adult version of Nate wasn't going to be as simple as dealing with the boy she'd known.

For one thing his eyes were no longer easy to read. No longer the warm honey filled with exasperated affection when he looked at her. It might have annoyed her that she couldn't read him but she got a little sidetracked by the sight of those sexy eyes in the bright light of day.

She knew he'd say they were brown, but not in any stretch of the imagination could such vibrant colors be called something as boring as brown. Brown made her think of mud or tree bark.

His eyes were made up of three distinct colors; honey, amber and onyx. Amber and onyx striations radiated out from the center and a thin onyx circle edged his honey-colored irises, growing or shrinking according to his moods. As a kid she'd been able know what he was thinking but the man had learned to hide his feelings really well.

From the world…or just her?

"I was thinking about the last thing you said to me all those years ago. You said you didn't want to see me again," Nate reminded her mildly, propping his shoulder against the door frame and studying her like she was a particularly interesting bug he'd just discovered.

Shame flooded her at the reminder of the words she'd flung at him that night.

"I was eighteen and a little tipsy," she said defensively, carefully propping her hip against the under-counter cabinet and placing one bare foot on top of the other. "I said a lot of stuff that night I didn't mean and you know it. Besides," she reminded him, "you called me a stupid spoiled brat and told me to grow up. I might have been spoiled and immature but I was *never* stupid."

"Really?" Nate said mildly as he placed a paper bag on the counter and folded his arms across his wide, hard—she wasn't ogling—chest. "Because I clearly remember you diving off Devil's Point into the sea one night to impress some young punk. That was a really stupid move."

"You, Jack and Ty did it," she pointed out. "Probably hoping you'd get laid by those brainless groupie bimbos you used to date. At least I won a bet."

"You won a broken arm too, but that's not the point. The point is Jack let you run wild just to make up for Frank and Gloria."

"Leave Jack and my parents out of this," she growled, feeling too fragile and exposed beneath those penetrating eyes to think about how inadequate she always felt when people talked about Jack. About how her parents had been so devastated at the death of their golden boy that they'd forgotten that she'd lost her brother too.

She'd tried to be there for them—still tried—but they were always too wrapped up in their grief.

And just like that she was feeling like the worst kind of person because after all this time she was still reacting like a jealous kid.

What kind of person was jealous of a ghost? What

kind of person was jealous of a brother she still adored five years after his death? But somewhere in all those mixed-up feelings of jealousy and anger and guilt was the certainty that everyone had set Jack up to die. They'd turned him into someone who'd felt that he should live up to everyone's high expectations by enlisting.

Besides, how better to live up to lofty expectations than dying a hero?

And here in front of her was yet another man who needed to prove himself worthy. Prove he was nothing like his father by becoming—you guessed it—a hero. A man who looked all hot and sexy while doing it. A man who saw her as an annoying little sister he was constantly rescuing from disaster.

Absolutely nothing sexy about that, despite that early-morning kiss.

She mentally rolled her eyes at herself. She really needed to forget that kiss. "Fine. I was spoiled and needed to grow up but I don't do stupid stuff anymore... unless saving you from a two-hundred-foot plunge to death is your idea of stupid." He opened his mouth, probably to say something incredibly manly and insensitive, but Frankie cut him off. "Besides, I don't want to talk about it." Her glare told him that included what had happened earlier that morning. *"Ever."*

He shut his mouth on a sigh and just looked at her for a couple of beats before saying quietly, "What happened to you, Francis?"

She didn't pretend to misunderstand. She'd realized after Jack's death that her self-worth wasn't wrapped up in someone else's opinion of her.

But she didn't tell him that. She also didn't know how to handle this quiet, serious Nate either. She shrugged one shoulder. "I grew up like you told me to. If you don't like what you see, Nathan, that's just too bad."

He casually lifted his hand to scratch his jaw but Frankie caught the quick smile he tried to hide. A low sexy chuckle was his only response to her dangerously narrowed gaze. Sexy because those amber bits in his eyes sparkled and sexy because tingles shot from the base of her spine, ending...well, everywhere.

She wanted to find him sexy about as much as she wanted to notice how the stark white cotton T-shirt contrasted with his tanned skin...or the way it stretched over some pretty awesome pecs, abs and biceps, inviting her hands to explore.

She didn't dare. No way.

His darkly amused tone zapped her out of her stupid haze. "Since when do you do what other people say?"

"Since never," she rapped out smartly, embarrassed to be caught having hot thoughts about him while he was laughing at her. "And I told you I didn't want to discuss the past so I'll say this just once—and if you ever bring it up again you're a dead man. You were...right." She practically choked on the word but forced herself to continue. "I needed to— What?" she demanded when he gave a dramatic gasp.

"Did you...did you just say I was right?"

Frankie swung away before she threw the coffee at him. She needed the caffeine fix more than she wanted to hurt him.

"You know what? Never mind. I take it back. You're not right about anything—except maybe the coffee. Which is delicious, by the way." She took another sip to show exactly *how* delicious and moaned with pleasure.

Instantly, Nate's eyes dropped to her mouth and

Frankie experienced that full-body tingle again—like it was possible he was having trouble sticking to his "brotherly" thoughts, no matter what he said. The thought made her knees weak and her head light.

The tense silence was interrupted when she finally caught a whiff of the food on the counter and her stomach decided to announce her hunger by growling… loudly. But she'd already rejected the breakfast and wouldn't be reduced to begging.

At least, not with Nate.

"I just want to be alone with my coffee so we can have our moment," she crooned, licking whipped cream from her lips, which curved in a delighted smile when his eyes instantly darkened. They went all heavy and half-mast and Frankie covered her smile with a yawn. He was definitely thinking non-brotherly thoughts. "But since you're still here, it might be a good time to repeat my question."

Nate's brows drew together over the bridge of his nose but his gaze was slow to return to hers. Probably with as much frustration as bafflement because, God knew, she had that kind of effect on men.

"Which question was that?"

"Why are you here, Commander?"

"I brought you breakfast and before you say you're not hungry, I heard your stomach growling. So don't think about spiting yourself just because I brought it. Besides, I bet you haven't considered that your body needs to recover."

"I *was* recovering," she reminded him. "But you interrupted my beauty sleep."

His eyes gleamed with amusement as he took in her wild red-gold hair, ancient T-shirt and soft, faded flannel PJ pants, and for the first time in her life Frankie wished she was wearing something sexy. Not because she wanted him to find her sexy but to prove to him that she was all grown up.

Okay and maybe just a little part of her wanted him to eat his heart out because she was no longer that brash, skinny, underdeveloped teenager jealous of all the attention he gave other girls.

"Don't say it," she warned.

"Say what?"

"That I need all the beauty sleep I can get."

He gave a low sexy chuckle that did annoying things to her belly. To convince herself it was just hunger pangs, she reached out and grabbed the paper bag from Sid's, a popular diner on the boardwalk, and drew it against her as though she was afraid he'd steal it. When she opened it and peered inside, she nearly swooned at the delicious aromas escaping. And if she wasn't mistaken, he'd brought her favorite breakfast. But then again Paige had probably told him.

There were two containers in the bag, one much smaller than the other. She focused her attention on the larger container because she knew what was inside.

"I thought you said you weren't hungry."

"I'm not," she lied, opening the container and practically salivating at what she uncovered. "But Sid's harvest eggs Benedict are the best in Washington. Team that with crispy bacon and mushrooms and I could almost forgive you for disturbing my beauty sleep. Besides, I figure if I eat something you'll leave and I can go back to bed."

"You're a terrible liar, Francis," Nate said mildly.

"Always were." He was quiet a moment before saying softly, "I'm glad to see some things haven't changed."

Not wanting to discuss changes, Frankie reached out to open the cutlery drawer and sucked in a sharp breath when the move reminded her that she'd tried to be a superhero last night.

"Looks like your stubborn streak is bigger than ever," Nate said dryly, and opened the drawer.

"Hey." She grabbed the fork he held out and jabbed it in the air. "I can fight my own demons, thank you very much. This morning I wrestled quite a few of my own—" Realizing what she was about to admit, Frankie shoveled a huge forkful into her mouth and prayed he didn't notice her almost-confession.

"Having nightmares?"

"Don't be ridiculous!" she dismissed, shoveling a piece of bacon into her mouth. But when Nate just looked at her she added casually, "Nothing a girls' night out won't cure." Or a hot and heavy bout of sex. But that was about as likely as winning the lottery.

"What?" she asked warily, quickly backing up when she realized that Nate had moved closer. He reached out and cupped her chin in his big warm hand, tightening his grip when she tried to jerk away.

"What?" she demanded, a little spooked by the abrupt intensity in his gaze.

"You had nightmares? About this morning?"

"Well, the kiss wasn't *that* bad," she tried to joke, but he just continued to hold her gaze until she was afraid he could see all the way to her soul. "Fine, yes," she sighed, shoving his hand away and stepping out of reach. "I had a few nightmares. Big deal."

"About? I'm only asking," he continued when she

rolled her eyes, "because it's better to talk them through. Keeps the dreams from becoming real inside your mind."

"Oh, please," she snorted dryly. "Now you sound like a shrink." No way was she talking about her dreams or nightmares. Especially not to him. Mostly because they'd been about him. About the fact that he'd slipped from her reach and disappeared into a stygian abyss.

"Is that what the Navy shrinks make you do?" she asked, to cover the fact that just thinking about him dying had left her with a hollow feeling of devastation. "Talk about your dreams?"

"Among other things," he murmured, and Frankie tried not to feel disappointed when his expression shut down and he drew away. Shutting her out. "But the other reason I'm here is to say thank you."

"For?"

His mouth twisted wryly. "For that stupid leap off the ledge."

"Stupid?" she demanded. "Is that what you call saving your dumb hide?"

"That's not what I meant," he said quietly. "I meant if you hadn't been attached to the safety line you would have gone over with me."

She rolled her eyes and shrugged. "I was attached, so what's the big deal? You think I should have just let you go over?"

"No, that's not—"

"Well, let me tell you something, Com-man-*der*." She jabbed her fork in the air with each syllable. "Maybe you've forgotten how things work around here. We look out for each other, we catch each other when we fall, we—"

"Thank you."

Frankie was silent a moment as anger and frustration drained away, leaving her exhausted.

"You're welcome," she said quietly, and sucked in a shaky breath. "Now, if that's all, I'm tired. I didn't get much sleep."

"Have you taken your medication?"

Frankie frowned and looked around the kitchen, trying to remember what she'd done with the prescription Paige had given her. "I went straight to bed… I haven't got it filled yet. I'll do it later," she said, trailing him when he turned and disappeared out of the kitchen. She found him in the hallway, emptying her purse onto the entrance table.

She rushed forward to stop him. "Hey! That's my purse. What do you think you're doing?"

He found what he was looking for and with her prescription in hand opened the front door and stepped onto the porch. "I'll see you get this," he said, and trotted down the stairs, heading for his shiny new toy.

"You're not the boss of me, Commander Big Shot," she yelled at his retreating back, furious that she allowed him to get under her skin. Why couldn't she behave like the sophisticated professional she was? "And next time don't expect me to save you. In fact, next time I'll help you off a ledge myself."

Nate couldn't stop the sigh or the wry grin that tugged at the corner of his mouth because dealing with Frankie was always like handling primed explosives.

Folding her prescription, he thrust it into his pocket and slid his aviators over his eyes. After the storm of yesterday, the sky was a clear cerulean blue so bright and clean that it hurt just to look at it.

During the past ten years he'd lost count of the times he'd dreamed of Washington skies after a wild storm. In the hot, dry climes of the Middle East, where every breath seemed to suck the moisture right out of you, he'd often found himself missing the cool humidity of his home town as much as he'd missed the people and his family. Missed Frankie.

But if he'd missed Frankie Bryce, it was because she'd been like a kid sister, he told himself. He'd grown up looking out for her, saving her from herself, and now that Jack was gone, Nate was left with a promise that weighed heavily on his shoulders.

Pulling open the driver's door, Nate looked across the roof of his truck at the wild woman glaring at him from her porch and sighed. He could feel the waves of irritation and frustration reaching across to him.

"Get some sleep, Francis," he said, knowing the name would irritate her. "You look like hell."

And before she could fling any more insults his way, Nate slid into the driver's seat, started the engine and shoved the truck into gear.

Besides, irritation was better than the cool indifference she'd treated him to since his return, even if he'd deserved it. It meant the old Frankie was still in there somewhere. The Frankie he hadn't realized he'd missed until he'd seen her again and discovered a poised, aloof woman with cool green eyes and a soft unsmiling mouth. A woman he didn't know quite how to deal with because she was nothing like the vibrant, feisty young girl he'd known.

That young girl he'd had no problem treating like a kid sister. The woman she'd become…well, not so much.

Besides, he had a debt to pay Jack and his family. They'd been there when Tom Oliver, Nate's father, had skipped town, leaving a devastated family to cope with a one-hundred-thousand-dollar debt on a high-school teacher's salary. They'd given an overwhelmed kid a place where he could be himself, had treated him as one of the family and showered him with the same love and attention they'd given to their son.

Love and affection they should have shown their daughter—but hadn't. Maybe Frankie's dad hadn't known what to do with a wild little girl, but he'd had no problem stepping in as the father figure Nate had needed, teaching him alongside his own son how to be a man—how to catch a ball, how to bait a hook and pilot a fishing trawler. Stuff his own father hadn't stuck around for.

Maybe it was guilt about that—or the fact that Jack was gone and it felt wrong somehow to think of Frankie as a woman—that had kept him away from her.

Besides, what did he have to offer a woman, anyway? He had too many responsibilities as it was, helping his mother pay off the huge debt his father had left behind, and helping take care of Terri.

In the past he'd felt suffocated by all the responsibility. It was the reason he'd left Port St. John's in the first place. To live his own life, get a couple of degrees and still be able to take care of his family. It was what a man was supposed to do. Not bail at the first sign of hard times.

Nate had always been determined to prove to everyone that he wasn't his father. Prove that he wasn't a womanizer who shirked his responsibilities or deliberately broke promises. And if that meant he'd have to avoid one feisty redhead…then that was exactly what he would do.

CHAPTER FIVE

EVEN THOUGH IT had been nearly twenty-four hours since he'd returned to Frankie's and dropped off her medicine, Nate still found his mind wandering back to her and to *that* kiss.

The only thing that was going to distract him was focusing on the other, less frustrating, women in his life so he offered to take his sister to her physical therapy session on his day off.

Terri had been as wild as Frankie and the inactivity of being a paraplegic drove her insane. She was doing an online degree in conservation because she wanted to be a forest ranger. If anyone could overcome a spinal injury, it was his sister.

After the grueling session that left her covered in sweat and snarling like a caged leopard, Nate steered them toward the Gelato Grotto on the boardwalk, hoping to put her in a better mood. But Terri knew exactly what he was doing.

"You know that I'm not a kid anymore, don't you?" she drawled dryly, after they'd left the shop with their purchases and headed for the harbor. The picturesque walkway was always filled with tourists and gave them a clear view of the strait. It was a sight Nate had missed more than he'd thought he would and it never failed to put his sister in a better mood. "Because ice cream doesn't fix a broken back."

"According to Paige, it fixes everything," he said absently, performing a few wheelies with her wheelchair and feeling his heart lift when she laughed. "Besides, I'm really enjoying your sunny disposition and was hoping to spend a pleasant afternoon in your company."

"Liar," she snorted, not in the least offended by his sarcasm. "You can't schmooze me like all your women, Nate. I'm too smart and I know you too well. You're giving Mom a break."

"Of course I am…and I'm spending time with my best girl."

Terri nearly snorted ice cream out of her nose. "If that's true then you need to get laid," she observed smartly. "Clearly you need more excitement in your life."

"I have enough excitement, thanks," Nate sighed, thinking of the confrontations he'd had with Frankie the last few times their paths had crossed. He knew it was mostly his fault but the woman was ornery enough to put a badger to shame.

Terri made a mocking sound in her throat. "That's for sure."

Nate frowned down at her in a way that usually made strong men pause. "What's that supposed to mean?" But she ignored his look and licked a dollop of ice cream.

"It's all over social media, you know."

That wasn't an answer that Nate had expected.

"What is?" he demanded curiously.

Terri made a scoffing sound. "Oh, come now, Com-

mander Coastie. Surely you've seen it? The man with
all the advanced engineering degrees?"

Nate stared at her in confusion, wondering if she was
on a sugar overload.

She rolled her eyes. "One of which is in computers?"

"What are you talking about?"

"Yeesh," she huffed out impatiently. "I'm talking
about last night, dummy."

At the mention of last night Nate froze, his mind
instantly going back to that kiss on Frankie's porch in
the early hours. Had someone seen them? Was his biggest mistake since coming home out there for everyone to see?

Frankie was going to kill him.

But showing any kind of weakness to his sister would
be like putting out a welcoming mat for an invading
army of Huns.

Instead he asked casually, "Last night?"

"Frankly, I think you should tell Mom before someone else does," she said shortly. "Before she freaks out."

Freaks out? Nate thought, feeling a little insulted on
Frankie's behalf. He'd thought his mother liked Frankie.
She was always talking about her. Francis this, Francis that. Now she was going to freak out because he'd
kissed her?

Or maybe she'd be mad Nate had taken advantage
of an old family friend.

"Just because I kissed Frankie doesn't mean—" She
made a choking sound and he whipped her around, cursing when he saw her expression. "We are talking about
that, aren't we?"

His sister was smirking as though she'd just tricked
him into revealing state secrets. "You kissed Frankie?"

She appeared delighted—and more than a little gleeful. "Well, it's about time."

"No, it's not," he said curtly. "Frankie's like a sister to me, you know that. Besides, she's nuttier than Mom's fruitcake."

Terri's expression was a mix of disgust and pity. "You're an idiot. Frankie's fun, not crazy. But in the spirit of full disclosure I'm talking about the way the woman-who's-like-a-sister dived off that ledge to save you."

"What?"

Terri rolled her eyes. "Oh, puh-*leez*. I'm talking about the fact that you nearly died last night and I had to learn about it online in a video shot by one of the guys on the chopper." She reached out to poke him. "I'm talking about Frankie saving your ass and nearly dying too... And all you can say is—" her voice dropped an octave "'—she's like a sister to me.' Are you insane?"

Nate shoved impatient fingers through his hair. "She was injured saving my ass, as you so elegantly put it, and I... I lost my head a little."

Terri paused with a frown. "She's okay, isn't she?"

Nate sighed and said more gently, "Of course she's okay. You know Frankie. She's like a cat with multiple lives."

"Nine lives, you mean."

He snorted. "She used up fifteen lives before she was ten."

"Well, she isn't a kid anymore," Terri pointed out unnecessarily. As if he could forget that after last night... and this morning. "I think you should buy her a ton of ice cream to say thank you."

"I took her breakfast."

"How about dinner and dancing…or maybe a sail along the coast with a picnic lunch? She'd like that."

Nate sent her a sideways frown. "Are you by any chance matchmaking, miss nosy?"

Her snort told him exactly what she thought about his suggestion. "Heck, no," she told him. "You're the last person I'd sic on Frankie. I *like* her."

He blew out an exasperated breath. "Why, what's wrong with me?"

She arched her brow and laughed. "Other than you have a hero complex and she hates heroes? A lot, believe me."

That surprised him. "She hates heroes?" He shook his head as if to clear it because Frankie was always trying to show she was the bravest and the most daring. "You know… Never mind. Why is this even relevant?"

Her expression became unreadable. "It isn't, I'm just saying." She shrugged. "I lived with you for thirteen years before you went off to become a hero. And for six months when you came back. I'm glad you moved into your own place. You're annoying. You eat all the good stuff, hog the remote and leave wet towels all over the place."

"No, that's you."

"Oh, yeah." She grinned and licked her cone. "My bad. So. Wanna see it?"

"See what?"

She gave a huge eye-roll that suggested he was a moron and pulled out her phone. "The video. It's pretty awesome now that I know you're safe."

While she was accessing whatever site she was looking for, Nate threw the last of his cone in the trash. He was wiping his hands when his phone rang.

"Hey, Paige, how's things?"

"Did you hear? Have you seen her?" She sounded out of breath.

He frowned at the odd note of anxiety in her voice. "Hear what? And if you're talking about your best friend, yes, I did. I took her breakfast, which she ate because I waited. Just as you ordered."

"That's great," Paige said impatiently. "But not what I'm talking about."

"What *are* you—"

"A call's just come in. There's been a fire and Fr—"

His blood went cold. "I'll be right there." He was already on the move when he remembered Terri. He grabbed her wheelchair and began speeding along the boardwalk. "I've got to get you home."

"What's wrong? Is something wrong with Frankie?"

"Yes. No... I don't know," he said, battling frustration, irritation and outright terror. "Paige just said something about a fire."

"A fire? Well, go, you idiot," she yelled, slapping at his hands on the wheelchair handles. "I can take care of myself."

"No—"

"I can get to the rehab center myself, Nate." She paused and then with extreme reluctance promised, "I'll call Mom, I promise."

After wrestling with his conscience for a couple of beats, Nate caved. "All right. But don't do anything stupid and don't talk to charming strangers."

"Yeah, yeah, I know," Terri said impatiently. "Go." She held up her phone. "See? Already calling Mom."

Nate paused only a moment before taking off. He

didn't trust his sister to call their mom so he put Ty on speed dial the instant he got back to his truck.

"I heard," Ty said the moment he picked up. "Is she okay?"

"Terri's fine but I wonder—"

"I was talking about Frankie. Did something happen to Terri?"

"No, I was just— Never mind." He shook his head to clear it of the panic that had taken root. "Can you pick her up? Terri, I mean. I took her for ice cream and a walk on the boardwalk after her therapy session and—"

"Already on my way," Ty interrupted, and Nate could hear the sound of keys and the slam of a door. "Get to our girl. I hear she got there before the fire guys and had to go in."

"Got there? Got where?" He gripped the steering wheel until his knuckles turned white. "I thought— Look, never mind. I'm nearly at her house."

"Let me know how—"

"I will," Nate said, and disconnected before he had an accident because he was taking corners on two wheels.

Fortunately, it was the middle of the afternoon and the roads were relatively quiet. He made good time getting from the harbor to Frankie's neighborhood and took a moment to thank the government for the advanced driver training he'd received as part of SEAL training.

As it was, all he really had to do was follow the signs of destruction. Or in this case the sound of sirens and the cloud of black smoke rising into the air.

That was Frankie, he thought with his heart in his throat. Always needing to show that she was ready to wade into the fray at a moment's notice. His gut clenching, Nate gunned the engine, barely missing taking out a couple of trash cans left on the curb.

His dread eased only slightly when he arrived at the scene and discovered her house still intact. Emergency vehicles blocked the road and a crowd had gathered but it seemed like all the excitement was over because a couple of firemen were already rolling up their hoses.

He didn't see Frankie anywhere.

Nate parked his truck and headed toward a couple of EMTs. He had to push his way through the onlookers and caught snippets of conversation as he went.

"It's a good thing she was home… I've never seen anything like it… She just waded into all that smoke and flames… I'd just put the baby down when I heard yelling… It was an age before she emerged with Mrs. Wallace… I couldn't believe my eyes. It was like something from a movie… Barely stopped before running right back inside for Mr. Wallace… I heard the EMTs say she suffered burns along with smoke inhalation…"

Nate sucked in a sharp breath and his heart clenched in his chest. Even if they hadn't mentioned her name, he knew they were talking about Frankie. All he could think of were the words *she suffered burns*.

Cursing himself for not keeping a closer eye on her, Nate approached the EMTs, only to find that Frankie had already been taken to the medical center, homeowner Mr. Wallace was in a bad way, and the worst of the damage was in the back of the house. The latter they'd told him in low voices because Mrs. Wallace was being prepped a short distance away for transport to the ER and they didn't want her to hear.

Nate thanked them and ran back to his truck, breaking the speed limit in his haste to get to the hospital. Offensive driving was one thing when you were dodging bullets and IEDs but another thing entirely when you were negotiating suburban residential streets.

He found parking and headed straight for the ER.

"Francis Bryce," he began, pausing when the duty nurse's eyes widened and her mouth dropped open.

"Omigosh, it's…it's… Nancy, it's *him*," she squeaked, as though Nate wasn't standing right in front of her. "Come quickly…it's him. The…the *guy*."

Nate felt his forehead tighten.

"I'm sure you have me confused with someone else," he began, only to be interrupted.

"Oh, no," the nurse said emphatically. "I'm pretty sure you're the one Frankie saved last night." Ignoring the reference to the previous night, Nate continued, "I heard she was brought in. Can I see her?"

"Oh…uh… I'm not sure—"

"Of course you can see her," Nancy announced with a bright smile. "She's in Room Three."

Nate thanked her and headed through the swing doors separating the waiting area from the examination rooms, and nearly ploughed into the small figure emerging. Paige Carlyle uttered a startled squeak and backed into the trolley beside the door. She would have gone flying if he hadn't shot out a hand and caught her.

"Hey, careful there, Dr. P."

"Nate? Oh, thank God you're here." Tears pooled in her large hazel eyes, turning his heart to mush and making his gut clench.

Man, he hated it when women cried. "What's wrong? Is it bad? How is she?"

She sucked in a deep breath and blinked rapidly a few times until her eyes cleared. "Well…" She gave a ragged laugh. "I swear when people say she has nine lives they aren't kidding but—"

Unable to wait any longer, Nate gently nudged her aside and shoved open the door, coming to an abrupt halt when he found Frankie sitting on the bed, covered in soot, her hair standing out around her blackened face like she'd stuck her finger into a socket.

An oxygen mask covered her nose and mouth and the only color in her face was the startling green of her eyes. They were red-rimmed and a little glazed.

She looked as though she'd been pulled out through a chimney—backward. But at least she was breathing. Well, sort of, he amended when she broke off sucking in clean air to hack up half a lung.

The ER nurse finished setting up a drip and sent her a concerned look. "Take it easy, Frankie."

Nate swept his gaze quickly over Frankie to check for injuries and when he got to her feet, which were wrapped in blood-soaked bandages, he sucked in a sharp breath.

The next instant he was abruptly sucked back into a time and place that had no bearing on the here and now; a place filled with the acrid smell of burning, mingled with dust and blood, sounds of the dying slowly filling his ringing ears.

As though she knew, Paige touched his arm, yanking him back to the present so fast his head spun and his gut heaved.

Every muscle in his body tightened.

"Don't freak out," she murmured, briskly rubbing his back. "It looks a lot worse than it is. She cut her feet on some broken glass, that's all."

The back of Nate's skull tightened as he struggled to

keep from being sucked right back into the battle that
had taken the lives of two of his crew and left another
an amputee.

"What the hell, Frankie?" he demanded hoarsely,
bringing up both hands to rub his palms over his face,
hoping no one had caught that flashback. Hoping no
one saw the fine tremor in his fingers or the fact that
he wanted to march over there and yank her into his
arms—prove that she really was okay.

Her reply was to roll her eyes and give a disgusted
snort as though he was an idiot, and the impulse changed
to wanting to shake her for scaring the life out of him.

"Of course I'm fine," she croaked hoarsely. "A little
singed, that's all." She coughed again and tried to hide
a wince, but Nate wasn't fooled in the least. She was
hurting from last night or this afternoon or both.

"Singed? Is that why you're running around in your
underwear?"

"My pajama pants caught fire so I ditched them."

His ears rang. "You're kidding, right?"

"Smoldering," she rasped quickly, at what she probably saw in his face. "They were smoldering, that's all."

"Don't try to talk," the ER nurse ordered sternly,
sending Nate a warning frown.

"Keep breathing that air, Frankie," Paige said
quickly. "And, Nate, if you're going to upset her, Ken-
dra is going to insist you leave."

"Me? I upset *her*?" He thrust a hand through his hair,
wondering absently if his fingers really were shaking.
"I think you have that wrong, Doc." He marched up
to the bed and gently took Frankie's chin in his hand,
looking her over. He noticed the reddened patches of
skin along her arms and legs.

"Your hair looks like it got stuck in a fire tornado," he growled, lifting a hand to feel the frizzled ends.

"Hey," she croaked, lethargically slapping his hand away. "Who asked you for fashion advice?"

"Some fashion," he muttered, and the nurse sent him a look that almost vaporized *his* hair.

"It's nothing a little visit to the salon won't fix," she soothed cheerfully. "In fact, Jasmine will have you looking like a cover model in no time." She glared a warning at Nate. "No time at all. In the meantime, I'll go check on my other patient. Dr. Carlyle, I need some advice about the woman in Room Four."

In the abrupt silence that followed their departure Nate heard Frankie's labored breaths and struggled to control his emotions. It ratcheted up his annoyance a couple thousand notches because he felt responsible.

"I leave you for a couple of hours and look what happens," he clipped out. "You go charging into a burning house. Do you have a death wish?"

The look she sent him suggested he had the IQ of a rock. "That's a stupid thing to say."

"Is it?"

"Of course it is," she rasped irritably. "I'm not the one who left home to go fight terrorists and get blown up," she pointed out. "Besides, I only did what anyone else would have done."

"Are you sure about that?"

She frowned and ignored the question. "I've known the Wallaces all my life, Nate. I couldn't just leave them in there." She took a moment to suck in a careful breath, before demanding on a wheezy sob that reached into his chest and ruthlessly squeezed his heart, "Have you seen what fire does to people?"

He had. A buddy in the teams had died when his chopper had crashed and burst into flames. The remains hadn't even looked human.

Frankie didn't wait for his answer. "Can you…?" she rasped before taking a few gasps of oxygen. "Can you check on Mr. Wallace for me? He…he was unconscious when I found him and Paige won't tell me anything." She stopped abruptly when she realized that Nate wasn't responding. Quick tears filled her eyes and she turned away. "Oh, God. He didn't make it, did he? I was too late." Her shoulders slumped and she lifted a hand to cover her eyes. "I called and called…but I… I couldn't find him." She swallowed hard and devastated him when a lone tear slid out from under her concealing hand. "And it…it reminded me…of…of—"

"Frankie," he rasped, reaching out to gently cradle her trembling hand in his. Her tears and pain made him feel helpless and angry because he didn't know how to deal with them. Besides, he knew she was thinking about Jack…that he'd died thousands of miles from home—in hostile territory—far from anyone who cared about him.

"I haven't heard anything about Mr. Wallace. Don't jump to conclusions, okay?" he urged, fighting the urge to pull her close and wondering when Paige would return. Women were much better at this kind of stuff. Men bumbled their way through, so terrified of saying the wrong thing that they invariably did.

Frankie was always so strong and feisty that seeing her looking fragile and battling tears alarmed him.

He gave her hand a gentle squeeze before retreating a couple of steps, shoving his hands into his pockets, feeling clumsy and inadequate. It was a new and very unwelcome feeling.

"By the time I got to the house you were already gone," he admitted gruffly. "I came straight here."

"You didn't have to, you know," she rasped kind of fiercely. "I'm fine." Then ruined her declaration by hacking up the other lung.

"You will be."

She sent him a suspicious look from red-rimmed eyes. "What's that supposed to mean?"

"It means," he said, pulling out his cellphone, "that I'm going to ensure you are."

"I'm a big girl, Nathan. I've been taking care of myself for a long time."

"Tonight you don't have to, unless the doctors are going to admit you."

"For what?"

"A psych evaluation would be a great start."

"Ha-ha. Funny. But you needn't concern yourself. Paige has already offered to babysit me."

"Paige? Seriously? You're willing to be the third wheel with the two lovebirds?"

"Hey!" Paige protested, appearing at the door. "I'll have you know—"

"That Ty would be happy with the arrangement?"

"Of course he will," she said firmly. "He loves Frankie."

"Not after a couple of days, he won't," Nate replied mildly.

"Hey!" This time it was Frankie who objected. "I can hear you and I don't need a babysitter. I promise to go home, get into bed and sleep for a week." Nate slid a sideways look at Paige, who was trying not to laugh and ended up rolling her eyes instead.

"What?" Frankie demanded.

"Nothing," Paige said innocently, and before Frankie could demand an answer, Dr. Luther entered the room.

"Okay, young lady," the older man said briskly. "Let's get you checked out." He fitted his stethoscope into his ears. "Dr. Carlyle, if you're not busy perhaps you could ask Nancy at the desk if she can scare up some spare scrubs. Our girl has given the town enough to talk about without wandering around in a hospital gown."

Nate sent Frankie a hooded glance and allowed Paige to nudge him out of the room. Besides, now that he'd seen she was okay, he needed a few moments to himself. Remind himself that she was okay.

"You okay?" Paige asked quietly, as though reading his mind. "Because Frankie is going to be. Okay, I mean," she babbled, rubbing his arm like he needed comforting. "She's a fast healer and—"

Nate shoved a hand through his hair and gave a ragged laugh that felt as though it had been torn from him. "Are you trying to convince me or yourself?"

"Well…" She expelled her breath in a loud whoosh. "Maybe a little of both. But she's not reckless, Nate, she's not irresponsible. Okay, so I maybe I overheard you talking," she admitted a little sheepishly when he arched a brow. "She'd never admit it but I think she feels guilty for being alive when—"

"When Jack's dead."

"Yes," she agreed quietly, looking upset. "I don't know her parents very well, but I think they make her feel that she should have been the one…to, well—"

"They don't mean it," Nate interrupted, knowing full well that they might not mean it but they had always tended to behave as if Frankie was somehow less important than Jack. His friend had always felt guilty about what was sometimes obvious to others and had tried his best to protect Frankie from it. He hadn't always succeeded. "I've seen many parents of soldiers that are KIA react in the same way. A bit of anger, guilt and what-ifs."

"And you, Nate? Are you suffering survivor's guilt?"

"We all have ghosts that haunt us, Paige," he murmured, and headed for the exit to call Ty. Most civilians had no idea what young men were expected to do in defense of their country, things that changed them and left indelible scars, both inside and out.

He had them too and had mostly learned to deal with them. But every so often something happened and he was flung back in time. These days he didn't have as many flashbacks, but early this morning when he'd finally slept he'd had a doozy of a nightmare, like the ones that used to plague him.

And then that flashback in the ER. He'd learnt years ago that there was little use in dwelling on things he couldn't control. Maybe Frankie was one of those things but she was just going to have to learn that his will was stronger than hers.

CHAPTER SIX

WOOZY FROM ALL the pain meds, Frankie not-so-meekly acquiesced to the wheelchair ride and then the indignity of being carried to Nate's truck. She might have been impressed by his strength if she hadn't been offended by his high-handedness, by the ease with which he'd swept her into his arms like Rhett Butler—all while ignoring her protests—if it hadn't annoyed the heck out of her.

Oh, yeah. And the way she reeked of *eau de* smoke when he smelled awesome—like fresh sea air and warm, sexy man.

Sheesh. Why was it that when a girl really needed to look *out-of-his-league* stunning, she ended up looking and smelling like smoldering roadkill—or like she'd been mudwrestling?

If it had been any other man—or if she'd been able to saunter out of the hospital under her own steam—Frankie might not have cared, but it was the man who'd been her first crush, the man who'd then crushed her. The man who now had the indecency to look like the hottest contender for sexiest man alive.

"You know my mother's more than happy to have you stay with her for a couple of days," Nate said, once he turned onto the highway.

"I love your mom, Nate, but she has more than enough to do without running after me. And Terri is exhausting," she admitted with a raspy chuckle. "Even in a wheelchair she has more energy than the rest of us put together." She yawned. "Besides, Paige said she'd come around after her shift."

Nate said nothing and Frankie finally turned her head to study his profile. It was the profile of a man who'd learnt to hide his thoughts and emotions well, a man who'd probably seen and done things in the past fifteen years that she couldn't begin to imagine.

He was no longer the boy who'd grown up trying to live down his father's reputation by taking on more responsibility than his thin shoulders could carry. And while his shoulders were now wide and heavy with muscles, he'd proved time and again that he could be counted on.

She remembered overhearing people talk about Tom Oliver and wondering how his wife put up with his womanizing ways. She hadn't understood what that had meant at the time, but if he'd looked anything like Nate, she could totally understand women finding the man irresistible.

She remembered how much Nate had hated being compared to his father and wondered if he still did or if he'd realized he was his own man. Besides, he was hard, rugged and intense—way hotter and more irresistible than any shallow pretty boy looking for a good time. He was a man a woman could count on when the going got tough. He was…

"What?"

She blinked when she realized he'd caught her staring. "Huh?"

"You're staring like you're waiting for me to morph into a mutant."

"Actually," she rasped, "I was hoping for Ryan Reynolds but no amount of squinting is helping."

A wry smile twisted his mouth. "Well, it's good to see your sense of humor remains unscathed."

"A little singed around the edges maybe, but gimme a couple days and I'll be a regular comedy act."

"Is that what you think people expect from you, Francis?"

She scoffed, "Well, not with a name like that."

"What's wrong with Francis?"

She grimaced and admitted with a raspy cough, "It sounds like I was conceived in a church and, let's face it, it's kind of girly."

He arched a brow. "I don't see the problem."

"Are you calling me a girly girl?" she demanded, unsure if she should be insulted or not.

Nate chuckled and turned away. "After living with women most of my life," he drawled, "I've discovered that answering a question like that is the same as wading through a muddy minefield. Explosions will happen, no matter what I say." He took a corner and accelerated up a quiet residential street where televisions flickered in lighted windows. "Let's talk about today instead, shall we."

Frankie immediately turned away because she knew what was coming. He'd accuse her of being reckless and not thinking about how her actions affected other people. Only thing was, she *had* been thinking about how her actions would affect others.

The Wallaces.

"Let's not," she whispered, because her throat hurt.

"Let's just agree to disagree. Just this once…until I get my zing back. Then you can lecture me all you want."

Nate fell silent, giving Frankie the opportunity to study him out the corner of her eye. His mouth was a firm, uncompromising line that reminded her of their kiss. But that was about as dangerous as leaping off a ledge without a safety line. Finally, he flicked her a sideways look and sighed, which drew a dry "Look at us, all adult and mature," from her.

"Well, one of us anyway."

Frankie wanted to roll her eyes but she yawned instead. "I know that was an insult but I'm going to ignore it. You can just drop me off. I can take it from here."

Nate continued to say a whole lot of nothing, which suited her just fine. She wasn't in the mood to talk either and when he turned into her driveway she couldn't stop a shudder from forming at the sight of the blackened evidence of the fire that might so easily have taken her elderly neighbors.

Even now Vince Wallace was in a coma and Thelma fighting for every breath. Tears pricked the backs of her eyes and, rather than cry in front of Nate, Frankie gathered up her bag of medical supplies and hopped out almost before the truck had come to a stop. The instant her foot made contact with the ground she was reminded of the glass she'd walked over.

She yelped silently, turning away to hide a pained grimace. *Great.* Even her exits lacked zing.

"Thanks," she rasped, before beginning to hobble up the path. The next thing she knew Nate was sweeping her off her feet and muttering something about her stubbornness.

Too weary to protest, she laid her head against his shoulder and let him carry her up the stairs.

She opened her mouth to say, *Thank you, I can take it from here*, but he ignored her, shoving open her door and heading up the stairs. Instead of taking her to the master bedroom, he made a beeline for the bathroom.

Frankie scowled at him, even though she'd also planned to make it her first stop. "Dr. Luther said I shouldn't shower."

"Yeah, and we all know you'll ignore his advice, so Paige gave me instructions on how to reapply your dressings," he clipped out, depositing her on the side of the bath as though he couldn't wait to get rid of her.

"Look," she huffed out irritably. "If I need help, I'll call Paige." Which was a total lie. No way was she bothering anyone with something as simple as showering.

"It's no bother," he said mildly, his sideways glance casual and more than a little amused as he reached into the shower stall and turned on the water. As though he knew she was lying to get rid of him.

It was the amusement that finally got to her. She stood and shoved him out the door. "Go. Away."

He took a couple of beats to study her before snagging the bag of medical supplies out of her bandaged hands. He nodded at the shower. "Call if you need anything."

Her answer was to slam the door and then curse the fact that there hadn't been a lock on it for about twenty-five years. Not since she'd locked herself in the bathroom when she was five and her grandfather had had to take the door off its hinges to get her out.

Frankie felt tears prick her eyes and ruthlessly suppressed them. She wasn't crying because she missed

Nanna and Gramps and she wasn't crying because Nate had left without a fight. She was…she was…*well*, a girl didn't need to have a reason.

Especially when her life was unraveling faster than ribbon at Christmas. Maybe…maybe she was just emotional because of the stress of the past twenty-four hours.

But Frankie knew it wasn't that. Her throat hurt, her back hurt from last night's scrapes and bruises and now, along with random patches of blistered skin, her hair looked like she'd crawled through the furnaces of hell.

She was a mess.

Her life was a mess.

And now…and now she'd chased away the last person alive that she really trusted.

More tired and miserable than she'd ever been in her life, Frankie stripped out of the borrowed scrubs and stepped into the shower.

The hot water hit her abused flesh and she quickly adjusted the heat to accommodate her scorched skin. After a minute, she planted her blistered palms flat against the tiles, closed her eyes and let the water wash away the soot and the memories of the past two days.

She hadn't realized she was crying until she heard a knock on the bathroom door and Nate's deep voice said, "Frankie…you okay in there?"

She had to swallow a couple of times before she managed a hoarse "I'm fine…go away," thankful that she would be able to blame the smoke for her red eyes and tight throat.

But the interruption had reminded her that crying never solved anything and she reached for the shampoo, determined to at least not look like a survivor of the Great Fire of London.

It took three washes to get the stench out of her hair and by the time she finally felt clean she noticed blood washing down the drain along with shampoo suds and shower cream.

She looked down at her feet and realized that the dressings had come loose. Oh, yeah, and she'd popped a few blisters on her right palm. Before she could start crying again, she reminded herself that it was okay, that these were things she could fix. Dressing a couple of cuts was basic stuff.

Everything else in her life? Well, that was another matter altogether.

She turned off the water and opened the shower door, reaching out to grab one of the thick fluffy towels that usually hung on the rail. When her hand grabbed air, she recalled that she'd left a pile of damp towels on her bedroom floor when she'd fallen into bed last night.

Great.

Huffing out an aggravated breath, she shoved dripping hair off her face and grabbed a hand towel, drying her hair as best she could before reaching for the hair towel—which of course wasn't large enough to adequately cover *anything*.

By the time she was reasonably dry, more blood stained the bathroom floor. But other than her towels, the only thing she had that would staunch the flow was her emergency stash of sanitary towels.

Shrugging, she reached into the cupboard under the basin. If football and hockey players could use tampons for nosebleeds, then there was nothing stopping her from using sanitary towels as makeshift pressure bandages.

Suitably padded up, Frankie covered the bare essentials with the tiny towel and hobbled painfully to the door. She pulled it open and stumbled back with a shocked squeak when she caught sight of a huge figure standing outside the door.

"What…what the…?" she rasped furiously, slapping one hand against her chest to keep her heart from making a break for it and the other on the wall, before recalling that her tiny towel needed help against the force of gravity.

Her shock turned to a panicked squawk as the towel slid silently southward. She made a frantic grab for it and caught sight of a wide, white grin at her futile efforts. The only course left to her was—

She grabbed for the door as a fiery blush covered every inch of exposed skin—of which there was a whole heap. For several seconds Frankie huddled behind the door, breathing like a racehorse after a two-mile gallop and coughing from all the smoke she'd inhaled that afternoon.

Finally, she caught her breath and peered around the door, half expecting to see Nate standing there, enjoying her discomfort. All she saw was a tanned muscular arm attached to a large hand holding out a pair of summer jammies.

She stared at the skimpy tank top and minuscule boy shorts for a couple of beats like they might bite her because this was a winter jammies kind of moment. The kind where a girl needed the comfort—and full-body concealment—of baggy flannel.

Considering it was either the towel or… With a muttered oath she reached out and snatched the tank and teeny shorts. She slammed the door to the sound of deep chuckles—*the jerk*—and hastily wrestled her PJs on, cursing herself for the way her body responded to the sound of that deep masculine sound.

Oh, yeah. And the fact that the man she'd once loved with every fiber of her eighteen-year-old being had just seen her naked.

In response, her skin was tight and sensitive, her breasts heavy and achy and…and the hot and heavy sensations turning her belly into a seething mess of dread, anticipation and nerves ratcheted her irritation up a couple gazillion notches.

She yanked open the door with a fierce scowl, only to find the passageway…empty.

"Seriously?" she muttered, before hightailing it to her bedroom for a sweatshirt because no way was she going down there looking like some sad attempt at a sex kitten. She heard a sound behind her and turned in time to see Nate standing on the top step, staring at her butt.

Resisting the urge to squirm or cover her bottom with both hands—heck, she wasn't *that* lame—Frankie cleared her ravaged throat and rasped in as cool a tone as she could manage, "Ex-*cu*-se me?"

Nate's gaze finally rose—crinkled at the corners as though he'd enjoyed running his eyes over her bottom and bare legs—and arched his brow at her tone. His eyes were unreadable, but with the knowledge that a minute ago he'd seen her *au naturel*—full frontal—Frankie felt her neck heat.

His amusement was soon replaced with a concerned frown as he stared at her feet.

"Your dressings came off."

Frankie shrugged and opened her mouth to say that it had been bound to happen, only to be interrupted by his curious "Are those…are those sanitary pads?" as he came closer. For some reason her blush deepened and she quickly turned away to hobble into her bedroom.

"They were handy," she called over her shoulder, heading to her closet for a zip-up sweater, which she hastily pulled on. Feeling a little more armed against his disturbingly intense gaze, she turned to find him filling the doorway, his hands shoved into his pockets.

Her heart leapt and then lodged in her throat because he looked like he was getting comfortable. And that meant—that meant her attempts to get rid of him had failed.

A shiver of something that couldn't possibly be pleasure, excitement and relief warred with irritation at his arrogance.

She scowled to cover her reaction. "What?"

"Lucky for you I'm handy too."

Her brow wrinkled. "If that is some sad attempt at seduction then you can just—"

He actually had the gall to laugh. "Relax, princess. I've had some training in field trauma so I'm sure I can handle a couple of bandages and burn gel."

"Don't be ridiculous. I'm an EMT. I can do it myself."

"Lucky for you, you don't have to," he countered mildly, stepping into the room. When she stubbornly glared at him, he murmured, "Either you go willingly or I sling you over my shoulder." His brow rose in challenge. "Your choice."

For a couple of beats Frankie considered defying him but the look in his eyes told her he wasn't kidding around. She uttered a growl of frustration and stomped toward him, hiding a wince at the pain in her feet.

"When did you get to be such a jerk?"

The question seemed to surprise him but he gave a soft snort before saying in a challenging voice, "When did I stop being a dupe, you mean?" His tone was wry. "You don't survive basic underwater demolition SEAL training by being a pushover, princess. Besides, what kind of friend would I be if I left you to fend for yourself?"

"The kind of friend who knows when I want to be alone," she said, trying not to show how much he was affecting her.

Nate made an exasperated sound in the back of his throat and before she could respond in kind, he'd lifted her off her feet and swung her into his arms.

She gave a growl of protest and tried to wriggle free but his curt "Be still before you break both our necks," had her stiffening in his arms.

He carried her down the stairs as if she weighed no more than a child, muscles bunching beneath his warm, taut skin.

To cover the shiver that started at the base of her spine and shimmied up to the back of her neck…then spread everywhere else, she growled, "Drop me and you're dead meat."

His answer was an exasperated snort. "Please. I've carried twice your weight up a mountain pass that was more of a goat trail in a snowstorm." He briefly dropped his gaze. "But keep squirming like that and there's no telling what might happen."

Conscious of the arm beneath her butt and the press of her breasts against his hard chest, Frankie stopped squirming and tried to hang onto her bad mood.

"I see your arrogance hasn't improved," she muttered, chagrined when amusement flashed in his gaze.

"No more than your reckless streak," he replied casually, but instead of getting annoyed she had to wonder if that was how people still saw her. And while it was true that she no longer did crazy things, she had to wonder if Nate truly believed Jack's death hadn't changed her.

Before she could ask, he placed her down on the kitchen counter and shoved a mug into her hands. "Drink," he ordered, turning away to look through her refrigerator. He made a sound of disgust and sent her a resigned look as he pulled his cellphone from his pocket. "When last did you go shopping?"

She thought about that a moment but couldn't remember.

He sighed. "Okay. Next question. When last did you eat?"

"Um…lemme see… This morning? Yep, this morning. I got breakfast delivered from Sid's. The delivery boy was rude and annoying."

"You probably forgot to tip him," he said.

"You can have the chocolate brownie," Frankie said magnanimously. "As much as I love Sid's brownies, they're bad for my thighs."

She wanted to kick herself for mentioning her thighs when his gaze took a leisurely journey over them, his mouth kicking up at one corner as though recalling what she'd looked like standing in the bathroom doorway with her towel sliding to the floor. Or maybe when he'd checked out her legs in her pj shorts.

Hiding her embarrassment behind the mug in her hands, Frankie took a sip and grimaced at the taste. "What the heck is this? Are you trying to poison me?"

"SEAL remedy for whatever ails you. Drink up. By tomorrow you'll be as good as new." His look said she'd better do as he said. He turned away to concentrate on ordering takeout and Frankie waited until he disconnected to ask curiously, "Do you miss it? Being a SEAL, I mean."

His eyes instantly became hooded and just when she thought he didn't intend to answer, he said neutrally, "Not as much as I thought."

"What do you mean?"

His expression told Frankie he did miss it. She knew because Jack had once told her that military brotherhood was something that couldn't be explained. She knew it had something to do with having to trust and rely on each other in dangerous situations and that it made for very close ties.

His jaw bunched and his eyes turned flat. "I got tired of losing friends."

Recognizing his pain, she casually changed the subject, "So, do SEALs have magic secret remedies for everything?" wanting to breach the wall he'd abruptly erected between them.

He wrapped his warm hand around her left ankle and lifted her foot, studying her makeshift bandages. "We don't have one for stupidity." She went to jerk her foot away because it was clear he was done sharing, but Nate tightened his grip and removed the "bandage."

"Whoa," he said, when he saw the condition of her foot. "Don't you have any sense?"

"Apparently not," she muttered, finally noticing the medical supplies he'd set out on the kitchen table. "Or I'd have done a better job running you off my property."

"Not with these feet." He chuckled, shaking his head when she stuck her tongue out at him.

He hooked a chair with his boot and pulled it closer, sitting so he could better see the bottom of her foot. She was tempted to plant her foot in his face and shove but he began to apply antiseptic cream and adhesive bandages with such gentleness that she was momentarily distracted.

"So…" she said casually, ignoring the tingles his long-fingered touch sent arrowing up her legs. "What's in this toxic beverage, anyway?"

His look was brief and amused. "If I told you I'd have to kill you."

Wrinkling her nose at him, she again considered kicking him but he was big and tough and her feet had been through enough. "You're a regular riot," she slurred, wondering why her tongue felt a little thick. The room spun lazily and she stared suspiciously at the mug. "Wha' ha' 'oo done?"

He rose fluidly and removed the mug from her nerveless fingers, catching her as she listed drunkenly. "Just a little herbal remedy, Red," he murmured, planting his wide shoulder against her midsection and lifting her as he rose to his full height. "Believe me, tomorrow you'll feel great."

Dizziness assailed her and she clutched at his back, fisting strangely lethargic hands in his shirt as he left the kitchen, walked down the passage and into the sitting room. He placed her carefully onto the couch, slid a couple of pillows beneath her head and pulled a blanket over her.

Frankie was already sliding into the comforting

blackness when she remembered something she needed to say. "Nate?"

The air shifted and she cracked her eyes open to see that he'd dropped to his haunches beside her. "What is it, princess?"

For a long moment she stared into his familiar face and wondered at the strange emotions roiling inside her. He lifted a hand and carefully brushed her damp hair off her face, the gesture tender and full of familiarity and affection.

Despite the tears pricking the backs of her eyes, she felt her mouth curve and allowed her weighted eyelids to fall. "I'm glad you're home," she slurred sleepily. "I missed you, even if you did just slip me a mickey."

"You sure?" he teased softly. "Because it seems like you think I'm a pain in the butt."

"I don't mean it, Nate," she murmured, so softly he had to bend down to hear her. "It's just…" She gave a huge sigh that told him she was slipping into slumber. "'S just that you're a sexy BAB…and those're the ones a girl's gotta watch…or she's toast."

He grinned. "Don't you mean babe? As in sexy babe?"

"BAB," she slurred softly. "Badass boy. And you're pretty bad…ass."

Nate couldn't prevent a soft chuckle from escaping. "You're no slouch yourself, Red," he murmured, staring down into Frankie's face feeling a confusing mix of annoyance and affection that squeezed his chest and lodged right beside his heart.

He'd never met a more aggravating female—no, make that person—but Frankie had always had a soul-deep reservoir of sweetness that emerged at the oddest times.

And in a blinding moment of clarity he realized that, no matter what he'd done over the past fifteen years, or where he'd gone, she'd stayed with him. Their…connection had stayed with him.

And it scared him, because the people he was most attached to…had a habit of dying on him.

CHAPTER SEVEN

BY THE END of the week Frankie was tired of staying home, and because she was ready to climb the walls with frustration, she'd snapped at everyone who'd dropped in to visit. Everyone except Nate, that is. And that was only because he'd been conspicuously absent.

Bored out of her mind, she did a couple of loads of washing, vacuumed the downstairs, and discovered her phone—which she'd thought she'd lost the night of the storm—in a container of basmati rice in her pantry.

With a confused frown, she reached for it and decided she must have been really spaced out on meds to put it there.

It wasn't until she'd charged the battery and accessed her messages—all one hundred and forty-three of them—that seeds of suspicion began to grow. Then she read Terri's message:

Frankie, you gotta see this. It's awesome. Thanks for saving the big oaf. I owe you.

The instant she clicked on the link, she knew with certainty that *someone* had deliberately hidden her phone to keep her from seeing it. And she had a sneaking suspicion it was the one person who'd been conspicuously absent since the night he'd seen her naked and then drugged her with some funky-tasting SEAL potion.

Nate. The man featured in the video titled "Daring leap saves coastguard commander from certain death."

The instant the grainy images began playing, Frankie's eyes widened and her mouth dropped open. Chills snaked up her spine as she watched herself leap for Nate the instant he'd gone over and she felt sick once more at the thought of what could have happened.

They'd have been retrieving his body from the bottom of the gorge. And she'd have been dealing with yet another devastating loss.

Nate was bossy and annoying but she didn't want to contemplate a world without him in it.

She was still stewing when Paige arrived, laden down with bags from a local supermarket. She let the other woman in and ignored her concerned frown as Paige headed for the kitchen and dropped the bags on the table.

"Why is your face red like you're up to something illegal?" she demanded, placing her palm on Frankie's forehead and checking her eyes. "Are you sick? Have you been taking your antibiotics? I hear you haven't been to have your wounds checked."

Frankie rolled her eyes. "I'm fine," she said mildly, and folded her arms, propping her hip against the counter. "Your turn to babysit?"

Paige made a half-hearted scoffing sound. "Even if that were true—and it's not, because you're a grown woman—you need your battle wounds checked and I thought we could spend some girl time together."

"So you're not here to cook for me just to make sure I eat?"

Paige looked surprised for a moment before resuming her chore with a snort. "Right." She chuckled. "Like I cook. But don't worry, the doctor has just the thing for what ails you."

"Wine?"

"And other stuff." Paige beamed with delight. "We're going to have ourselves a party."

"What are we celebrating?"

The look Paige sent her was filled with censure. "Since when do we need a reason to drink wine, eat ice cream and watch chick flicks?"

Hours later, Frankie watched hockey on the sports channel while Paige slept, curled up on the sofa like she'd entered hibernation. They'd watched a rom com first, during which Frankie had sneered at the soppy moments, predicting exactly what would happen next and hooting with laughter at the clichéd dialogue.

At first Paige had tried to shush her but the plot had been so corny they'd ended up rewriting it in the most outrageous ways they could think of.

They'd made dinner and returned to watch an action adventure movie but Paige had soon fallen asleep. It was a movie Frankie had already seen so she'd switched over to sports.

The game had just gone into overtime when she heard a faint noise outside, followed by the clatter of a trash can falling over.

Grabbing her brother's old baseball bat, Frankie padded to the front door and pressed her ear against the wood. Just when she thought the noise might have been one of the neighborhood raccoons, scavenging for an easy meal, she heard another thud, followed by soft cursing.

Whipping open the door, she stepped out and hefted the bat over her shoulder in a classic batter's stance. "Make another move, buster," she snarled, "and I'll use your head for batting practice."

Another curse had her tightening her grip and peering into the darkness as a large shadow materialized out of the night. Her pulse skipped a couple of beats and she swallowed a stupid girly squeak that would have mortified her if it had escaped.

Realizing that her neighborhood prowler was someone she knew, someone even more dangerous to her body and mind, Frankie demanded, "What are you doing sneaking around like a pervert?"

Nate lifted an arm to swipe at his face and it took only an instant to discover why. He was soaked, his uniform sticking to his skin like he was a hunky seal-a-meal.

Yum.

No, Frankie lectured herself silently, studying the man standing with one foot on the bottom step looking hotter than any man had a right to look in the middle of the night. *Not yum, dummy.* She was mad at him. Mad that kissing her and then seeing her naked had made him run away like she had a contagious disease.

"Run into any sprinklers while you were out playing covert ops in my garden?"

Nate made a rough sound of frustration in his throat and stomped up the stairs, his expression morphing from disgruntled to enquiring as he took in the baseball bat resting on her shoulder, her opposite hand resting on a canted hip.

"Expecting someone?"

"It's how I greet unwelcome guests," she replied smartly, sucking in a sharp breath when he came closer and the ambient light from inside illuminated his face. "What the heck, Nate?" she demanded, nudging him in his wide chest with the bat. "Have you been beating up the big boys at the Seafarers again?"

"Hey, careful with that," he complained, smoothly grabbing the bat as though he expected her to use it. Not that she wasn't tempted, but it looked like he'd just gone a couple of rounds with an LA street gang. "That was seventeen years ago and in case you haven't noticed, I *am* one of the big boys."

Of course she'd noticed. She'd have been an idiot not to see that he'd become a big badass boy. A name she'd called him—maybe—the other night in her drugged and weakened state.

She ran her gaze over him, telling herself that she wasn't noticing how his soaked clothes clung to every inch of muscle, sinew and bone, every inch of awesome masculine perfection.

"All I'm seeing is an idiot dripping on my ma—" She stopped abruptly when she noticed a darker stain marring the wet fabric of his shirt. "Omigod, you're… *bleeding*?"

He sighed and worked his jaw as though he was gritting his teeth. "It's nothing."

Nothing? Who was he kidding?

She sucked in a furious breath before saying tersely, "I'll be the judge of that," determined not to give him the satisfaction of falling apart like the silly heroine in the rom com she and Paige had watched earlier. But the awful truth was the sight of his blood instantly reminded her of how dangerous his job could be. Of how fragile human life really was. Of all the years worrying about him and Jack, only to have her worst fears confirmed with her brother's death.

"Come in and take off your boots," she ordered to cover her reaction. "I just cleaned."

He winced and held his side as he bent to unlace one tactical boot. "I thought you were supposed to be taking it easy."

"I was taking it easy," she retorted, bending to brush his hands aside so she could unfasten his boots herself. "I only vacuumed."

She watched as he toed the boots off and left them beside the door before he stepped inside.

"Paige here?" he asked.

"Why?" she demanded suspiciously, wondering if he'd come specifically so the doctor could fix him up. But, then, of course he had, she reminded herself irritably. And since he'd stayed away lately, she had to wonder if he'd been worried she'd get romantic ideas.

"Her car's in the driveway. I was about to leave when I heard the trash can go over and decided to check it out." He entered the kitchen and squinted in the bright light. "Since when do you open a door without first checking who it is?"

"Shh," Frankie warned in a low tone. "Paige is sleeping. I was about to head off to bed when I heard you stumbling around like the three stooges after an all-night bender."

"I'm too old for benders and I'll have you know I'm

an expert at moving among the enemy without them ever knowing I've been there."

She didn't want to think about him sneaking around enemy territory. It gave her nightmares and made her act badly.

"You've clearly lost your edge," she snorted, ruthlessly suppressing a quiver when his eyes went dark. Dark in a look she knew all too well. Maybe hadn't *seen* in a good long while, but still recognized—especially when his mouth curved into a sensual smile that had her knees wobbling and her belly doing the Highland fling on hot coals.

For years she'd watched him ensnare women of all ages with his dark good looks and bad-boy smile, but he'd never looked at *her* as anything but Jack Bryce's little sister.

She swallowed. How the heck was she supposed to handle this older, hotter, brooding version of the boy she'd once adored? A man with sexy eyes and sexier mouth?

"Ya think?" he drawled dryly, but there was an edge to his voice that confused Frankie and she turned away before he saw exactly how he affected her. Limping to the refrigerator, she yanked it open, wondering if this was his way of keeping her off balance.

That it was working annoyed her no end.

"What are you doing here at this time of night looking like…?" She waved her hand at his face. "Like that?"

Nate had done a lot of crazy stuff in his lifetime, often—tonight, for instance—disregarding his own safety to protect others. But he'd never made a habit of visiting women where he wasn't sure of his welcome.

He'd been with a lot of sophisticated, beautiful woman but when he'd looked up and seen Frankie standing on her porch, the light spilling over her body like she was a kickass heroine in an action movie, it had hit him right between the eyes.

Standing there with her legs spread for balance, a baseball bat gripped in one hand and resting on her shoulder, she'd made his world tilt on its axis. Her hair was wild and messy and as far as he could see there wasn't a lick of makeup on her face. Her natural beauty was patently obvious.

It reminded him of exactly why he'd stayed away— because he wasn't nearly as immune to her as he'd thought. But, then, he hadn't meant to come here at all, fully intending to go home to a hot shower and bed.

Weary, he leaned against the counter and watched as she reached into the refrigerator to pull out a beer. He didn't even want to think about the fact he was suddenly allowing himself to see her as the sexiest woman he'd ever met. She was annoying, reckless, contrary and could be downright belligerent when she wanted to be.

But she was also tall and curvy, every man's living fantasy, even dressed in snug shorts, a baggy T-shirt and thick socks. She'd also piled her luxurious red-gold curls atop her head in a style that was both messy and incredibly appealing.

His hands itched to explore but before he could reach out and bury his fingers in the heavy mass, she turned and silently handed him the beer. With a look that was hard to read, she disappeared down the passage, leaving him to wonder if she'd seen where his gaze had been.

Not that he cared, Nate assured himself. He was a
red-blooded male over thirty and could look where he
wanted.

Except there, a voice in his head reminded him.
There you'll find only trouble.

But Nate ignored the voice and tried to decide what
it was about her that kept throwing him off balance. She
was all grown up, sure, and there was still that streak
of recklessness…but she'd changed.

Or maybe…maybe his years in the SEALs—seeing
and doing things ordinary people couldn't imagine—
had changed *him*. And perhaps *that* had changed the
way he saw her. Maybe he was being kept off balance
by the brief flashes he saw of that lively young girl in
the very put-together woman she'd become.

Before he could ponder it further, she was back with
her emergency medical kit, demanding "What?" when
she caught his somber gaze.

He shook his head and the sensation of his world
tilting on its axis faded. "I wanted to tell you before
you heard it from someone else." He paused, wondering how to mention the other big headache in his life.
The video that made *her* look like a kickass superhero
and him…well, not so much.

She put the backpack on the table and flashed him a
wary look. Free of cosmetics, her skin was smooth and
dewy and infinitely touchable.

"Tell me what?"

He lifted a hand to scratch his jaw, wondering why he
was noticing her skin now. Deep down he knew, though.
After that kiss…the taste, scent and feel of her skin had
been burned into his mind and his senses.

Realizing what he was thinking, Nate lifted a hand to massage the band of tension tightening around his skull.

Get a grip.

"There's a video clip online," he growled, wondering what he'd thought he was doing when he'd found himself outside her house. He should have put his truck back in gear and got out of there. He should have listened to his gut, which had been screaming like a five-alarm fire. But, no. He'd had to go all super-soldier when he'd heard the trash can falling. As though he *wanted* to be the hero Frankie said she didn't want or need.

She gave a short derisive laugh and for a horrifying moment he thought he'd voiced his thoughts out loud.

"What?"

Her gaze was mocking. "I've seen it, Nathan. Terri beat you to it."

"How did you— Never mind." He sighed and rubbed the back of his neck where his muscles bunched with tension and fatigue. "Just don't answer any calls or talk to anyone. Publicity will handle it."

She unzipped the emergency kit and began pulling out supplies. "I know you hid my phone," she said, flashing him a look that dared him to deny it. "And swore everyone to silence." She narrowed her gaze. "The question is why?"

Nate watched her toss a packet of alcohol swabs onto the table. He didn't want to analyze his actions so he went with, "I didn't hide it. I put it in rice because it was wet and forgot to tell you." It was the truth. Just not the full truth, which was that he'd looked like a rookie who had needed saving.

Her snort conveyed her opinion of his lame explanation. "Are you sure it wasn't because the big badass SEAL needed saving…by a girl?"

"Of course not." He managed a chuckle, thinking that Frankie had always been too sharp and perceptive for her own good. "I think my ego and rep can handle that." He broke off to yawn. "Besides, you needed the rest."

"Looks like you should take your own advice."

His mouth twisted into a wry smile. "Yeah, well." He rubbed a hand over his face before murmuring, "Hard to get any rest when you're boarding dark unmarked vessels carrying human cargo."

Frankie stilled and her eyes widened. "You mean like…traffickers? Here? In Port St. John's?"

Nate grunted and folded his arms across his chest, wincing at the pain radiating from where a bullet had grazed him. He'd been conducting night stealth training when they'd come across the battered vessel a little too close to the coast for comfort.

"We intended to surprise the crew, only to find il-legals hoping to sneak into Canada via the islands."

"Does MSRT handle that sort of thing?"

"If there's a threat alert but we were already out on maneuvers and decided to check it out." He ran his fingers through his hair, scattering water droplets in every direction.

Eyes searching, she gestured to his face. "Is that where you got on the wrong end of a fist, Commander I-Used-to-be-a-Badass-Navy-SEAL?"

His mouth twitched because a teasing Frankie was always hard to resist. "It's Lieutenant Commander, as you well know. And I'm still a badass."

She smirked but ignored the chastisement, asking instead, "Hungry?"

"You offering to cook me a meal, Red?"

She rolled her eyes and made a scoffing sound. "In your dreams. I only cook for people I like."

He allowed a smile to tease the corner of his mouth and addressed the issue—or *one* of the issues—between them. "Is that why you told me the other night that you were glad I was home? Because you don't like me? Or is it because I'm a sexy BAB?"

Wild color appeared beneath her creamy skin, making him want to touch it, see if it was as soft and warm as it looked. "Don't be ridiculous," she drawled ironically. "I was drugged out of my mind. Besides, I thought you were someone else."

Nate just chuckled because he knew she was lying; knew she was embarrassed by the momentary vulnerability.

"There's leftovers from dinner," she continued after a hard stare. "Why don't you ditch the wet clothes while I rummage around?"

"Did…did I hear you right?" he demanded, pretending to be shocked. "Did you just tell me to undress?" He waited until she lifted her gaze. "Trying to get me naked by offering to feed me, Francis?"

She rolled her eyes. "You forget I've seen you in swimwear, Nate," she drawled smoothly, and turned away, but he caught the deepening flush that rose up the back of her neck. "Nothing I haven't seen before."

He gave a soft snort and reached for his buttons, reminding himself that the reason he was removing his shirt was because he'd been wearing a wetsuit instead of tactical gear when he'd climbed aboard the unmarked vessel.

Immediately sensing something off, he'd reacted a

split second before gunfire had erupted from the stern. He'd shoved the rookie with him aside but hadn't managed to avoid the bullet himself. Fortunately, it had just grazed him but his fall over the trash can outside had reopened the wound and it had begun bleeding again.

"That was over a decade ago," he said referring to her insult about his body. "Before I joined the SEALs."

"Don't be ridiculous. I saw you—" She went abruptly quiet, as though realizing what she'd been about to admit. "On second thoughts, you're right." She waved her hand, dipping her head to pretend interest in the medical supplies, which meant some red-gold curls slid across her rosy cheek to hide her expression.

Amused by her reaction, he said softly, "Been spying on me, Red?"

She stiffened, high color staining the edge of her cheekbones. He doubted many people got to see Francis Abigail Bryce blush. "Th-that's…that's ridiculous," she spluttered in outrage. "It's not spying if you're strutting around half-naked in public for everyone to see."

"Public?" His eyes narrowed in confusion that quickly cleared when he remembered catching her and Paige—along with half the female population of PSJ—hanging over the boardwalk railing, watching beach training and cheering them on a few weeks ago. "Oh, right." He chuckled. "Beach training."

"And it wasn't you I was looking at, anyway. So don't go getting a big head." She swept a scornful gaze over his wet T, her expression changing to one of horror when she caught sight of the blood staining his shirt. "And, dammit, Nate, I thought you were done being a hero."

"It's my job, Francis. I was a little off my game, that's

all. Besides," he continued impatiently, because the reason he'd been off his game was standing there looking sexy and annoyed. He never used to have problems focusing, but lately he'd been preoccupied. It scared him because if being in the teams had taught him one thing, it was that when a man allowed himself to be distracted people died.

He'd nearly died a week ago because he'd dropped onto that ledge and found not just any rescue worker but the woman he'd promised to protect. But how the heck was he expected to look out for her if she was still wild and reckless?

"It's just a scratch."

After a brief battle of stares, Frankie snapped, "Fine. Then you won't mind if I check it myself."

He silently weighed his options and decided that letting her patch him up was better than a trip to ER.

He sighed and shed his outer shirt. Reaching for the T, he sucked in a sharp breath when he felt Frankie's smooth, warm fingers brush his wet skin.

For a blinding moment he imagined she was undressing him for something entirely different but then his head cleared because her expression was anything but seductive as she grabbed the hem and lifted. He was forced to raise his arms or get whacked on the nose and took over with a warning growl, whipping the shirt over his head while Frankie muttered something about a "shoddy patch-up job."

Annoyed because he'd done it himself, he demanded, "You think you can do better?"

"Of course I can do better," she snapped, sounding offended. "I have several advanced diplomas to say that

I can do better." She carefully pulled away the clumsy bandage and sucked in a sharp breath.

"Omigod!" Her gaze rose to his, stunned and furious. *"That* is no scratch."

CHAPTER EIGHT

NATE SIGHED AND waited in resignation for her to state the obvious. He didn't have to wait for more than a couple of beats.

"You've been *shot*?" Frankie accused, her voice rising. "You've been shot and you didn't tell me?"

"It's no big deal—" he began, only to become distracted by the luxurious length of her lashes and the way they made thick lacy curtains on her cheeks. He was so entranced by them it was a couple of seconds before he noticed that her moss green eyes had turned stormy.

Stormy and sexy and—

"You let me think it was a matter of you being clumsy," she clipped out tersely, totally dispelling the idiotic vision growing inside his head. A vision that was far more dangerous than getting shot by modern-day pirates.

Nate blinked to dispel the sensual web she was weaving around him and sucked in air to clear his head because *what the hell was he thinking*?

"It's no big deal," he growled, lifting a hand to pinch the bridge of his nose. He was more annoyed at himself than at her and was starting to wish he'd never given in to the stupid impulse to come.

Before he could explain, a sleepy Paige appeared in the doorway. "What's going on? I heard voices… Oh," she said, spying him. "Hi, Nate."

Grateful for the interruption, Nate turned his attention to the petite doctor. "Hey, Dr. P. How's it going?"

She took in the sight of him sitting shirtless on the table, and Frankie standing with an alcohol swab in her hand looking like she was contemplating murder.

"Better than you apparently." Her brow wrinkled as she wandered closer, going still when she saw his injury up close. "That's a—" Her eyes widened as what she was seeing dawned on her. Her mouth dropped open and the sleepy look vanished. "You…you've been shot? What happened? Why didn't you go to the ER?"

"See," Frankie said curtly, jabbing a finger at him. "I'm not the only one who knows a gunshot wound when they see one."

He grabbed her hand before she could drill him with a fingernail.

"I didn't go to the ER because it's no big deal," he growled, wondering at the jumble of confusing emotions making him behave like an idiot who didn't know the score. Especially the ones that urged him to pull Frankie close and prove just how okay he was. And maybe have those long-fingered hands slide all over his body.

Stunned by the abrupt need knifing through him, Nate dropped her hand and scrubbed a hand over his face, hoping to scrub away the images in his mind. Maybe he was just tired, because there was no way he was contemplating tangling with Frankie.

No way.

"I've had worse. A lot worse."

His assurances did nothing to appease her. She looked ready to punch him. "Seriously, Nate," she snapped, her eyes going all squinty, "now is *not* the time to remind me how much you like playing hero."

He opened his mouth to deny he'd been a hero but she ignored him, muttering something about heroes being no good to anyone when they're dead, and he knew she was referring to Jack.

"This was just me being clumsy, really," he soothed when she looked ready to snatch his beer bottle away. "I didn't get out of the way in time."

She spun away, eyes shadowed and her mouth pressed in a tight line of unhappiness. "What about next time, genius?"

He sighed and reached out to brush escaped strands of silky curls off her face but she jerked away, looking like she might bite his hand off at the wrist. He suppressed a smile mostly because, despite her insistence that she didn't like heroes, she'd been drawn to saving people too.

Tipping the bottle to his mouth, he taunted softly, "Aw. Worried you'll miss me, Francis?"

She reacted just as he'd predicted. "Don't be an idiot," she snapped, and he suppressed a private little smile that at least some things hadn't changed. But then she sprayed his side with disinfectant and demanded, "Why would I miss you? You're annoying and juvenile and—"

"There won't be a next time," he interrupted, hissing out a pained breath when he realized she'd used Merthiolate to cleanse his side. Probably because—*yowza*—it would sting more than a million fire ants.

With her eyes hot and upset, she demanded, "How can you know that, Nate?"

"Next time I'll be in full tactical gear," he rasped through gritted teeth. "Any stray bullets will do nothing but make a hole in my vest. And maybe if you're lucky, a nice bruise to remind me what an idiot I am."

"If they have any brains they'd aim for your stupid head," she muttered, squeezing a generous amount of antibiotic cream along the shallow furrow and confirming his suspicions that she'd used Merthiolate to punish him.

He caught her hand to get her attention. "Did you hear the words *tactical gear*, Francis?"

"No," she snapped, pulling away and taking the large adhesive bandage Paige handed her. "All I heard was blah, blah, blah… I'm a stupid macho idiot, trying to get myself killed."

"Jack didn't *deliberately* get himself killed, Frankie," he said gently. "It's just a hazard of the job. A hazard we all accept."

"Not me," she rasped. "And you shouldn't either."

Battling frustration, Nate dropped her hand and shoved his fingers through his hair, resisting the urge to pull out chunks because dealing with Francis always made him a little crazy.

"Well, there's a tactical helmet too," he continued as though she hadn't spoken. "It won't stop a point-five slug, but pretty much everything else."

Paige was silent throughout the exchange and when Frankie fell into a fuming silence she asked Nate, "You okay?"

"Never better," he practically snarled.

Amusement tugged at the corners of her sleepy

mouth and her hazel eyes sparkled with amusement. "I can see that." She shifted her attention back to Frankie. "Need any help?"

"I've got this," Frankie said curtly. "You go back to sleep. You're off the clock and there's no need to patch up idiots in your free time."

"You're sure you don't need me…?" She paused a moment and when Frankie shook her head, she nodded and said, "Okay, then," and cleared her throat as though fighting a laugh. She looked around. "Have you seen my car keys?"

Frankie's head came up. "You're leaving?"

"Hmm?" Paige said, looking around absently. "Exhausting day in the ER on top of the baby clinic." She gave a huge yawn that looked suspiciously fake. "I could sleep for a week. Besides, you're a disgustingly early riser and I want to sleep in tomorrow morning."

Before Nate could ask the petite doctor what she was up to, Frankie said, "You don't have to go. Nate is leaving."

"No, I'm not," he contradicted mildly. "You said you'd feed me. Plus, I figured that you owe me for getting injured chasing down bad guys for you."

"It's okay," Paige said on a chuckle, and leaned forward to kiss Nate on the cheek. "Don't go catching any more bullets, big guy, you're clearly not bulletproof." She hugged Frankie, said "I'll see myself out," and disappeared down the passage. There was a short silence before they heard the sound of the front door closing.

Frankie frowned and looked at the wall clock.

He wondered why he hadn't taken the opportunity to escape when it had presented itself. Clearly he wasn't as smart as all his advanced engineering degrees said he was. He silently drank his beer while Frankie applied a couple of Steri-Strips to the cuts on his face.

Sound filtered through from the TV that was still on in the sitting room but otherwise the house was quiet.

And then it hit him.

They were alone…in a dark, empty house in the middle of the night.

Not only were they alone but, despite Frankie's attitude, he had a feeling that she was just as determined to ignore the simmering tension, just waiting for one wrong move from either of them to explode.

"Relax," he said wearily, wondering if he was referring to Paige having headed out on her own or…well, the growing tension between them. "This is Port St. John's. People don't get blown up here, Francis."

"But—"

"Believe me, I've seen bad and this isn't it."

She frowned, clearly not convinced.

Nate studied her beautiful face; close enough that if he wanted to he could turn his head and their lips would touch.

He froze, the beer bottle halfway to his mouth. Where had these dangerous thoughts come from all of a sudden? Because they were the absolute last thing he needed right now, especially as he had enough problems juggling all the other responsibilities in his life. Messing with Frankie would be both stupid *and* dangerous.

She frowned. "You okay?"

Oh, yeah he was great, just great. He'd left the SEALs because he'd lost too many people he cared about. He'd transferred to the US Coast Guard for the same reason—to protect those he loved. His mom, Terri, Ty and Paige, and all their friends and colleagues…and

Frankie. He couldn't do that if he allowed himself to get distracted. Which meant… His jaw clenched. It meant that he needed to stay away.

For her sake as well as his.

"Peachy."

Which also meant that he had to leave now. Because resisting Frankie's grown-up allure was becoming increasingly difficult. Especially as they were alone in a darkened house and he hadn't participated in any recreational activities with a woman in far too long.

Staying was just asking for the kind of trouble he didn't need or want.

Coming to an abrupt decision, Nate placed the half-empty beer bottle on the table and with a palm flat against her belly he nudged her back a couple of paces, slid off the table and reached for his wet shirts.

He caught her baffled frown out of the corner of his eye. "Where are you going? I haven't finished. Besides, I thought you were hungry."

He studied her face silently before turning to head for the front door as fast as he could. "Oh, I am, princess," he tossed over his shoulder. "But not for food."

After a short stunned silence, she demanded behind him, "What's that supposed to mean?"

With frustration beating at him, he drawled roughly, "It means that if I stay I'll take you up on more than your offer of free medical care and leftovers."

He heard her sharply indrawn breath and turned in time to catch the odd look that flashed across her face before a shutter came down, hiding her thoughts from him. Instead, amused challenge replaced the soft, uncertain—very un-Frankie-like—expression.

"Oh, please," she scoffed, folding her arms beneath

her breasts and cocking one hip to the side. "The big badass Navy SEAL can't *handle* anything more than leftovers. Not that I'm offering," she said pointedly. "Especially not to you. Not again. Not ever."

Ignoring her reference to her eighteenth birthday, he drawled mockingly, "I don't accept *anyone*'s leftovers, princess. I'm an all-or-nothing kind of guy."

But right now none of that mattered because her pose reminded him that barely five days ago he'd seen her naked. Naked and lush and every man's fantasy. Something that had tormented him because he knew he wouldn't get another chance.

Shouldn't get another chance if he intended to keep his promise to his friend. He needed to keep his mind on his job. People depended on him to keep them safe. Not just his mother and sister—but his men too.

Then she challenged his masculinity with a taunted "You couldn't handle it anyway, Nate." And something snapped inside his head.

Knowing he was making a mistake and suddenly not caring—because, God knew, she drove him completely insane—he retraced his steps, stalking her like a leopard stalked its unwary prey.

Something in his expression had her backing up a step and putting out her hand like a traffic cop. Dark amusement joined the frustration because she actually thought that would stop him.

She was right to be wary, because something dark and tumultuous was driving him.

"Are you sure about that, princess?" he drawled softly, advancing slowly, forcing her to retreat another step. "You're not the only one who's changed. How do you even know what I can handle anymore?"

When she realized he'd all but boxed her in between the wall and the coat rack, she growled, her eyes narrowing a warning that he ignored. To her credit she didn't try to escape, instead letting him advance until his chest bumped against her outstretched palm.

"Nate," she said, tilting her head to stare at him as though he'd grown three heads. "What are you doing?"

Yeah, Nate. What are *you doing?*

Ignoring her and the voice in his head, Nate stepped in, pushing her against the wall, forcing her hand to flatten against his chest. And as he stared into the darkening depths of her moss green eyes, the heat of her palm seeped into his flesh and spread warmth and warning across his skin.

He welcomed the warmth…ignored the warning.

"I'm showing how much you don't know about me, babe."

Her back snapped straight and she thrust out her chin.

"Oh, please," she scoffed. "You're a man. You couldn't handle me as a child. What makes you think you can handle me now, Commander Big Shot?"

Fire began to race across his skin. Against his better judgment he found that he loved that about her—that damn-your-eyes challenge. His muscles tightened and bunched and the skin across his scalp prickled. But Nate was accustomed to ignoring distractions and focusing on his mission. Mostly.

Right now his mission was to warn her off—*hell*, warn himself off.

"Someday, princess," he murmured, reaching up to brush his knuckles along the clean line of her jaw, "someone might take that challenge seriously."

She gasped in outrage, her eyes flashing with a defiance that lit a slow-burning fuse to his long-buried need.

"Oh, yeah?" she rasped, giving him a not-so-gentle shove. "And I suppose you think *you're* the man to do it?"

A rough laugh escaped him, his gaze drifting from her defiant green eyes to her soft mouth. "I'm not *that* crazy, princess. You think you're tough enough to take me on, but you aren't. Nowhere near."

Shoving him with both hands this time, she growled, "And *you* are, Commander I-Think-I'm-So-Tough?"

His heart rate doubled and his skin prickled a primitive warning that he ignored because he suddenly knew why he'd come tonight. He wanted—no, *needed*—this…this wild flood of reckless exhilaration. Something he hadn't experienced in too long.

"I'm plenty tough, Red." He leaned forward to growl in her ear. "Now…" his mouth brushed against her neck and he felt her go still, her breath hitching in her throat as though she couldn't believe his audacity. His mouth curved against her soft skin "…let's see just how tough *you* are."

The tension thickened and Nate swore he could see sparks zipping through the air between them. He opened his mouth on her delicate skin and a voice in the back of his mind yelled, *Pull back, pull back.*

But then Frankie's nails dug furrows in the skin of his chest and the warning abruptly faded. Drawing back, his gaze locked on her mouth a couple of inches beneath his, the curves soft, plump, moist…*inviting*. Then her breath quickened in the heated silence and with a muttered curse Nate caught her mouth in a punishing kiss. Although who he'd intended to punish wasn't so clear,

especially when the taste of her filled his mouth and—
oh, yeah—sent his senses reeling.

She gasped as though he'd caught her by surprise.
Hell, he'd surprised himself too, so sure that he could
taunt her and then leave, unscathed.

He still could, he assured himself. He'd kiss her
breathless and rid himself of this overwhelming need
crushing his resistance, making him forget long-held
promises. And because he felt driven by something buried too deep to analyze, he wanted to teach her that
messing with him came with consequences.

Consequences he suddenly couldn't recall, but was
all too willing to face…later.

Much later.

Once he'd had his fill.

Thrusting his hands in her hair to hold her so he
could wage a sensual war on her soft, pliable mouth,
Nate promised himself that he would leave soon. After
another few tastes…another few deep drugging kisses…
then he would leave. Just as he had last time. Besides,
he was the master of control, the master of his own des-
tiny. And he'd prove it.

In another minute.

Frankie gave a shocked, furious gasp and managed
to shove him back a couple of inches, her gaze fiery and
defiant. But as their ragged breathing filled the quiet
hallway, her warmth seeped into his skin, setting off
a chain reaction that could have only one conclusion.

Frankie's entire system jolted as his kiss had her gasping in outrage and a wild excitement that had her pulse
trebling and her senses scattering like autumn leaves.

Hot prickles flashed across her skin as Nate captured

her hands and pinned them to the wall next to her head, and she had no idea what it said about her that she was a second away from orgasm.

"Get *off* me...you big...*oaf*," she snarled breathlessly, horrified that her limbs had turned to cooked noodles and that her belly was clenching with alarm and anticipation.

Anticipation?

No way. There was no way she was anticipating tangling with Nate, physically or verbally.

But deep down she knew—*oh, boy, did she know*—that she was lying. Every strand of DNA rejoiced that she was once again up close and personal with all that hard flesh and satin-warm skin.

CHAPTER NINE

WITH NATE PLASTERED to her and her hands trapped, there was only one thing left for Frankie to do.

Turning her head, she sank her teeth into his naked shoulder and bit down. Hard. If she'd expected him to curse and pull back, she was a little surprised when he just laughed, a deep thrilling sound that sent tingles scattering across her skin, liquefying her bones and laying siege to her resistance.

His hard thigh flexed between hers, blasting heat deep in her belly. Muscles clenching against the shockingly intense sensations, Frankie knew she needed to do something before he swept away all her resistance.

Drugged by the taste of him in her mouth, she bit him harder. Nate simply flexed his shoulder and taunted softly, "Like what you taste, Red?" in her ear. And even if his breathing was as ragged as hers, it was Frankie who shuddered because he was right. She did like what she tasted. In fact, she was hungry for more.

"Because, let me tell you," he breathed and gently closed his teeth on the skin between her neck and shoulder, searing a line of fire across her flesh that landed with a jolt in her liquid center, "I sure like the taste of *you*."

A shaft of panic sliced through the ratcheting excitement. *If he doesn't leave soon*, she thought, *there's no telling what I'll do*. Not with the equal mix of fury, pleasure and anticipation pouring through her.

"Y-you…y-you…" *Really? Now you're stammering?* Sucking in a ragged breath, Frankie steadied herself, determined not to let him know how he affected her. "I know you, Nate," she rasped defensively. "You're only doing this to punish me for daring to challenge your fragile male ego."

He stilled and for an instant she thought her words had done what her struggles could not—send him out the door. But then he lifted those sexy dark-gold eyes, glowing with a wild recklessness that was terrifyingly exhilarating.

Kind of like free-falling out an airplane at fifty thousand feet.

"Is that what you think, babe?" he murmured, dipping his head to swipe his tongue across her bottom lip. "Just goes to show that you don't know me at all."

A sob of need caught in her throat but the last thing she wanted or needed was to be vulnerable to him. Frankie didn't do vulnerable. For any man. Especially a man who'd already crushed her tender heart.

"I don't want you," she snarled, twisting her head to evade his tormenting mouth. *Why the heck did he have to be so darn…irresistible?*

"Little liar," he breathed on a soft chuckle. "You want me. You want me bad."

"Why you arrogant, self-important—" she spluttered, only to have her words cut off when he opened his mouth over hers in a kiss that just about knocked her socks right off her feet. It started out as a hard, demanding kiss that quickly escalated into a hot mating of mouths that sucked the breath out of her lungs.

With a low helpless moan, she strained closer.

Nate tightened his grip on her and sucked her bottom lip into his mouth, knowing just how to render her a helpless, quivering blob of sensual need.

"Nate," she gasped, feeling her knees buckle, feeling the hot ache in her core build until it was all she could do to keep from moving against the hard thigh between hers, against the growing evidence of his arousal. "*Nate*…s-stop."

No, don't stop. Don't ever stop… Because he was big and thick and hard against her. And getting bigger and thicker and harder by the second and…and she hadn't felt this good in a long time.

"Stop?" he teased softly, clearly preoccupied with tasting her skin, helping himself to her mouth; because instead of stopping he hummed in the back of his throat and moved to another spot. "You sure that's what you want, babe?"

Of course she wasn't sure. Only that it would be smart because after Jack's death Frankie had promised to make smarter choices with her life. Choices that didn't include being vulnerable. To anyone.

Then Nate's thigh flexed, dragging a ragged whimper from her throat.

"See," he murmured softly, his mouth tormenting hers. "It's too late for that, Red. Way…too…late."

And then he released her wrists, sliding his big hands down her arms, her sides, to grasp and lift when he reached her bottom, forcing her to wrap her legs around him. Then he settled, big and hot and hard right where she ached, and she was about a second away from orgasm even though they hadn't even reached the good part yet.

Nate tightened his grip and took the kiss deeper… deeper, hotter and bolder than any she'd ever experienced. And before she knew it, Frankie was moving against him, making embarrassingly hungry sounds that might have mortified her if he hadn't growled a response that was as hungry as hers.

She'd forgotten what it was like to be kissed with such savage hunger. Okay, so maybe she'd *never* been kissed with such single-minded intensity—as though he wanted to consume her. Or maybe make her forget every other kiss she'd ever received.

It was working because she couldn't even recall her own name, let alone anything else. When he finally broke the kiss and pulled back, his breathing was as ragged as hers.

"Francis…" he breathed.

And she thought, *Oh, yeah, that's it. That's my name.* But then she became aware of his heart, pounding against hers with the same jagged rhythm.

"No talking," she ordered, fisting his hair and pulling his mouth back to hers.

His lips curved. "Francis…"

"I said no talking," she growled irritably. Because if she let him talk, he might change his mind…and she might remember what a bad idea it was to let Nathan Oliver into her life again.

He chuckled at the same moment he rocked his hips into hers, drawing a low moan from her throat.

Nate gave a laugh and backed away from the wall. He took a few steps toward the stairs then stopped. One hand slid up her back to fist her messy topknot. He pulled her back a couple of inches and growled, "This *is* what you want?"

She blinked at the question. Was he kidding? Of course this was what she wanted. Couldn't he feel how much she wanted him? *She* could certainly feel how much he wanted *her*.

"Frankie."

She didn't know why her nickname on his lips did something to her but she stopped trying to get at his mouth. One look into his searching, solemn gaze had her hands sliding up to cup his strong jaw. "Yes," she said with a certainty that couldn't be misunderstood.

His unreadable gaze remained on hers for a long moment before going as hot as the sinfully badass smile curving his mouth. "All right, then," he murmured, and bounded up the stairs as though he wasn't carrying a woman taller than most men. It both shocked and excited her, eliciting a gasping laugh as she tightened her thighs, only to instantly loosen them again when she recalled that just a half hour ago she'd treated his bullet wound.

"Your side," she managed to croak.

Only to be interrupted by his grunted "Is fine," as he tightened his arms, pressing a most impressive erection against her. The jolt of electricity had her eyes crossing and her back arching.

She managed a stuttered, "B-but—" before closing her teeth on his shoulder again when she realized to her horror that she sounded all breathless and desperate.

His growled response filled her darkened bedroom as he headed unerringly for her bed—as though he could see in the dark. Probably could, she thought, giving a startled yelp when she flew through the air to land in a graceless tangle of limbs and pillows in the middle of it.

She lay blinking up at him, a large, dangerous presence in the dark room. And although she knew he'd never hurt her, a quiver of unease moved through her. Partly because there was always the fear that he'd leave her in a state of raging hormonal discomfort—as he had the night he'd kissed her senseless on her doorstep then sauntered off to his stupid truck—but mostly because when it came to Nate Oliver, she'd always been vulnerable.

He moved, but instead of leaving he leaned forward. Soft light spilled across the bed and just like that all Frankie's girlish insecurities returned. She was once again that skinny, freckled girl wishing she was like the beach babes Nate gravitated toward and hating herself for wanting to be one of a crowd.

Maybe she wasn't that girl, hadn't been that girl for a good long while, but she still found herself looking down at the less-than-attractive picture she made in her ratty oversize T-shirt and thick socks. How pathetic was that?

She felt the skin across her forehead tighten. She hadn't meant for this to happen, and she was fairly certain neither had he, but maybe—

"Francis…condom?"

For one panicked moment she couldn't remember the last time she'd even needed one—*even more pathetic*—before another thought occurred—this one much more satisfying. "You don't carry condoms?" His gaze narrowed. "I thought SEALs always came prepared?"

He made a rough sound of impatience and shoved shaking—*yeah, they were shaking*—fingers through his hair, but even in the low light Frankie could detect the faint redness creep up his neck.

"Top drawer," she snickered, and watched as he yanked open the drawer with barely leashed violence. He didn't comment on the fact that the box was un-opened and she snatched it from him to tear impatiently at the packaging.

It abruptly gave way, scattering condoms over the bed and across the floor.

Nate gave a low laugh as he snatched up a small foil square. "Impatient much, babe?" he rasped, and tossed it to her.

"Lose the pants, Oliver," she ordered, and when he didn't react fast enough, she reached out impatiently. The next few moments were a flurry of hands until Frankie became distracted by his eight pack, by the cut muscles on the sides of his hips and the way his skin felt beneath her fingers—all hot and taut and smooth.

She gently ran a fingernail around the startling white dressing over his wound, her mouth curving with de-light as goose bumps broke out across his skin.

Nate cursed, a sound pain-filled and impatient. It had her hands stilling and her hungry gaze rising, past his defined abs and pecs, his shoulders, up his strong tanned throat and hard jaw to his dark, burning gaze.

It promised a universe of sensual punishment.

Frankie gulped. "Does it hurt?"

"Don't feel a thing." His mouth curved in a wicked smile. "Well, not there, anyway."

Rolling her eyes, she leaned forward and swiped her tongue across the taut skin south of his abs, delighting in his sharply indrawn breath and the fine tremor in the fingers that gripped her shoulders.

She gave in to the urge to nip his belly too, laughing at Nate's ragged curse. The next instant he shoved her back onto the bed and pushed his pants and boxer briefs to his feet. His erection sprang free, big and thick and hard, but Frankie had only a couple of seconds to admire it before he was joining her on the bed.

"You're overdressed," he growled, pushing her flat and sliding his big palms up her thighs to the curve of her bottom. She tried to sit up, get her mouth and hands on him, but Nate made a sound of impatience and pressed her flat.

Capturing her wrists, he lifted them over her head, ratcheting her excitement up a couple dozen notches.

"Dammit, Nate," she grunted breathlessly. "I want to—"

"Shh," he murmured, pinning her with one heavily muscled leg and silencing her protests with his hot mouth.

The kiss—a lush, deep mating of mouths—made her forget her need to control things and she found herself kissing him back like a starving person.

Gradually the hot demand of his mouth softened until his lips were sliding against hers in soothing, gentle swipes. He finally lifted his head and after a long heated moment breathed hoarsely, "God… Frankie, look at you." His breath escaped in an explosive rush, as though he was struggling to contain his emotions.

A confused frown drew her brows together when she caught him staring at her with an expression she'd never seen before.

"Wh-what?" There was that stupid adolescent uncertainty again.

"You're beautiful," he murmured, kind of distracted

but with more than a hint of annoyed wonder. "So beautiful...you take my breath away."

"I thought—" She broke off to swallow past the emotion clawing at her throat. "I thought you didn't like redheads?"

The question momentarily distracted him from examining the shoulder he'd managed to reveal in the wide neckline of her T-shirt. He shook his head.

"I never said that."

"You did. I was seven and you said red hair was the sign of the devil."

He had the audacity to laugh at her disgruntled tone. "I was twelve," he said, as though that explained everything. "Besides, you'd probably done something annoying or reckless."

Okay, so maybe Frankie had made it her mission in life to annoy Nate, Jack and Ty because it had been the only time they'd paid any attention to her.

"And now?" she said softly.

His mouth curved into a sinful smile that would have melted her bones if she hadn't already been lying flat on her back in a puddle of lust.

He slid his hand up under her shirt and cupped her breast. "Can't you feel how annoyed I am?"

The sensation of his warm hand cupping her aching flesh had a moan sliding right up her throat. It also had her nipple tightening into a painful bud and she bit her lip.

Nate hummed with pleasure and shoved up her top to watch his thumb brushing the pebbled peak. Both the look on his face and the feel of rough skin on hers had waves of pleasure and impatience rolling through her. Before she could ask if he intended to take his sweet

time, he growled, "Look at you…all grown up and finally mi—" He broke off abruptly and rose to his knees,
his rough hungry growl kind of thrilling.

"I wish you could see yourself," he said hoarsely,
making her belly jump because she'd caught sight of
something in his eyes, something she didn't normally
see when Nate looked at her—desire…raw and naked
and hot.

Her breath whooshed out. If she didn't have him in
the next five minutes she would explode—all by herself.

Planting her socked foot against his chest, she purred,
"Need any help, Commander Big Shot?" and gave a not-
so-gentle shove. Nate slid off her sock in one impatient
move, his smile sending her temperature soaring, then
the other. He stilled when he caught sight of her bandages and he kissed her feet with a gentleness that had
her throat tightening.

Nate's eyes glittered as he let his gaze slide up the inside of her leg, pause and then take in her naked breasts
and the flush of arousal making her skin glow. She shivered when he dropped a gentle kiss on her hip bone.
Then, cupping her bottom, he leaned forward and kissed
the tip of one breast as he whipped off her shorts. Finally, he leaned over her, hands planted either side of
her head.

Frankie should have felt a little threatened by his
size—by the latent power in the big body caging hers.
The truth was she wanted him closer. Much…much…
closer.

She slid her hands up his arms, ropey and tough with
muscle, and curved them over his shoulders, her fingers soothing the teeth marks clearly visible beneath
the satin-smooth tanned skin. Then she not-so-gently

scored her nails down over his pecs, unable to prevent a tiny smile of triumph at his sharp inhalation.

"I've heard that SEALs are all talk and no action," she taunted softly, but Nate just chuckled as though no one would believe such a claim. A little annoyed by his arrogance—and, she had to admit, more than a little excited—Frankie shoved at his shoulders.

"All right, Commander Big Shot. Why don't you put your money where your big mouth is?" Her lips curved in a challenging smile. "Words are meaningless if you can't back them up with action."

One moment his breath escaped on a laugh, the next he'd made himself at home…right between her thighs.

Bending her knees, Frankie felt her eyes cross as the long, hard length of him slid against the tiny bundle of nerves right at her damp center. She caught her breath and bit down on her lip to prevent a moan from escaping.

"Fine by me, babe." He grinned, knowing—*the jerk*—exactly what he was doing to her. She must have been doing something to him too because he drew in air before dropping a quick kiss on her mouth. Then he rolled his hips and through the explosion inside her skull she thought she heard him murmur, "But I warn you… SEALs take no prisoners."

And then Frankie got lost somewhere between having her mouth possessed and her breasts ravished. She moaned through the torture of his lips sliding slowly down to her belly button, whimpered when he nibbled at the insides of her thighs, and gasped—her fingers clutching the sheets—when he took her in his mouth.

She came embarrassingly fast and then came a second time, almost as quickly and only just a little less violently. Flushed and panting, and eager for the feel of him inside her, she reached out to wrap her hand around him, but he growled. "Keep that up," he rasped hoarsely. "And it'll be all over."

With impatience he ripped the condom package with his teeth and fitted the latex to the bulging tip of his shaft with shaking hands.

She tried to help but he caught her hands and slid his fingers through hers. Then he crushed her mouth in a kiss that meant to consume…and thrust deep.

Surprise had Frankie jolting, her inner muscles tightening at the sudden invasion. Muttering a low curse, Nate stilled, his body hard and tense as though he was exercising enormous control. Through clenched teeth he bit out, "Francis? *You* okay?"

Shifting to relieve the slight discomfort—*he was a big guy*—Frankie bit her lip to keep from wincing. "It's…it's been a long time," she managed weakly.

He was silent a long moment before huffing out a low laugh. "Yeah. Me too… But don't worry," he promised softly, thrusting home when he felt her inner muscles relax to accommodate his size, "I think I can remember what to do next."

And then he proceeded to show her that he did indeed know what to do. In fact, when she came with him buried deep inside her body, it was so spectacular that she lost herself there for a moment…or five.

And she might even have heard herself cry out.

Maybe.

And when he crushed her close and followed her over, his breath escaping in a long low groan of completion, Frankie thought very briefly that this…this was what she'd been waiting for her entire life. But then her

thoughts slid away and all she could do was feel the heat
and strength that surrounded her.

Seconds, minutes or hours later, Nate finally stirred.
Realizing that she was wrapped around him like cling
wrap, Frankie loosened her grip and took her first
breath.

Wow…but that had been…*wow*. Words seemed inadequate to describe what had just happened and she
needed a moment to gather herself because it had im-
pacted her far more emotionally than a simple physical
release was supposed to.

He'd touched something deep inside that was beginning to unfurl—and it scared her.

The trick here is to distance yourself, she lectured
silently. *Hide your emotions…before he sees how much
it meant to you.*

Fortunately, Frankie had had plenty of experience
with that. Opening her eyes, she was a little unnerved to
find him closer than was comfortable, studying her with
an expression that had her belly instantly clenching.

The breath she'd just taken whooshed out. "Um,
sorry." Even before the words were out, her brow tightened. *What the heck was she apologizing for?*

Annoyed, more with herself than him, she shoved
at him and sat up when he finally rolled aside. Turning
away, she pushed her hair off her face and noticed that
her hands were shaking. "I guess…" She hid a grimace
and casually reached for the sheet, suddenly feeling
more vulnerable and exposed than she liked to admit.
"I guess I got a little carried away."

Sprawled beside her and looking like he'd conquered

the world—or maybe just hers—Nate folded his hands beneath his head, his mouth curving in a sensual smile as he continued to study her.

"I liked it."

"You…um, did?" she asked, before she could censor herself. Since when did she get all girly and insecure after a bout of hot, spectacular sex?

Nate gave a rough laugh and sat up, thrusting his fingers through his tousled hair. Hair she remembered clutching as her world spun completely out of control. He dropped a quick kiss on her exposed shoulder and rose. "Give me a couple of minutes," he growled in a sex-rough voice that had her inner muscles clenching. "And I'll prove exactly how much."

Struggling for nonchalance she was far from feeling, she picked at a loose thread, looking anywhere but at the sight of him disappearing into the bathroom.

Okay, so she totally watched his hard buns flex as he moved across the floor. Partly because he had a world-class ass…all high and tight with those little dents on the side, but mostly because she'd half expected him to dress and leave.

"Are you sure you can do that again, Nate?" she asked, sounding skeptical. There was a moment of silence before he reached out to curl one large tanned hand around the door frame. He slowly turned his head and Frankie could see by his stunned expression that no one had ever thought to question his stamina before.

"I mean, you're, what, thirty-five?"

For a long moment Nate studied her with an unreadable expression before he turned and disappeared into the bathroom.

Stifling a giggle, Frankie rolled onto her back and allowed her eyes to drift closed. She could practically feel the waves of outraged masculinity coming from the bathroom.

There was absolute silence for a couple of beats then the air changed subtly and she opened her eyes to see a spectacularly naked Nate standing beside the bed, staring down at her with hungry heat and a wicked smile.

Trying for confidence she was far from feeling, Frankie let her gaze wander down his impressively sculpted chest and abdomen to another impressive feature.

"You were saying?" he taunted softly, looking so pleased with himself that Frankie pretended to yawn. "Big deal," she murmured, closing her eyes. "Talk is cheap."

In the next instant she was flipped over onto her belly as though she weighed nothing more than a pancake. She gave a startled yelp and before she could laugh or demand to know what he thought he was doing, Nate had given her backside a smart slap and hauled her up onto her knees before him.

"Never let it be said," he murmured softly before giving her shoulder a punishing nip, "that a SEAL couldn't rise to the challenge."

Despite the stars exploding behind her eyes and the excitement gathering in the pit of her belly, Frankie laughed. "Actions," she teased again breathlessly, "speak louder than words."

His deep chuckle vibrated in his chest, sending tingles erupting across her sensitized flesh, and when he moved his lips from her shoulder to her ear, a shudder of excitement began as a deep humming in her core.

"It's a good thing, then," he murmured in a voice that made her body melt and her mind slip away, "that I'm a man of action, isn't it?"

CHAPTER TEN

JUST BEFORE DAWN, Nate carefully rose from the bed and scooped his pants off the floor as he headed for the door. His intention was to leave before Frankie, sprawled facedown across the bed in careless naked splendor, awakened, but it took all his SEAL discipline not to slide back against that warm, curvy body for another bout of spectacular sex.

And it had been spectacular. In fact, he couldn't ever remember sex being that good, but she needed her sleep and he needed a change of clothes as well as a shower before he headed off to work.

But it wasn't just work that drove him from her room without a backward glance. It was a desperate need to get away before she wormed her way any deeper under his skin.

Oh, yeah. And then there was the promise he'd made to his best friend. He wasn't sure "looking out for her" meant doing it up close and personal. During the past six hours, he'd conveniently forgotten that and hated what that said about him—that it was possible he was more like his father than he cared to admit.

Ignoring the pain in his side, Nate paused on the landing to pull on his still-damp uniform pants over his bed-warmed flesh. If the worst he suffered was a cold, wet ass, then he'd got off lightly because he'd spent the last thirty-five years trying to distance himself from his father's legacy and had no intention of starting to act like the man now. He'd taken advantage of someone he'd known his whole life, someone who trusted him, someone who'd been like a sister.

And he couldn't take it back.

That she'd taken advantage of him too—spectacularly—was beside the point. She didn't know about The Promise and she didn't know how much keeping that promise meant to him. Besides, he had enough responsibility in his life and should have known that coming here was a bad idea. But the sight of her standing on her front porch, looking like an Amazon princess on a war raid had floored him. He'd kind of lost his mind, ignored the little voice in his head warning him that he would only find trouble here.

The kind of trouble he was facing now. The kind a man found himself in when he discovered that his wild night had been more than just sex. More than a release of tension. What that more was exactly wasn't quite clear. What was clear, however, was the need for space.

But even as Nate scooped his damp bloodstained shirts off the entrance floor and quietly let himself out of the house, he knew he running. From the past few hours and from the fact that what he felt for Frankie might be more than he'd bargained for.

From the darkened window, Frankie watched a shirtless Nate pause and look up over his shoulder. And though there was no way he could see her, she froze, holding her breath, the hand clutching the sheet between her breasts tightening until her knuckles ached.

Light from the streetlamp poured over his tall, muscled frame, gilding half his body and face while leaving the other in total darkness. Even from this distance she could tell his expression was all hard lines and angular planes, unsoftened by any hint of a smile—by any hint of emotion—his posture all but screaming a remoteness, a distance she wished she could breach.

For some reason he wasn't ever going to let her in. The realization left a pinch in the region of her heart and Frankie spun away to sink back against the wall. Squeezing her eyes shut, she told herself that she wouldn't watch him leave. Not again.

Yet her ears strained for the sound of his truck and when it eventually came, the well-tuned purr competed with the rush of blood in her ears.

After it faded, she let out the breath she was still holding and pushed away from the wall. She absolutely did not care that he'd sneaked out without a *Thanks* or a *See ya around* as though she meant nothing to him but a couple of orgasms.

But that was fine, she told herself fiercely. At least he'd saved her from having to throw him out because she was done with him too. He'd given her exactly what she'd needed and had left before he could annoy her with his big body and bossy attitude. Great. Good. She hated sharing her space almost as much as she hated bossy alpha males.

Ignoring the little voice in the back of her mind calling her a liar, Frankie firmed her jaw and headed back to the bed, determined to get a couple more hours' sleep even if it killed her. But when she approached the rumpled covers and spotted the foil packets scattered across the floor, the thought of sliding back between sheets that smelled of him was suddenly more than she could face.

Because what had been an impulse brought on by heightened emotions had become so much more.

With a growl that sounded suspiciously like a sob she dropped the sheet she was still clutching like a lifeline and reached for a clean oversize T-shirt.

Emotions locked firmly away, she pulled it over her still-tingling flesh and stripped the bed, ripping everything off before stomping downstairs to dump the whole lot in the washing machine.

She added washing powder, set the program to sterilization and then headed upstairs to sterilize her body and scrub away the memory of the past five hours.

It was still dark when she left the house and set off on foot, her wallet and car keys tucked into her pockets as she headed for the hospital five miles away where her car was still parked.

She needed to do something or else she would go insane, and after being cooped up the past week she had a desperate need to head up the coast—to get out of Port St. John's.

She knew—from experience—that she couldn't outrun herself. But, hey, she would give it a darn good try.

It felt good to be in the crisp predawn air and Frankie sucked in deep lungs full of cool air redolent with salt and hints of the dark nearby forests. Walking at a fast clip, she ignored her still tender feet and willed her mind blank because that was the only way she was going to handle this.

Yet even the full force of her will couldn't lock away images of the past few hours. Images of Nate's hot gaze holding hers as he drove her out of her mind with pleasure. Of the rough scrape of his jaw against her sensitized flesh…of the heavy weight of his body as he uttered a long low moan and collapsed over her, breathing roughly, heart thundering, muscles twitching in the aftermath.

You got me into this mess, she told her body furiously when her good parts tingled and melted. *You should have let me kick his ass instead of exploring all those yummy muscles with my hands and mouth before licking him from head to toe.*

Arrrgh. Pressing her fist against the pressure in her chest, Frankie told herself she didn't need all the conflicting signals he constantly sent out and she certainly didn't need his bossy, annoying attitude. She didn't *need* anyone. Least of all a man who'd ignored her for the past twelve years, pretended she didn't exist the months he'd been home, and then stormed back into her life, thinking he could order her around.

Nope, she didn't need him.

Want, however, was something else entirely. Something her body was all too eager to remind her of. And her mind…well, it seemed just as rebellious as her stupid body.

Fine. She wanted him. Big deal. He was pretty to look at and he had some awesome skills in the bedroom. But it was over now and she—and her body— could just get over themselves. They'd had him and once had been enough.

More than enough.

But even as she thought it, a growing feeling of misery lodged like a hot ball of lead in her chest. As for her heart, well, its job was to pump blood around her body and that was all. It had no business yearning for things that would never be. *She* would never be the kind of woman Nate wanted.

A few days after the biggest mistake of his adult life, Nate caught sight of Frankie walking out of the ER ambulance bay looking like a warrior goddess in the dark blue EMT jumpsuit. She'd immediately caught his attention—along with that of just about every other guy in the car park, including the rookies he was escorting to get their routine shots because their medic hadn't yet been replaced after his unexpected heart attack.

With her head thrown back as she laughed at something the young guy she was with said, she looked more carefree than he'd ever seen, but it was the overly familiar body language of the other man that roused some very dark, very alien emotions in Nate's gut. Especially as Frankie seemed to be enjoying the closeness—a little too much for a woman who just a few days ago had been all over *him* like he was the frosting on a huge piece of chocolate cake and she was ravenous.

His mind instantly conjured up images of Frankie and the guy that had his teeth practically cracking under the strain of his clenched jaw. Oblivious to the tension humming through his body, the rookies had completely embarrassed themselves and the uniform by letting out a couple of wolf whistles.

Frankie had instantly turned her head and her eyes had locked with his for a couple of beats—no smile of recognition in their leafy-green depths. But even as he'd felt his heart rate speed up and his mouth begin to curl into an involuntary smile, she'd turned and walked away; without acknowledging him in any way other than that one brief unreadable glance. Without a sign that just a few nights ago he'd rocked her world.

Without even a *Hey, keep your pets in check* quip he'd half expected.

And as he watched her slender back and swaying hips disappear, he was tempted to follow and punch the guy before grabbing her and pushing her up against the nearest wall. He wanted to kiss her—remind her of the other night—until her eyes went soft with arousal and she made that little hitching noise in her throat that drove him wild.

The fact that he'd been at the hospital in his official capacity and that he was back on his promise wagon stopped him. Oh, yeah, and the fact that she'd think he'd lost his mind and have him committed.

And even if he'd felt as though he had, Nate Oliver was an ex-Navy SEAL. SEALs completed their mission—no matter what.

And his mission: to honor a promise to a dead man.

But although Nate had tried, going back to the way things had been was more difficult than he'd anticipated. He might have washed her scent from his skin but no amount of scrubbing could rid him of the feeling that he'd messed up. Watching her climax had been the hottest, most erotic experience of his life, and if he'd wondered why it had happened with Frankie of all people, he was going to ignore it because dealing with her had always been like negotiating a minefield. One misstep and everything could blow up in his face.

In one thing she *was* predictable, though, he mused wryly. She was *un*predictable, and in the days that followed he found himself tensing every time his phone rang or chimed an incoming message. But Frankie never

called or texted. In fact, she seemed completely un-
fazed by something that had rocked him to his emotional foundation: that their night had been more than
a quick release after months of abstinence.

He'd heard that she'd been partying it up at the Seafarers and what he experienced could only be described
as jealousy. It was an emotion he'd *never* once felt when
it came to women. And he didn't like it.

Not one little bit.

CHAPTER ELEVEN

IT WAS TOWARD the end of the following week that Nate admitted he was in serious trouble. First he zoned out during a meeting and then he nearly passed out on a routine swimming exercise, drawing a concerned reprimand from the base commander and orders to get himself checked out.

Since the base medic had still not been replaced, Nate was ordered to go to the ER for a checkup. He didn't need a doctor to tell him that his wound was infected but since it would only be fixed by a course of antibiotics and expert wound care, he simply nodded and left the base. No way would he make the mistake of going to Frankie, though. Not after what had happened the last time.

Sighing, he drove to the hospital, hoping he wouldn't see the redhead currently making his life a living hell.

Prepared for a long wait, he was surprised to find the ER relatively quiet as he headed for the admissions counter. The nurse who'd been on duty the night of the fire looked up as he approached.

She straightened her navy shirt and batted her eyelashes in such a blatant attempt at flirting that Nate smiled, despite the pain and fever racking his body.

"Here to let me make your dreams come true, sailor?" she asked boldly.

He managed a chuckle and a pointed glance at her wedding band before rasping, "Since you're already married, my dreams will have to remain unfulfilled."

"Your loss." She laughed. "So, what can I help you with, handsome?"

Nate seriously thought about leaving, but reluctantly admitted, "I need to see a doctor."

Her gaze sharpened and she must have seen something in his face because she instantly came round the counter to take his arm. "Let's get you into one of the bays and I'll find you one."

Unwilling to admit just how wobbly he felt, Nate shook his head and locked his knees. "I'll wait here."

After a long searching look, the nurse disappeared, leaving Nate to lean against the counter as a wave of prickly heat and dizziness washed over him. The next thing he knew someone was calling his name and shaking his arm.

"Nate? Nate, what's wrong? Can you hear me?"

He cracked open his eyes and Paige's concerned face swam into view. "Nate, are you sick?"

Embarrassed by the display of weakness, he quickly straightened and scrubbed a hand over his face, hoping to clear his head. One minute he was hot and feverish, the next racked with sweaty chills. He'd felt this way only once before in his life, when he'd been in the field, nursing a gunshot wound.

Abruptly aware of their curious audience, Nate lowered his voice. "Can we have some privacy, Doc?" he rasped. "I need...um..." Swaying, he sucked in air and admitted quickly, "I need medical assistance."

Paige's eyes widened and quickly flashed over him, probably expecting to see blood. Seeing none, she grabbed his hand and steered him toward the swing doors. "Nancy, which bay is clean?" she called out, practically dragging him along like she was afraid he'd bolt.

Another nurse popped her head out a doorway and straightened when she saw Nate. "Bay Seven is clear. Dr. Reyes is on his way."

"All right. It's okay, Nate, we've got you," she said, shoving Nate ahead of her into the unoccupied bay. As she drew the curtains she demanded, "It's the gunshot wound, isn't it?"

Frankie pulled the ambulance up to the emergency entrance and shoved the vehicle into park before hopping out and hurrying to the rear. Her partner, Dale Franklin, was ready with the collapsible gurney, jumping down the instant she opened the doors.

Grabbing the ventilation bag with one hand and using the other to assist with the dismount, she quickly checked the mobile heart monitor, cursing when she realized their patient was crashing again. It had been like this since they'd arrived at the scene.

She yelled, "He's crashing again," as she and Dale took off through the doors. "High-voltage burns to hands and arms. ACLS protocols observed, patient unresponsive and intubated on signs of respiratory muscle paralysis. Fourth-degree burns to right hand, third and second degree to left hand and both forearms. Possible fractures to phalanges and ulna."

Dale added, "Catheter inserted with no immediate

signs of MGB. Kidney function appears to be coping with increased fluid treatment."

"Cranial and spinal injuries?" Dr. Thornton demanded, striding down the passage toward them as they rushed the patient into the trauma bay.

"He was thrown over twenty feet in an explosion and appears to have a lump on the back of his head," Frankie reported. "Pupil reflex is normal at this stage but I'm more concerned with tetanic injuries and damage to his heart. We've struggled to keep him stable."

The next fifteen minutes were spent in controlled chaos and shouted instructions. Frankie assisted in the transfer, answering the terse questions quickly and concisely.

They'd arrived on the scene where the patient and his partner had been conducting routine maintenance on the city's main power supply. As far as she could tell, something had gone wrong with the safety switch, resulting in an arc explosion. It wasn't clear why he hadn't been wearing his safety gloves and if his hands had been damp, but he'd been thrown twenty feet in the explosion. His partner had immediately run to his aid and started CPR until other personnel had arrived on the scene. They had cut the smoking coverall fabric away from his hands, which were a mangled mess of burnt flesh and damaged tissue.

He'd been covered with a space blanket and his burned hands wrapped in sections of cut-up space blanket to await the EMS.

Immediately on arrival, Frankie and Dale had activated ACLS, or advanced cardio-life support, and intubated him at signs of respiratory paralysis. They'd then removed the rest of his coveralls to assess the damage, inserting a saphenous IV in his groin instead of a PICC in order to bypass the injured arms and exit wounds on his feet.

Once they'd fitted a neck brace they'd moved him to a spinal board and performed a twelve-lead ECG. He'd gone into cardiac arrest twice, forcing them to use the paddles.

Once Dale could handle him on his own, Frankie—having more advanced driver training—had taken the wheel.

After returning the equipment to the ambulance and submitting their procedure report to the ER staff, Frankie headed toward the EMS offices, wishing she didn't have a ton of paperwork to get through. It had been a really busy afternoon and she was tired, hungry and needed a shower in the worst way.

She also hadn't been sleeping lately and blamed the heat wave for it because no way would she admit that *he* was responsible. No way would she admit that the minute she closed her eyes she relived that night over and over and over again until she wanted to scream with frustration that was as much temper as sexual frustration.

She spotted Dale heading toward her, carrying a two-cup tray and stuffing his face with a Boston cream donut. Another donut was perched on top of the cup he held out to her.

She took the cup and tossed him the donut. "How many times do I have to tell you these things will kill you? They're loaded with sugar, GMOs and trans fats. You're better off eating cardboard."

"Yeah, yeah," he mumbled, licking cream off his lip

as he bit into the second donut. "My liver appreciates your concern but even with my diet of champions I'm likely to live a long life. Even if it's just to watch you get all bent outta shape over your boyfriend."

Not willing to discuss her pitiful love life and sound even lamer than she was, Frankie snorted, stepped around him and continued walking. She should have known that Dale wouldn't take the hint, and within seconds he'd caught up with her.

"An interesting reaction there, Ms. Bryce."

"Not that interesting," she said dryly. "Considering I don't have a boyfriend." No one knew about Nate or that night and although Paige suspected, she didn't know for sure. Frankie was all too happy to pretend nothing had happened.

"That's not what I hear," he said, casually chewing on the greasy pastry and sending her a curious sideways glance.

"Yeah, well, maybe you shouldn't believe everything you hear." She lowered her voice. "Besides, the only reason I let people think it's true is to get rid of guys like that," she added, nodding as the new EMT, Hank, pushed his way through the ER doors.

"New guy been making a nuisance of himself?"

Frankie lifted her coffee to her mouth, making a humming sound of agreement.

"Want me to beat him up?" Dale demanded out loud when, sure enough, the other man swaggered up.

"No." Frankie chuckled and nudged his shoulder affectionately. "But you know you're my hero, right?"

"What about me?" Hank demanded with a smirk that often made Frankie want to smack him. "Am I your hero too?"

"There's only place for one in my life," she said smoothly. "And that's my partner."

Hank sent Dale a dismissive glance before turning back to Frankie. "Seems like a henpecked husband to me," he snorted. "If not me, then what about that coastie guy I hear you're dating?"

"Now, there's a *real* hero," her partner piped up smugly. "He's an ex-SEAL and probably knows a hundred ways to kill a man and make it look like a natural death."

"People talk about those guys as though they're superheroes," Hank argued, getting a little red in the face. "But I know for a fact that your guy isn't bulletproof."

Frankie stiffened. "What does that mean?"

"I'm talking about the fact that he's been shot." He laughed. "I heard he even fainted."

For a moment Frankie's breath froze in her throat. Her heart lurched in her chest before settling down into a ragged rhythm. "That was last week," she said as casually as she could, a tremble of relief escaping along with her exhalation. "And he didn't faint or even pass out then so I can't see him doing it now."

Dale's eyes widened and he quickly grabbed the donut out of his mouth before it fell.

"He got shot? For real?"

She shrugged. "It was just a flesh wound." He'd come around for some first aid, stayed long enough to rock her world before leaving without saying goodbye, *Thanks for rocking my world* or even a *See ya around, babe*.

He seemed to have forgotten everything about her, including where she lived, a point he'd hammered home by not calling, texting or even sending a message in a bottle.

Frankie was smart enough to know what that meant. He was done with her now that he'd done her. *Jerk.*

"Hmm."

Hank's smirk was enough to draw an impatient "What?" from Frankie, in a tone that usually sent people running. But it seemed the other man's ego kept him from picking up on verbal cues because, instead of backing off, he said, "Just that maybe he isn't as invincible as you think. Lieutenant Thinks-he's-a-Badass is in Bay Seven, being fawned over by a bunch of nurses. Your friend Paige is there too, looking suitably concerned."

What? Nate was here? Frankie's blood ran cold then hot then cold again.

"It's Lieutenant *Commander*," she snapped. "Why the hell can't people remember something as simple as a man's rank?" And before the two men could do anything more than gape at her, Frankie spun on her heel and headed for the ER.

She would not to lose it, she told herself, because losing it meant she cared. And why would she care about someone who thought so little of *her*?

But she did care, she thought as a strangled sob caught in her throat. More than she wanted to. And the news that he was in the ER, hurt and possibly bleeding to death, had Frankie flying down the passage toward the ER bays, her stomach a ball of dread, her nerves jittering like she'd guzzled a gallon of coffee.

She reached Bay Seven and whipped aside the curtain, only to find it empty.

Spinning in a fast circle, she spied an intern lounging at the nurses' station and called out, "The guy in Seven. Have you seen him?"

"The gunshot guy?" He looked up with an absent frown. "Gone."

She halted in her tracks as his words sank in. *Gone.* There was a buzzing in her ears and her world abruptly tilted on its axis. "Gone?"

"Yeah. Departed." He must have seen something in her face because he shot to his feet. "I mean not gone gone," he hurriedly explained. "He left on his own two feet."

The pressure around her forehead eased. "And you didn't stop him?"

He gaped at her. "You're kidding, right? That guy is built like a cyborg. Besides, he was looking…" he narrowed his eyes at her "…kinda like you're looking right now. Scary. Are you okay?"

"What about the attending physician?" she demanded, barely resisting the urge to head over there and throttle him for making her think that Nate was… well, gone. Permanently.

The intern shrugged apologetically and went back to whatever he'd been doing before she'd interrupted him.

Feeling as though her brain was about to explode, Frankie took another look into the empty bay and decided that since there were no signs of blood, Nate was most likely in one piece.

She expelled the breath she'd been holding. He was okay. He was alive and walking. "Men are stupid," she muttered to herself, wondering how long ago he'd left and if she would find him passed out in the car park.

A dry feminine voice said behind her, "You won't get any argument from me," and Frankie spun around to see an ER nurse pushing a teenager in a wheelchair.

He was bruised, bloodied and was hugging both his left arm and a battered skateboard to his skinny chest.

"Alpha flip or pop shuvit?" she asked, hoping to calm her crazy before she found Nate.

The kid's torn lip curled. "Those are for little kids," he scoffed. "I was trying the new hospital flip."

"Guess you tanked it, huh?"

He looked a little sheepish as Nancy shook her head and rolled him into an open bay.

Frankie headed down the passage to the nearest exit and pulled out her phone to call Nate. It went directly to voice mail and with a muttered curse she shoved it into her back pocket just as she rounded a corner and nearly collided with Paige.

"Frankie, did you hear—"

"Yep, and now he's not answering his phone." She lifted a hand to the headache blooming into life behind her right eye.

"I'm sorry. I offered to drive him," Paige admitted, "but he acted like I'd insulted his manhood and stomped off."

"Idiots," Frankie muttered, and rubbed her forehead. "Men are such idiots."

Paige sighed her agreement. "But we still love them, right?"

"Right," Frankie said dryly, before expelling her breath in a loud whoosh. *Not going there*, she thought. "Maybe I should go make sure the big oaf doesn't wrap himself around a tree."

"Need some help?"

Frankie snorted and strode toward the exit, pretending she wasn't in a hurry. "Please, like I can't handle an idiot guy with my hands tied behind my back."

"You sound just like him, do you know that?" Paige called out, making Frankie feel just a little insulted.

"*I* am not the idiot that left after passing out in the ER. I just don't want any witnesses when I kill *him* for being one."

"Good luck with that," Paige snorted. "There's an entire race of males you'll have to take on."

No, there wasn't, Frankie fumed as she hurried down the ramp toward employee parking. After she'd checked—because that's what friends did—that he hadn't passed out behind the wheel of his brand-new truck and smashed into a tree or driven over a cliff, she was done with men. Finished. Kaput.

Especially the ones with hero complexes. The ones who kissed you like you were the missing piece of their soul, like they wanted to consume you one kiss, one greedy bite at a time, gave you a few mind-blowing orgasms—then left without a single word.

Oh, yeah, she was done.

For the rest of freaking eternity.

CHAPTER TWELVE

THE SUN WAS dipping low on the horizon when Frankie turned west and headed along the coastal road to Rocky Bay, creatively named because of the many rocks littering the cove. She'd never been to Nate's house, but knew from Terri that he'd bought a fixer-upper overlooking the small bay.

Turning off Ocean Drive, Frankie had only gone a couple of hundred yards when she came across Nate's truck, abandoned on the side of the road a good half-mile from his house.

Chest abruptly squeezing, she pulled in behind the truck and shoved her car into park before hopping out to check—half expecting to find glass, crumpled metal and a bleeding unconscious alpha.

She found the vehicle empty and allowed her breath to escape in a loud whoosh. Okay, so no crumpled metal and no unconscious alpha…which was good. Also good, she decided when she tried the door, was the discovery that it was locked. It meant Nate couldn't have been too out of it if he'd remembered to lock his precious truck. But then again he was a guy, and guys tended to treat their vehicles better than they treated people.

She tried his phone and heard ringing coming from

inside the cab. Cursing, she got back into her car and shoved it into gear. Driving slowly, she craned her neck and squinted into the deepening shadows on both sides of the road for any sign that he'd wandered off and passed out in someone's yard.

Or fallen into a ditch.

Houses on this side of town were spaced further apart and the forest tended to encroach, which was why she missed Nate's road and had to reverse before finally locating Gull's Way. Bouncing over the rough spots, she totally understood why he'd bought the truck.

His house was at the end of the beach access lane, a sprawling log cabin that in the gathering gloom looked like it had been neglected but showed recent signs of renovation.

Light spilled from the neighboring houses but number eight Gull's Way was in darkness—a fact that set her nerves jangling because it meant he hadn't made it home.

Where was he?

Working to not go into a total freak-out, she sat, thumbs tapping the steering wheel and nerves jittering at the image of him taking the stairs built into the side of the cliff and tumbling down onto the rocky beach fifty feet below.

Her breath backed up in her throat. Or…what if he'd gone onto the front deck, fainted again and fallen over the railing? What if—

"Stop already," she snapped, swallowing her heart, which had lodged in her stupid throat. The words, spoken aloud, settled her and she turned into his driveway and pulled up a few yards from the wooden porch.

She shoved the vehicle into park, telling herself that

the wide open front door didn't mean that his place had been burgled and she wasn't about to walk into a crime scene. It just meant she'd been watching way too many cop shows on TV. Port St. John's still had that small-town feel and people rarely locked their doors. Besides, bad guys had most likely heard that Nate was an even badder guy than they were and were keeping away.

Shaking her head at the idiocy of the male species, Frankie grabbed her phone and got out, then took the stairs and stepped over the threshold into the dark house.

"Nate?"

In the ambient light, she could see very little in the way of furniture, as if he hadn't bothered to decorate the place. But when she ventured in a little further and caught sight of a sawhorse, piles of planks and machine tools, she was reminded of all the DIY scenes she'd been called to because guys thought that having a Y chromosome meant they could use power tools without reading the safety instructions.

What if…?

Stop it, she ordered silently. *He's fine. He's an ex-Navy SEAL, for God's sake, and…and he'd better be fine.*

Or she was going to kill him herself.

"Nathan?"

Being greeted by further silence, Frankie did a quick tour of the living room, kitchen, study—which had been turned into a home gym—and headed down the short passage to the master bedroom. Half expecting to find him passed out on his bed, she was surprised—and more than a little concerned—to find it not only empty but as neat as a pin.

Beginning to panic, because it seemed more and more likely that something bad had happened to him, Frankie retraced her steps. She was just about to call 911 when she heard a soft sound coming from the deck. She whipped her head toward it and noticed that the French doors were standing open.

The newly built deck was in darkness when she stepped out and looked around before heading for the flimsy makeshift railing. Carefully peering over the side, she hoped she'd be able to see him if he'd fallen over the edge…but equally praying that she wouldn't see anything but rocks.

The sun had by now dropped into the sea and she could see…absolutely nothing. She gritted her teeth. It meant she'd have to get her flashlight and do a little night recon. Muttering to herself about stupid alpha guys and their stupid big egos, Frankie turned to retrace her steps when a deep, rough bedroom voice growled, "Get away from the damn edge," nearly giving her a coronary.

She gave a startled yelp and stumbled backward— right into those flimsy bits of wood. There was an ominous crack as a plank abruptly gave way behind her. She opened her mouth to gasp, *"Seriously?"* and tried to grab onto something solid, but her heel caught the edge of some planks and she felt herself begin to fall.

She had a flashback to the night of the storm, thought, *Well, this sucks*…fully expecting to go tumbling backward onto the rocks below when hard fingers closed around her wrist and she was yanked forward against a hard body with enough force to knock the breath from her lungs.

"Oomph," she said.

At the same time an irritated male voice snarled, *"What the hell, woman?"*

Adrenaline flashing through her at warp speed, Frankie clung to the only solitary, steady, solid thing in a dangerously unstable world. Then again Nate had always been a rock—a really big, hard, yummy rock. A rock whose heart was pounding almost as hard as hers and muttering curses that ended with, "It's a full-time job keeping you out of trouble."

Reminded that she was giving up men permanently, Frankie snatched her hands off him and glared up into the achingly familiar face above hers. Only, instead of the hot sexy expression he'd been wearing the last time she'd been this close, he was scowling at her as though she was the last person he wanted to see.

Before she could stop it, hurt sliced through her and in reaction she shoved away from him...only to be roughly yanked back and forcefully removed from the edge of the deck. *"What's wrong with you?"* he growled roughly. "Do you have a death wish?"

Slapping at his hands, she gulped and gasped at the same time, which should have been impossible but totally wasn't. Realizing she was trembling—from relief at the near disaster, she told herself and not because he was warm and she was tempted to bury her face in his neck—Frankie planted her palms on his chest and shoved, aggravation ratcheting up a couple of notches when he remained as steady as a mountain.

Steady, when she felt as though she was floundering in quicksand.

He pulled back with a look that said she was crazy before saying, "You're welcome, by the way, for saving you." He sounded a little rough around the edges, like maybe the fact that she'd nearly died had affected him. But then she took in his tousled hair and the pillow crease on his cheek and realized he'd been napping.

Taking a freaking nap while she'd been on the verge of panicking.

He gave her a little shake and demanded, "You think I should have given you a nudge instead, Francis?"

Frankie realized in a blinding flash of awareness that he hadn't needed to give her a nudge at all. She sucked in a horrified breath as she realized that she'd gone and done what she'd promised herself she wouldn't.

She'd fallen. Flat on her face. All by herself.

Again. For the only man on the face of the planet to drive her completely crazy. Only this time it was no teenage crush.

She backed away, realizing this was the second stupidest thing she'd ever done. Actually, no, she amended. Falling for Nate was by far the stupidest thing she'd ever done because all she'd got for diving off Devil's Point other than the nickname Fearless Frankie had been a broken arm. This was…well, she'd be lucky to survive without a broken heart.

Something that was a lot harder to fix.

Furious—at herself more than him—Frankie spun away to stalk across the deck, breathing like she'd run up the north face of the Olympic mountains. She needed a moment—heck, she needed a whole bunch—and maybe to hide in the dark too, because that penetrating gaze always saw way too much.

Frankly, she'd rather throw herself off the deck than have him see what she'd only just discovered herself. Something that was as doomed now as it had been when she'd been a kid.

"What is wrong with you?" she demanded, momentarily unsure whether she was asking him or herself. Spinning around to face him again, she decided to handle him first. She'd deal with herself later.

And *then* there'd be hell to pay.

"You don't answer your phone. You abandon your truck ten miles away and then when I get here your front door is wide open and you're nowhere to be found. I was about to call 911, thinking you'd fallen off your deck, you...you—"

"I felt a little queasy and decided to walk," he interrupted roughly, and Frankie was glad because she couldn't think of a bad enough name to call him. But he'd already lost interest in her, turning to inspect the broken railing and muttering something about "damn fool women"...or was that wo*man*, as in singular?

She yelped, "Excuse me? *I'm* not the idiot here. *You* are, thinking you're so tough and invincible."

Ignoring her, Nate grabbed a nearby plank and a discarded hammer and went to work repairing the rail. "What are you doing here, Frankie?" he demanded in a voice that was as tired as it was distant.

Momentarily distracted by the play of muscles in his back and arms, Frankie thought, *Okay, so he doesn't want to talk. Fine.* He could darn well listen—but it would have been nice if he'd at least pretend to be happy to see her.

"I heard you fainted at the hospital and then refused to let Paige drive yo—"

"I did not *faint*," he interrupted, straightening with a snap and sounding as though she'd just insulted his manhood. "Women faint, and even if Paige hadn't been busy I..." He lifted one hand to press a couple of fingers into his forehead like he had a headache. "Look, I don't need a babysitter, okay? I'm fine."

"And I *do*, is that what you're saying?"

His sigh sounded more than a little impatient. "All I'm saying is that I'm an adult. I don't need anyone checking up on me like I'm ten."

She snorted and stomped closer. "Right. That's why you left your truck on the side of the road? Because you're an adult?" His fleeting glance was unreadable before he dropped the hammer into the nearby toolbox.

Incensed by his air of masculine superiority, Frankie cocked one hip and shoved her hands on her hips to glare at him. "Oh, right, silly me. I forgot for a moment that SEALs are immune to the same weakness that occasionally afflicts the rest of humanity."

He nudged her away from the edge, put himself between her and the flimsy rail, then folded his arms across his mile-wide chest and stared down at her as though she was speaking Swahili.

"You're human, Nate," she snapped. "You hurt, you bleed. Not…" she poked his pec with her finger "…a cyborg. Or some stupid superhero dodging bullets or healing in the blink of an eye. Someone who should accept a hand from his friends once in a while, instead of thinking he's everyone else's self-appointed protector."

He arched a dark brow. "You wanna go there, princess?"

It was Frankie's turn to demand, "What is *that* supposed to mean?"

He sighed and squeezed the bridge of his nose. "Nothing. Look, I'm fine, okay? And for your information, I'm no hero." He gave a harsh laugh and folded his arms across his chest. "You, better than anyone, know exactly how *human* I am."

She opened her mouth to ask what he was talking about and shut it with a snap when he just arched a brow, clearly reminding her of the other night when he—

Face flaming, she sucked in a sharp breath, suddenly grateful for the darkness that hid her expression from those golden-brown eyes. Eyes that seemed to see everything yet gave nothing away.

"Aaargh," she growled in frustration. "Trust a stupid man to bring that up." She squeezed her head between her hands and turned away but then something occurred to her and she spun back round. "And since you did, let's talk about that, shall we?" She lowered her hands and scowled at him. "And the way you left. Sneaking out like I…" She swallowed an unpleasant notion. "Like I'm something you're ashamed of."

His expression abruptly closed down and his mouth firmed into a tight line of irritation, leaving him looking about as approachable as a grizzly. "Let's not."

"Fine," Frankie snapped, and before she could stop it, the implication that he *was* ashamed of her lodged like a sharp ache right beside her heart.

He must have seen something in her expression because he sighed and looked pained. "Frankie—"

"No, it's okay." She gave a shaky laugh and spun away. "I mean, it's not the first time I've disappointed someone—or you, for that matter. And given my track record, it's not likely to be the last."

"It's not *you*. It's—"

She turned on him with a warning snarl. "Finish that and I'll gut you like a fish."

He sighed as though she was a huge pain in the butt. "Just drop it, okay?"

"Why? Because *you* said so?" She asked, annoyed with his calm inscrutability when she was certain steam was escaping from her ears. "Because you're an ex-Navy SEAL who can kill with a single blow?" Furious and hurting, she couldn't stop the words pouring out of her mouth. "Because 'heroes' don't need to have a reason or explain themselves to lesser mortals?"

He closed his hand over hers and the ease with which he managed to render her immobile had Frankie's simmering temper igniting.

"I thought…" She drew in a shuddery breath and yanked her hand away, surprised when Nate released her. She wrapped her arms around herself as though to protect herself from the memory of losing someone she cared about. She'd loved her brother and his death had hit her hard, but she knew losing Nate would devastate her. "*We* were worried about you, Nate." *I was worried about you.*

"I'm fine." His tone was coolly dismissive, as was the way he folded his arms across his chest. "Look, it was a…mistake. I blame myself because it shouldn't have happened." Frankie blinked and opened her mouth to ask him what he was talking about when Nate continued. "You and I?" He waggled a long masculine finger between them. "Not going to happen again. Ever."

For a long moment Frankie stared up into his face—half-hidden in shadows—and felt herself go cold because she'd just realized something horrifying. Something so mortifying that it left her feeling exposed and raw…because somewhere buried deep she'd harbored the small, fragile hope that one day—

Oh, hell, no.

Swallowing past the burning lump of humiliation that lodged in her throat, she gave a short, ragged laugh. "You…you arrogant, self-important…*ass*." Her reaction must have surprised him because a wrinkle appeared between his dark brows and he was suddenly looking at her like she was live ammo likely to go off any moment. "What makes you think *I* want a you and me?"

He didn't reply but one dark brow hiked up his forehead.

Infuriated, she gasped, "You're joking, right? *You…*" she jabbed a finger at him "…are the last man on earth that I'd want *any*thing with. The last man I'd *look* to for anything other than a few quick orgasms."

His expression hardened. "Why, because my father was the town loser who lied and cheated his way into every woman's bed? A man whose word meant about as much as his marriage vows?"

"What?" Frankie's mouth dropped open. "Have you lost your mind?"

He sighed and thrust an impatient hand through his hair, leaving it more rumpled than ever. "Maybe. But *my* word happens to mean something."

What? Frowning, Frankie curled her hands into tight fists and then folded her arms beneath her breasts when her fingers itched to smooth all that thick silky mess. She shook her head to clear it. "You're not making any sense. Have you been drinking?"

Hands shoved into his pockets, he turned to stare out at the bay. In the darkness, Frankie saw his jaw flex and for a long moment thought he wouldn't reply. Finally, he said quietly, unemotionally, "I made a promise."

Okay, so that wasn't what Frankie had expected. "A what?" She shook her head, confused. "I mean, to whom?"

He sent her a brief unreadable glance. "I promised Jack I'd look out for you."

She stared at him, more than a little stunned by the news. "J-Jack? Wha—"

Somehow Frankie had known this moment would come, when she would be forced to talk about Jack.

She stared at Nate, hoping for some sign of softening, but his profile might as well have been carved in granite. "The night before we shipped out that first time," he said flatly, "he made me swear that if anything ever happened to him, I'd look out for you."

"Seriously? I was a *kid* then, Nate, something I no longer am—in case you haven't noticed."

"I broke my promise to my best friend," he continued with quiet intensity. "A promise I swore to keep, no matter what."

"Jack's dead."

"Which is why I—"

"He's gone, Nate," she interrupted abruptly. "Gone, trying to be a damn hero."

"He *was* a hero," he said with quiet intensity.

Frankie sucked in the sharp edge of grief that threatened to overwhelm her and spun away. "Yes. And look where that got him."

He sighed, the sound heavy with apology, regret and his own grief. "I'm sorry."

"Yeah, me too." Sorry for so many things. "But I'm not thirteen anymore, Nate," she reminded him tersely. "I'm a big girl now. I have a job, pay all my own bills and manage to dress and feed myself every morning."

She pressed shaking fingers to her temples, where a blinding headache had finally exploded into being. "Besides, the Jack I knew would hardly expect you to honor some silly adolescent pledge for all eternity."

"Then you didn't know your brother," he drawled in a tone that said she was being overly dramatic and difficult. "He meant it and so did I."

"Arrrgh!" Her frustration emerged as a growl. "I don't *need* some *man* thinking I need a keeper and it's… it's insulting that you think I do."

"It doesn't matter what you think," he said quietly, implacably, confirming what Frankie was beginning to realize. Nate viewed her as one of his responsibilities.

Only she didn't need saving. She never had.

"I am *not* your responsibility, Nate," she snapped. "I'm no one's responsibility." Struggling to control her breathing, Frankie wondering if her hair was smoking because it felt like her brain was boiling inside her skull. "Who do you think you are?" she continued when she could form words.

"Frankie—"

"How dare you! What right do you have to assume responsibility for *me*?"

"Jack—"

"Don't you dare," she interrupted furiously. "Don't you dare add me to the rest of your responsibilities, Nate. In fact…" She blinked back tears and spun away from him, determined that he never know how much his words, his attitude tore at her. Never know that she felt as though she'd been gut shot.

Sucking in a shaky breath, she headed for the doors. "In fact, you can just write me off as a…a loser and forget you ever—"

Before she'd taken two steps, Frankie was spun around and slammed up against his hard body. She gave a surprised squeak that was instantly swallowed as his mouth covered hers in a kiss filled with such fury, frustration and wild need that she instinctively brought up her hands to soothe.

She had a moment to think, *What...?* before he growled, "And don't *you* dare call what we did 'just sex', Francis," he growled, pulling away and leaving her swaying at the abrupt assault on her senses.

"Go home, Frankie," he said quietly, wiping his hands down his face as though he was beyond weary and, without another word, turned to face the darkened bay—obviously done with the conversation.

Obviously done with her.

Hurt burrowed deep and for several beats she stared at his wide, tense shoulders, her heart squeezing at the image he presented. Big. Tough. Distant. As isolated as the mountain peaks he faced. A man alone, shouldering the burdens of everyone around him.

But he didn't have to and *she* didn't want to be a weight he carried on his shoulders. She was a strong, independent woman who could shoulder her own burdens—and maybe some of his.

She opened her mouth to tell him but another look at the implacable set of his shoulders told her that he'd never let her close enough to help. Never let her close enough to care.

"You know what I think, Nate?" she said after a short silence during which she struggled with her battered emotions. She had to swallow past what felt like a huge shard of glass in her throat. "I think you use that stupid promise to evade the real issue here." When he remained silent, she gave a tight laugh and continued, "For all your medals, for all your bravery and courage, you're a coward. Too scared to let yourself care, let yourself be vulnerable to anyone, because they might leave you like your father did. Like Jack and your team did. Well," she reminded him fiercely, "I'm *still* here."

His answer was a whole lot of silence that had Frankie flinging at his head, "But, then, I guess you think no one can function without you around to protect them. Even from themselves." The backs of her eyes stung and she swallowed the sob rising in her throat, threatening to cut off her breath and humiliate her.

She wouldn't cry. Not in front of him. In fact, he wasn't worth the swollen eyes, stuffy nose or blinding headache.

"Well, let me tell you something, Commander Big Shot," she said fiercely. "I survived just fine without your 'protection' for the last twelve years, and I'll survive the next fifty. So you can just scratch me off your Things-I-Have-to-Take-Care-Of list." Her throat finally closed as she spun on her heel and left before she broke down.

Broke down and begged him to love her.

At the French doors, she paused and sucked in a steadying breath. With one hand on the wooden frame, she looked back over her shoulder. Nate hadn't moved and the set of his wide shoulders was as tense and unapproachable as his attitude.

She firmed lips still tingling from that last kiss. "Just stay out of my life," she said with quiet intensity. "I don't need or want your protection." Then she turned and walked away.

CHAPTER THIRTEEN

FOR THE NEXT few days Nate kept telling himself that he'd done the right thing. He didn't have the time or the space in his life for the responsibility of a woman who couldn't—or wouldn't—see how much keeping a promise to his best friend meant to him.

Jack had refused to believe that Nate would grow up to be like his father and even when he'd screw up, his friend would remind him that he wasn't Tom Oliver.

Remind him that he could be anything he wanted.

Well, he'd wanted to be a Navy SEAL, be a part of a something that meant something more—brothers-in-arms fighting for a just cause. It had been a way to earn a few advanced engineering degrees and the pay had helped his mother make ends meet. What he'd never told anyone was that he'd decided it would give him discipline and goals—something his father had lacked.

But the cost had been high. Jack and too many of his brothers-in-arms had paid the ultimate price.

He missed the close bond he'd had with his SEAL team, but he didn't miss having to deal with losing them. Didn't miss having to hold them while they breathed their last.

Yet, even as he told himself he'd done the right thing

by keeping his promise to Jack, he couldn't get the look on Frankie's beautiful face out of his head. The quick glint of tears ruthlessly suppressed. The stiff, proud back disappearing out the door.

Almost immediately he'd wanted to stop her because he'd hurt her—something he'd promised himself he'd never do—and when Frankie was hurt she almost always did something reckless.

He'd waited until the next day to call her but she didn't answer or return any of his messages. He went to her house but it was locked up tight and her car was missing. Her partner Dale hadn't heard from her either but, then, he hadn't expected to as they both had a few days off. Nate then called Paige, because if anyone knew where Frankie was it would be the petite doctor. Paige, however, had been quick to deny knowing anything but Nate could tell she was lying. When he called her on it she told him, "I love you but you're an idiot," and disconnected.

Frustrated, he called Ty, whose first words were, "What did you do?"

"Me?" Nate's tone was indignant. "I didn't do anything."

"You must have," Ty said bluntly. "Frankie doesn't just go off without telling anyone."

"Frankie *always* goes off without telling anyone," he reminded him.

"Not anymore. She *always* tells Paige."

"She did tell Paige," Nate pointed out impatiently. "Now, go be a man and get it out of your woman."

"Are you insane?" Ty sounded scandalized. "I prefer sleeping with a soft, warm woman, thank you very much. Go find Frankie yourself and be prepared to beg."

"What the hell, Ty?" Nate swore, frustration beating at his temples because he'd done nothing that required him to beg. You'd think people would appreciate the fact that he could keep a promise, that he was a responsible man. Unlike the other men in his family. "You let that sweet little doctor walk all over you?"

"Of course not." His snorted then added in a low voice, "But she says you need to wake up and see what's right under your nose. I'd listen to her, if I were you."

"You're a wuss," Nate said with disgust, but he could hear Ty laughing as his friend disconnected.

Frustrated, he went to work on his deck, needing to finish installing the railings before someone got hurt.

She's already hurt, numbskull.

Yep. He was scum and he felt really bad. Especially now that he knew exactly how she tasted and felt wrapped around him.

He cursed. *Especially* as it wasn't going to happen again.

But if she wanted to go off and sulk, who was he to interfere? She'd told him to stay out of her life and that's exactly what he intended to do. There were plenty of women in town who'd be more than happy to keep him warm at night. Women who weren't wild and reckless and annoying.

Is that what you want? The voice in his head demanded.

"Yes," he said out loud. "That's exactly what I want." But he knew he was lying. Maybe he wouldn't allow himself to think about Frankie but if he was honest with himself, he didn't want to be—couldn't see himself—with any other woman. She'd told him to stay out of her life but that didn't mean he couldn't keep an eye on her from a distance.

Yeah. You're certainly good at distance.

"Shut up," he snarled.

Great. Now he was talking to the voices in his head. Voices that had become as annoying as the woman they were defending.

Maybe he should make an appointment to see a shrink or just get himself committed because he was clearly losing his mind.

So Nate pushed himself, hoping the physical labor would silence the voices and let him sleep without dreaming about Frankie. But working with his hands always left him with far too much time to think, and when a big storm hit the area he moved inside to work on the floor.

With nothing but the sound of the wind and rain, and the monotonous movements of the floor sander, all he *could* do was think.

About Frankie. About the little sounds she made when he was buried deep inside her tight body and the way she'd made sex not just fun but intense. About the way she laughed—completely without artifice and un-caring if people stared. He thought about the way she liked to hog the bed and the way he'd felt with her in his arms.

Like he was where he was meant to be. Like he was the hero she said she didn't want.

"Are you waiting for the carpenter fairies to finish the job or are you mooning over a certain wild redhead who's MIA?"

At the unexpected interruption, Nate's instincts—honed through years of training and combat—reacted with split-second timing. He rose to his feet and spun toward the threat in one smooth move; nail gun locked and loaded for action.

He took one look at Ty lounging in the doorway and cursed. Nate hadn't reacted like that in months, which told him he was losing it. Big time.

And he knew exactly whose fault it was.

Straightening from his combat-ready stance, he lowered his "weapon."

"Do you have a death wish?" he demanded for the second time that week, a bit shaky at the thought that he'd nearly shot his best friend. "I could have nailed you between the eyes a dozen times before you could blink," he growled, shoving one hand through his hair and hoping the surgeon didn't see the fine tremor in his fingers. "Didn't you ever hear about knocking, or announcing your presence? Sneaking up on a SEAL is guaranteed to *seal* your fate."

Ty lifted one dark eyebrow, his bright blue eyes gleaming with amusement. "Wow, I'm impressed," he drawled, brushing raindrops from his dark hair and wandering over to inspect Nate's handiwork. "Two puns in two sentences. And for your information I did knock, *and* call out, but you were too preoccupied with X-rated thoughts."

"Who said they were X-rated?"

"The goofy, lovestruck look said it all."

"I was frowning," Nate pointed out.

Ty dropped down to run his hand over the satin-smooth floorboards. After a couple of beats he looked up and smirked. "Yep, definitely mooning."

Nate snorted and folded his arms across his chest. "I don't moon. Mooning is for saps like you."

"Oh?" Ty straightened, regarding Nate politely. "Is that a Navy SEAL thing or a Nathan Oliver thing?"

"It's a no…thing," Nate growled, dropping his arms and heading for the doorway. "Just minding my own business." He glared over his shoulder when Ty made a scoffing sound. "You want a beer, or what?"

Without waiting for a reply, he stomped into the kitchen and yanked open the refrigerator. By the time he'd pulled out two beers, Ty had joined him. He'd rolled up his sleeves and loosened his tie as though he intended staying a while.

"Why are you here again?" Nate asked, lobbing a beer through the air. Ty snagged it and twisted off the cap with his left hand. The scars on his right hand were still fresh and Nate knew the surgeon was hoping to regain complete use of his hand so he could resume surgery. "Don't you have a fiancée to go irritate?"

"Paige's working, so I thought I'd irritate you instead." He lifted the bottle in a silent toast and took a deep pull, his eyes studying Nate. "It's what buddies do." He swallowed again and licked his lips. "I'd ask what crawled up your ass but since I've been there, I'll give you a piece of advice I wish someone had given me."

Nate gave a rough snort, telling himself that what he was experiencing was a reaction to all the unsolicited advice people kept giving him. It was the only reason his gut burned. The only reason he felt jittery, as though something bad was about to happen. "You're hallucinating, Doc. Probably from sniffing too much happy gas."

"You're a funny guy, Nate," Ty drawled. "But not too bright. At least, not when it comes to Frankie."

"Frankie has nothing to do with this."

"Frankie has *every*thing to do with this but you're just too stubborn to admit it."

Nate casually leaned against the counter and drawled, "Admit what?"

"That you've got it bad and you're too scared to face it."

"What?" He gave a hard laugh and lifted his beer, pointing the bottle at Ty. "That's complete and utter bull, and you know it. I'm not scared, I'm—"

"In love with her." Ty nodded. "Yep, I know."

"Are you out of your freaking mind? I love her, yes. Like a sister. But *in* love?" He made an impatient sound in the back of his throat and shook his head. Because what he felt for Frankie defied description. It couldn't possibly be love.

Could it?

Lust and deep affection, yes…but love? He shook his head emphatically. Nope. No way. "You're insane," he growled, unsure who he was addressing, but just in case it was Ty he added, "I'd have to be certifiable to love a woman like that. She's annoying and opinionated and she makes me crazy."

"Good crazy or bad crazy?"

That's the million-dollar question, isn't it?

He growled, "She frustrates me so much sometimes that I'm tempted to throttle her, so…yep, definitely bad crazy."

Ty's face made it clear he didn't buy it and neither, apparently, did the voice in Nate's head.

You want to wrap your hands around her all right, the voice taunted. *But not to throttle her.*

Ty must have agreed with the voice because he snorted and stared pointedly at Nate. "Yeah…" he smirked "...I can totally see how bad crazy she makes you." He made some kissy noises that ratcheted Nate's annoyance up a couple of hundred notches and made him grit his teeth.

"What are you, twelve?"

Ty snickered before sobering. "It's the best kind of bad, Nate. And if you're really lucky, a woman as fiercely loyal as Frankie comes into your life and has your back."

"Have you forgotten how wild and reckless she is?" Nate demanded, because the thought of him and Frankie...well, it terrified him. "She's a disaster waiting to happen. Just looking out for her is a full-time gig."

"Who says you need to?" Ty asked mildly. "Seems she's done just fine on her own."

The words, spoken by Frankie just a few days earlier, made him scowl. "I don't need that kind of aggravation in my life," he argued curtly. "Frankie isn't like Paige. She's not a comfortable woman to be around." *Hell.* Just thinking about her made him damned *un*comfortable. The kind of uncomfortable that tempted him to push her up against the nearest wall and put his hands and lips all over her. It was why he needed to stay away from her. "In fact, she can be downright belligerent and...and messy."

Ty grinned. "That's women for you."

Maybe, but Frankie wasn't like other women. She was wild and fiery...and so passionate he had a hard time pushing her from his mind.

His breath whooshed out.

Could he really be in love? With Frankie?

That would be insane and Nate had always prided

himself on his cool rationality. But what he felt for Frankie wasn't rational.

Life with her would never be boring. She was too vibrant for that. Too full of life. Too stubborn. They'd fight because she was so...so contrary and opinionated, but the makeup sex would be spectacular.

"*She* saved *your* life, remember?" Ty pointed out, unknowingly slicing to the very heart of what really bothered Nate. Exposing his weakness, his secret shame. "Not the other way around. Or have you forgotten?" Ty demanded. "Because if you have, I still have that video." He pulled out his phone and waggled it. "Wanna see?"

"No. I do not want to see," Nate growled irritably, taking a swig of beer in the hope that it would drown out the sudden realization that he'd resented her for besting him at his own game.

She'd rescued him—instead of the other way around. The way it had always been between them. The way he was comfortable with. He didn't know how to deal with this Frankie, the Frankie who rose without hesitation and threw herself at him. He recalled in perfect detail the horror and devastation in the green eyes locked with his when she'd realized that he was going over; the memory of how her body had felt wrapped around his as they were hoisted into the chopper, and the cuts and bruises she'd sustained saving him.

And not once had she reminded him of it. Not like *he* always seemed to do.

"I don't need to see it to be reminded of that night." He dreamed about it. But in his nightmares their roles were reversed and every time she slipped through his fingers to disappear into the black abyss below. He'd wake drenched in sweat, his heart pounding in his chest and the pain of desolation echoing in his soul.

"The guys at the station remind me often enough, thank you very much."

"Yeah," Ty drawled. "I can see why you'd find that so unsettling."

"What exactly do you mean?" Nate demanded.

"It means that you liked being a SEAL because you got to do all the saving. Frankie's right, you do have a hero complex."

"That's just bull and in case you've forgotten, I'm no longer a SEAL."

"No, you're a coastie. Apples and pears are still fruit, Nate. You're the man sworn to protect and care for everything and everyone around you—your mom, your sister, your country, your teammates… Frankie. It proves to everyone that you're not your father."

"I never had to prove that to anyone," he said curtly, the conversation beginning to really annoy him.

Why, because it's the truth?

"No, just yourself," Ty agreed mildly. "*We've* always known what you could never see. Just because you share his DNA, it doesn't mean you're going to wake up one morning and suddenly *become* Tom Oliver."

"I know that," Nate snapped, then sighed tiredly. He scrubbed his hands over his face before admitting, "I can't love Frankie… I promised Jack."

Ty's eyebrows shot into his hairline. "You promised him you'd never love her?"

"Buddy rule number one—sisters are off limits. But that's not what I meant," he said wearily. "I promised Jack I'd look out for her—keep her out of trouble. I can't mess with Frankie and keep my promise to Jack."

"Then don't."

"Don't what?" he growled impatiently. "Don't keep my promise? Because I can tell you, I am *not* my father."

"Don't be a moron, Nate. I meant don't *mess* with her."

"But you just said—"

"Jack always knew you loved her," Ty drawled with a glint of amusement.

"Wait. What? She was thirteen, for God's sake. *I* didn't even know I loved her until—"

"You were like brothers," Ty reminded him. "Of course he wanted you to look out for her. But before he died, he knew that you were *in* love with her. He told me."

Nate's jaw dropped open. "*What?* That's cra—"

His instinctive denial was interrupted by Ty's phone.

Ty's mouth curled into a sappy grin as he answered. The look of intimacy, of shared laughter and history told Nate who it was. It also made him feel just a little bit jealous because it was what he wanted too.

And not with just anyone, he finally admitted to himself. He wanted it with Frankie.

She might be wild and unpredictable but she'd always have his back, even—his mouth curled—when she wanted to kill him. She might have saved him from falling off the ledge that night, but he'd gone and fallen anyway.

Hard and completely.

Wham!

He'd been half in love with her for years, but that night…the feel of her against him after so many years, the light of combat in her eyes, the damn-your-hide attitude…had been like coming home.

Ty was right. Frankie was his heart. She was the reason he didn't want to spend time with other women. She was the missing piece of his soul but he'd been too blinded by his need to prove that he wasn't like his father—that he could and would take care of those he loved.

"Babe," Ty's calm voice cut through Nate's revelation. "Calm down, okay?" His gaze, suddenly unreadable, locked with Nate's but it was Ty's next words—"Now, what was that about Frankie?"—that had his blood freezing in his veins.

He was already reaching for his truck keys and heading for the front door when Ty ended the call.

"Before you go off half-cocked, Frankie's fine," he said, grabbing his jacket as he followed Nate out. "She called Paige an hour ago from the ferry to say a woman was in labor. But Paige said they just got word that there's been some kind of accident on board and they need all available medics. I'm heading over there to help."

Nate paused. "And Frankie?"

Ty shook his head, his voice steady. "No one's heard from her. But that doesn't mean she's hurt," he added when Nate cursed. "It just means she's probably busy. You know Frankie. She's probably hip-deep in all the action."

But Nate wasn't listening. All he could think about as he dashed through the gusting rain toward his truck was that Frankie was in the hot zone—with no one covering her six. He'd made her believe she was nothing more than a promise to be kept. That he cared more about a memory than a fiery, vibrant woman who owned his heart—and very possibly his soul.

CHAPTER FOURTEEN

ON THE LAST leg of the two-day trip to the local islands, Frankie braced her feet against the pitching deck and tried not to think about the huge waves crashing over the lower decks of the ferry. A huge storm system had hit two days earlier than expected, with gale-force winds whipping the seas into a frenzy. It might not have been so bad if the ferry's stabilizers hadn't been damaged by submerged debris a few hours earlier, rendering the vessel all but unsteerable in the heavy seas.

But right now she had bigger problems than heavy weather and rolling decks. A ferry officer she'd gone to school with had asked her to help out when a man had collapsed, complaining of chest pains and muscle weakness. Then a pregnant woman had gone into early labor and she was soon treating the small band of people injured by the rolling of the ship.

She'd called the hospital to alert them of the emergency—but that had been before lightning had struck, frying all the equipment and starting a fire somewhere in the engine room. Before she'd lost her cellphone when panicked crowds had begun streaming onto the decks, letting rain and sea water pour in through the open doors.

Help was on its way but Frankie had a feeling that time was running out for Serena Porter, who had all the signs of preeclampsia, a dangerous condition for both mother and child.

Then she'd overheard the crew talking about a fire in the cargo bay and had to wonder if they were going down. Smoke had already begun making its way to the upper decks and Frankie prayed help arrived before cars and trucks started exploding.

She also couldn't help hoping that Nate was working on his house and not getting ready to join the rescue. Maybe she was still mad at him for treating her like a one-night stand, but she didn't want him opening up his healing wound.

The knowledge that she was nothing more to him than a responsibility had been a blow to her ego as well as her heart. Discovering that she was in love— a soul-deep connection that throbbed like an open wound—with a man who saw her as just a promise he was honor-bound to keep had devastated her and she'd needed to escape for a while. But running away never solved anything and she couldn't avoid going home forever. Port St. John's wasn't that big and she was bound to run into him sooner rather than later.

Unless she moved to Australia.

Australia had the Great Barrier Reef and she'd always wanted to scuba dive and learn to surf.

"Evac ten minutes out, Miss Bryce," an officer said, popping his head around the door. "Let's get your patients upstairs."

"Upstairs?" Frankie demanded, grateful for the interruption. "I thought they were being airlifted from the port-side deck."

Officer Paul Murray shook his head. "Too many people. The captain is worried they might panic and try to get on the first chopper. We've gotta move your patients to the top observation deck ASAP before we let the rest up there."

Conditions on the upper deck were worse than Frankie had feared. Lightning slashed at the sky, briefly illuminating the wind-driven rain that soaked them instantly. With limited visibility, it took a couple of moments for her to get her bearings and make out the direction of the approaching choppers. Relief had her exhaling in a quiet whoosh when she saw lights appear out of the darkness.

As the nearest chopper lost altitude, figures in protective gear dropped onto the deck and ran toward them, even before the skids made contact. "Medic's waiting in the chopper, Ms. Bryce," someone yelled as they passed. "It's like hell out there, so let's roll."

Paul caught Frankie's shoulder and leaned close to her ear. "I'm going to start directing people up here to the choppers," he said. "Get moving and good luck." Then he was gone.

Frankie quickly ushered the group to the waiting chopper, bending low as rotor wash and lashing rain made it almost impossible to see the hands reaching to pull them to safety. Once the last of her charges was on board, she stepped away and motioned for them to take off.

"You're not coming?" the copilot yelled through the open door. When she shook her head and took a couple more steps back, he lifted his visor. "Nate said to make sure you got on this chopper," he yelled. "Don't make me go back without you. He knows a hundred ways to kill a man and make it look like an accident."

She rolled her eyes at him but the words stung more than the pelting rain. Even after everything, he was still insisting on being her big brother, her big bad protector?

"Tell the SEAL he's not the boss of me," she yelled back, but as she splashed her way through the torrential rain toward the stairs, she wondered if she would ever get the chance to prove to him that she was worth loving.

"There's been an explosion," the pilot reported abruptly into his comms as they headed back out to the stricken ship, causing Nate's gut to tighten into a fist of dread. "The fuel tanks are starting to explode, so look sharp, men. Those left on board don't have a lot of time."

It was just after eleven and most of the passengers had been airlifted onto waiting coastguard cutters or taken to the medical center, but of Frankie…there was still no word.

Several people had reported seeing her and Nate had begun to worry that she'd insist on going down with the stricken ship. She'd refused all opportunities to leave with the choppers and wasn't on any of the cutters. He'd checked—countless times—until the shift commander had ordered him to "Get out there and find her, Oliver."

Grateful for the man's understanding, Nate had hopped on the next flight out, hoping Frankie was smart enough to stay out of danger and praying he got the opportunity to tell her how he felt.

They were a few minutes out when another huge fireball ripped through the night sky, briefly illuminating the dangerously listing ship.

"Move in. *Move in*," he barked into his headset. "Tell them to get the last few people aboard onto the decks so we can evac them now."

He could hear yelling through the comms and saw people spill onto the upper deck. He had time for one horrified thought—*Where the hell is Frankie?*—before finally catching sight of her tearing across the upper deck with several others in pursuit, just as another explosion ripped open the port bulkhead.

They felt the force of it as the chopper slewed sideways and Nate felt terror grip his throat. *"Get them off. Now!"* he yelled, watching in horror as the ferry lurched sideways, water rushing across the upper deck on which Frankie was scrambling to regain her footing.

He saw dinghies streaking across the water toward the stricken vessel even as people began falling or jumping into the water from the stern.

Frankie and the others were still scrambling up the listing ship, grabbing onto the railings to keep from sliding into the water.

"I'm going in," the pilot yelled, banking sharply to the left. "I'll try to get abreast of their position and hope the rotor wash doesn't sweep them overboard."

"Make sure your lines are secured," Nate ordered as his men scrambled into position. "And get the safety sling ready in case someone doesn't make it."

Ruthlessly squashing the fear that tried to rise up like the angry sea, Nate deliberately slowed his heartbeat and tried to pretend this was just another mission, just another rescue. But as his eyes locked on Frankie with grim determination, he knew he was lying to himself. This wasn't just any rescue. This was about rescuing himself as well.

He caught her expression and knew she understood what they were about to attempt. He saw rather than heard her shouting as the chopper moved in. This close he could see how young they were—probably all ferry staff—and terrified. She shouted, "Jump, they'll catch you," just as another wave broke over them.

The chopper edged closer and one by one the frightened staff were hauled to safety until there was only Frankie and a young uniformed kid left on the deck.

Above the rotor noise, Nate heard another muffled explosion and the next instant the deck pitched dangerously. The pilot jerked the chopper sideways in an attempt to maintain enough rotor distance and Nate saw the kid start to slide. Frankie shouted a warning and shot out her arm to snag the back of his uniform and haul him up.

Eyes white with terror, the kid flailed as he tried to regain his footing as the ferry slid down another few feet.

"She can't hold on forever, LC," the winch operator yelled, tossing a sling at them. It fell short of its mark but Frankie couldn't have grabbed for it anyway. Terrified that they were both going to slide into the churning water, Nate quickly hooked himself to the safety line and scrambled onto the skid. "Give me a little slack," he barked into the comms. "And get as close as you can."

Once the line played out, Nate leaned forward, his arms spread out as though he was flying. Spray from the surging sea instantly covered his visor, making it impossible to see.

Although they were designed to repel water, Nate shoved it up because he couldn't afford to screw up. Not with two lives relying on his experience and training.

Not with Frankie hanging on by one arm while holding onto someone else with the other.

He could literally feel the collective breaths being sucked in behind him as he leaned out over the turbulent water. His gaze locked with Frankie's and all the fear, exhaustion and grim determination in them hit him with a one-two punch.

"Hang on," he yelled, snatching at the swaying rescue sling. "Grab it and if you can, slip it over your head and under your arms. We'll do the rest."

Out the corner of his eye he saw Frankie's face go white with pain and desperately wanted to yell at the kid to hurry up. At the third attempt he managed to snag it and slip it clumsily over his head and under his arms, and Nate finally took his eyes off the kid to shout, "Frankie, let go now and grab my hand."

Eyes on his, her mouth moved and he thought she said *I love you* just as a huge wave broke over her. The sling line abruptly tautened and the boy swung free, jerking at Frankie's body. She wasn't going to be able to hang on against the drag.

"Pull him up and give me four feet," Nate yelled frantically as he watched her struggling against the pull of the water. He instantly felt his line play out and hooked his feet over the chopper floor as he fell forward, catching her just as she lost the battle against the sea.

"I've got you," he said, although he knew she couldn't hear him. Through his comms he heard cheers and, "Oh, my God, he actually did it. Nate's a freaking super bat."

"He's got her, Lieutenant," another voice yelled. "Let's get out of here."

Nate immediately felt the chopper gain altitude before banking sharply away from the sinking ferry.

Using his upper-body strength, he tightened his grip on her arm and pulled her up until she could grab onto his harness.

"You came," she said simply.

And just as simply Nate replied, "Always."

The instant they were hauled aboard, Nate pulled a wet and shivering woman into his arms, only vaguely aware of the excited commotion around them.

He needed a moment. Hell, he needed a whole bunch of moments to get his heart rate down from stroke level and take in the reality of the woman pressed against him. To enjoy the feel of her warm breath on his throat and let the fact that she was alive and safe register. Someone dropped a blanket around her shoulders and after a couple of beats he loosened his grip to wrap it around her icy body.

"I've got you, babe," he murmured, his throat tight and the band of fear around his heart finally loosening. Now that he had her safe he could admit to himself that he'd been scared. Terrified that he would lose the best thing that had ever happened to him.

And looking into her beautiful face he pulled her into his warm body and swore *And this time I'm not letting go.*

After a couple of beats he realized that she was trembling and lifted his head to press his lips against her temple, giving thanks that beneath the delicate skin her pulse beat strong and sure. "You're shaking."

Frankie made a sound between a laugh and a strangled sob. "No," she whispered. "That's you."

It took him a few moments to realize that she was

right. He *was* shaking but then again it had been close... too close for comfort.

"I thought I'd lost you," he rasped, pressing his cheek against hers. "I thought..." He sucked in a steadying breath and admitted, "I don't think I'd survive losing you too. Not you, Frankie."

"Hey," she said, pushing back a couple of inches to take his face between her icy palms. "I'm here. I'm not going anywhere."

"You're right," he said firmly. "You're not, but—"

"You saved me," she insisted gently. "Just like you promised Jack. But it's over now, Nate. I'm safe and your debt is paid. Let it go. Let *him* go... It's time."

Hell if she wasn't right. Jack would never be forgotten but maybe it was time to let go of the past, let go of the grief and the guilt of being the one to survive when Jack, the best of them, had died.

"Yes," he admitted, taking her icy hands in his and pressing them against his heart. "And it's also time for you to stop giving me heart failure." He gave a rough laugh. "I can't take much more."

"Me?" she croaked, as though her vocal cords had seized. "What about you?" Huge green eyes glowed eerily in her white face. "What was that? What the heck was that move?"

Now that she was safe and they'd come to terms with Jack's death, he could smile. "Admit it, that move was awesome."

"No," she practically snarled. "It wasn't. It was reckless and stupid and—"

No longer able to keep his relief and joy under wraps, Nate started laughing and quickly dropped a kiss on her surprised mouth, effectively silencing her. "Exactly what you would have done. It's what SEALs call thinking on your feet," he drawled, lowering his voice. "It's what's called being creative and doing whatever you need to do to save the woman you love."

"Well, I call it male stupidity," Frankie said, with a lot less heat. "What were you thinking? What if your line had snapped? What if…?" Her eyes grew huge and she sucked in a shocked breath. "Wha— What did you say?" she whispered hoarsely.

"You heard me. I love you, so damn much. And as to what I was thinking?" he murmured, abruptly serious. "I was thinking that I can't seem to live without you. I was thinking that maybe you were right and I was using my promise to Jack as an excuse to keep you from getting too close." He sucked in a deep breath. "But it's too late. You're already so deep nothing short of a soul transplant will get rid of you."

Frankie looked as though someone had punched her in the head. "You…you l-love me?" she whispered, looking more stunned and vulnerable than he'd ever seen her.

"Hell, yes," Nate declared emphatically, pulling her against him and tucking her face against his neck. He waited until she lifted her head to say, "I love you, Frankie. With everything that's in me. Seems like I've always loved you, even when you're mean and bossy and drive me completely insane. Besides…" he chuckled when she pushed him lightly "…who else will put up with you?"

A snort of laughter filled the silence. "You might be a superhero, Nate," someone said. "But you sure need lessons in romance."

He caught her hands and lifted them to his mouth.

"I'm not the most romantic guy, Frankie, but you're my happy. Without you I'm only just going through the motions."

"Oh, wow," one of the woman survivors sniffed. "If that's not romantic, I don't know what is."

Frankie's hands rose to cup his face. "I don't need romance, Nate," she said, eyes shining with tears and laughter. "I just… I just need you."

"And you'll do as I say?"

Frankie snorted rudely and to Nate it was the most beautiful sound he'd ever heard. Frankie was everything he needed; everything he'd ever wanted, wrapped up in silky-soft skin and prickly attitude. His heart.

"As if, Commander Big Shot," she scoffed. "But," she added when he opened his mouth to object, "I will if you will."

"Be mine," Nate said, oblivious to the whoops and sighs around them.

With a laugh, Frankie yanked him closer, and just before her mouth took his in a passionate kiss she murmured against his lips, "I already am."

* * * * *

MILLS & BOON

Coming next month

BOUND BY THEIR BABIES
Caroline Anderson

People joked all the time about sex-crazed widows, and there was no way—*no way*—she was turning into one! This was *Jake*, for heaven's sake! Her friend. Not her lover. Not her boyfriend. And certainly not someone for a casual one-nighter.

Although they'd almost gone there that once, and the memory of the awkwardness that had followed when they'd come to their senses and pulled away from the brink had never left her, although it had long been buried.

Until now...

Emily heard the stairs creak again, and pressed down the plunger and slid the pot towards him as he came into the room.

'Here, your coffee.'

'Aren't you having any?'

She shook her head, but she couldn't quite meet his eyes, and she realised he wasn't looking at her, either. 'I'll go back up in case Zach cries and wakes Matilda. Don't forget to ring me when you've seen Brie.'

'OK. Thanks for making the coffee.'

'You're welcome. Have a good day.'

She tiptoed up the stairs, listened for the sound of the front door closing and watched him from his bedroom window as he walked briskly down the road towards the hospital, travel mug in hand.

He turned the corner and went out of sight, and she sat down on the edge of his bed, her fingers knotting in a handful of rumpled bedding. *What was she doing?* With a stifled scream of frustration, she fell sideways onto the mattress and buried her face in his duvet.

Mistake. She could smell the scent of him on the sheets, warm and familiar and strangely exciting, could picture that glorious nakedness stretched out against the stark white linen, a beautiful specimen of masculinity in its prime—

She jack-knifed to her feet. This was crazy. What on earth had happened to her? They'd been friends for years, and now all of a sudden this uncontrollable urge to sniff his sheets?

They had to keep this platonic. So much was riding on it—their mutual careers, if nothing else!

And the children—they had to make this work for the children, especially Matilda. The last thing she needed—any of them needed—was this fragile status quo disrupted for anything as trivial as primitive, adolescent lust.

It wasn't fair on any of them, and she'd embarrassed herself enough fifteen years ago. She wasn't doing it again.

No way.

Continue reading
BOUND BY THEIR BABIES
Caroline Anderson

Available next month
www.millsandboon.co.uk

LET'S TALK
Romance

For exclusive extracts, competitions
and special offers, find us online:

f facebook.com/millsandboon

⊙ @millsandboonuk

𝕏 @millsandboon

Or get in touch on 0844 844 1351*

For all the latest titles coming soon, visit
millsandboon.co.uk/nextmonth